Chosen

Chosen

LUCY COATS

ORCHARD

ORCHARD BOOKS
First published in Great Britain in 2016 by The Watts Publishing Group

1 3 5 7 9 10 8 6 4 2

Text © Lucy Coats, 2016

The moral rights of the author and illustrator have been asserted.

A CIP catalogue record for this book is available
from the British Library.

ISBN 978 1 40833 417 1

Typeset in Minion by Avon DataSet Ltd,
Bidford-on-Avon, Warwickshire

Printed and bound in Great Britain by Clays Ltd, St Ives plc

The paper and board used in this book are made from wood
from responsible sources.

Orchard Books
An imprint of Hachette Children's Group
Part of The Watts Publishing Group Limited
Carmelite House
50 Victoria Embankment
London EC4Y 0DZ
An Hachette UK Company

www.hachette.co.uk
www.hachettechildrens.co.uk

For Juju, Bestest of Friends for longer than either of us
care to remember, and all-round Worker of Marvels,

com amor e beijos.

L.C.

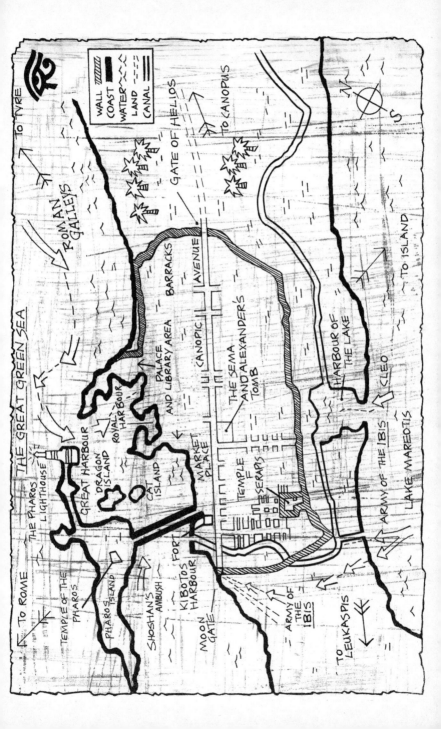

PART ONE

1

Escape from Alexandria

My camel was dirty white, and stank of old pee, dusty dung and sun-roasted fur. It also spat gobs of greenish mucus backwards at every opportunity, spattering my robes with foulness. I didn't care that it clearly hated me, though, nor that its gait was that of a lurching, one-legged beggar. The great city of Alexandria lay far down the road behind us. We had escaped, but we were still not safe. Even though the bright orb of Ra's chariot was riding high in the sky, I could feel the gaze of the Pharos statue through the shimmering midday heat, accusing, judgemental, its eyes boring into my back like burning coals.

Only one Pharaoh, it seemed to say. *Your fault.*

It *was* my fault, too. A few hours before, both my half-sisters had been alive. Now one of them was dead, and I'd provided the means. The knowledge lay in my belly like a jagged-edged stone – hard, sharp and unavoidable.

I'd managed not to think about it while we were running from the palace, and after that I'd had to concentrate on the practical things, like how we were going to get eleven people on seven camels. Once we were disguised in our merchant robes and through the Gate of Helios, though, I hadn't been able to avoid it.

Tryphena was gone, and Berenice was the only Pharaoh in Egypt.

I hadn't meant for Tryphena to die, at all. I wanted to believe it must be some terrible mistake, and I still couldn't work out exactly how it had happened. I thought I'd been so careful. The potion was only meant to send her into a death-like sleep, not into death itself.

'Berenice must have added something extra to it,' I muttered. Smelly Camel spat again, viciously. Maybe it felt the same about the one remaining Pharaoh as I did.

'What are you mumbling about?' asked a voice in my ear. It was slurred with tiredness. Charm – best friend, body servant and all-round fount of everything amazing in my life – stirred behind me, clutching at my waist as the wretched beast stepped in yet another hole in the road, making both of us slide forwards on the covered wooden saddle. At least we weren't galloping any more, though we weren't dawdling either. I could feel blisters already rising on my inner thighs from the rub of the rough, nubbly wool padding. I didn't want to think about how Charm's thighs must be feeling. She was already battered and bruised enough.

'Nothing,' I said. 'Don't worry about it.'

She leaned forward, digging her chin pointedly into the hollow in my collarbone. I could feel her breath on my cheek, smell the dried sweat in her hair, underlaid with the faint tang of herb ointment and roses.

'I can hear you thinking, Cleo. Don't pretend you aren't.'

I never could fool her. We'd been together since I was a tiny child.

'It's just...I don't see how she's dead. Cabar promised me the potion would work.' I didn't have to say which she. Charm had heard Tryphena's death-horn as well as I had, and seen the people wailing and tearing their clothes in the streets.

'What are you talking about? What potion? What have you done?'

With a jolt I remembered. Charm didn't know about my earlier side trip to the poison expert, Sister Cabar, in the Pharos temple – none of them did. Not even Khai.

Khai.

My eyes slipped sideways to the camel just in front. There he was, with my former fan bearer, little Mamo, cradled tenderly in one arm. His long, black hair fell down his back, and I could see the crusted scabs on the ankles sticking out from under his brown merchant robes. I shivered a little, remembering just how he'd got those wounds, remembering the damp dungeon and how close he'd come to being eaten by the vile demon god Am-Heh's vicious crocodiles. At least my bargain had had one good consequence. Khai was alive and with me, and he was no longer dressed in embalmers' red.

'I…I promise I'll tell you soon. I need to tell Khai too. There are things you both need to know.'

As if I'd reminded it, the magical map tucked into my breastband gave a tug, startling me. Without any instruction from my brain, my right hand pulled hard on the rein, making Smelly Camel give a grunting *hooaaaooor* of protest as it swung round, its clumsy two-toed feet trampling and tearing the silvery-green gum cistus bushes which stretched out beyond the road. There was a shout from behind, and the thudding sound of a galloping camel. Captain Nail appeared beside me in a cloud of damp brown dust. He looked strange without his leather breastplate and silver-embossed warrior shield.

'Where are you going, Chosen?' he asked. 'Canopus is that way.' He pointed to the left with one calloused finger. 'We are nearly there, but we need to hurry if we are to hire boats before sunset.'

'Yes, what are you doing, Cl— Chosen?' said Charm. 'You nearly had us both off with your stupid—'

'I don't know,' I said crossly, interrupting her. 'I don't seem to be in charge here. It's this Isis-blessed map. It's telling me to go this way.' I tried to tug on the left rein, but my hand simply wouldn't move. 'Let's get off the road.

I think there might have to be a change of plan.'

By the time we'd all gathered the camels in a loose circle in the middle of a grove of withered date palms, among some dying vines, my fingers were dripping sweat, making the plaited leather between them slippery. After I'd explained what our goddess and the Old One had said to me down in the secret archives of the brotherhood, and where they wanted me to go, the whole of me was damp with remembered fear, and all my audience but one had their mouths open with amazement and awe. The one was Khai, of course. He had been there with me. I heard the words in my head again.

We await you. Bring what you hold in your hands to us before the month of Mechir begins. You must hurry!

All at once I wanted to urge Smelly Camel to gallop southwards till we both dropped. What if the map stopped guiding me? What if its power all drained away before I could get to Isis and the Old One? My two goddesses weren't exactly known for their patience.

'Are we not to go back to Philäe, then, Chosen?' asked Captain Nail. His black eyebrows were pulled down into a frown I knew all too well.

The map pulsed against my breastbone like a second and more urgent heartbeat.

'I don't know!' I said again. 'All I am sure of is that our goddess's map is pulling me south and eastwards, so that's where we're headed for now.'

'We will follow where you and our goddess lead, then, my Chosen,' said Khai, his voice soothing my frayed nerves like bee balm on a graze. For a second I wished I was on the other camel cuddled up against him. We had been through so much together in the past days, and I felt closer to Khai than ever. But then Charm's hands tightened round my waist, clinging to me, and I remembered what she had suffered too. I reached back and clasped her cool, dry fingers with my sweaty ones.

'You'd better guide us right, O Great Mistress of Maps,' she whispered in my ear as I booted Smelly Camel in the ribs, guiding it forward through the brown and diseased grape tendrils towards the blue-green sparkle of Lake Mareotis in the distance.

'I'll do my best, but only if you let me breathe, O Most Worthy Waist Strangler,' I said. Her breath huffed out in a tiny laugh, but she didn't loose her grip on me.

We would have to find shelter and make camp before night fell, but at least both my hands were obeying me now that we were moving in the right direction. Leaving the road meant that we had to pick our way carefully, taking detours to avoid marshy hollows and pockets of floodwater. The workers among the vines stared at us curiously, their reed baskets filled with wispy dry clippings, and their curved knives hanging limp at their sides. Their faces were pinched and old, and their eyes were hungry. The vines should have been green and vibrant at this time of year, the faces of the people fat with the eating of good grain. That they weren't was a very visible reminder that my goddess was not able to protect Egypt as she should. I must restore her powers soon, or it would only get worse. One more season like this and half of Egypt would starve to death. That was what the map was not-so-subtly reminding me.

I huddled into the brown hood of my robe, hoping that no one would remember my hair or eyes. I didn't know whether Berenice would send her Nubian mercenaries searching for us. I hoped that maybe she would just be glad to see the back of me. Right now, though, she would be distracted, and her guards too. The Alexandrians would see Tryphena's death as a bad omen – and there might be rioting in the streets. The first signs of unrest had already started as we left. The distracted guards at the Gate of Helios had waved us through with no more than a perfunctory glance in the misty dawn light. They had been too busy watching the crowds pouring into the city for signs of trouble to bother inspecting a train of merchants on their way out of town.

By dusk, the light of the Pharos fire was a muted glow on the northern horizon behind us. We set up camp outside a small village above flood level, beside a huge pile of broken potsherds and smashed amphorae. It was still hot and humid, and the flies crowding round the camels' eyes also buzzed around us, settling on our faces till we slapped at them. All of us were slightly unsteady on our feet after the long ride, and I could feel the liquid inside my thigh blisters slide and chafe as I walked.

After a quick consultation with Captain Nail, we sent Dhouti, my one remaining eunuch, to knock on village doors to try and buy bread and wine.

'No sense in using up all the supplies just yet, Chosen – not if we don't know where we're going,' Nail said, the very slightest edge of disapproval in his voice.

I put back my hood and smiled at him, showing teeth. 'Quite right, Captain. I'll leave all that sort of thing to you to organise, then.'

He scowled, taking my point immediately.

I knew nothing useful about camel care or camps, but I attempted to help anyway, even though everyone tried to stop me. I waved away their protests with a smile and a few firm words. I might be a princess and the chosen of Isis, but we were all together on this journey – and I didn't need to follow protocol here as strictly as I had in the palace. Nor did I need to wear my impassive princess mask. It was a relief to strip it all away, really, to go some way towards being ordinary Cleo again, for as long as I could. So I unbuckled straps and gathered firewood and unrolled blankets till Charm lost her patience with my ineptness.

'If you must do something useful, go and find some water to wipe that camel gob off yourself, Cleo. You smell like something died on you.' She handed me a cloth and pointed off towards the edge of the camp. 'There's water over there. Use it.'

I sighed. She was right about the smell, so I walked a little distance away from the bustle and hurry of unsaddling and firemaking till I came to a small irrigation channel. The emerging stars were like tiny white lamps overhead. Over the reek of camel, I smelt salt and green things on the air, as well as the sour tang of fermenting grapes, and heard the tiny high-pitched whine of mosquitoes. I bent over and wet the cloth, then wiped at the green streaks, but it didn't make much difference. Now I just smelled of damp camel gob.

As I finished I heard a soft, limping footstep behind me, but I didn't turn. I knew who it was. He didn't touch me, but he stood close enough beside me that I felt the heat of his body mix with my own like oil into warm water.

'Khai,' I said, then stopped. I didn't know what to say, and he remained puzzlingly silent.

I reached for his hand, just as another footstep sounded – a lighter one this time. I knew who that was too.

'So, are you going to finally tell us what you've done?' Charm asked, her voice soft. She knew I wouldn't want the others to hear this. Khai still said nothing, but his fingers squeezed mine, the small pressure encouraging me.

I didn't want to tell them, but I knew I had to.

'I've broken *ma'at*,' I said bluntly. 'I didn't mean to, but I think I have. I've killed Tryphena and made Berenice the only Pharaoh on the throne, and now that blood-drenched god of hers will have free rein to do whatever he wants until I go back and fix it.'

There was no question that I would have to go back and undo the evil I had caused. I just couldn't see the path to it yet.

'How did you kill her?' Khai asked. I knew he wasn't sad – he couldn't be, given how he'd hated my eldest sister – but there was something in his voice that made me want to growl all the same.

'I didn't do it myself,' I said. 'Cabar made me some stuff which was supposed to make her sleep, not die. I gave it to Berenice. She must have tampered with it somehow. Or Tryphena had a bad reaction. Or Cabar got the dose wrong.' My voice rose. 'I don't *know*! But it was my fault she died, however it happened.' I turned, gripping the front of Khai's robes, trying to make him understand. 'You know I only did it to save you and Charm. You were there when Berenice and I made that horrible bargain. I didn't have a choice.' My breath was catching and hitching in my throat now, and my heart rattled and banged in my chest like a pebble in a rushing river.

Khai put his arms around me, just as Charm did the same at my back. Suddenly I was enclosed by the two people I loved most in the world. It felt safe, but only for a moment.

'All the gods will hate me now,' I said, my voice muffled

in the front of Khai's robe. Charm's hands moved to my shoulders abruptly and she stepped back a pace, pulling me away from Khai, giving me a little shake as I turned to look at her.

'I'm not going to let you wallow in self-pity,' she said. 'You did what you had to do. The gods, blessed be their names, will understand that. Count your own blessings for a second, Cleo. You've got the map, you've got a brand-new magical gift from the Old One, Isis is pleased with you, and we've escaped from Alexandria. What on Ra's earth are you complaining about?'

Khai stiffened slightly. He'd never heard Charm in full flow before.

'You can't talk to the chosen like—' he started, but Charm hadn't finished.

'Yes, I can, and don't you encourage her by bowing down like some palace flunkey, Spy Boy,' she said. 'She doesn't need that from either of us. It's about time she woke up and realised that Isis chose her for a reason. There's a job that needs doing and only Cleo can do it.' Her fingers dug into my skin so hard I could feel the pinch of her short nails. 'You need to start believing in yourself, Cleo. We all believe in you, otherwise we wouldn't be here, following you into Osiris knows where.'

One hand left my shoulder to slap at a hovering mosquito as Khai laughed.

'Now, *that* I can agree with,' he said. 'And when Isis has

her power back, she will protect you from the other gods. I'm sure of it, Cleo.'

'I wish *I* was,' I said. 'I keep expecting Horus or one of the other gods to send a falcon to peck out my eyes or something.'

'And what about me?' Khai asked, his voice suddenly serious. 'Do you think I don't wonder if Seth is going to send his hyenas to tear me to pieces, or strike me with lightning?' He opened the neck of his robe to reveal a bright red burn, blackened at the edges and weeping a clear liquid. It was where the god's amulet had hung. 'I think this is proof enough that he doesn't like me very much, don't you?'

'Yes,' I said slowly. 'Yes. I suppose it is.' A wound like that could be very dangerous if it wasn't properly cared for. It was another worry to add to the many I already carried.

'Well, if you two have quite finished moaning about which of you the gods hate more, I think Dhouti is back. I'm going to see about something to eat,' said Charm, already on her way back to the fire.

Khai's arms tightened around me again.

'She's quite something,' he said.

I laughed. He'd finally noticed how amazing my best friend was, then. 'She's been more of a sister to me than either of those two Evil…' I stopped suddenly. There was only one Evil Sow now.

'Don't worry about it, Cleo,' he said gently. 'What's done is done. Now, come on, we'd better go back.' He made a movement towards me, and then pulled away. Was it deliberate?

I'd expected him to kiss me – had wanted it so badly that my lips began to part of their own accord. But instead he turned me round and gave me a little push in Charm's direction, following closely at my heels. The disappointment was a jab of ice in my heart, but I was suddenly too tired to ask him what was wrong. Maybe it was just that he was worried about Seth's vengeance. Maybe it was the smell of camel gob. I didn't blame him on either count.

Isis, Osiris, Ra! All you great gods. Please forgive me, and protect us, I prayed. It couldn't do any harm to ask, could it?

As I lay down after our meal, full of warm bread and sweet wine, Captain Nail ordered Warriors Sah and Rubi to take the first watch of the night. I could see Khai on the other side of the fire, sitting blanket-wrapped and gazing into the flames, a brooding look on his face. I wondered if he was remembering Tryphena. He had been her boy toy – and most probably her lover too. There had been a connection between them, however much I hated the thought of it.

'Stop staring so hard at His Gorgeousness,' Charm whispered from the blanket beside me. 'Your eyes will fall out.'

I ducked my head, blushing. Had it really been that obvious? He *was* gorgeous, though – all shining dark hair, brown eyes deep enough to drown unwary girls in, and those slightly chapped lips whose roughness tempted me to rub my own against them. Why hadn't he kissed me when he could? I fell asleep worrying about it.

In the middle of the night, the Old One's voice came to me in my dreams.

Use my gift, Beloved Daughter. Unroll the map and let it show you the path you must take.

Half-awake now, but not quite knowing what I was doing, I fumbled the map out from between my breasts. It was glowing with the pure white light I'd seen when I first took it from its hiding place in the ebony box down in the embalmers' archives. Bodies lay peacefully asleep around me, some of them snoring, and I could just see the tall figures of the guarding warriors outlined by the risen moon. Their backs were to me. They wouldn't notice this new evidence of a goddess's favour, and I was guiltily glad. Being the chosen of Isis, being set apart from other mortals, was already enough of a burden. I didn't think I could take any more awed looks from my warriors if they saw this.

I sat huddled over the map scroll, hiding it with a fold of my cloak, and unrolled it with trembling fingers. At first, all I saw were old lines of ash and blood, clumsily drawn in by a finger – the marks of Tebu, the traitorous embalmer and priest of Seth who had murdered the priestess guardians of the Old One's tomb and scattered most of my goddess's power to the stars. Then, creeping in from the edges of the scroll, came a wash of light, which erased those shameful scrawls, replacing them with a shining line of gold, flowing across the page like a tiny river.

Unfortunately, it made no more sense to me than the ash and blood daubs had.

Use my gift…

I stared at the map for a while, thinking hard, then closed my eyes, still holding it. Previously, the Old One's gift had come to me when I was asleep. Maybe it would again. Holding the golden line of the map in my head, I drifted off again. Almost immediately I felt the tug in my solar plexus and found myself hovering above the camp, a silver cord anchoring me to my sleeping body. Next to it was a brighter line – a golden one, which stretched away into the distance. Quicker than a thought, I was flying along it, seeing a long lake; marshes; salt pans; the sinuous, still-bloated waters of the Nile; towns; small villages; cities at the Nile's edges; night-green farmland with another lake at its centre; a mysterious building which thrummed with life underground; stony hills; leagues of desert; a huge oasis; more desert; another even bigger oasis – and then a great flat lake of sand with a mound in the middle of it that sparkled in the moonlight and into which the golden thread plunged and stopped about half way up. Each place, each landmark, seemed to pulse in my blood. I opened my eyes to find the map had disappeared. A wisp of light was all that remained in my hands and, as I watched, it formed itself into an arrow and plunged into my breast, just above where my heart lay. It didn't hurt, just fizzed a little, like a blazing golden spark.

You are our living map now, Beloved Daughter. Listen to the whisper within your blood. Come to us. Time is short. War comes on swift wings.

I wanted to cover my ears, and yet the words hadn't been spoken aloud. The voices of my goddess and her grandmother echoed through my head, the belling of hunting dogs, the sweetness of wild honey, and the cool of long-hidden waters all mixed together into a command I couldn't ignore. I raised my palms in worship, bowing my head.

'I will come, Great Ones,' I whispered.

I knew that it would be a long journey, and that we would indeed have to hurry if we were to get there by the beginning of the month of Mechir. But I could have walked every step of it with eyes closed and blindfolded now. I was indeed their living, breathing map. The urge to start at that very moment was strong, and a restless energy filled my bones. I wanted to run, to leap, to never stop till I reached where I needed to be. But I was only human. I needed rest, and so did my companions.

I didn't close my eyes, though. Instead, I stretched out on my back, looking up at the immensity of the sky above me. The waning moon was lower now, and holy Thoth was doing cartwheels around it, pulling the occasional star out of his pocket and flinging it down to earth in a streak of silver-white light. It was the first time I'd been properly still since our flight from Alexandria, the first time I'd really had to think about something Isis and her grandmother had said to me at the moment I'd first held the map.

We have great plans for you, Cleopatra Chosen. Have courage.

What plans? What would I need courage for? Would what I had to face in the future be worse than Berenice, than Am-Heh and his crocodiles, than Seth and his red-robed priests? I shivered despite the warmth of the night air. When two of the greatest goddesses in Egypt had big plans for you, it was best to be prepared for anything. It wasn't the most comfortable of feelings, but I knew there was nothing I could do now but accept my fate – whatever it was to be.

2

The Road to Naucratis

'Stop arguing,' I said impatiently, standing by Smelly Camel, who lay saddled and ready, chewing cud and dribbling disgustingly. 'I know where we're going now, and how to get there. We're wasting time here.'

'But Chosen,' Captain Nail said, 'if we go that way, towards Lake Mareotis, we will pass by the southern reed beds.'

I shrugged. What was wrong with reed beds? They were everywhere around the lake. Before I could open my mouth again, Khai was speaking from beside me.

'It's a well-known area for bandits, my Chosen. We don't have any proper weapons now, remember? It would be hard to protect you with only our daggers and belt knives.' He carefully didn't say that I would be putting everyone in danger, but I heard it anyway.

I sighed. It was no good. I would have to tell them about

last night – make them understand that I was following the path the immortals had set out for us. I cleared my throat.

'Listen,' I started, and felt the power of both our own goddess and the Old One tinge my voice with truth. It seemed that I couldn't be just Cleo any more: I had to be the chosen of Isis *and* her grandmother – even with those I trusted most.

When I'd finished, they looked at me differently – as I'd been afraid they would. I could see they believed me absolutely. A fragment of both Isis and the Old One was within me now and they had heard it. The awe in my warriors' faces was coupled with a hint of fear, and little Mamo had turned a greyish brown, his eyes rounder than moon pebbles. I didn't dare look at Charm on my right, nor at Khai on my left. If they too feared me, I didn't want to know about it.

'Our goddesses will protect us,' I said, more confidently than I felt. 'They wouldn't have marked out a path which meant our deaths.'

There was no more to be said. Charm and I mounted Smelly Camel, which rocked to its feet, grunting and roaring as we leaned back and clung on. I felt a blister burst with a silent damp pop, and wondered fleetingly if it would be too much to ask Isis to heal my aches and pains. Then I felt that unmistakeable surge of gold in my blood, pulling me onwards.

A few hours later, the southern reed beds lay misty and

damp to either side of us. A stench of decomposing vegetation and wet mud rose from them, coating the back of my throat with a slimy layer of rot. There were small fishing boats further out on the lake, but I couldn't see anyone close by. Only the *jeet jeet jeet* of a flock of yellow wagtails bobbing and flitting in the reeds broke the silence.

On the camel in front, Captain Nail was turning his head from side to side like a dog shaking its ears, his whole body tense and ready for trouble. Despite my confident words, he wasn't taking any chances, and he was right not to. Suddenly, the reeds to either side of us erupted with a rustling splash. All in a moment we were surrounded by about fifty black-encrusted, dripping figures, their heads wrapped in linen so that only their eyes showed. Each held a long spear with a curved hook on the end. All the spears were pointing at us.

As Khai shouted a warning behind me, I just had time to notice that some of our attackers were women before Captain Nail and the two warriors in front of us wrenched their camels round in an attempt to protect me and Charm. The bandits were too fast for them, though. Some had immediately run to the camels' heads, and now held all their collars in a tight grip, Smelly Camel included.

One of the remaining bandits stepped forwards – a woman, I thought, from the way her hips swayed.

'Please to give us your valuables, dear travellers. There is a toll for using this little reed road of ours. Did you not know?' Her voice was melodious but menacing, and her thick Delta accent hard to disentangle.

Cold rage rose in my chest, and before anyone else could reply, I spoke, my voice icy.

'I am the chosen of Isis, bandit. Do you dare to interrupt the business of the goddess?'

The bandit bowed low.

'But Great Lady, as you see, the goddess is not here to prevent us interrupting you, and we have many expenses. See it as a small matter of business between us. Hand over your money, and then you may be on your way.'

I closed my eyes, the ice melting and turning to uncertainty.

Great goddesses, I prayed. *You have put these people in our path for a reason. Please – show me what to do.*

Above the reek of rotting reed, a small breeze brought me the scent of hot sand and wild desert places, caressing my cheek.

Turn them to our service, my Chosen. They will be needed. They will be the first troops in my secret army. War is coming.

Isis's voice was muted thunder and the softness of rain inside my head. I was confused by her words. Secret army? What secret army? And what war? This was the second time she'd mentioned war. But then rage took me.

'Kneel before me,' I said, my voice a whisper of fire. It was a whisper that could have been heard above the fiercest storm. 'Lay down your weapons and swear to serve me. For I am Isis-on-earth. I am Cleopatra the Marked and Chosen and I will make you mine. I will have your loyalty now and forever.'

I dropped the reins, slid down off Smelly Camel, and looked the mud-spattered woman in the eye, feeling the gold in my blood heat and focus, split into many small burning branches and shoot out of my fingers like tiny lightning bolts. Her eyes widened with sudden pain. Then she and all the other bandits let out small muffled shrieks and dropped their weapons, clutching their hands to their breasts. The haft of every spear smoked and glowed red in the misty light of Ra's rays. They dropped to their knees as one, now raising their open hands in worship. The Knot of Isis was burned into each and every right palm, and as I saw it, I felt Isis leave me. I snatched my hands back and put them behind me, digging my fingers into the leather of the saddle girth, willing myself not to fall over. My goddess had just acted through me, and I felt the power of it like boiling lead in my bones. Charm trembled above me. I could feel her through the leather, shaking harder than an acacia leaf in a high wind.

'Swear to Isis!' I said to the kneeling figures, the fire of rage still in my voice.

'We swear, O great Cleopatra, O Chosen and Marked,' said the bandit leader, prostrating herself. 'We did not know. We will make offerings to the goddess. We will serve you. Only let us go. Do not kill us.'

'I will not kill you. You too are marked by Isis now, and she is merciful and just to those who worship her.' I looked down at the back of her head, still wrapped in black linen. 'Get up. Uncover your face and tell me your name.'

The woman went very still, then got to her feet, unwrapping the binding around her face. She was fairly young, not yet twenty-five, I thought, and her mouth was set firm and determined in a proud face – not beautiful, but very striking, with high cheekbones and flashing dark eyes.

'I am Shoshan of the Spear,' she said, meeting my gaze. 'And my weapon, and those of my people are yours, Holy One.' I believed her.

'Hold yourselves ready for my word, then, Shoshan of the Spear. If I send a messenger, you must come.' I hesitated for a moment. Should I tell her? Yes. It felt right. 'You and your people will be the first troops in our goddess's new army. Be silent and secret, but prepare. War is coming.'

She nodded.

'I smell it in the air, Great Lady. Not yet, but soon.'

I felt the gold in my blood move and stir again. I knew where it wanted me to go. 'Now, Shoshan, will you guide us by the quickest ways to the city of ships? We must be silent and secret.'

She nodded, giving swift orders, taking the bridle of Smelly Camel herself and leading it to the head of the line.

I nodded to Corporal Geta and Warrior Haka, and to Captain Nail as I passed them. They saluted swiftly, but I noticed they all kept their eyes cast down, unable to meet my gaze. I knew Khai was on the camel right behind. I wondered desperately what he was thinking, wanting to reassure myself that he was still there, but fear kept me from allowing myself to turn round and look at him. What if he thought I was too different now – as untouchable as our goddess herself? I would show him that I was still Cleo underneath, I vowed – just as soon as we had a moment to ourselves again. But the memory of his stepping back from me last night left a small, cold spot in my heart.

As the camels squelched forward again over the muddy ground, the silence around me was like a weighted blanket. Nobody spoke. Shoshan and a tall, thin bandit walked on either side of Smelly Camel, but the others had melted into the reeds as swiftly as they had come. Charm's trembling had calmed a little, but now she clutched me again as if I was the only solid thing in her world. I unclasped her hands and moved them apart a little, stroking the soft backs with my thumbs. I could feel the small bones underneath the skin, tense and stiff with holding on.

'Don't worry,' I whispered. 'I'm still me.'

'I know, Cleo,' she whispered back. 'It's just…a little scary, that's all. Hearing you speak like that – you sounded just like your father used to – just like a Pharaoh. It's… it's really happening now, isn't it? What you said

I couldn't mention, I mean. Back in…in Philäe, that night the kite came.'

I could hear her words as if they'd been spoken yesterday.

If it's the goddess's will, how can you fight it? If Isis wants you to be Pharaoh, you will be – and you'd better start getting used to the idea.

I wished I could turn round and see her face, but I spoke to Smelly Camel's ears instead.

'Yes,' I said softly, the throne mark on my shoulder throbbing and burning. 'Yes, I still don't want it to be, but I think it really is.'

It made me feel sick, though, the thought of being Pharaoh. I couldn't sit on the Double Throne with Berenice – but who else was there to share it with? My father was far away across the Great Green Sea with my little half-siblings Arsinöe, Len and Tol. If I wanted one of them beside me, I would have to go to Rome and fetch them. And when I came home again it would have to be with an army at my back, because Berenice and her hound-headed demon god would not give up the throne without a fight. Was that what Isis had meant by her warning that war was coming? I didn't think Shoshan's muddy bunch of reed-dwellers was going to get me very far against the trained Nubian guards in the palace – nor against the Pharaoh's own battalions. But where could I find enough soldiers for a whole secret army to stand against them? How could I lead grown men and women into a bloody battle?

I turned the problem over and over in my head all the way to Naucratis, but I was no closer to a solution as we came into sight of the port city. As we came near to civilisation again, I called down to Shoshan to halt, beckoning her towards me.

'We will leave you here. Remember!' I said. 'Come when I call you.'

She bowed gravely.

'I will remember, Most High. War is coming. We will be prepared.' And with that, she and her companion turned and slid back the way we had come, disappearing into the twilight like eels into mud.

Captain Nail came up beside me.

'Where to now, Chosen?' he asked. I was thankful that his voice sounded just as gruff as normal.

'We need to find boats to take us upriver past Memphis,' I said. 'And I for one will be grateful to get off the back of this horrible animal.' My blisters had all burst now, and I was sure I could feel fresh ones forming underneath them. Smelly Camel grunted and spat ferociously. Then there was a pattering sound underneath us, and I smelt the acrid scent of hot, fresh pee.

'Disgusting beast,' I muttered, and Charm laughed, the sound of it startling after the heavy silence of the last hours.

'Disrespectful, too,' she said. 'I don't think it's a worshipper of the goddess, do you?'

'No,' I answered. 'And I don't think she'd want it to be.

'I'm pretty sure camel gob isn't high on her list of desires.'

The small town of Naucratis was busy, even at dusk. The sound of Greek voices filled the air as we passed temple after temple dedicated to Hera, Apollo and Aphrodite, and I could just see the flicker of votive lamps inside. The Greeks had been here centuries before great Alexander set foot in Egypt, trading silver and timber for linen and papyrus, and they had brought their gods with them.

We got off the camels in a small square, and Dhouti went to seek out a merchant to sell them on to. It didn't take long. They were healthy beasts, and soon his purse was heavy with silver and copper coins. I wasn't at all sorry to see the hindquarters of Smelly Camel swaying off around a corner. I hoped it would be less revolting to its new owner than it had been to me.

Just as I was about to go over to Khai, Captain Nail came up beside me. His face was stiff and his black eyebrows locked together in a deep frown. I saw his throat work, once, twice, and then he fell to one knee before me, bowing his head. One arm was outstretched, and in it was a dagger, sharp-edged and deadly.

'I have failed to protect you twice now, Chosen,' he said, and I could hear the emotion choking him. 'My life is forfeit. I am not worthy to be captain of your warriors.'

I knew he meant it. The burden of guilt he was carrying must have been intolerable for my proud, capable captain to humble himself like this. I would have to tread very, very carefully to give him back a sense of his own honour. I took the dagger, weighing it, thinking, then I made a small nick in my index finger.

'Give me your hand,' I said, as the blood began to run. He held it out wordlessly. I made a nick in his index finger too. He didn't flinch as the blade cut. I didn't expect him to. Then I pressed our two bloody digits together.

'There will be no death today, Captain. Isis knows your worth, and she binds the blood of her Chosen with yours to pay tribute to the warriors who serve us both. If you had failed in your duty, she would know it, and so would I. You did not.'

I bent forward and pulled him to his feet. His black eyes were almost soft as they stared down at me, bemused, and I knew he had expected to die. Did he know me so little? I smiled, just a quick twitch of the lips to comfort him.

'If you want to atone for not protecting me, I know nothing of building armies, so you must do it for me. That is the path our goddess has laid out for you, Captain. She doesn't waste the lives that belong to her. War is coming. I want you at the head of our troops – when we have some.'

He straightened, shoulders back, and saluted me.

'As I said, Chosen – my life is yours, as is my blood.' He looked down at his finger wonderingly. 'It feels like molten gold. I…I never expected…' He broke off and cleared his throat, his usual gruffness falling around him again like a familiar military cloak.

'Very well, then. First of all we must have new weapons and shields, Chosen. There are bands of mercenaries here who will sell them to us. Though they will not make us look like proper warriors of Isis again, they will at least give some protection if we need to fight. Will you come to an inn and let us order food and beds for the night while I and some of the others go and seek them out? There will be no boats till morning, I think and anyway, it will take time to find one big enough to take us all.'

I nodded. It made sense, and the thought of lying down on a bed was very seductive. Especially if the inn was so small that Khai would have to be in the same room as me.

I suspected that the hostelry we ended up at had a sideline as a brothel. The serving girls were suspiciously pretty, and the skinny innkeeper eyed Charm and me up as if we were tasty new merchandise. The room we were shown to had two well-worn pallets, and the telltale scent of cheap ambergris and patchouli lay heavy in the air. The wooden furniture was basic, and there were strings of blue pottery scarabs hanging everywhere on the walls, which were painted with vines and small birds. The captain ordered Warrior Sah to stand guard outside the door, and Corporal Geta to stay downstairs on the look out for any trouble, while he took the rest of my warriors on the search for weapons. Dhouti went to see about a boat to take us upriver, and I sent Am, my lanky food taster, and little Mamo to find food and bring it to us.

'And what would you like me to do, my Chosen?' Khai asked. There was a slightly bitter edge to his voice. I didn't like it. Something had been strange between us since last night, and I wasn't going to wait to find out what it was for a minute more.

'I'd like you to stay here, please, Khai,' I said. 'I need to talk to you.'

He folded his arms and leaned against the wall by the door while the rest of them went about their business.

Charm took one look at both of us and tutted.

'I'll just be getting some hot water,' she said. 'Try not to make her too angry while I'm gone, Spy Boy. I don't want to have to scrub your blood off the floor.'

I nearly laughed, but then I saw Khai's face. He wasn't amused.

'What is your problem?' I asked, as soon as the door closed behind her. 'You've been strange with me ever since last night in the village. Have I done something wrong?' I stopped, a sob rising in my chest. 'C-can you not bear…'

With two long strides, Khai was across the room, his hands on my shoulders.

'Cleo…my Cleo. Don't cry. Of course you haven't done anything wrong. It's just…' He wrenched himself away from me and went over to the wall again, slapping his palms against it as if he wanted to punish it, then leaning his forehead against the painted wood. 'It's just that I don't know who I am any more…what I am. I have no value to you here. I was useful in Alexandria. I was a spy. I helped rescue people. But what use am I now? I'm not a warrior. I'm a scribe, a librarian. But there is no Great Library here, and no scribing or spying to be done. I—' He broke off, his voice catching as mine had done.

I went over to him and wrapped my arms around his back, leaning into him as I spoke into his hair.

'What matters is that we're here, together. Isn't that enough for now?'

'I don't know, Cleo,' he said, and my heart shattered a little.

I took my hands off him, very deliberately, and moved back across the room to sit on the pallet. Ice was moving outwards from my chest, spreading all along my arms and down into my belly.

I wanted to curl up and die.

3

Up the Nile

'I'm sorry,' I said, retreating behind my princess mask so as not to scream out loud. 'Perhaps I misunderstood it when you said you loved me.'

'Oh, Cleo! I love you – of course I do – but…'

'There's no need to explain, Khai,' I said between my teeth. Buts were never good, and I didn't want to hear any more. Had I really risked everything for this?

He whirled round and came to me, squatting in front of me, seizing my hands. I tried to turn away, to pull them free, but he wouldn't let me. He took my chin in one hand, made me look at him.

'I need to make you understand, Cleo, my Chosen. Love of my heart. I am a man, not a lapdog. I need a job. I need to have a purpose. I want to be your lover – more than anything – but that cannot be all I am. Do you see?'

I did see. The spectre of Tryphena and what she had

done to him stood between us. The ice melted into a flood of truth.

'I won't make you my lapdog, Khai – not like *she* did. You are the one who understands my soul. If you can't see that then you're blind. You and Charm are the only people who can see beyond the Chosen to who I am underneath. Do you know how important that is? How precious? I need you to take me back to myself. To remind me that I'm Cleo.' I leaned forward, pressing my forehead against his. 'If Isis hasn't shown you the path you are to take, it's because she's not ready to. But there is a path for you – a use, a task for you to do, and we will find out what it is together. I promise it in the name of our goddess's sacred blood.'

The ball of his thumb stroked my cheek, the roughness at the edge of the nail a tiny scratch on my skin.

'Together, then, if we can, and trusting in our goddess. I know you don't break your promises, Cleo. You proved that back in Alexandria.'

His lips touched mine, unsure at first, and then, as his arms went round me and we fell back onto the pallet, rougher and more demanding. I kissed him right back, locking my arms round him and pulling him down till he lay sprawled on top of me. I didn't need gentleness from him. I just needed to feel real again.

He lifted his head, wrinkling his nose.

'We're both all camelly, but you still smell good right

here,' he said, nuzzling his nose into the hollow under my throat. 'Like new grass and honey. It makes me want to bite you.' He bared his teeth and his long fingers stroked down the tender inner skin of my arm, making me shiver, and then he lifted it to his mouth, nipping at the bend of my elbow, tasting it with the tip of his tongue.

I couldn't help it. I giggled.

'What?' he said, raising his head. 'Now you're laughing at me?' He grinned, and my heart nearly stopped dead at the gorgeousness of his dimples.

'It tickles,' I complained. 'Come back up here. Kiss me again.' He did, driving all thought out of my brain till we were just Khai and Cleo, a boy and a girl in love.

'Ahem,' said Charm's voice from the doorway. 'Not that I want to interrupt or anything, but Warrior Sah is right outside, and Am and Mamo will be coming upstairs with the food right after you've washed.'

We jerked apart, frantically straightening clothes and hair.

'I'll...I'll just go and find my own water, shall I?' said Khai, his voice hoarse and strangled as he leaped off the pallet and across the room like a thrown spear.

Charm stood in his way deliberately, preventing him from leaving. Steam from the bowl of water she held rose in front of her face like a veil, so that she looked mysterious, like an oracle.

'Oh, no, you don't, Spy Boy. Not yet. I've got a few

things to say before you go and wash that camel stink off.'
She fixed him with a glare, set the bowl down, and advanced
towards him. 'First of all, if you ever hurt Cleo, I'll kill you.
Second of all, if you get her with child, I'll strangle you.
Slowly. And, third of all – your robe is all rucked up at the
back and I'm not sure I'm ready to see what's under there.
You might want to sort it out before you go down.'

Khai plucked at his robe, disentangling it from his
loincloth. I'd rather liked the view, myself. The long line of
his thigh and the taut roundness above was very distracting.
Then he turned round to face me, his face serious.

'I'd never hurt you, Cleo. You know that, don't you?'

I nodded. I knew he wouldn't – not intentionally,
anyway.

'And…and…' I could see a dark red tide rising from the
neck of his robe. 'Well…I wouldn't…' He made a confused
gesture, then pushed past Charm and out of the door.

'Thanks a lot, Charmion,' I heard him mutter.

Charm shut the door behind him and brought the bowl
over to me.

'You had to say it, didn't you, O Empress of
Embarrassment?' I demanded, blushing just as hard as
Khai had. 'What are you? My mother?'

She scowled, wringing out a cloth and handing it to me
as I hastily stripped off my camel-stained robe.

'Someone needed to. You've never been with a man,
have you?'

'No,' I said. 'You of all people ought to know I haven't. And we didn't...' I stopped.

'Well, then, O Chieftainess of Canoodling,' she said. 'Next time you might. Or the time after that. And... and you need to think about it. I don't think Isis would be very pleased to have a baby Chosen on the way. She didn't choose you as a mother-to-be, did she? You've got a job to do. You need to concentrate on that, not on...you know. Sex.'

My whole body was still tingling and buzzing from Khai's kisses, so I did know.

'I promise,' I said. 'I will take care. We will, I mean.'

'It'll have to be you, Cleo. Men don't always stop. Even if you really, really want them to. They're stronger than us, so even if you struggle they...' She shut her lips tight and busied herself with getting another robe out of our bags for me.

I suddenly realised what she meant. I went over to her, turning her round to face me, remembering the fingermark bruises I'd seen on her inner thighs. Gooseflesh stood out on my damp body – and not only from the cooling air.

'You know what happened to you when you were captured wasn't your fault, don't you?'

Charm had been held by the priests of Am-Heh and badly beaten a few days before. Now I knew for certain that there had been more than a beating, and inwardly I cursed those monstrous sons of a hyena's vomit with the vilest words I knew.

She stiffened, but she didn't shake me off.

'Yes,' she said slowly. 'I know. I still don't want to talk about it but...' Her hand went to her belly. 'There's a chance I might be... I won't know till the moon is full again.'

I wanted to hug her, but I knew it wouldn't be a good idea right now. I squeezed her shoulders instead.

'Whatever happens, we'll get through it together,' I said.

Her hands came up to meet mine, squeezing in their turn.

'I know,' she said. 'And that's what keeps me going, O Bestest of Friends.' She stepped back from me, pasting a smile on her face that made my heart nearly break. 'Now get dressed. His Gorgeousness wouldn't like it if Am and Mamo caught you in your undies, O Carefully Chosen of the Goddess.'

The boat Dhouti had found for us was a high-sterned felucca of the old-fashioned kind with only one steering oar. Although it had a deckhouse in the centre, the acacia-wood planks that made up its walls were crooked and ill-kept, and the whole vessel smelled strongly of old fish. Most of its crew were scattered and drunk on barley beer after a long voyage downriver from Thebes, but Dhouti had bribed the helmsman to sail with only two of the more sober ones, telling him that the warriors would help out if they were needed.

'The wind will be with us, Chosen, however far upriver we need to sail,' he said, wringing his hands as if they were wet washing, and apologising for the meanness of the accommodation. 'That is the best that can be said.'

I didn't care what kind of boat it was, so long as we were on our way as soon as possible. I had woken, my muscles stiffer than sun-dried wet leather and my skin itchy from what I hoped weren't bedbugs, with the all-familiar onwards tug pulling at me urgently. I could almost hear a whisper fading in the stifling air.

Come to us, Beloved Daughter. Hurry. War unfurls its wings.

I wish it would bloody well furl them again, then. I caught the thought just as it streaked across my brain, hoping my goddesses hadn't heard it. If war was really coming, there was nothing I could do to stop it.

It hadn't taken long to rouse everyone, and we were down at the port just as dawn broke. The warriors were now armed again, and they'd bought substantial-looking knives for the rest of us, including a silver-hilted one for me, with a sheath made of embossed leather.

'Just in case,' said Captain Nail, handing it to me with a bow.

I weighed it in my hand. Charm had taught me how to strike – up and under the left-hand ribs, or into a kidney at the back – but I wasn't at all sure I wanted to find out what it felt like to kill someone face to face. I belted it over my robe anyway, thanking him.

As we clambered aboard, I noticed little Mamo, drooping and sad as he helped to bring our luggage into the boat. I beckoned him over to me when I was settled.

'How is it with thee, boy child,' I asked in his native Amharic.

He wiped a dirty hand across his nose, smearing a snail trail of slime over his upper lip.

'Mamo cannot say his sadness out loud, Great Lady,' he whispered, shrinking back. 'It is too hard.'

The whip weals from where Berenice had struck him were still not healed properly. He would bear the scars till he died. Was he afraid of me? I guessed the answer was yes. He had every reason to fear the Ptolemy family – though I had hoped he would trust me at least by now. Perhaps seeing lightning come out of my hands had not exactly helped, though. Then I remembered. Berenice still held his brother – who was probably dead by now, or would be as soon as she found out her little spy had fled with me. Now I knew why Khai had cradled him so tenderly as we left Alexandria.

'Oh, Mamo,' I whispered, holding out a hand to him.

He looked at me like a frightened mouse, then straightened his back and picked up another bundle, scuttling into the stern with it as if one of Bastet's fiercest cats was after him. I had ordered him drugged and taken with us so that he wouldn't betray our plans to my sister. Now it was most likely I had the shadow of another death hovering over my conscience. I felt the weight of it settle on my shoulders, squared them, accepted the guilt. If there was to be war between Berenice and me, it would not be the last such shadow, and there was nothing I could do to change it now. All I could do was to make sure that my small fan bearer was safe, and hope that he was young enough that the grief would pass in time.

I had travelled on this part of the river quite recently, on my way up to Alexandria. How long ago it seemed already. I was a different girl from the one I'd been then. I had faced down a god, caused a Pharaoh's death, broken *ma'at* – and learned how it felt to kiss and be kissed. Now I was being pulled towards a fate I'd never asked for, filled with the gifts of two goddesses.

I spent most of that first day, and some of those following, at the prow, listening to the flap and crack of thick linen behind me as the sail bellied and swung in the stiff breeze that carried us upriver. The gold in my blood pulled and pulled like a current, sweeping me onwards, causing me to curse on the many days when the wind dropped to nothing and the oars had to be used. I didn't sleep much, but when I did, my dreams were full of flying ibis wings, dark underground mazes full of shining silver spears and, always, the flat landscape of sparkling sand that was our final destination.

When I was awake, it was hard for me to be in such close quarters with Khai and not touch him or talk to him in the way I wanted to, and Charm's constant whispered teasing about His Gorgeousness didn't help. After I'd snapped at her a few times, and she didn't shut up, I realised she was doing it to keep from worrying about other things, and so then I just let her carry on.

I didn't think Khai liked our situation much either. From the moment we got on the boat he was utterly correct with me, keeping a distance of at least two cubits between us at all times. We could never be alone, so at the beginning our eyes did the talking and touching for us when no one else was looking, which was hardly ever on such a crowded vessel. I noticed that he threw himself into rowing with a kind of fierce passion, which told me how frustrated he was. I understood that it was at least a job, something to do, something that made him feel less helpless. When the sail was up and the oars were shipped again, he stood near me, his hands grasping the rail till his knuckles whitened, gazing out at the ravaged land we passed with blank, unseeing eyes. But as the voyage went on, he looked at me less and less and then he began to avoid me, though he was often huddled in a small knot with Captain Nail and the warriors. I tried not to let it hurt.

I was shocked at how much worse the land had got in the short time since I'd last seen it, and kept on wondering guiltily if the power Isis had had to expend helping me in Alexandria had contributed to the speed of my country's decay. I'd been warned over and over again that her power was waning, that Egypt and its people were in danger – been told that I was the only one who could bring it back to her. Was it too late already?

There was a constant miasma of rot hanging in the air. The groves of date palms we'd seen heavy with fruit were now showing signs of grey, fluffy mould on the orangey-green bunches. Fat crocodiles, having gorged on the bloated bodies of dead cattle and goats, lay on the banks, occasionally thrashing away in a flurry of stinking mud as an oar came too near. Towns and villages, built on ground normally immune to the floodwaters, lay damp and empty, the folk who lived in them having fled to higher places, or drowned.

Even great Memphis, city of the old Pharaohs, with its towering pyramids and houses of the dead, had not escaped.

There was a continuous wailing and praying in the streets and beside the old palaces, and all the temples were full of the smoke of burnt offerings rising to Ra, to Osiris, to Hathor, to Thoth. Charm and Dhouti came back from the market talking of a jagged bolt of lightning that had come out of a clear blue sky and hit a woman and her children, leaving them as smoking blots of death on the street. Khai, using his spying skills once more to listen at doorways and on the edges of small, frightened knots of inhabitants, told tales he'd heard of spirits rising in the night from the necropolises; of shrieking curses, of long-dead animals leaving their tombs; of trailing linen wrappings, clattering to bone and dust as the rays of Ra hit them in the morning dawn. He reported the stories as if to a senior officer, eyes looking somewhere over my left ear.

Well, two could play at that game. If he wouldn't look at me, then I wouldn't look at him either. I turned an angry shoulder to him and began to issue orders.

'On,' I said, urging them aboard again with their meagre bundles of bread, beans and beer. 'We must go on.' I could feel the green spaces of the Great Lake waiting upriver, beckoning to me, and I knew that it was there we must leave the river and travel out into the thirsty desert.

What I wasn't prepared for when we arrived at Herakleiopolis the Great was a reception party of priestesses, each with a silver Knot of Isis pinned to the cloth covering the outer slope of her left breast.

I was even less prepared for the sight of High Sister Merit. The leader of the Sisters of the Living Knot stood silent and impassive at their head, and rank upon rank of warriors of Isis stood behind as far as my eyes could see, the silver knot emblems on their shields sparkling and their spear tips bright. There must have been two thousand of them at least. As I looked out of the deckhouse window and saw her standing there, I bit back a tiny whimper of shock. The Eye of Ra was dipping into the west, and its fading rays kissed the dark cobweb scars on her face and the pristine whiteness of her robes with pink. I was grubby from weeks on the boat, not dressed as a priestess of Isis, nor as a princess of the House of Ptolemy. I was entirely unready to meet the scariest woman in the world – the one who had commanded the loyalty of my warriors before I ever met them.

'Oh, no,' breathed Charm over my shoulder. 'What's *she* doing here? And who are all those other priestesses?'

'I think they're most of the sisterhood, given what they're wearing,' I said, answering the easy question first. 'I've no idea what Merit is doing. But one thing I do know. I won't let her trap me. Whatever spiderweb she plans to tangle me in is not as important as the job our goddess has given me.'

I looked round for our bags.

'Quick, Charm. I must change. I'm not meeting her looking like this.'

'It's me that'll take the blame if you do, O Mistress of Messiness,' she said. 'Help me look in the bags for your priestess stuff.'

Like whirlwinds we went through every bundle, throwing everything out onto the dirty floor. Then Charm gave a cry of triumph as she dragged out my best white robes – slightly creased from travelling, but clean.

I stripped, then threw them over my head, smoothing the folds into place and tying the girdle. Working fast around me, Charm pinned the Knot of Isis between my breasts, coiled my hair into neatness and threw a gold-beaded net over it. I missed the jewellery I'd had to leave behind, hidden in great Alexander's tomb. It was the only thing I had left of my mother. It would have given me comfort to have worn it. Instead, I folded back the shoulders of my robe, tucking them under, exposing the throne glyph that marked me as Isis's chosen. I'd need all the authority it gave me if I was to tackle the woman Isis had picked to lead her secret sisterhood – the implacable, unyielding wall of granite that was Merit of the Pharos.

Charm looked at me seriously.

'You can do this, Cleo,' she said, as the boat glided into the almost-flooded dock.

'Maybe,' I answered. 'But it's Merit…'

'You can do this,' she repeated firmly. 'Now go out there and be the Chosen. It's time.' She gave me a little push.

Charm was right. I needed to face Merit, but there was something else I had to do first. I straightened my back, walked out with her comforting presence behind me and beckoned to Captain Nail and the warriors. They were hurriedly grouping themselves on the stern deck, putting on what armour they had, and retrieving spears and weapons. I looked for Khai but he was nowhere to be seen, avoiding me as usual – as were Am, Dhouti and Mamo.

They must be helping the crew at the front. The flapping sail came slowly down the mast, hiding us for a moment.

'Are you mine?' I asked the captain bluntly. It was a question for them all, really. They didn't look like the neat rows of pristine warriors who waited for us on the dock any more. Their few pieces of armour were more a mish-mash of leather straps than proper breastplates, and their shields were just round pieces of hide-covered wood with a few metal studs. Their spears had sharp tips, though, and I knew the edges of their blades had been honed till they would cut through flesh faster than a striking cobra could spit.

Five clenched fists thumped into five brawny chests.

'We are yours and our goddess's, Chosen,' said my captain, very softly, as the boat banged suddenly into the wooden pilings, making all of us lurch. 'Whatever happens next.'

The other four nodded.

'Yours and Isis's till we die, Chosen.'

I closed my eyes for an instant, relief flooding my bones. I'd been afraid they'd go back to Merit, revert to the proper warriors they'd been before they were assigned to me all those months ago in Philäe. But my powers were stronger than hers, I reminded myself. I held our goddess's map inside myself. I had shot fiery lightning out of my fingers. Perhaps I was the scary one now.

My captain stepped in front of me and Charm

deliberately, with Warriors Haka and Sah to each side, and the other two falling in behind us, along with Khai, Dhouti, Am and Mamo, as we reached the prow. Then he led us ashore.

That walk over the rough, slippery planks felt as if it took forever. My inscrutable princess mask was clamped in place only by my own will, and a brief churning in my belly made me clench myself inwardly for a moment, hoping I wouldn't disgrace myself right there on the dock.

My only true comfort was that I could feel the pulse of gold still beating in my blood, telling me that this was right, this was meant, this was Isis's will. It made me ignore my roiling gut, stand even straighter, walk taller and more confidently. I was not the confused girl I had been when Merit and I first met, straight after my initiation into the Sisterhood of the Living Knot. I had passed through far worse than that now. I was stronger, harder, more powerful. Our goddess had spoken through my lips, used my fingers to channel lightning. I would not let the High Sister beat me down in the way she had before. The throne glyph on my shoulder began to glow gold as I stalked towards her.

To say I was surprised when the head of the sisterhood dropped to her knees and raised her palms was an understatement. If the Eye of Ra had started travelling backwards in the sky, I could not have been more astonished. Every sister behind her did the same, and the warriors clashed spears on shields. It was a deafening sound of approbation. I held my jaw upwards and closed with extreme difficulty.

'Blessed be Isis. Hail to her chosen and marked,' said Merit, her voice high and cold as ever.

'Blessed be Isis. Hail to her chosen and marked,' echoed voices all around me, making the air shake with the sound.

There was only one thing I could do. I stepped forward, past Captain Nail, took Merit's hands and raised her to her feet.

'Hail, beloved and blessed High Sister,' I said, pulling her round so that she stood beside me.

Then I looked out at the kneeling bodies before me, all gazing at me with a devotion I was not sure I deserved. 'I bring greetings from our goddess to you all. She sees you and marks your loyalty and devotion.'

They cried out with joy, prostrating themselves.

I turned my head sideways, as if to kiss Merit's cheek.

'What in the name of Isis is going on here?' I hissed.

4

Iras

Merit stepped back and away, almost as if my touch repulsed her, but I turned sideways, gripping her arm, forcing her to face me. The sisters and warriors in front of us were still flat on their faces, but behind me Charm, Khai and the others remained on their feet. I could see Captain Nail and my other warriors out of the corner of my eye, hands on spears, bodies alert and tense, watching.

The high sister glared at me. The cobweb scars on her face stood out, dark lines criss-crossing her otherwise smooth cheeks. Her black eyes were like a hawk's, piercing and fierce, and they bored into mine as if she wanted to drill a message into my brain.

'There is much to tell you, but not here,' she whispered, her words only a breath on my cheek. 'Let me escort you to our rooms in Heryshaf's temple before darkness falls, Chosen,' she said loudly. 'There is food and rest there for all of you after your long journey – and fresh gear for your warriors.' She sent a sideways glance at Captain Nail, and one nostril flared with a disgust she couldn't hide from me. 'I don't know what you've done to them, but they're a disgrace to the name,' she said, her voice lowering again.

That was more like the Merit I knew and didn't love.

'Our Chosen's rest is more important than ours,' said my captain in his gruffest voice. I knew he had heard her. 'We will see her settled and safe before we take heed of our own comfort or appearance.' His voice lingered on the word 'safe'.

'Very well,' I said. 'Warriors, Charm and Khai with me. The rest of you, bring the bags to wherever we are going.' I gave Merit a steady look. 'I'm sure the high sister here will send someone to show you the way.'

She nodded, then turned. 'Rise,' she commanded. 'Let us do our Chosen honour.'

As one, the sisters and warriors got to their feet, stepping aside and forming two long columns with a passage in between. I walked through, Merit at my side snapping out orders. She did not quite dare to take my arm, and I didn't offer it. I also didn't look back to see if Khai was following.

Heryshaf's outer temple yard was full of baaing sheep, appropriately enough for the ram-headed god. It stank of lanolin and dung, and I wondered why Merit had brought us here. We were soon past the woolly bodies and into an inner courtyard, though, where it was quieter. She gestured me through a painted wooden door, and into a large room set with low cushions and benches, carpeted by woven reed mats and lit by oil lamps. The walls were painted with a frieze of Heryshaf's deeds. In his hand was the Knot of Isis – I took that as a good sign. I raised my head and peered into an alcove beyond the main chamber. Abruptly my mouth watered as the appetising scent of mutton roasting over charcoal wafted into the room. I hadn't realised I was so hungry.

We stood there while Captain Nail and Corporal Geta searched the room, and gave quick orders for my other warriors to fan out into the adjoining chambers beyond, or stand guard outside the door. Merit tapped one foot with impatience.

'Do you really think I would put our Chosen in danger, Captain?' she spat out, finally. 'I thought you knew me better than that.'

He turned a cushion over, looked carefully underneath it, and then replaced it before he answered.

'I have learned not to take anything at face value since I last saw you, High Sister. I would not forgive myself if I failed in my duty.' Only I heard the unspoken 'again' at the end of his sentence.

'Very commendable, I'm sure,' she said tartly. 'But you don't—'

'Captain Nail will do as he must,' I interrupted her, just as sharply. 'What I have learned is to trust his judgement in all matters of my safety.' I smiled at him. 'Do what you have to, Captain. We will wait.'

Khai and Charm had moved to either side of me while I was speaking. Merit looked at them with raised eyebrows.

'You will not need slaves or servants here, Chosen. You may dismiss them.'

It was too much. I stepped right up to her, till my nose was nearly touching hers. I spoke very clearly, each word falling into the warm room like a small, sharp spear of flame.

'Charm and Khai are neither slaves nor servants. They are my friends. I would trust them – have trusted them – with my life. They are my right and my left hands. You will treat them with courtesy and honour, or we are finished here. Do you understand?' I hoped Khai understood too. I valued him and Charm above all others.

She moved back abruptly, a look of wary respect on her face.

'I understand. And I apologise if I have misunderstood, Chosen. I thought—'

'I know what you thought,' I said through my teeth. 'Unthink it. Because right now there are only four people I trust in this room. Tell me why you are here.'

Merit would never droop – she was too proud for that – but some tiny shift in her body let me know I now had the upper hand. The feeling of power was a small rush in my veins, and I secretly liked it a bit too much. I tried not to let it go to my head, though. I picked the least uncomfortable-looking bench and sat down, patting the cushions to either side of me. Khai sat immediately, straight-backed and wary, but Charm shook her head.

'I will go and find your taster, Chosen,' she said. 'And see about food. You need to eat.' She didn't say that the kitchen here was not to be trusted, but the purse-lipped sideways glance she cast at Merit spoke volumes. She went through the alcove, and I heard her begin to ask questions of someone on the other side. Captain Nail and Corporal Geta stood rigidly against the walls. I knew they wouldn't leave till I told them it was safe to do so.

'Very well,' said Merit, taking the bench opposite. She paused, then drew in one sharp breath, squaring her shoulders. 'Over the Ahket season, our goddess has spoken – to each one of us personally, Chosen. Every sister who is here. It has been…' She paused and her eyes went distant and dreamy for a moment. 'It has been the greatest honour of all of our lives. I cannot even describe to you how it felt.'

I knew very well.

'Like the music of a desert storm, like smooth, sweet honey dripping from the comb,' I said, and she nodded.

'Like that, and yet…not. The message was the same for all – meet you here around the seventh day of Choiak, bring every warrior we could without leaving the temples completely unprotected.' There was another pause. 'She told us to do you honour – and to…' She swallowed as if something unpalatable was stuck in her throat. 'To obey your every command.'

I could see how hard it was for her to say it.

'Did she tell you what happened with the map?' I asked, to buy time. Isis wanted all of them to obey my command? She had sent me warriors? My dreams of an army of shining silver spears in dark mazes underground came back into my mind. I knew there was something I should remember, some piece of information from long ago that plucked at my mind.

'She did not,' Merit said abruptly, breaking into my thoughts. 'Will you do me the honour of telling me, Chosen? I expected you to come back to Philäe, but then my own summons came soon after you left us, and I have been travelling ever since to get here in time.'

'I will,' I said, 'but first, I need to know something. Are there any underground mazes round here – or something similar?'

She stared at me in speechless astonishment.

'What do you—?' she started, but a voice from the alcove interrupted her.

'There are.'

A very short girl, with the roundest face I'd ever seen, stepped through. She was wearing a sand-coloured tunic cut to mid-thigh, and had a small blue amulet at her throat. I just had time to wonder how she had sneaked past the outer guard before Khai was up and thrusting me behind

64

him, and Captain Nail and Corporal Geta were in front of us, spears pointing at her. All in a moment she ducked, flipped forwards in a somersault and was past them. She prostrated herself, grasping my ankles as Khai flung himself at her, and my warriors whirled, about to run her through.

'Stop!' I shouted. 'Do not harm her!'

It was not my voice. It wasn't Isis's or the Old One's either. It sounded like dark, deep water, the clarion call of trumpets, the still moment between life and death. I did not recognise it at all, but it was definitely the voice of a god, and that made all the hairs along my spine stand up, bristling like small, cold needles.

The two warriors froze, spear-tips bracketing the girl's kidneys, then backed off, one careful step at a time. Khai scrambled up and moved to one side of me again, a quiet rock of strength. In my heightened state of awareness, I could feel the *thump thump* vibration of his heart, even though he wasn't touching me.

I breathed out hard through my nose, as the unknown deity within me faded and vanished. My own heart was thumping just as hard as Khai's. Even though I'd seen gods for as long as I could remember, it was only ever Isis and the Old One who'd talked to me – and only Isis who had been within me, taken over my voice. Who was this new god? Was he a threat or an ally? And how had he taken me over so easily?

I looked down at the girl who still lay prone at my feet,

determined not to show any fear. The skin on her palms felt unusually warm on my ankles, but she looked perfectly ordinary – not someone to invoke the direct protection of a deity.

'Get up and tell me who you are,' I said, keeping my voice steady with an effort. 'You do not belong to Isis, do you?'

Merit took one step towards us. I hadn't seen her move, but she was halfway across the room, a deadly-looking curved knife dropped on the reed mat at her feet. I held up one finger and shook my head slightly. I needed to deal with this myself.

The girl jumped to her feet all in one graceful movement, strangely agile for someone who seemed all curves and roundness, and stood facing me.

'I am Iras of Crocodilopolis,' she said cheerfully, in a surprisingly deep voice. 'And I am sent by Blessed Sobek himself to take you to his labyrinth. Among other things.' She grinned at me, and her teeth were whiter than summer clouds. 'But first, let us eat. I'm hungry, and that mutton out there smells good.' She smoothed her hands over her hips lovingly. 'As you see, there's a certain amount of me to keep up.'

I shook my head, trying to clear it. She had wrong-footed me completely.

'Sobek,' I said stupidly, trying to make sense of her, to take back control of the situation.

At least I knew which god had taken over my voice now,

even if I didn't yet know how or why. I wasn't sure whether I felt honoured or violated by his attention.

'Sobek sent you? Why should the crocodile god want to aid me? And what is the labyrinth?'

She grinned again, her eyes crinkling to slits.

'All in good time, chosen of the goddess. First we eat. All that being the voice of the god stuff takes it out of you, doesn't it?' She winked at me as if we were co-conspirators, put two fingers to her lips and whistled shrilly. 'Hurry up, you through there,' she shouted. 'Food, and plenty of it! Let us rejoice in the blessings of both our gods.'

Her joyfulness was infectious, and without meaning to, I found myself smiling back as Khai's tense body relaxed at my side. I nodded at my warriors to stand down. Merit, of course, was frowning, but for the first time ever she looked more than a little unsure of herself, and as confused as I felt. I could see she desperately wanted to speak, but just as she opened her mouth, Charm came in, several serving women at her back, laden with steaming dishes. Her face was like a thundercloud as she directed them to set everything down in the centre of the room. As she dismissed them, I had just time to wonder why she looked so cross, when she scowled at Iras's back and came over to us.

'You!' she said, poking her in the shoulder. 'Was that you, whistling and shouting at us? You nearly made these women drop everything! Who are you, anyway? How did you get in here?'

'Charm,' I said. 'Don't...' But Iras had stepped back, nearly treading on my toes. Suddenly I saw a dark tide sweep up from Charm's neck, over her cheeks and upwards. Tiny beads of sweat sprang out on her forehead, and then I noticed the same flush had formed at the nape of Iras's neck, just under where her tightly coiled and plaited hair lay. I raised my eyebrows and tried not to stare at them staring at each other. What was going on here?

'D-do I know you?' Charm stammered, sounding more flustered than I'd ever heard her.

'Not yet,' said Iras, her eyes suddenly unfocused. 'Not yet. But Sobek says you will.' The words sounded charged with a layer of meaning I couldn't quite decipher. Charm made a single, unintelligible noise and edged away.

'I'll just go and see if they've brought everything from the kitchens then,' she muttered, and fled back the way she'd come.

'Where is your taster, Chosen? Your sla— Charmion seems to have misplaced him.' Merit's snow-cold tones fell into the heat, dispersing it as if it had never been. I looked round for Am, then remembered. Charm had gone to look for him.

'Perhaps you can go and direct some of your own warriors to search for my other servants, and see them safely to me,' I said, my voice just as icy. I had asked her to take care of my people already, and heard her order it done. But it hadn't been. I wasn't going to have her blame Charm for it.

'Very well,' she said, and glided out of the room, stick-straight back radiating disapproval. Into the small silence after she left came a loud rumbling. I realised it was my own belly.

'I am too hungry to wait, and it sounds as if you are too, Chosen. I will be your taster,' said Iras, grinning at me again and patting her own ample stomach. 'The people of Heryshaf are not likely to try and harm you, but it is best for you to be sure. And it will show you that I am to be trusted.' She squatted by the many dishes, and spooned a little of each into her mouth before I could say anything. Her round, muscled arms were bare – there were no hidden powders or potions she could slip in without one of us noticing.

Khai leaned towards me. 'She could have taken an antidote!' he growled, as we waited for any reaction. He was right to warn me, of course, but I had a growing instinct about this girl, the kind of instinct I always trusted. A god had protected her. She had been sent to me tonight for a reason. This was not my time to die from poison. I touched his arm briefly, hoping he'd understand that I wasn't dismissing his warning lightly. Nothing had happened to her. The food was most likely safe, but I needed to be sure.

'Will you serve me, Iras?' I asked quietly. 'Will you swear to keep me safe on the life of your god?' My question was laden with more than one meaning.

She looked back at me over her shoulder, then picked up another spoon and filled a bowl for me.

'I will, Chosen,' she said, holding my gaze with her own in a way that answered me as I had wished. 'That is one of those other things my god has sent me to do.' With that, she handed me my food and waved the spoon at Khai. 'Dig in, Inky Locks!' she ordered. 'Don't let it get cold.'

I had to smile at the look of shock on my very proper lover's face. Khai cared about appearances and respect in public, if not in private. Iras's informality had thrown him, as it had me, at first – but now I thought I rather liked it.

Just as I had persuaded my warriors to put aside their weapons and eat, one at a time, Charm came back. She helped herself to food, then slid in beside me, carefully not looking at Iras. A spark of curiosity lit within me. I wondered if either of them would blush again. Perhaps I should test it.

'Charm, this is Iras,' I said, 'sent to us by Blessed Sobek himself, though his messenger has not told us why yet.' I cocked my head at Iras enquiringly.

Charm merely nodded at her, and Iras belched politely behind her hand, nodding back. Neither of them blushed at all. Maybe I'd imagined it.

'If you're sure we shouldn't wait for that cold streak of disapproval who went off to look for your taster?' Iras asked. Both Charm and Khai choked and even Captain Nail coughed into his bowl.

'No, no,' I said, biting the inside of my cheek hard so as not to laugh. It was the perfect description of Merit. 'I'm sure she'll catch up.'

I cleared my throat and made my voice serious. I did not know this girl from a grain of desert sand, and yet the hairs on the back of my neck told me that her life and mine were now entwined like vines on a thorn branch.

'If you are truly here to serve me, Iras of Crocodilopolis, then tell me what you know, and why you have been sent.'

'Very well, then,' she said simply, and began, her deep voice sing-song and mesmerising.

'I was the voice of my god. I was the one known as the Crocodile Child until I was eleven years old. He spoke through me to the priests and to the people of the lake. I rode the lake waves on the backs of his crocodiles, and none harmed me. I knew not mother nor father, because all the people of the lake were my mother and father. But then, as is the custom, when my moon bleeding began, the voice of the god passed to another. It was then that I started my proper training and left Crocodilopolis. Sobek loves the thrust and cut of war, and so I honoured his role as god of military might. I can wield sword and spear, dagger and knife. I can kill in a thousand different ways, but I can also heal in ten thousand more. I can live in the desert, find water in the driest place, food where none seems possible, shade under the highest sun. All these things a true soldier of Sobek must be able to do, and more. I passed all the tests, and then came the final one.'

She leaned closer to me, lowering her voice to a mere breath, so that I had to strain to hear.

'The ordeal of the labyrinth, we call it, for it takes place in the secret spaces under the temple. And that was where my god came to me three days ago. He said that I was to meet you and bring you and your warriors and priestesses there, for his purpose and your goddess's are as one when it comes to war; that I must tell you that I am the pathfinder; and say that I am to serve you and holy Isis for the rest of my days, until the very end.'

Her face shone with remembered awe.

'I am to be your light in darkness, your guide and your guard.'

She unfolded herself and knelt before me, hands outstretched in the sign of homage to a Pharaoh.

'Will you have me, Cleopatra Chosen?' she asked simply.

Charm and Khai shifted beside me, and I glanced at them.

Khai looked even more troubled and unsure than usual. I had to act quickly, before either of them saw Iras as an unwanted intruder.

I reached for their right and left hands, taking them and pressing them tightly together between mine. I was fumbling towards what I needed to do, going on instinct alone. I hoped it would work.

'Close as Isis, Osiris and Horus are we three,' I said softly, holding their eyes with mine, 'and nothing can break that. But Isis could not have put her son's butchered body back together without the help of Blessed Sobek.' I stretched out the hand that held Charm's and took Iras's, adding it to the other two, holding all three in the circle of my own, a small pyramid of faith.

'Where there were three are now four. I accept the gift of your god, Iras.' I looked into her eyes, seeing only trust and gratitude for the task she'd been given. 'I am glad to have you at my back.'

The gold within my blood throbbed and swelled with approval.

We all felt it, I thought, though in Khai's case I wasn't totally sure. He relaxed for a brief second, and then went tense again. But whether we liked it or not, we four were now bound with an unbreakable bond, shackled by the immortals till they chose to let us go. I wondered suddenly if they ever would.

With one last firm squeeze I released them. It seemed to me that Khai's hand left mine reluctantly, dropping between us, index and middle fingers drumming restlessly on his thigh, but it was Charm I noticed most at that moment. Her hand turned and clasped Iras's, clinging to her for an instant like a lost child to its protector. I felt her sigh, a small breath on my cheek, and then she too let go. I would get her alone before we slept and find out what was happening. But just now, I needed another question answering.

'So, Iras,' I said. 'Tell me about this labyrinth.'

She dropped back to the reed mat and settled herself, reaching for her bowl again and dipping a piece of flatbread into it to wipe up the remaining meat juices.

'It's not that I don't want to tell you,' she said, around a mouthful. 'I do. It's just that I—'

Khai leaned forward and interrupted her.

'Did you or did you not just swear on the life of your god to serve the chosen?' he asked, his voice clipped and slightly aggressive. I didn't understand. Was he jealous of her, even after what had just happened? Or was it something else? I noticed that he wasn't calling me 'my' chosen any more. It hurt more than I would have expected.

'Keep your hair on, Inky Locks,' she said, that irrepressible grin popping out again. 'I was about to say—'

But he interrupted again. 'Don't call me "Inky Locks",' he said fiercely. 'My name is Khai. Use it.'

'All right…*Khai*,' she said. For the first time I saw wariness in her posture. She wasn't quite sure how to deal with him. Right now she wasn't alone. He was definitely being extra moody and strange again.

'As I said, I want to tell you, even though it is forbidden knowledge for anyone outside Sobek's inner circle of initiates. What goes on in the labyrinth is almost never shared with strangers. It is a place of mystery and danger, but my god has bidden me to bring you and all your people there. It is best you see it and judge for yourselves what it is. It…it…' She hesitated as if unsure. 'It shows different faces to different people.' She raised her head and looked at me directly. 'We will go tomorrow, Chosen. All of us. Sobek, blessed be his name, told me to say this to you directly: "War is coming. You must be ready."'

War is coming.

Those were the exact words Isis had spoken to me. An icy fingernail trailed down my back.

'Tomorrow then,' I said.

'I will go and prepare the way,' said Iras, just as Merit swept in again.

'Your servants have placed the baggage where it needs to be, Chosen. There was a misunderstanding at the dock. They are all safely here.' Her lips were pursed tighter than a dog's backside, and I pitied whoever had misunderstood her orders. I bit down on a yawn, clamping it tightly behind my lips till my teeth clenched. Suddenly the food sat like a lump in my belly and I knew I needed to sleep.

'Do we all rest here, or is there another chamber?'

Merit looked a little shocked. 'Another chamber, of course. It should be ready by now, Chosen,' she said. 'Come with me.'

Beckoning Charm to follow, I went with her eagerly, and not just because I was tired. I could feel Khai's brooding gaze on my back. I thought we'd dealt with his issues back in Naucratis, but apparently not. Whatever was going on with him would have to wait till morning, though. I just couldn't handle a big argument right now.

I badly needed to talk to Charm.

Alone.

5

Crocodilopolis

'I don't know,' Charm said, flapping her hands at me in a shooing motion. 'It just…I just…she… Oh, why do you have to make everything so complicated, Cleo? I blushed. She blushed. So what? It's not a crime, is it?'

She began to swish around the plain, whitewashed room impatiently, shaking out bedding with a crisp snap as I took off my tunic and washed as best I could in the small basin of lukewarm water which had been provided. Everything smelled slightly of sheep and damp plaster, and I could hear sleepy baaing from the far courtyard. Captain Nail had left Warrior Haka on guard outside the door. His slow voice rose to a momentary sharpness as someone passed, then fell into silence.

'Anyway, what about His Gorgeousness?' Charm went on. 'Has a hornet crawled up his backside and stung him or something? I thought he was going to bite that Iras's head off back there.'

I debated for a moment as to whether I should let her get away with changing the subject. The very fact that she'd done so told me she had something to hide when it came to her reaction to Iras. But I knew she'd only tell me when she wanted to. It had always been that way with my stubborn Charm. She could give rocks lessons in obstinacy.

'I think he's jealous of her, to be honest,' I replied. I hesitated. Would it be breaking Khai's confidence? But I really, really needed to talk to someone – and Charm was the only one who'd understand my worry. 'He's a bit unsure of himself right now, and that's why he's been so moody, I think. When we last talked properly, back in Naucratis, he said he feels like a...like a spare leg on a camel. I tried to reassure him that Isis has a role for him in all this – and I did promise he wouldn't be my...er...lapdog.'

'Not like he was your sister's, you mean?' she said, putting her finger right on it as usual.

'Yes,' I said, the gloom coming down on me again like a blanket. 'He's used to being busy, to being a hero and rescuing people from death by crocodile, to being a spy for Isis. Just being at my side isn't enough for him, I don't think, even if he says it is.' Saying it out loud made my stomach clench. 'Haven't you noticed how he avoided me on the boat, how he doesn't look at me properly any more? He did defend me tonight, when he thought Iras was an assassin, but afterwards... I don't know if he even believes what I said back there. About us all being bound together, I mean.'

I looked at her uncertainly.

'You felt it, Charm...didn't you?'

'Of course I did, Cleo!' she said, rolling her eyes. 'I'd have to have been dead not to feel that. It was amazing. Like a wash of warm gold or...or...well, I can't really describe it properly. But then I've been bound to you forever, haven't I? I've known that since I first met you. If your destiny is to be the Great and Wonderful Pharaoh, then mine is to be the Great and Wonderful Pharaoh's Handmaid of Wondrousness.' She said it so matter-of-factly that it took me aback for a moment.

'You're my...' I started, but she interrupted, with an eye roll that made my lips twitch.

'I know. I'm your best friend, too. That kind of goes without saying by now, Cleo. But I'm not ashamed of being your handmaiden, either. Stop trying to make me feel better about it. We're not all born to rule the multitudes, you know.'

'I'm not at all sure I was born to do that,' I admitted. The thought of maybe having to be Pharaoh continued to send cold icicles down my spine.

'Of course you are,' Charm said. 'Don't be an idiot, Cleo. You're a Ptolemy, aren't you?'

I couldn't argue. It was true. Generations of my family had ruled Egypt. But I wasn't Pharaoh yet. And I had more pressing problems to deal with.

'Never mind that now. What am I going to do about Khai?' I demanded.

Charm tutted, frowning.

'Men!' she said. 'Always trying to make it about them. He should get over himself and his moods. If anyone is going to feel jealous of Iras, it ought to be me, but I don't. She's…she's…' Charm stumbled to a halt.

'Pretty?' I suggested mischievously, as she blushed again.

'No!' She batted a hand at me crossly again. 'I mean yes, but…that's not what…' She cleared her throat. 'She's necessary, is what I mean. She has a job to do for you, and so do I. If you trust her enough to do what you did tonight, then we all should too.'

'Yes, but that's just the point, Charm. Don't you see? I told you already – Khai thinks he *hasn't* got a job. He feels as if he's just a useless hanger-on. It's not about trust, it's about jealousy and insecurity.'

She looked at me, one eyebrow raised.

'When did you get so wise?' she asked. Now it was my turn to blush.

'I'm not,' I said. 'I know how he's feeling, but not what to do about it or how to make him feel better. This eternal black mood of his is driving me mad, to be honest.'

'Then give him something to do,' she said simply.

'Make him into your king of spies or something. Use his talents. Make him feel he counts. That's all he really wants. Apart from the obvious, of course.' She wiggled one eyebrow suggestively.

She was a genius. She'd also made me blush again, but I decided to ignore it. I wasn't so sure Khai did want the obvious any more, either. We hadn't had much of a chance to find out lately.

'I love you, you know, O Bright and Brilliant One. Why didn't I think of that?'

'Because your brain is full of higher things, O Empress of Erudition. Like getting us through the desert to find Isis and all that stuff. Now, if you've finished playing with that water, leave it alone so I can wash. Get into bed. I have a horrible feeling there may be more camels in our future tomorrow. You'll want all the rest you can get.'

'Thanks,' I said. 'As if the sheep weren't bad enough. Now I'll probably dream of Smelly Camel and his friends.'

I didn't. Instead, I drifted through mazes deep underground, searching, always searching for the jewel at their heart. There was the sound of chanting, of clashing weapons, the feeling of many bodies pressed together in the darkness – and always underneath everything, the murmur of my goddesses.

Come to us, come to us. War is coming.

It didn't exactly make for a restful night. I woke a couple of hours before dawn, irritable and still not really knowing what to do about Khai, with the smell of sheep dung in my nostrils and on my skin, and the feeling that my eyeballs had been rubbed with fine grit. Charm lay beside me, her mouth slightly open, making a tiny whiffling noise in her throat. Asleep, I could look at her properly. I studied the last faint traces of purplish-yellow bruise on her face. Those made me not just irritable but angry.

I will *repay you in full for all the hurt you caused, Berenice*, I thought to my Pharaoh sister, back in Alexandria. *If war is coming, you and I will definitely be on opposite sides.*

I made it a promise as I slipped out of bed, trying not to wake Charm. I needn't have bothered, because just then there was a loud triple knock at the door. Charm sat bolt upright with a start, looking about her wildly, and I scowled as Iras's cheerful shout sounded over the growly challenge of Warrior Sah. The guard must have changed in the night.

'I bring breakfast, Chosen. Hot bread and fresh dates. Open up.'

Charm slipped past me, pulling on her tunic, fighting to get the shoulder fastening done up, before she flung open the door.

'You,' she said, hands on her hips. It was a pose I knew well. 'Yelling about the food again. Are you always this noisy? You should have more respect.'

Iras grinned at her. 'You'd better get used to it,

Pretty Girl. Nothing is more important than a good breakfast in the belly.'

'Or a good midday meal or dinner either, it seems,' Charm muttered, half snatching the tray from her and turning to set it on the low table in the room.

'A soldier marches on her stomach,' Iras replied gravely, though a twinkle remained in her eyes. 'The next meal may be a long time coming. I eat where I may, and give thanks to Mother Isis for blessing the fields so that we may have food.' She looked at me. 'I have messages. The Cold Streak wishes to know when we will leave, and Inky Locks wishes a private word with you at your convenience.' She winked, not very successfully.

I knew I shouldn't laugh. I really did. But her informal good humour was so infectious that I couldn't help a small snort bursting from my nose.

'Ah, good,' she said, beaming. 'I like a girl who can laugh. Laughter is good for the blood and—'

I cut her off. 'Charm is right,' I said, trying to make my voice severe. 'You do need to learn a little respect, Iras. Merit is a high priestess of Isis – and Khai is…well, he did ask you not to call him Inky Locks, you know,' I said, my words trailing off into silence.

She hung her head, but only a little. 'I am sorry, Chosen. I am only a rough soldier girl. I will try to mend my manners.'

I didn't believe she was only a rough soldier girl

for an instant, but I let it pass.

'How soon can we travel to Crocodilopolis?' I asked.

'As soon as you are ready, Chosen,' she said. 'All is prepared. You have only to say the word.'

'Then we'll leave as soon as everyone has eaten. Tell Merit, and then please send Khai to me.' I hoped he'd asked to speak to me because he wanted to clear the air between us. Maybe if I put Charm's suggestion into action that would help. I didn't think I could stand even one more minute of his dark moodiness – I had enough to worry about without that. As soon as I had woken, the insistent pull of the map in my blood had told me that we needed to go onwards as soon as we could.

Iras bowed. 'From your lips to my ear. I hear and obey, Chosen of Isis.'

I sat waiting for him on the bed in my chamber. Iras had come to tell me that everything was ready, and she and Charm had taken the last bags to load. From outside I could hear the faint final bustle and clatter of things being strapped down into mule carts and onto camels. Merit's ice-cold tones were raised in reprimand, directing her warriors and priestesses, as well as the servants. None of it really penetrated, though. I was thinking, and I didn't much like where my thoughts were taking me.

It was almost a relief when Khai came in, brows drawn together in a black scowl. His whole body was stiff and awkward-looking, practically vibrating as the door shut behind him.

It seemed to me that he was looking for another fight. I decided to go on the attack before he could.

'I thought we'd sorted this out, Khai. Do you think I feel any more sure than you do?' I asked, low and fierce, as I rose to my feet. 'Do you think you're the only one here who doesn't feel scared about the future? Or is it that you're jealous of Iras?' He whirled round, eyes suddenly slitted with fury, mouth open to speak, but I held up a hand. 'Be quiet and let me finish, Khai. Our goddess has given me a job, yes. She has shown me the path to get to her. But what happens after that, after her power is restored? Do you think I know how to build her an army? To restore *ma'at*? How do I do that?'

I clenched my fingers into fists, trying not to rub them across my suddenly damp eyes. I didn't want kohl halfway down my cheeks for the rest of the day. It wouldn't be a good look for the chosen of Isis.

'If I somehow tip Berenice off the throne, and become Pharaoh myself, what then? There would still only be one of me. *Ma'at* would still be broken. So do I leave her where she is? Go across the Great Green and fetch my father back to be Pharaoh beside me?' Saying that out loud was terrifying. I took a deep breath. It trembled in my throat, and my voice wobbled.

'I can't do this alone, Khai. I need you and Charm, and

yes, probably Iras too, since Isis and Sobek have decreed it. But you've avoided my eyes for weeks, you hardly talk to me, and I don't even know if you felt what happened to us all last night. If you didn't…' I stopped, unable to go on.

He took a deep breath, squeezing his eyes shut, pressing his lips together. Then his shoulders slumped, and all the stiffness went out of him as he blew the air out in a great sigh.

'Yes, Cleo. I felt it, Isis help me. For one long, blessed moment. It's the only time since Alexandria when I haven't been in pain.'

That wasn't at all what I'd been expecting him to say.

'In pain? But what…?'

He met my eyes properly at last, and folded back the neck of his tunic, his fingers trembling. The mark of Seth's amulet was still there. It should have healed by now – but it was still as red and angry as the day it had been burned into him, and it had spread, creeping silently towards the mark of Isis he wore secretly on the right side of his chest, as if it would swallow it up. The red-streaked flesh looked dirty raw, and sticky yellow fluid was seeping from it.

'Oh,' I said quietly, my mouth dry and suddenly bereft of any other words. I should have remembered. I should have made sure…

'"Oh" is right,' he agreed, his mouth a thin, drawn line. 'I spend all my time fighting the pain of it now, and it's getting worse and worse. Since before Memphis I've been feeling as if…as if… I think Seth wants me back, Cleo. I think he wants to punish me.' His voice dropped. 'That's why I've been avoiding you. I don't…I don't want to bring his curse anywhere near you, Cleo. I…I need to stay away from you. I've been thinking lately that maybe he wants me more than Isis does, and I wonder whether I should just give in and go back to the brotherhood – let them do what they like to me.' He bent over suddenly, hands on his knees, panting hard.

I felt like the lowest kind of sewer rat. I'd ranted on about myself, accused him of being jealous, thought hateful thoughts…and all this time his moodiness had been caused by the wound Seth had given him. I'd misread the language of his body entirely. It wasn't anger but pain which had made him avoid me, and the desire to shield me from Seth, protecting me as he always had. I wasn't worthy to be in the same room as him.

Isis, I prayed silently, biting my lip so as not to sob out loud. *O, Isis. Please heal him. Please give him a sign that you care. Please don't let Seth win.* But there was a deafening silence from our goddess. I would have to try to help him on my own. It was an all too familiar feeling.

I went to him, laying one hand on his heaving shoulder. Surely I would feel it if Isis's mortal enemy was anywhere near him? But there was nothing apart from the burning heat of his body.

'You idiot,' I said gently, my heart too full of guilt to

think of anything sensible to say. 'Why didn't you tell me it wasn't healing? I could have...'

'You could have what, Cleo?' he asked, straightening up with a grimace he tried to hide. 'Cured me? I think only Isis can do that. Last night I hoped she had, just for that one tiny moment. But then...then the pain came back.'

'Let me look at it properly,' I said, reaching out. He stepped back.

'It won't do any good. I've tried everything. Washing it in sacred Nile water, putting grease on it – the captain even gave me some Isis-blessed herbal stuff the warriors carry to use on wounds, but that just made it burn worse than fire. I tell you – it's Seth's punishment for betraying him.' He sat down heavily on the bed and put his head in his hands. 'I'll have to go back to Alexandria and give myself up to the brotherhood. It's the only way.'

'You will not go back,' I said, my voice rough with tears. 'I won't lose you again – and especially not to Seth's horrible priests.' My brain was working furiously, sifting through the bits and pieces of what I'd learned in my healing lessons at Philäe. As far as I could tell, everything he'd done to treat his wound was wrong. Maybe, just maybe, I could fix it after all.

'Did you cover the burn with clean cloths every day, and boil the Nile water before you used it?' I asked him. He raised his head and stared at me as if I was madder than a crazed jackal.

'No. What good would that have done?'

I shook my head. 'Doesn't matter. I'm going to find Iras. She said she was a healer. It may not be Seth at all...' I hurried towards the door.

'Don't leave me, Cleo,' he said. 'Please.' His voice was a harsh, pleading rasp, and I knew how much it must have cost him to ask.

So I poked my head round the door and sent Warrior Sah to find Iras instead, then went to sit on the bed beside him. His hand was dry and desert-hot in mine. He definitely had a fever.

'How could it not be Seth?' he asked. There was no hope in his voice at all. I tried, not very successfully, to explain basic healing to him until Iras bounced into the room, followed by Charm.

'What's up, Chosen?' she asked in her cheerful way. 'Are you ready to go?' Then she saw Khai and her eyebrows rose at the sight of our clasped hands. Charm let out an exclamation as he abruptly keeled over and slumped against me. She ran over and together we laid him back on the bed, with Iras helping by picking up his feet.

'He's sick.' I explained to both of them what had happened to him back in Alexandria as quickly as I could. 'You said you could heal ten thousand wounds, Iras. I need you to heal this one.'

Khai's forehead felt like a small, hot furnace under my fingers. His eyelids flickered. 'He's coming for me...' he mumbled. 'I can feel his fire. Don't let Seth burn me, Cleo. Don't leave me.'

'I won't,' I said. 'I'm not going anywhere, Khai.' But I wondered numbly if he would leave me instead. He couldn't die. He just couldn't. I wouldn't let him. Iras was now on the bed beside him, her nose close to the wound, sniffing, as she uncovered it.

'How bad is it?' I whispered. She raised her head, looking serious for the first time since I'd met her.

'Not good,' she said. 'I have only the most basic healing stuff here, but there are things which must be done at once. I need to get willow-bark essence into him right now to bring down the fever, and clean the wound out properly. Then we must lay him in a shaded cart, and keep him cool with cloths soaked in water. When we get to Crocodilopolis…well, my teacher, Nanu, is very skilled. If anyone can cure him, she will.'

One hot tear slipped down my cheek, falling onto his. It dried immediately, leaving a small, pale mark.

'I won't lose you, Khai. I won't!' I said, my voice fierce. 'But you have to fight.'

'Am fighting,' he mumbled. 'Always fighting for you, Cleo. Love you.' It was all I could do not to fling myself across his body and try to dissolve my guilt in tears.

Instead, I squeezed his hand really tightly.

'Do what you have to, Iras. And Charm, please will you fetch Merit? We won't be leaving just yet.'

'Oh, joy,' she muttered. 'Our favourite Cold Streak will be delighted to hear that.' But she stroked my arm as she left. I knew she understood.

Merit was coldly efficient as always, once she saw I was determined not to leave Khai to the mercy of the healers at the Temple of Heryshaf. All was arranged very quickly, and once Iras had done what she could to make him more comfortable, Warrior Sah lifted Khai into a cart, and laid him down on the soft bedding I had ordered to be brought. Reluctantly, I agreed that Charm should be the one to tend him on the journey.

'It is important that you show yourself as our chosen,' Merit said briskly. 'You must ride with me at the head of the line.'

I was about to shake my head obstinately – I had promised not to leave him, after all – when Khai spoke, his voice hoarse with the aftermath of screaming. The cleaning of the wound had not been pleasant.

'Go on, Cleo. I'll be all right with Charm.' It was a mark of how ill he felt that he called me by my name in front of everyone. Charm smiled at me from beside him.

'I won't let him get away with anything,' she promised. 'Like dying on you.'

'I wouldn't dare,' he said, one corner of his mouth twitching up to show the brave ghost of a dimple.

'You'd better not,' I said, meaning it. Then I left, putting all my feelings into one last look at both of them as I followed Merit out into the chaos of the outer courtyard.

A beautiful white desert mare was waiting for me in what was now the full light of day, with a saddlecloth made of thick, silver-embroidered linen. Merit stood beside her, her face a mask behind which impatience danced.

'A gift from Heryshaf's people,' she announced. 'Her name is Swift. I hope you can ride, Chosen.'

I hadn't done so since I was a child, but it couldn't be much harder than riding a camel, could it? I'd remembered how to do that perfectly well, though I winced slightly at the thought of more thigh blisters. The last ones had only just healed. So I nodded, and Corporal Geta knelt in the dust and made a cup for my foot. My scramble into the saddle wasn't quite as dignified as I would have liked it to be, but the mare stood docilely enough as I took the reins. I patted her neck and we moved off in a fairly disciplined mass of donkey carts full of sisters, and laden camels and marching men. Captain Nail, Iras and my warriors fell into step around me, and out of the corner of my anxious eye I saw Khai's covered cart join the throng.

I had to fight not to crane my neck round every five minutes to see if he was all right.

I worried about Khai all the way to the Temple of Sobek – but mostly I had to try and put that particular worry to the back of my mind. I had enough trouble trying not only to work out how to steer my mount but also to fend off intrusive questions from Merit about what had happened during my time in Alexandria. At least the small, urgent tug of the map within me had subsided to a quiet pulse now that we were on the road again.

Apart from crossing a small strip of desert sand, we rode through lush green land, shaded by palm and fig trees. All the way, I noticed the ever-present signs of rot and disease.

'Is it really like this everywhere?' I asked quietly. Merit nodded.

'This is not so bad,' she said. 'Some of our sisters have told me of entire villages lost to starvation and disease. Our goddess's influence is waning,' she said, fixing me with a severe glare. She couldn't hide the worry which lay behind it, though. She might be cold and distant, but she did care.

'Isis will fix it all, you know,' I said. 'Once she has her power back.' I'd told her what had happened with the map when she'd demanded to see it. I wasn't sure she believed me entirely. She didn't have to. She just had to heed our goddess's command to obey me.

'Shouldn't you be on a fast camel, heading for the desert, then, instead of fussing about that boy?' she asked. 'Or am I missing something, Chosen?' Somehow, she made my title into a small drip of acid sarcasm as it came out of her mouth. I think it burned her more than me. I chose to ignore her dig about Khai.

'What is it with you, Merit?' I asked, more curious than angry. 'Are you never happy?'

'Not really,' she said. 'Why should I be, when Egypt is dying as we watch? And you haven't answered my question.' She was like a jealous street dog with a bone. I sighed.

'I'm not on a fast camel, because, apart from needing to get Khai better, there is something Isis needs me to do at Sobek's temple first. Were you not listening to Iras?'

'You sent me away, if you recall,' she said stiffly. It was true. I had.

'Let me explain then…'

We arrived on the outskirts of Crocodilopolis as Ra's chariot was sinking into the west. We rode up a long processional avenue lined with enormous statues of Sobek. His crocodile head should have made me shiver, given my experiences with foul Am-Heh and his bloodthirsty beasts but, somehow, Sobek had a fierce but benevolent gaze which made me feel safe instead of scared. The temple itself lay ahead. It was vast, a soaring pile of columns and sun-kissed white stone blocking out the sky. Everywhere about it were more statues, and endless pillar paintings of the god and his snake-wife, Renenutet – and everywhere were priests, each carrying a spear, as well as many, many people. I could sense Merit at my side, getting stiffer and stiffer when Iras began to wave and greet everyone as we went, stopping for a word here and there, her voice loud and cheerful. The priests and people waved back and bowed low, murmuring her name. She was clearly well-known and well-loved here.

As we came to a halt before the shallow steps leading up to the vast temple doors, an imposing figure was waiting to greet us. The head priest's robes were embroidered with gold and gems, and his face was hidden by a golden crocodile head with eyes made of huge rubies. Beside him stood a child of about eight years old, dressed in a short green robe made of what looked like scales. Iras skipped up the steps and knelt before them.

'I bring you the chosen of Isis, O Crocodile Child, O mouth of Sobek. Will you welcome her?'

A drum boomed out, and Swift shied under me. I gripped her with my knees and whispered calming words as Captain Nail sprang to her head. Then the child's voice floated down to me. It was surprisingly deep, just like Iras's.

'Approach, beloved and blessed of Isis. I greet you in the name of the Lord of the Waters, the Rager, He Who Combats Evil.' She beckoned with one small finger. 'Come. It is time.'

6

The Labyrinth of Sobek

Time for what? I wondered, as I slid off Swift's back. My legs felt like floppy strings of hemp from riding for so long, but I stiffened them. All I really wanted to do was to run to Khai and see if he was still alive. But I made myself step forward onto the first temple step without looking back. My warriors fell in behind me, but Sobek's high priest held up his hand.

'You need no protection here, Chosen of Isis.' His voice sounded like gravel grinding underwater. It was somehow familiar to me, and I recognised the echo of his god within it. 'Is not Iras to be your light in darkness, your guide and your guard?'

Iras turned and looked at me expectantly. She had moved up the steps now, and stood smiling at me from near the door of the temple.

'She is,' I said, knowing it was true.

'Then let her help you find the path to where you must go, to the place of visions. Let her take you to the lair of Petsuchos.'

I felt Captain Nail jerk at my elbow.

'It'll be all right, Captain,' I said softly. 'Let me go. Isis will protect me here.' I felt the truth of it with every heartbeat, even though I had no idea yet who Petsuchos was.

'Please, Chosen...' he said, but I waved him back, not turning, not wanting to see the expression on his face.

I walked past the Crocodile Child, past the jewelled head priest, until I was level with Iras. She looked at me and laid a hand on my arm.

'Don't worry, Chosen,' she said softly. 'Your boy is being taken straight to the infirmary. Nanu herself will tend to him.'

I closed my eyes and took a breath.

Please, Isis, as Sobek healed Osiris, please let his healer do the same for Khai.

No breath of wind touched my cheek, no voice echoed in my head, but I suddenly felt as if a deity was watching me. I straightened my spine.

'Let's go,' I said. 'No sense in putting it off.'

In uncharacteristic silence Iras led me onwards past the glare of a hundred lamps, the gaze of a thousand painted eyes, and on into the tunnels which lay under the heart of Sobek's temple.

There was no getting around it: the lower levels smelt strongly of rotting fish and damp. I took shallow breaths, trying not to remember the last time I'd been underground on the way to meet a crocodile. I fixed my eyes on Iras, striding along in front of me, turning left and right and left and right through the maze of twisting passageways without any hesitation. The sight of her sturdy back was oddly cheering. She had no fear here, so I would try not to be afraid either. It was hard, though. I kept flashing back to vile Am-Heh's vicious crocodile executioners, and the poor, wretched girl they had torn to pieces before my eyes. I sent up a brief prayer for her soul, wishing yet again that I'd been able to save her.

Suddenly, as we turned yet another corner, there was a sharp flare of light, and we emerged into an enormous shrine with a high, arched ceiling painted with a papyrus-fringed pool that was surrounded by stars. The walls were full of alcoves ablaze with golden oil lamps. Within them lay mummified crocodile babies, crocodile eggs and other offerings of various sorts – small clay figures, bowls of grain, glass beads, precious stones, spices and bolts of bright cloth. In the centre of the shrine there was a real pool, echoing the shape of the one above. It lay on an island reached by a narrow stone bridge covered with the signs of Sobek, and right in the middle of it there lay a behemoth of a crocodile, its armoured coat shimmering with jewels, its claws painted gold, and its slitted eyes alert and watchful under their heavy lids. A huge Nile perch, a quarter the length of its entire body, lay half-eaten at its feet, and as we entered, its jaws opened in what looked like a wide, toothy grin of welcome.

'Greetings, Petsuchos,' Iras called, running over the bridge to fling her arms around it.

I hung back, staying a safe distance away. I wasn't ready to hug a crocodile quite yet. Actually, I was pretty sure I never would be.

A primeval roar shook the shrine, making the lamp flames shudder and shimmer. I leaped back, my whole body flooded with a terrified energy that told me to run, to hide. But Iras's throaty laugh rang out above it.

'Don't be afraid, Chosen. Petsuchos greets you and welcomes the beloved of Isis to his lair. Come and meet him. He's an old softy really, aren't you, my sweet?' And she scratched the beast under its chin as if it was one of Bastet's temple cats. It grinned even wider. I could see the shreds of fish, caught between its teeth.

Making my feet walk forward onto that bridge was very nearly one of the hardest things I'd ever done. I forced my hands and arms to hang loose at my sides, but the fear sweat was trickling down my temples and down my spine, soaking the back of my tunic and stinging the corners of my eyes. I hoped against hope that the great beast wouldn't scent it – but I knew it would. It was the earthly incarnation of a god, after all. I could see the shimmer of Sobek's presence all around it.

All at once, the god's voice was in my head and I was drowning in dark, deep water. I gritted my teeth and tried to keep breathing.

Good! You are a fighter I see, little Isis girl. Now, let us look further into your soul. What are you made of?

I couldn't move my feet. Petsuchos had laid its enormous head down on them. Its jaws were as heavy as stone, and I could feel the damp huff of its nostrils against my shins.

Look into my eyes.

I had no choice. I gazed into those mud-green orbs, and fell deep into their black slits. I wasn't alive, I wasn't dead – I just *was*. And the god knew me from the thinnest hair on my head to the smallest, meanest thought I'd ever had. I was there for eternity and for no time at all. Then Sobek spoke again.

She Who Bears Up the Throne has chosen her vessel well. A diamond with flaws, but a diamond nonetheless. Bring me the seeds of your army, then, child of Isis. If I find them worthy, I and mine will help to build a force which will break Egypt on its spears and build her anew. The false crocodile will fall, and with him, the false Pharaoh. But mark me well, war is coming, whether you will it or not. If the Throne Bearer is weak, none of this will come to pass. You must make haste to leave here before Ra rises, two dawns from now, or all will be lost.

I found myself on my knees, panting, brow to jaws with Petsuchos. Its breath reeked of rotting perch, and its sharp lower teeth pressed into my forehead so that I knew I would feel the deep indents of them in my flesh when I got up. I backed slowly away and raised my head to find Iras looking into the distance, head cocked to one side, as if she was listening to something. Then her eyes fell on me, and she nodded decisively, coming forward to stand by the great, grinning head, her hand resting on a gigantic ruby.

'There is a door,' she said. 'We of Sobek call it the Way of Judgement. Your people must pass through it, one by one. If they are found worthy, they will be taken to the heart of the labyrinth. If not…' She hesitated.

'If not, then what?' I asked, and my words sounded creaky from disuse, as if I hadn't spoken for a season.

'If not, then those with impure hearts or purpose will be taken to the lake and given to Sobek's crocodiles, to do with what they will.'

I shuddered. I couldn't help it. Would I too have gone to the lake if Sobek hadn't found me worthy? I could imagine crocodile teeth meeting in my flesh all too well. But the god had spoken, and I must obey.

'What about Khai…and Charm?' I asked. 'Do they have to go through the door too?'

Iras nodded. 'Yes. All must pass. But not until dawn tomorrow, when Ra first drives his chariot up over the lake. We have a little time.'

She and I both bowed to Petsuchos. She kissed it on the nose. I did not. Then we both left the way we'd come.

* * *

I should have gone straight to Merit, really, or to the high priest. That was what a proper princess, a proper sister of the Living Knot would have done. But I didn't want to be a proper princess or sister until I had to. I knew what my duty was to my goddess, and I would do it willingly, however hard it was. But right now I wanted to see Khai, to check with my own eyes that he was being looked after properly.

Iras just laughed when I told her what I wanted.

'Am I not to be your guide?' she asked. 'I know every loop and twist of this place. We will go out the back way and find Nanu and your Inky Locks. I can easily sneak you back in again. No one will know how long we spent with Petsuchos. Isn't he beautiful, by the way?'

I nodded as she chattered on. It was beautiful in its way, but I didn't think I'd ever feel as enthusiastic about it as Iras did. Finally, we were outside under the stars, and Iras turned to the right, where a long, low building lay at the back of the main temple. The risen moon was a few days off being full, and I remembered with a jolt: Charm. She would be worrying, checking her body for the signs of difference she was desperate not to see. How bad a friend was I to have forgotten that, even for a moment, amid my own worries? I didn't think it was selfish that I quickly raised my palms to the night sky and asked Isis to make sure Charm wasn't with child. Then, of course, I wondered guiltily if every prayer of mine drained away a little more of my goddess's power.

'Wait here in the shadows,' Iras said, breaking into my thoughts. 'I'll see where he is.' I huddled against a pillar, still warm from the heat of Ra's rays, and felt the pain of sore muscles and a very long day crash in on me. I closed my eyes and willed myself to stay upright. Luckily Iras soon returned.

'This way,' she said. I followed her down a dimly lit hall and into a small room which smelled of herbs and something sweet and sickly. Khai lay asleep on a bed, his chest wrapped in linens stained with green. His breath rasped through his chapped lips, and there were dark shadows of pain round his eyes. Charm was on her feet and she came to me, putting her arms round me and holding me tight.

'He's not dying yet,' she said, knowing what I wanted to hear most. 'Nanu gave him a sleeping draught, and burned a pellet of poppy under his nose to help with the pain. She'll check on him soon, and all through the night. She was very cross with him for not getting a proper healer sooner. And she tore a strip off Captain Nail and made him give her all the warriors' ointment. She threw it away and said she'd give them something that might actually work. I've never seen Captain Nail look so much like a kicked dog before!' Her voice flowed on, soothing me like a river of calm, letting me come back to myself.

Finally, I disentangled myself from her arms and put a finger to her lips.

'Did you speak to Nanu about your...er...about you?'

I asked quietly, glancing at her belly.

Her eyes narrowed and I felt her grow stiff, casting a wary glance at Iras. 'I did,' she said. 'You're not to bother yourself over it. It's my problem. I'll deal with it if I have to.'

I sighed. There was my obstinate Charm, back again as if she'd never been away. 'All right, then, but if…'

'Yes, if,' she said, her voice brisk and unyielding. 'If isn't here yet. Now tell me what happened with Pet— what's his name?'

Iras cleared her throat.

'His name is Petsuchos, and you should have more respect, Pretty Girl.' She grinned, and my mouth twitched upwards for a fleeting second as Charm's dark skin flushed with red. The tables had been turned on her very neatly.

'Respect has to be earned,' she said tartly. 'And crocodiles and their priests aren't my favourite thing since I…well…they're just not.' She bit her lip, and I knew she hadn't meant to say even that much.

Iras had that faraway look in her eyes again, and then I saw her wince. She put out a hand to Charm, laying it for just a moment on her bare arm.

'I understand,' she said. 'But I will show you that in the way of the true crocodile, the way of Sobek, there is nothing to fear and much to love.'

Charm pulled her arm away abruptly, and I saw her swallow hard.

'You couldn't possibly begin to understand,' she snarled,

just as Khai began to thrash and moan. I ran to the bed, kneeling down on the hard floor, taking his hands in mine. They were burning hot, dry as *simoom* sand.

'No,' he moaned, tearing himself free from me. 'I won't. I can't. I'm not yours, I'm hers. Leave me alone…' The words trailed into incoherent babbling, and then he tried to throw himself off the bed. It took both Charm and me to hold him down.

'Fetch Nanu!' I spat the words at Iras like spears, but she was already out of the door and running.

Nanu came within minutes, together with an older man. The two healers bound Khai to the bed with linen straps as he screamed, then Nanu forced a funnel into his mouth and poured in a bright blue-green liquid, stroking his throat to make him swallow. I could do nothing but stand there helpless, listening to the choking sounds, holding Charm's hand so tightly that I could feel the bones creak. Memories flickered through my head: Khai in the Great Library, Khai in the feasting hall, Khai in the embalmers' archives, Khai saving me from snakes…on and on the images went, and in all of them he was alive, vibrant, strong. He couldn't die now. He just couldn't.

Isis! I called in despair. *Isis! Please!* But my goddess was silent, unable or unwilling to intervene. I felt a tap on my shoulder.

'What?' I snapped, pulled out of my morbid thoughts. It was Iras.

'I'm sorry, Chosen,' she said. 'But it is getting close to dawn. It is time for you to lead your people to the door of the Way of Judgement.'

I shook my head, frantic with fear.

'No. No. I won't leave him.'

Then the diamond will crack, and She Who Bears Up the Throne will fall, roared Sobek's voice into my head. Do your duty, little Isis girl, or all Egypt is lost. I will watch over the boy, if he is so important to you. And then, when all is done, I will judge his worth for myself.

'He is,' I whispered, falling to my knees. 'Oh, he is. And you will find him worthy. I know you will, great Sobek.'

We shall see, said the god. And then he was gone.

Iras and Charm helped me to my feet.

'I'll stay with him,' Charm said. But Iras shook her head, looking serious.

'You too are summoned to walk the Way, Pretty Girl,' she said. 'You wouldn't want to keep Sobek waiting.'

As Ra's chariot edged up over the horizon, I stood before the door of Sobek's Way of Judgement. Charm was just behind me, with Captain Nail and his men behind her. Their weapons – and those of all the warriors – were left in a neat heap against the wall of the temple. The high priest and Iras had made it very clear that everyone should go in unarmed. My captain had not been at all happy about that, and had said so, loudly. I could feel his brooding gaze on my back even now. Merit and every other sister and warrior were gathered further back, waiting in neat, silent ranks in the clear pink-grey haze that preceded the dawn.

The door itself matched the immensity of the temple. It was made of cedarwood, overlaid with bright bands of beaten yellow gold and red copper polished to a high shine, and you could have driven four oxcarts through it, side by side. The lintel and pillared door frame were of purple porphyry carved repeatedly with the crocodile hieroglyph of the god, and a vast painted figure of Sobek himself stood on either side of it, jaws agape. As the first ray of Ra's light struck it, the door swung silently open to reveal the child who was the voice of the god.

'Enter!' she said, her voice deep and strong as a struck gong. 'Enter with pure heart and strength of purpose. Sobek will guide the steps of the righteous.'

I noticed that she didn't say what Sobek would do to the unrighteous; though, of course, I already knew.

Iras had instructed me to go first, even though the god had already seen deep into my soul.

'Where you lead, the others will follow, Chosen,' she had said, as we hurried back towards the temple.

I hoped they would. Merit had tried to argue with me as soon as I was within a cubit of her, of course, but I had commanded her to be silent, reminding her of what our goddess had ordered her to do. In the end she had just bowed her head and sighed in a very un-Merit-like way.

From the shadows under her eyes, I thought she had had as little sleep as I had. I had been brutal with her, overridden all her objections, not spared her feelings, just as once she hadn't spared mine. Blocking my worries about Khai was taking up all my energy, and I had no room in my heart right then for anything but enforcing Sobek's orders.

Just before I went through the door, though, I did put my hand behind me, hooking Charm's fingers with my own and squeezing hard. It was as much for my reassurance as hers. Sobek had to find her worthy. He *had* to.

I felt the child's eyes on me, wise beyond her years.

It was time.

I couldn't delay any longer.

With a silent breath I stepped forward, bowed my head to the child, and entered the Way of Judgement.

It was not like the realm of Isis, except for the initial darkness, and I had survived darkness before. I felt a faint brush against my mind, as if I'd walked through a large cobweb, and then my feet were stumbling forward along a path of unearthly green light, flickering as if it was underwater. I tried to track the twists and turns as I went, but time slid sickeningly back and forth, lurching and fragmented, leaving my memory full of holes and my stomach on the verge of turning itself inside out.

I could not remember how I had reached the heart of the labyrinth. When I came to myself, I was sitting in a pool of green light at the feet of a huge golden statue of

Sobek, in a place I thought I recognised from my dreams. Painted pillars soared upwards into blackness, and rank upon rank of silver spears hung beside each opening in the walls, along with stacks of rectangular shields, and piles of sharp-edged bracelet weapons from the tribes of the south. Each shield was marked with the sign of the ibis, Isis's sacred bird.

As I rose to my feet, Charm came flying though an entrance to my right, her eyes wild and staring. Then she saw me, stopped, and took a gasping breath. Her shoulders slumped.

'Cleo! I...he wants me to...I saw...but I won't... I can't...' The incoherent words poured out of her like water, and then she shook her head as if to clear it, walking to my right side on trembling legs. 'I don't understand what just...' But although I was desperate to know what she had seen and what the god wanted from her, I put a finger to my lips, and reached for her hand once more. This time it was her squeezing till *my* bones creaked.

Out of the middle doors, one by one and in total silence, poured the sisters of the Living Knot. Each paused to take two of the strange bracelet weapons, snap them open and fit them on her wrists. Then came the warriors, also silent, headed by my own captain and his men, with Dhouti, Am and little Mamo close behind. All except Mamo took an ibis-decorated shield and a silver-tipped spear. Every face was filled with purpose, glowing in that preternatural green light. Last of all, and after a considerable pause, came Merit. Her robes were rent, and there was blood pouring from a cut on her cheek. She ran to me and knelt at my feet.

'I serve,' she croaked. 'Please believe me. I...I serve, Chosen.' Her black eyes were haunted with pain and remembered grief, but a pure light now shone in them, a light that I recognised as the sign of our goddess. I raised her up and wiped the blood away with my thumb, pressing on the cut to seal it. Then I embraced her and kissed her gently on both her scarred cheeks, as an equal.

'We both do, Sister,' I whispered, turning her gently to stand on my left. 'We both do. Our goddess knows it.'

Suddenly there was a strong smell of burning metal and ozone at my back. The statue behind me became both cold and hot at the same time. Slowly, Charm, Merit and I turned to face it. The gigantic golden crocodile head opened its eyes. The human hand raised its palm in blessing. The jaws creaked open, and seven drops of blood fell from them, splashing my robe. Then, as we all fell to our knees, prostrating ourselves, the child voice of the god appeared between Sobek's legs.

'The unworthy are cleansed, the three spies of Seth, the four vile servants of the false crocodile have all met their doom. They will be weighed now in the scales of Ammit and must answer to great Osiris, Lord of the Dead. You who are not found wanting, you who have taken up the spear and shield, you who now wear bracelets of death, must remain here in the temple, to train with us. You are now reborn, you are now the army of the Ibis and you each have your orders. Blessed Sobek and She of the Throne command you to serve, obey and be ready. War is coming.'

The sisters' voices mingled in an unearthly ululation, which howled around the immense space, echoing and growing, as the warriors leaped to their feet, clashed spears on shields and let out a deafening yell of praise.

'War is coming. We are one. We are the ibis-born. All praise to Blessed Isis and the great crocodile!'

'War is coming. We are one. We are the ibis-born. All praise to Blessed Isis and the great crocodile!' shrieked the sisters in their turn, shaking their bracelets in the air with a clash and a rattle.

Merit stirred beside me as we scrambled to our feet.

'I will need my own bracelets, I think,' she said quietly. 'If I am to lead the sisters of the Living Knot to become warrior-maidens once more.' She flexed her fingers and her face hardened, the spiderweb scars standing out on her skin. 'It will be good to come out of the shadows, to learn again how to kill the enemies of our goddess.'

Her voice was hoarse, as if she had been doing a lot of screaming, and there was no ice in it now, only pain. 'My pride was nearly my downfall, Chosen. But in the end, my love of Blessed Isis tipped the balance. It was not...' She swallowed audibly. 'It was not a pleasant experience.'

I reached for her hand, knowing she wouldn't reject me

now. She hung onto it almost as tightly as Charm had.

'Blessed Sobek is a god of war,' said Iras from behind us. 'He doesn't make mistakes with his weapons, even if he has to strip you down to your bones and rebuild you. I think you have been stripped harder than most, Merit of the Pharos. I think all the ice has been washed from your soul.'

'Not all,' said Merit, her old crisp tone almost back. She pulled her hand from mine. 'Not in the least bit. Now, if you'll excuse me?' She turned and walked away towards her sisters, reaching for the last two bracelets as she went, jamming them onto her wrists with careless hands. The blood bloomed at her fingertips as she winced.

There was a moan from the shadows, and I saw that Khai was there, lying on a stretcher of wood and hide. Nanu was standing beside him, silent and stern-faced, but as I ran to him, uncaring of any watching eyes, she turned and left. Khai was still unconscious, but no longer babbling nonsense. Suddenly I remembered. Sobek had said he would judge Khai's worth 'when all was done'. Was that time now? With a shiver, I remembered those seven drops of bright traitor's blood falling from the god's golden jaws. Who had the spies been? Who among us had served foul Am-Heh and Seth? Had I known any of them? What if Khai was right? What if Seth was taking him from me, from our goddess? What if he didn't pass Sobek's testing?

What if another drop of blood fell?

'I won't let you eat him,' I said, glaring over my shoulder

at the golden statue. 'I won't.' Behind me was silence. All the sisters had disappeared, and the warriors too, even Captain Nail and his men. Only Charm, Iras, Khai and myself were left. Even the child voice of the god was no longer visible.

Khai screamed and arched on the stretcher, his body rigid as a drawn bow. Blue-tinged froth appeared at the corners of his lips. Then a greyish miasma, like a miniature sandstorm, but tinged with the red of old blood, seemed to pour up out of his wound, through the linen wrappings. Sobek's golden hand reached for it, crushed it into a ball. There was a small pattering of red-grey dust and then I heard a strangled roar in my head. It sounded like an angry thunderstorm, full of spite and fury. Pain cut into my brain like a blunt, jagged blade. I couldn't help myself – I flung both arms over my ears, pressing hard, trying to claw it out of my skull, fighting against its influence with every speck of courage I had.

Enough! roared Sobek in my had. Enough! The boy's soul has the throne's protection and mine. Begone, Lord of Storms. I rule in this place, and I say it shall be so!

It was too much. I fell to the ground, twitching, stars of green and gold flickering in front of my eyes before everything faded and went black.

7

Into the Desert

When I woke, I was in the infirmary, and the fading light falling across the bed told me it was nearly dusk. I sat bolt upright and then swayed as a wave of dizziness hit me.

'Gently, Chosen,' said Iras. She was sitting in a chair beside me, and she had her arm around a sleeping Charm, whose head was pillowed by her shoulder. Across the room lay Khai. He was still bound to the bed with linens, but his body was so still and straight that he looked as if he had been prepared for a journey to the afterlife. Only the almost invisible rise and fall of his chest told me that he was still alive.

'What happened?' I asked, rubbing my temples to rid myself of the last pangs of the god-given headache that lingered in my skull.

'Not much. You fell. We brought you here. You slept through more of your boy's screaming. Pretty Girl here was so frantic that Nanu gave her a sleeping draught. I don't think even an elephant stepping on her would wake her now.'

There were so many things I wanted to know. But right now Khai was my first concern.

'Is he...' I screwed up my eyes trying to remember. 'Has Sobek...?

'Blessed Sobek has taken him back from the god of storms, if that's what you want to know. But he's still very sick. Nanu says it will be weeks before he recovers his old strength.' She looked at me silently, waiting while I put it together.

'He can't come with us, can he?' I asked, hating the words even as they came out of my mouth.

She shook her head, and my throat hurt with the pain of choking back my tears.

'I'll come back for him,' I said. 'After I've done what I have to. I...I need him. We've been through so much together.'

Iras laid Charm down tenderly, taking the time to raise her feet and slide them onto a nearby stool. Then she came and knelt beside me.

'I know how hard it is to leave him behind,' she said, laying a hand on mine. 'I'll guide you back to him, I promise, Chosen.'

I tried to smile at her, but my mouth trembled in the middle of it. She was a good person. Even though I had only just met her, I knew that to the depths of my bones. I looked into her round, brown eyes. They had a hint of amber in their depths, like those of a leopard.

'My friends call me Cleo,' I said. 'And I need all the friends I can get right now.'

Iras winked at me.

'You do me great honour, friend Cleo,' she said. 'But I have another name for you too, of course.'

I groaned, remembering the horrible nicknames I'd been given at Philäe.

'Well, as long as it's not "Stuck-up Stick Girl" or "Her Snooty Flatness"…'

Her eyes ran over my curves, once…twice.

'Now, why would I ever call you that?' she asked, raising an impudent eyebrow.

We left in the cool and lucent grey-mauve of the predawn light, Charm, Iras, Corporal Geta, Warrior Sah and I. I had heard the map's voice whispering within me ever since I woke from my god-induced faint, stronger than it had ever been before, tugging me onwards, always there underneath everything I said and did. Also with us were fourteen heavily laden camels and their five handlers, veiled to the eyes and dressed in the deep blue robes of the tribesmen of the western deserts. We were quite a caravan.

I had said goodbye to Merit and Captain Nail in the darkness. They would stay behind at Crocodilopolis to train the new army of the Ibis. Am, Mamo, Dhouti and the rest of my warriors would remain with them. Nail had wanted to come with me, but I refused him.

'What did Sobek tell you to do?' I asked, staring him down till he bowed his head. I was pretty sure I knew.

'To build you and our goddess an army, Chosen,' he said. 'To obey. To be ready for your return.'

'And would you disobey the direct order of a god?'

He shook his head and sighed. 'No, Chosen. But I still don't like letting you go with just two warriors to guard you. Corporal Geta is steady, but Sah is very young…'

'I am very young too,' I interrupted him. 'However, I will do my duty to our goddess, and so will he. Don't worry.' But I knew he would anyway.

Khai had still not woken when I went back to the infirmary. I kissed his lips, his forehead and his hands over and over. It felt like kissing a stone statue. There was no fire in him now – he was cool to my touch. Nanu assured me that he would be well looked after, and that he would recover his senses in time.

'He has had a high fever,' she said. 'He carried the poison of that wound for weeks. His blood is still purging itself.'

Not to mention the three gods warring for his soul, I thought. But I didn't say it out loud. I left a part of my heart with him when I walked out of the door, dry-eyed only by will and determination.

'I will come back to you, Khai,' I whispered as I left. 'I vow it by the blood of Isis.' But he did not answer me.

I wondered whether he ever would again.

Being on a camel again didn't fill me with joy. However, although this one was also white, it seemed to be more docile than Smelly Camel. It certainly spat less, and the handlers appeared to have washed it down before I mounted it. I wouldn't name it yet, though – not till I knew what its character was. I saw Charm sway as she scrambled onto hers – a brown one with ragged clumps of wool at its rear. Her eyes were heavy and still dream-filled. She had only just woken from her day and night of drugged sleep. I looked at Iras, who stood ready at my right foot. She was dressed, as we all were, in a rough white robe which covered everything except hands and feet, and her head was wrapped in a linen cloth with a long tail of material hanging down over one shoulder, ready to cover face and eyes against the dangers of a sudden sandstorm.

'Will you ride with Charm?' I asked. 'I don't want her to fall off. She's not that used to camels.' Her eyes went to my friend, and I saw something in her face I knew I should recognise. Was it perhaps tenderness? Then her normal cheeky grin popped out.

'It would be my pleasure, Cleo Blue-Eyes,' she said over her shoulder as she strode away. 'I'll take care of Pretty Girl, don't you worry.'

Cleo Blue-Eyes. It was definitely better than those other nicknames. In fact, I rather liked it.

The camels lurched to their feet with the usual chorus of face-pulling *hoooarrrrhs* and pink-gummed lip curling. I settled the reins in my hands, shook them once and we were off.

The lush green of the oasis soon stopped, as if a line had been drawn, and then we were into the desert. I could see no discernable track among the black stones and the rocky hillocks which dotted the sandy landscape. Our guides, however, led us sure and straight. The gold in my blood throbbed and pulled in the same direction, lulling me into a daze. But as Ra's chariot rose in the sky in front of me, higher and higher, I began to sweat inside my robes, and I felt the familiar chafing on the inside of my thighs begin. I would have blisters again before the day was done. I took frequent gulps from the large water skin which hung on the front of the saddle. By noon, when we stopped to rest in the scant shade of some thorn bushes spread with blankets, it was all gone, and my mouth was parched and dry. I turned it upside down to show the emptiness, and held it out to one of the tribesmen. He jerked his head aside and spat, before snatching it from me and breaking into a fury of guttural words, shaking it angrily in my face.

I couldn't understand what he was saying, but I knew when I was being scolded. Iras hurried over to me. She averted her eyes slightly as she reached me, biting her lip.

'I'm sorry, Chosen,' she said, 'but he says you have used up your whole day's supply already, and the worst heat is still to come.' She hesitated, biting her lip harder.

'That wasn't all he said, was it?' I asked. I was pretty sure a lot of it had been name-calling and I wanted to know. I wasn't used to having a translator – but this was not a desert dialect I was familiar with. 'Tell me all of it, please.' Iras flushed.

'He…he said you…' She stumbled to a halt, then cleared her throat and straightened her shoulders, looking at me squarely now.

'You ask, Cleo Blue-Eyes, so I will answer. They are not my words. The man said you were a she-donkey's liquid excrement, with no more sense than a sand devil, and that if you kept on drinking like that you would swell up like a desert gourd and die. He also said that he would not see his camels or his companions suffer from your thirsty ways. It is a long way till the next oasis, and the wells are not always certain.' Letting out a tiny snort that might have been laughter, she dropped her gaze.

I bowed my head to the tribesman gravely, acknowledging my fault.

'Will you tell him that I did not know, that I am ignorant of the ways of the desert, and that I will do better. I would not have his camels, or any living creature in our party, suffer from my thirsty ways,' I said.

Iras nodded, and as the harsh sounds spilled from her

lips, I tried to hear them properly, to make sense of them, but nothing was familiar. I felt my old thirst for knowledge wake within my mind, making me almost forget my very real physical thirst. Maybe learning a new tongue was the way to make time pass quicker on this journey. I would ask Iras to teach it to me. Then a sudden movement beside the camels caught my eye, and I saw Charm sway and clutch at her belly as she staggered towards me. I ran to her, despite the heat, catching her and laying her down in the tiny patch of shade, my eyes quickly scanning for snakes or scorpions.

'What is it? Charm! Talk to me!' Iras appeared, close at my shoulder. I could feel her breath under my ear.

But Charm was smiling as well as grimacing from pain.

'It's nothing, Cleo,' she whispered. 'Or rather, it's everything. My moon blood has come early, thank the goddess and praise her forever. Isis has answered my p-prayers...' Her breath caught on a sob of relief. 'I'm not...I'm not...' Our hands met and gripped tightly as I closed my eyes, my own relief welling up inside me like a warm spring. She wasn't with child. There would be no permanent physical reminder of her ordeal at the hands of Am-Heh's priests. The bruises were gone. Now perhaps she could begin to heal the mental scars. Now perhaps she would be able to talk about it and to purge the poison.

'Thank you, Isis,' I whispered. Maybe my goddess *was* still hearing prayers.

I could hear Iras behind me now, shooing the men away.

'We will care for her,' Iras said loudly, in the face of Corporal Geta and Warrior Sah's worried questions. 'Be off with you. She is well, just tired from the heat.' This was women's business, but we couldn't say that openly. The proper thing to do at the moon blood time was to rest in the women's quarters, but that wasn't possible for Charm right now. She would have to manage as best she could and hope the jackals didn't scent the blood when we stopped for the night.

I helped Charm tidy herself up, as Iras spread her robe wide and made a screen of her body between us and the men. Then I gave my friend some willow bark to chew for the pain. She screwed up her face at the bitterness.

'Ugh!' she mumbled around the wad of medicine. 'You know I hate this stuff.' But I could see a new lightness in her, as if a long-carried burden had been lifted.

'It's either this or the bellyache, O Champion of Complainers,' I pointed out. She smiled at me hazily.

'It's a welcome kind of bellyache, O Dispenser of Disgusting Drugs,' she whispered. 'It's come at an inconvenient time, but I wanted this so badly.'

'I know you did,' I whispered back. 'O goddess, I know you did, Charm.' There was no need to say any more.

We each had a mouthful of bread and soft curd cheese and a short rest. Then we got on the camels again. The heat was even worse now, as predicted, shimmering across the sands like silken mist, making far things seem near at hand. Iras showed us how to fold a thin strip of linen over our eyes against the glare. My water bottle had been refilled, but I was determined to let my mouth get to the stage where it was so dry that I nearly couldn't swallow before I took even a small sip. I would not be scolded by the tribesmen again.

We stopped in the dusk beside a small well, just a rough round of stones on the ground, with a larger flat stone as a cover. I groaned as I hit the ground, wincing at the stiffness. The blisters were indeed back.

Corporal Geta, Warrior Sah and two of the tribesmen busied themselves with lifting the stone and seeking water. The man who had scolded me started to unpack rough tents, while the rest tended to the camels.

Soon there was a small fire burning, fuelled by dried dung and thorn bushes. The temperature had dropped now, and while it was still hot, I could feel that the middle night would be chilly. By the time we had eaten more bread, and the warm and by now slightly sourer cheese and some dates, I was more than ready to crawl into the tent with Charm. Corporal Geta and Warrior Sah would take turns to stand guard over us through the night, and Iras would sleep in the doorway.

I fell asleep under the light of a full moon, watching Thoth dance in its silver rays through the tent's open doorway. When I woke, an hour before dawn, Charm had moved down the tent and had one outstretched leg draped half-over Iras's arm. Her face was pressed into my solar plexus and she was clasping my wrist with both hands, as if to reassure herself that I was close by.

I could hear noises outside, so I unwrapped her hands and eased myself out from under her head, trying not to wake her. Iras's eyes flew open at the first movement, coming to rest on that outstretched leg. Her mouth opened in surprise, and then she smiled, putting out a tentative finger to stroke the smooth skin of Charm's foot.

'Time to wake up, Pretty Girl,' she croaked, tweaking at her big toe. 'Time to get on that camel again.'

'Ra-cursed camels,' Charm said, her voice muzzy with sleep. 'Leave me alone. Annoying pest. My thighs are agony.'

Iras said nothing, but began rummaging in the bag she had beside her.

'Here, Pretty Girl,' she said. 'Rub some of this on. Nanu gave it to me. It's good for camel chafe.' She looked at me. 'You use it too, Cleo Blue-Eyes. I saw you waddling last night.'

'I did not waddle,' I started indignantly, then I saw her grinning at me. 'Oh, you're impossible!' I said, starting to pull up my robe. If her salve helped the blisters, I wasn't going to say another word about her impudence.

The days passed, running one into the other in a daze of

heat and sand. Sometimes we slept by a well, sometimes in a tiny oasis, sometimes just in the lee of rocks. With the help of Nanu's ointment my blisters healed and my muscles got used to riding so that I no longer felt it when I got down at night. My white camel was as steady and uncomplaining a beast as Smelly Camel had been foul. I decided to call her Lashes, for her long, curly eyelashes, though Iras told me that the tribesmen called her Pearl of the Sand. Charm and Iras continued to share the brown camel, until Iras too was scolded and told it was too great a burden for one beast to carry. In those early days of our journey, I could hear them talking together, but once they were separated, we all travelled in silence, conserving the scant liquid in our mouths by keeping them shut. Silence became a habit, the creak of leather and the crunch of gravel and shale under camel feet the sounds that punctuated our lives.

I learned the tribesman's words for 'camel' and 'water' and 'fire' and 'sand', but not much more than that. It was too hot for learning, and I was too tired. We all smelt of camel stink by the evening of the second day, and then, used to it, we didn't even notice it any more. Sand crept into all the crevices of our bodies, into our hair, into our eyes, but there was nothing we could do about it, so we endured, and wrapped our robes tightly about us when the wind blew, as it often did. The camels also endured, their ribs becoming more and more prominent as the water became scarcer, and three wells in a row had no water to speak of. Corporal Geta developed a boil on his chin, but bore it stoically till it burst. Warrior Sah avoided lying on a somnolent snake by inches, and we all laughed, voices rusty from disuse as he ran like a gazelle from it. Sometimes we met other caravans, but more often we were alone. The nights were full of flame and starlight and the strange, wailing songs of the tribesmen, and in most of my dreams the goddesses whispered my name, and beckoned me onwards, pulling me towards them, tugging at my heart with the golden string of the map which lay within me.

Hurry, Cleopatra! Hurry to us, our Chosen. War is coming. Time is short.

'Yes, blessed ones,' I whispered in my sleep, over and over again. 'I'm on my way. I'm coming as fast as I can.' I awoke each dawn covered in another layer of sweat but shivering from the intensity of their eagerness and their worry.

The moon waned in the sky, shrinking little by little until just after its midpoint had passed. We rode up out of the black sand in the heat of the afternoon and arrived at the oasis the desert tribes called Shore of the Sea. Amun and his son Khonsu reigned here, along with Thoth of the Moon and Hathor, Lady of Cows. My ancestor, great Alexander, also had a temple here, and I vowed to go and visit him before I left and renew my prayers for him to look after the city that was named after him. I had not only heard my goddesses in my dreams. I had also seen a dark cloud stalking the night streets of Alexandria, prowling the corridors of the palace, leaving pools of blood behind it, and the shrieking sound of Berenice's laughter. Am-Heh's power was growing, and my sister's with him. They could be stopped only if Isis and her grandmother were returned to their full glory. It was up to me to make that happen.

The camels started to run as soon as they smelt the fresh water, and the tribesmen whooped and hollered, spotting friends and relations in the camp of tents which lay to the left of the mud-brick houses, below a stand of rocky hills. The green was intoxicating to my eyes, and the smell of it was almost an assault on my nostrils. I slid down from Lashes as she dipped her muzzle to the water, snorting, shaking her lips and blowing great clouds of bubbles and froth as she slurped and sucked. I was eager to get to the women's bathing place and scrub the sand and stink off.

Corporal Geta came over to me, his thin face worried, his eyebrows drawn down.

'There are soldiers in the garrison here, Chosen,' he said. 'And also functionaries and scribes who send weekly reports up to Alexandria and Memphis. I do not think our guides are aware of your rank and purpose, but if you were seen, someone might recognise you... Word will have got out about events in Alexandria by now. People gossip, and this is a major trading post.'

I had been about to unwind the cloth from my hair, but

I stopped. He was right. Even though it was extremely unlikely, it was a risk I couldn't take. Given what I'd seen in my dreams, the less Berenice knew about my movements, the better. There was nothing I could do about her right now, but I didn't want to tempt snake-headed Shai who weaves all our fates.

'Thank you, Corporal,' I said. 'I'll be careful. I'll continue to dress as I have been doing, and cover my face. It's fairly brown from being outside now, so hopefully anyone who sees my eyes will think I have the pale blood of the Temehu tribes. You and Warrior Sah must cover your shields, and you must put your spear-tips in the fire to make them less bright.' He bowed.

'It shall be done, Chosen.'

I looked round for Charm and Iras and found them waiting just behind me.

'Shall we go to the bathing place?' I asked. Charm nodded eagerly.

'We stink worse than a crocodile's backside,' she said without thinking, and then clapped a hand to her mouth as she caught Iras's eye. 'I'm sorry,' she said. 'No offence intended to your precious Petsuchos.'

Iras laughed.

'None taken,' she said. 'And you smell *much* worse than a crocodile's backside, Pretty Girl. I think it'll take quite a lot of holding your head underwater to scrub the stink off you.' She gestured to her left. 'It's this way. Follow me.'

* * *

On the way to the bathing place we bought new robes, loincloths and breastbands from a trader in the small market. She sucked the four brown teeth in her wrinkled face and rolled her eyes as Iras bargained her down to a reasonable price.

'You will ruin me, young lady. My children will starve, and there will be no food for my husband to come home to. Have mercy on a poor old woman.' But her eyes twinkled under her head covering, and she was clearly enjoying herself.

The water which bubbled out of the women's spring on the Hill of the Cow was slightly warm. Iras stood guard as Charm unbraided my hair and scrubbed at it, ladling water over it till it ran clear and clean, and then I did hers. Dirt and dust ran off our bodies like brown rain. We put on our clean robes and stood guard in our turn while Iras washed. I caught Charm stealing glances at her. The warrior girl had a fine body, curvy but strong, with breasts that stood proud and high. I nudged my best friend.

'It's rude to stare, O Admirer of Maidens,' I whispered.

Charm jerked her eyes away, blushing. 'I wasn't,' she whispered back. 'I'm not. Don't be silly.' But the tide of rising red at her neck gave her away, despite her continuing denials. I still wasn't sure what exactly had happened when she and Iras had first set eyes on one another. All I knew was that Charm hadn't been acting like herself when she was around Iras since then – and it had nothing to do with what she'd suffered in Alexandria. Could she really be falling in love, or was it only lust? I knew of such things, of course – there had been girls both at Philäe and in the women's quarters where I grew up who were more than friends – but I'd never known Charm to take so much interest in a girl before. But then she'd never thought of anyone of either sex in a romantic way, as far as I knew. We'd giggled over the acolytes at Philäe, and their blatant attempts to get the attention of the young priests, and she'd teased me mercilessly about my dreams of Khai, but there had never been anyone special for her – till now. It was past time that I got her alone again. We'd been too tired, and there'd been no privacy to talk properly on the journey, but now there were things I needed to know – like what Sobek had said to her in the labyrinth to make her so flustered.

Right now she was gathering up our soiled clothing.

'I'll go and find the laundry pools,' she said, avoiding my eye. 'The sooner they're washed, the sooner they'll be dry. I suppose we'll be stuck back on those Ra-cursed camels again before we know it.'

Before I could even open my mouth, she was off down the hill like a hurrying hare. I glared at her back.

Avoid me all you like for now, O Sorceress of Scrubbing, I thought. *But you can't do it forever.*

8

Seth's Storm

Corporal Geta and Warrior Sah were leaning on their now dull spears, waiting for us at the bottom of the hill. The corporal was frowning again, but he straightened and bowed as he saw us approaching.

'Please, Chosen. Don't run off like that again. There's only us two to guard you, and we can't do it if we don't know where you are.'

I sighed. Clearly the corporal was going to prove as much of a pain in my behind about security as Captain Nail had been.

'I just went to wash…' I started, when Iras flashed past me and did something so fast that before I could blink, both warriors were flat on their backs. Iras stood between them, both spears in her right fist.

'Still think our Chosen will be in danger if you're not around, spear-carriers?' she said, her voice challenging.

'Did you forget that I am a trained soldier of Sobek, and that I have vowed to guard her with my life?'

Both warriors scrambled up out of the dust, humiliation mixed with respect written all over their faces as Iras handed them back their spears.

'How did you do that?' Warrior Sah asked, in his gruff-squeaky voice. 'You're just a—'

Corporal Geta elbowed him sharply in the ribs.

'I wouldn't finish that sentence if I were you, lad. She might throw you over the nearest palm tree.' He rubbed his tailbone, grimacing.

'I won't forget again, Lady Iras. And maybe...' He hesitated. 'Maybe you can teach us some of your tricks. They might come in handy if we have to fight outnumbered.'

'I'm no lady. Just Iras will do,' she said, nodding at the corporal. 'But, yes, I will teach you if you want. You are part of the army of the Ibis, after all.'

'Did you have to do that?' I whispered, as we walked away, the warriors a few paces behind us.

'Yes, I did,' she said, totally unrepentant. 'I've learned that a swift, practical lesson teaches men who think I'm just a girl far more than plain talk. I can take down an enemy just as fast as they can – probably faster – and now they know that. It saves time all round.'

She had a point. I would probably have done the same. Ra's chariot was descending now. I wanted to visit the temple of my ancestor before it fell below the horizon. Iras knew the way, so there was no need for me to ask. The blue Ptolemy eyes were bad enough, I didn't want my accent giving me away as not of the tribes, causing questions. There was a big Greek community here, and I didn't want anyone tattling that there was a stranger who sounded like them around.

Alexander's sandstone temple was not as big as the one dedicated to the thirteen gods that lay some way away, but it was richly decorated, with cartouches, carvings and paintings of my ancestor with the gods on its walls. Its priest was only too delighted to receive my offering of silver when I laid it on the red granite altar which stood a little way away, down the hill. It was already piled high with cucumbers, pomegranates and other fruits from the oasis. My stomach rumbled, reminding me that I had existed on a diet of camel milk, flatbread and dates for almost our whole journey. But my hunger would have to wait.

I stood in front of the statues of Amun, Alexander and Horus, palms lifted, praying.

Please, great Alexander, son of Amun, protector of my house, take care of your city. Don't let foul Am-Heh and my sister destroy it. Rise up out of your tomb. Show yourself to the people. Defend them till I can bring my father home. And please, Blessed Amun, divine Horus, protect Khai till I can get back to him. Forgive me for breaking ma'at. *Help me to put things right.*

I stared up at the statues wordlessly, my eyes pleading.

And then I swear I saw one of Alexander's golden lids blink, just once. I couldn't be sure, though, because suddenly tears were overflowing from my eyes, and everything was blurred. I dashed them away crossly. Tears wouldn't help anything, but my worry about Khai suddenly beat at me with harsh wings, breaking out of the place where I had caged it. Was he awake yet? Surely he must be after so long. Was he regaining his strength? I had tried and tried to reach for him in my dreams, but the Old One's gift was not one that I could control. It came when she wished it to, not when *I* did. That is the trouble with divine gifts. They are never quite what you thought they were.

It was a long walk back to the camp, and the corporal had to purchase a lamp to light our way for the final rocky stretch. Charm was pacing up and down between the camels and the fire, craning her head to peer into the growing darkness.

'Where did you go?' she asked, her voice gone high and thin. 'I was worried. I told Geta where you were, but then you'd all disappeared by the time I got back from the washing pool.'

'Sorry,' I said, putting an arm around her. She shrugged it off crossly. 'I went to Alexander's temple to pray for… well, you know…for all our safety.'

She eyed me sideways. 'Praying for Spy Boy again, I suppose.' I blushed. She never missed anything.

'Not only him,' I said, then changed the subject hurriedly. 'Now, what's that smelling so good on the fire?'

We ate till our stomachs hurt. They were not used to such plenty. Roasted squab, tender and crisp (if a little charred at the edges), flatbreads cooked on the hot stones, sweet figs, and crunchy green cucumbers mixed with camels' milk yoghurt. There was no sign of want or decay here, and I was glad that at least somewhere had escaped the devastation that I'd seen elsewhere on our travels. It gave me hope.

Over the next two days I tried to get Charm alone several times, but she avoided me neatly, claiming that she needed to sleep or shop for provisions or do washing, or any of a number of excuses not to be with me. It wasn't that she wouldn't talk to me. She did that when we were all together often enough, and in her usual teasing manner. It was just that she simply wouldn't talk to me in private. When I saw her chatting to Iras alone, and laughing with Sah and the corporal, I began to feel surly and hurt and shut out, all at the same time. I didn't understand why she was treating me like this. Hadn't we always told each other everything? I didn't know what else I could do, other than sit on her and force her to talk. It wasn't very mature of me, but I was too proud to beg. So instead I snarled at Iras when she made one of her ridiculous jokes, and I snapped unnecessarily at poor Sah when he came up on me unawares to ask me some question from the guides about where we were going next.

'West,' I said. 'Tell them always west. I don't know any more than that. All I've seen is desert, desert, Seth-blasted desert, an oasis with blue lakes and then another until we reach the last of them. One even bigger than this one. Tell them to take us there.'

He walked off, giving me a reproachful look, and I was immediately flooded with guilt. It wasn't his fault that I missed my private talks with Charm, and that I was so worried about my wounded lover that I'd started again to gnaw the skin on the sides of my thumbs till they bled. It also didn't help that the map was reminding me every second that we needed to leave, tugging me towards my goddesses. The month of Mechir was not far off now, but however impatient I was to get going, the camels needed rest, and we needed to reprovision properly.

It was Iras who came up to me as I stood by one of the many pools in the late afternoon light, scratching my multitude of mosquito and sandfly bites and staring moodily at the small boys shinning up the palm trees to cut dates. I hoped none of them got bitten by the numerous scorpions and snakes which lurked in the dead leaves.

'Pretty Girl had a big shock in the labyrinth, you know?' Iras started.

I whirled round to face her. 'No. I don't know. She's been avoiding the subject with me, in case you hadn't noticed.'

Iras half put out a hand towards me, then drew it back

hurriedly. I suspected I might have looked as if I was going to bite it off.

'It's hard for her,' she said abruptly. 'What she was shown there has turned everything she knew about herself upside down, and she can't get her mind round it.' She clasped her hands behind her neck and blew out a deep breath. 'By Sobek's armour, but she is so stubborn.'

I laughed. I didn't want to, but her frustrated face forced it out of me, even as I squashed down a spark of jealousy that Iras knew something about Charm that I didn't.

'And you only just noticed this?' I asked. 'I'm pretty sure there are mountains round here that are less stubborn than Charm. What in particular is she being stubborn about with you?'

'Oh, you know.' She waved a hand at herself. 'Apart from the labyrinth, me. Us. The...the thing between us.'

I shouldn't have found it funny, the strong, confident warrior girl being lost for words. 'Do you mean the fact that she's falling in love with you and doesn't know what to do about it?' I asked bluntly. I wasn't going to let her evade this. If I couldn't talk to Charm about it, I'd talk to the person on the other side.

'Well, yes...er...' Iras's round face lit up like the Pharos. 'Is she really, do you think?'

I nodded. 'I'm pretty sure. I don't know about whatever-it-is with Sobek and the labyrinth, but she doesn't know how to get her head around you and her, either. Charm's never had anyone special before. She's always…' I stopped. 'She's always had me to tell things to, I suppose. But it's never been like that between us. She's my best friend and…well…all the real family I have, apart from Khai. I…I don't do well without her,' I admitted.

Iras stepped closer and took my hand. 'You have me now too, Cleo Blue-Eyes,' she said. 'But know this. I will never take Pretty Girl away from you. She is as precious to me now as my right hand. I just wish she would let me in to tell her so.'

'Me, too,' I said, gloom washing over me again. We looked at each other for a long moment.

'Perhaps a double-pronged attack,' Iras said thoughtfully. 'We of Sobek's army call it "the horns". When you herd an unsuspecting opponent between two wedges of soldiers, and then close the trap on them.'

'We'll need to do it tonight,' I said. 'We leave again before dawn.'

In the end it was easy. As we were making our way back to the camp, Charm came towards us, carrying a big bundle of clean robes, bleached white again by Ra's golden light. Without any warning, Iras and I each took an elbow and steered her away, towards the pool again. There was nobody near. We were alone.

'What are you doing?' she asked, sounding flustered. 'I've got to put these away. And then there's the flatbread to make.'

Iras gave her left arm a little shake.

'Time to stop avoiding things, Pretty Girl. I know you won't like me for it, but you need to tell Cleo Blue-Eyes here what you told me about the labyrinth and what you saw there, however uncomfortable it makes you. She deserves to know.'

Charm wrenched her arm away, spilling all the robes on the sandy ground. She couldn't escape me, though. I held onto her with a grip like a lion fastening onto a bushbuck's neck.

'How dare you?' she spat at Iras. 'It's up to me, not you. I don't want to tell her. She doesn't need to know. I won't do it, anyway. I can't.' With an angry sob she tried to pull herself away again, but when she couldn't, she flung her arms around me and held me tight, sobbing properly now. 'I won't, Cleo. I w-won't.'

I got my hand under her chin and pushed it gently upwards, so that she was looking at me. Her eyes were brimming over and her face was full of shadows. 'What won't you do, O Sultana of Secrets? What is so very bad that you can't tell me? You're not going to stab me in the night or something, are you?' I felt her jerk with shock, and I stiffened. 'What? You *are* going to stab me in the night?'

She shook her head in frantic denial. 'No. No, Cleo. Never. It's nothing like that.'

I let out a small breath, knowing she felt it.

'Then what is it? You know I'll make you tell me

eventually, so you might as well do it now. What did you see in the labyrinth? Please, Charm. Whatever it is can't make me feel worse than not knowing.' I made my voice calm, soothing, knowing that nothing made Charm more obstinate than a direct order to do something she didn't want to do.

She sighed, letting go of me and scrubbing the back of one hand across her wet eyes like a child before letting it fall to her side. Then she cleared her throat.

'Mostly it was like having my heart torn out and examined under that piece of crystal you once showed me when we were still children – the one that made everything look bigger. I felt all turned inside out and upside down, and I was so frightened. Then there was this voice in my head. It was Sobek, at least…at least Iras says it was him. He told me that the god of my own people had a warning for me. Then Apedemak the lion came. I'd nearly forgotten him…it…it's been a long time since…' She cleared her throat again, a rasping sound. It was always difficult for her, thinking about the time before she was captured.

'Anyway, he showed me a picture inside my head, except that everything was moving, not still, like in a dream. There…there was a basket with a snake in it, an asp, I think, and I reached in and I picked it up, and…' She stopped and swallowed hard. I could see she was forcing herself to continue.

'You were there, but you were so much older and you

looked really sad. I almost didn't recognise you. I…I…gave you the snake and you put it to your breast and then…' She gave a great moan, as the words rushed out of her mouth. 'And then it bit you, and you fell down, and Iras was there too, lying by the bed, all still and cold, holding out her hand to you, and…and you…no! It's too horrible. It won't happen, it can't. But…but I don't know how to stop it.'

Iras came to stand at Charm's back, putting both hands on her shoulders and squeezing so that I saw the flesh give.

'Tell our Chosen the rest of it, my brave one,' she said.

'The great lion said I could make the picture different. He said there was a choice coming for you soon, within the next four seasons – well, he said "the diamond", but I knew it was you he meant – and that I could help you take the right road. The road that led away from that horrible picture, from the fate that snake-headed Shai has planned for you. There would be one moment, just one, when I could stop you doing something, but that if I let you make the wrong decision, then the chance would be gone forever, and Shai would make sure that what I saw in the picture would happen whether I wanted it to or not.' She grabbed my hand, raining kisses on it.

'How will I know, Cleo? How will I know if I've got it right? How could Apedemak ask this of me? What if it's my fault that you and Iras die? What if I can't prevent Shai giving that fate to you? You know what they say: there is no one who can ignore Shai. But I won't be the cause of your death. I w-won't!' She began to cry again, great choking sobs that made her chest heave and her breath catch in her throat.

I pulled her to me, rocking her, stroking her hair, desperately trying to think what to say. I'd never really considered the possibility that Shai, god of fate, might be actively meddling with my future – he was a deity who kept himself to himself. However, I knew exactly what it was like to have a god load you with that much responsibility. I had to live with it every day, and I'd known from a very early age that my destiny and Isis's were entwined. Charm had never had that experience – till now. She must be absolutely terrified. I had no idea how she'd held herself together for this long – except through sheer stubbornness. And that was it, of course.

'Shai might be in charge of all our destinies, but he wouldn't dare argue with you, Charm, because his stubbornness is nothing to yours. You've never helped me make a wrong decision, and Apedemek knows you're not going to start now, or he wouldn't have asked you. I'll listen to whatever you tell me, and we'll get through this together, Shai or no Shai.'

She gave a tiny hiccup. 'Like we always do,' she said, her mouth twisting up at the corner as if she didn't believe me, but wanted to desperately.

'Like we always do,' I agreed. 'And we've got Iras to help

us now too. She won't let us do anything stupid.'

'Never,' Iras said. 'Sobek wouldn't be very pleased with me if I did.'

She scooped up the robes and shook them out with a snap.

'I believe these are yours,' she said, handing them to Charm with a flourish.

'I believe they are,' Charm answered, with a wavery smile. 'And if they're full of sand when we put them on, Cleo and I will know exactly who to blame. Come on. You two nosy girls have delayed me enough. I've got flatbread to knead.' With that, she marched off towards the fire again, her back straight and her head held high.

'Brave as well as stubborn, by Blessed Sobek's eyes,' Iras said admiringly. 'I'm glad he chose her for me.'

'The god may have chosen her for you, and maybe even you for her,' I said, a little tartly, 'but I think you'll find that Charm has a mind of her own. You'll have to have a better line than "Sobek said so" to win her, that's for sure.'

'Thanks, Cleo Blue-Eyes,' she said, dancing backwards in front of me, and doing several tumbling somersaults. 'If my god's command doesn't charm my Pretty Girl, I have plenty of other tricks up my robe.' She wiggled her eyebrows suggestively.

'I'm sure you do,' I said. 'Please do me a favour and don't tell me any of them.'

* * *

We left before dawn as usual the following morning, and fell into our desert routine again with surprising ease. That is, we did until the first of the sandstorms hit, nearly a month after our departure from Crocodilopolis, and a few days after we had left the blue salt lakes of the next oasis.

I had been uneasy and restless all day, watching the watery orb of Ra appear and disappear behind grey clouds. I could almost see the golden line of the map with my waking eyes now, but Isis and her grandmother had been unusually silent within me. I had got so used to their voices that the lack of them bothered me more than I liked to admit. Then, about midday, the tribesmen stopped and huddled together, glancing around in a worried way, before leading the camels off towards a barren stand of hills.

'What are they doing?' I called to Iras, my voice croaky and parched as usual from not drinking enough.

She shouted loudly at them, but the men just beckoned us forward, replying with what sounded like a single word.

'A sandstorm is coming, a *haboob*,' Iras called. 'We need to get to shelter if we can. It's going to be a bad one.'

I had more than an uneasy feeling now. I always knew when a god was lurking about, and there was one here now. It wasn't hard to guess which one. Seth was the lord of the desert, the bringer of storms. This *haboob* was his, and I was very much afraid it might be directed at me. Not only had I invaded his territory in Alexandria and stolen something he considered to be his, but I was carrying that thing within me now. I tried to dampen the tug and rush of gold in my blood. I commanded it to hide itself. But it would not. Surely it must be like a beacon to one who could see such things?

Isis! Where are you, beloved goddess? I asked within my mind. But she didn't answer. Where had she gone? I must be close enough to the Old One's resting place that she could hear me, but there was not a flicker of a reply. Was Seth blocking my goddesses from me somehow? I remembered the lightning streaking from my hands in the marshes. Where was that power now? Did I still have it within me? And could I call on it against one of the strongest gods in Egypt? Seth had killed Osiris, chopped him up into little pieces. What chance had I against him?

I called on Isis again, more desperately this time. But still there was no answer. We were off the floor of the desert now, and climbing among the rocks. Just before we reached the top, on a narrow, rocky plateau, the tribesmen made the camels lie down in a rough semicircle, taking off the saddlecloths, tying down any loose bundles, and checking the ropes. Last of all, they wrapped the camels' heads in cloths, tucking them firmly underneath their halters. The wind was rising fast now, and small grains of sand whirled and snapped against my exposed skin, like tiny stinging whips. Iras struggled over to me, Charm close behind with my two warriors.

'Put this in your nostrils,' she said, handing each of us a small pot of grease. 'And then huddle down by the camels, on the leeward side, away from the wind, facing the rock. Wrap your head completely and cover your eyes, and pull your robe down over your feet. Don't move, don't speak, and make yourselves as small as you can.'

'Also, pray to our goddess and Sobek, and any other gods you like,' I said. I didn't tell them my fears about Seth – there was no point in everybody being terrified.

Almost as soon as I was settled in a tight, huddled ball, my back squeezed up tight against Lashes, the storm hit in earnest. Mostly I kept my eyes shut, because even through the cloth, the dust got in and blinded me. But on the rare occasions I did open them, I was sure I could see sand demons dancing around us, lit by immense flashes of lightning. I listened to the beast song of death and oblivion, and knew I'd heard it before somewhere. There was no rain, but above the scream and pull of the wind's fury I could hear great bangs and crashes of thunder, even as my body was battered by the blows of small rocks and stones flying through the air. I began to worry about flash floods: I knew that people could be swept away, even in the driest places. Mostly, though, I just prayed to Isis, to her grandmother, to Sobek, to protect us all from Seth's wrath. I could feel Lashes' ribs moving at my back as she breathed, and the occasional vibration of a disgusted grunt. Otherwise my world was reduced to noise and fury and the need to endure till it was over – if it ever was.

Hours and hours later, in the darkness of night, the sandstorm finally abated.

I moved cautiously, painful patches of bruising flowering all over my body, making their presence known immediately. I felt a strange, cold heaviness on my shoulders. Sand slid away from me as I sat up, spilling onto the ground. Between my fingers, inside my robes and mouth, on my eyelashes, within every pore of my body I could feel grit, and my nose was clogged with it where it had hit the grease and been caught, making it hard to breathe. Carefully, I unwrapped the cloth hiding my face and wiped it away. I could see nothing at all. I fumbled for the water bottle, trying not to let any sand into the narrow neck, took a small swig and spat, then another to ease my throat, dry as a desert bone.

'Is anybody there?' I whispered into the now eerily still, silent air.

9

Sand and Riddles

'Me,' rasped a thread of a voice to my left. It sounded like Charm, but I couldn't be sure. I groped my way over to her by feel. She too was covered in sand, huddled into a miserable knot. I heard the patter of it falling off as she moved.

'Here,' I said. 'Have some water.' Her dusty hand met mine, and moments later I heard her spit too, and drink thirstily.

'Pah!' she said. 'My mouth feels like the inside of a donkey's armpit. Gods, but I hate sand.'

'Me, too,' said another voice: Iras this time. There was a brief spark, then another, and finally a small flare of flame that lit the scene of devastation for one frozen moment before going out. 'Oh, by Sobek's teeth,' she said as the darkness fell again. 'I've dropped it.'

A little time later, a small fire had been lit, crackling and spitting, as we surveyed the damage. Two of the camels at the outside of the semicircle had run off – one of them carrying both water and food. One of the tribesmen had a possibly cracked ankle, smashed by a boulder. He sat stoically while Iras poked at it, then cleaned away the blood and bandaged it. Warrior Sah had taken a blow to the head, and was looking dazed. Apart from that, only a few saddlecloths, a tent and some of our fuel had blown away. It could have been so much worse, and I began to wonder if Seth had really known I was there, or whether the presence I had felt had just been delighting in the chaos and destruction of the storm. I prayed it was only that. I didn't want to think that he'd been playing with me for fun.

We ate a few dates and drank some milk from one of the female camels. Then we wrapped ourselves in our bedrolls and lay down with the camels again, the three of us girls lying together, head to toe, with a warrior on either side, at a proper distance. We slept deeper than the dead in their tombs and awoke to a clear, pinkish dawn.

There were three more sandstorms before we reached the Oasis of the Oracle, but none of them was as bad as that first one. Although I sensed Seth each time, I came to believe that my instinct was right: he just liked the chaos and terror of it all. It did not seem to be personal, and for that I was mightily thankful. On the other hand, the sound that first met us at the Oasis of the Oracle was the loud braying of many donkeys. Donkeys, as everyone knew, belonged to Seth, and the noise took me back to a dangerous place. It had been the bray of a donkey which betrayed Khai and me on our first visit to the brotherhood. It was an uncomfortable reminder that we were still deep in the god's territory, and would be going in further still.

Now that we were so close, I felt it like a fever. I wanted to rush on, to finish the task I had been given, to restore my beloved Isis to her full strength. But I also knew that if I pressed on alone, I would die.

My goddesses continued to be silent, so I decided to visit the oracle, as great Alexander had done before me. It was here that he had found the blessing of his father Amun, and become the first Greek Pharaoh. I hoped that I might find a blessing here too, before I set out on the last part of my journey. This was the last oasis before the Great Sand Sea, and that was where the throb of my blood told me that the Old One and my goddess lay hidden.

'Shouldn't I come with you?' Charm asked. 'What if this is the thing, the decision? I should be with you.'

'All right,' I said. 'And you can ask the oracle to bless you too, to help you know what you have to do. It can't do any harm.'

Iras nodded.

'Why not?' she said. 'And I'll come along to guard both

your backs. Geta here can stay with Sah and practise.' She fixed them both with a stern look. 'I expect you both to have that underhand knife move improved by the time we come back.'

'You've made us practise it over and over, but I still can't get it,' Warrior Sah grumbled, his voice going high on the last word.

'Practise it some more,' said Iras, unsympathetically. 'When it's as good as your trip and flip, I'll teach you another one.'

'I was happy with my spear,' Corporal Geta grunted under his breath.

'And look where that got you,' Iras said over her shoulder as we left, tucking her arm into Charm's.

Charm was more comfortable around Iras now, but she untucked her arm at once, giving Iras a gentle push.

'Guards need both hands free, don't they?' she asked in a prim little voice, that made me stifle a laugh. 'If they're to guard properly.' Iras promptly went into a leopard's stalk, looking around exaggeratedly with her hand shading her eyes.

'Seven small children, three old ladies, five donkeys and a man with a cart. I could beat all of them at once with one hand tied behind my back, Pretty Girl. Want me to try?'

Charm swatted at her. 'No. And behave. We don't need to be noticed.'

'She's always scolding me, Cleo Blue-Eyes. Can't you

persuade her to be nicer to me?' Iras came up to me, eyes big and pleading.

'Perhaps you should try some of those tricks you told me about,' I whispered.

'I already have,' she said with a sigh. 'They're not working.'

The oracle's temple was set high on a flat rock, overlooking the oasis. When we climbed up to it, we found the open court outside it was mostly empty. A man with a scarred eye socket and dirty robes was waiting in one corner, his back to the wall, rocking and chanting, and a black-clad priestess was milking a goat in the other. There was the faint sound of a beaten drum coming from within the temple. I peered round, and then went over to the woman.

'We've come to consult the oracle,' I said to her in a low voice. 'Where do we leave our offerings?'

She jerked her head. 'Go through the first hall, and into the second. Someone will be there to take whatever you've brought. One at a time into the sanctuary, mind. Did you fast before coming?'

'No,' I said, surprised. 'We didn't know it was necessary. But we haven't eaten since this morning.'

'That'll do,' she said. 'Never find it makes any difference to Blessed Amun, myself, but I'm supposed to ask.'

We followed her instructions, the noise of the drum becoming louder the further we went in.

Tap tap tap thud-thud it went, *tap tap tap thud-thud* over and over, and I felt the sound pull at me. As we entered the second hall a veiled priestess came forward and took the small purse I held out to her.

Tap tap tap thud-thud went the drum. *Tap tap tap thud-thud.*

'How many?' she asked.

'Two,' I said. 'Unless...' I looked at Iras. 'Unless you have a question for Amun's oracle?'

She shook her head.

'Then just two of you,' said the priestess. 'Drink this.' She handed us each a small cup that contained a milky liquid. I looked at it doubtfully. What if it was poisoned?

'Drink,' she said impatiently. 'It is quite safe. It is just to open your ears to the god's voice.'

I didn't tell her that mine probably didn't need opening all that much, but I raised the cup and tipped the liquid down my throat anyway. It was both sweet and bitter at the same time. I saw Charm drink too, making a face at the taste.

'Who will go first?' the priestess asked. Charm looked at me. Her face was tense, and I knew what she was thinking.

Should it be her or me? O, Isis! How I hated that this extra burden had been put on her.

'I-I'll go,' Charm said through stiff lips, and stepped forward and through the rough linen curtain which hid the sanctuary without giving me a chance to argue about it.

Tap tap tap thud-thud.

The drumbeat got into my head, and I became aware of a faint murmuring sound, deep and rich and full of both the heat of Ra's golden light on a summer day and of the coldness of the deep stars of night. It was the voice of Amun speaking through whatever lay behind the curtain, but I couldn't make out what he was saying. I found myself swaying on my feet, rocking back and forth as the man outside had done.

Tap tap tap thud-thud, tap tap tap thud-thud, tap tap tap thud-thud.

Almost without my being aware of it, Charm was out, and I was swaying towards the sanctuary on feet that seemed to be floating. The roughness of the linen curtain brushed over my face, and then I was on my knees, palms raised to the huge stone lion mask in front of me. Its eyes were those of a living being, and in its mouth it held a huge round emerald, set in gold studded with more emeralds and other gems, which glittered and flashed in the light of several lamps. Sweet-scented smoke rose from these, making me dizzier than I already was. I could no longer hear the drum, which seemed distantly strange to my muddled brain.

'Speak your question, O Chosen, child of Isis,' came a harsh whisper, overlaid with the voice of the god.

I didn't mean to say it. I meant to ask about my goddess, ask whether I would reach her in time. But I didn't. What came out was the question I'd had buried in my heart ever since we left Crocodilopolis

'Will Khai come back to me?' I asked, my voice catching on a sob.

There was a pause, and then the harsh voice of Amun spoke again.

'Green waters lie between the ibis and the rat. Seek truth at the heart of the fiery tower, chosen child of Isis.'

'W-what?' I stammered. 'I don't understand...' But an irresistible force was bringing me to my feet, turning me, thrusting me through the curtain again.

As soon as I was back in the second chamber, the drum started up again. *Tap tap tap thud-thud, tap tap tap thud-thud.* I saw Charm rocking and swaying, Iras at her side.

'Get out,' I said. 'We need to get out.' I stumbled back into the first chamber, and then into the open courtyard, taking great gulps of air as I reached it. The one-eyed man was still rocking, now silently, and the priestess with the goat had gone. My head began to clear, and although I still felt wobbly on my feet, I could think again. Charm too was taking great gulps of air. I clutched at her.

'What did he tell you?' I asked. 'What did you ask him?'

'Not here,' Iras said, taking both of us by the arm and steering us down the hill. It was nearly dusk now, but luckily the place where we had camped was not far. We walked towards it in silence, Charm and I still breathing heavily. The smell of the incense sat heavy in my nostrils and I could still taste the vile brew the priestess had given us. When we were on level ground again, Charm stopped.

'It didn't make any sense,' she said. 'It wasn't any help at all, not really. All that lion thing said was, "Beware the silver voice floating on the waves." What does that mean? How can a voice float on waves?'

'Mine wasn't much better,' I said. 'And I asked the wrong question too.' Suddenly I didn't want to tell them. They'd think I'd been stupid to waste such an opportunity. But I did it anyway. They deserved the truth.

'So,' said Iras, when I'd finished. 'That was why I didn't go in. Amun's oracle is known for its cryptic answers. Are we any further forward than we were this morning?'

'Not much,' I said. 'But if he mentioned waves to you, Charm, then maybe we're safe for now. The Great Green is a long way from here.' Charm just looked at me.

'It said that stuff about "green waters" to you too,' she said. 'I don't think that's a coincidence.'

Iras put an arm round both our shoulders.

'I've never seen the sea,' she said. 'It'll be an adventure.'

But I didn't want any more adventures. And now I had something else to worry over. Were the ibis and the rat me and Khai? And if the fiery tower was the Pharos, what truth would I find there? And when?

* * *

Late in the night, my goddesses came back to me.

Arise, Chosen, they said within my dream. *Your second time of testing is upon you. Follow your blood. Come to us. If you can.*

I opened my eyes and saw gold streaming out of me, a thin line leading out north and west, into the Great Sand Sea. All was silent, apart from the breeze rattling the palm trees. Even Corporal Geta's snoring was stilled. I felt as if the world was waiting, time paused till I set it in motion again. I slid out of my bedroll, careful not to wake Charm or Iras. I looked over at Warrior Sah, who was supposed to be on guard, but his head was slumped on his chest.

I squatted beside my covers, in the dirt and sand, and wrote one word very carefully, in the demotic script I knew Charm would be able to read.

WAIT

As I sketched a quick Knot of Isis beside it, I hoped it would be enough, and that she would understand.

I did not know how to saddle Lashes without noise, so I simply took the halter laid with the rest of the harness, and went towards her, apprehensive lest she made a fuss. She didn't, just blinked sleepily at me, grunting a little at being woken, but otherwise accepting the halter in her usual docile way. The water bottles had been filled, so I took eight of them, together with a bag of dates, tied them together with a long strip of leather and slung them over her neck. Then I clambered onto her hump and urged her

157

to her feet. Still nobody woke, and I began to realise that nobody would. I was on my own, as I had been before in Isis's realm. My throat tightened with fear, but I urged Lashes forward anyway, and didn't look behind me. I knew if I did, I would turn tail and run back to my bedroll, where it was safe.

Come to us. If you can.

I'd heard those words from Merit before my first testing, but this time they had the force of two goddesses behind them. I'd had no choice then, and I had none now. I would pass this second ordeal and find my goddesses, or die trying.

The gold still poured out of me like an arrow pointing straight between the camel's ears, so I followed its path. There was nothing else to do. Despite the message I'd left, I knew that my friends would be frantic in the morning when they woke, but my goddesses' call was undeniable. Charm and Iras couldn't come with me – I had to do this on my own.

By the third day, I was rubbed raw from slipping and sliding down Lashes' hump, and running out of water. There was a scant half-measure left in the last water skin. I sucked on a date stone, desperately trying to make my mouth produce saliva, but it only made the thirst worse. Black spots were dancing among the gold now, as Lashes plodded on, past dune after dune, no shelter, no shade, only desert. I held out as long as I could before I shared the last sip of water with the camel, and then it was all gone. Unless I found the Old One's cave soon, I was as good as dead.

Hours later, as darkness fell, I still hadn't found it, and by now poor Lashes was stumbling and groaning with distress. I slid down her neck, my sandals hitting the sand with a thump. Immediately the stored heat of the day scorched through my soles, but I hadn't the strength to climb up again. I set my teeth and followed the gold, one painful step after another. Soon my lips were even more parched and cracked, and my feet were bleeding, but still I carried on, Lashes a few steps behind me.

I will not give in. I will not give up. I will not give in. I will not give up. Over and over I chanted the words in my head, till they became the only crutch I could lean on.

Just as poor Lashes foundered behind me and sank to her knees with a pathetic moan, Thoth's moon rose, full-bellied and yellow in the sky. Ahead of me lay a great flat lake of sand, with a mound in it which sparkled in the moonlight. The golden thread plunged into shadow and stopped about halfway up. I wanted to run forward, but I had no strength left. So I fell to my knees and crawled. The top layer of sand was still hot, but as my hands and knees sank into it, I felt a cooler layer underneath. I sank and struggled with each movement, but I was so close, so near now, I couldn't fail. I couldn't.

Upwards I went. The sand smelt of heat, drying the insides of my nostrils till they burned. Upwards and upwards, further and further, feeling rock scraping my skin even more raw, tearing the flesh off my bones.

What seemed a day, a week, a month later, without even knowing how, I reached the place where the gold dived into the mound, and sank back on my heels, gasping for air – except that I couldn't gasp, because my throat was swollen from lack of water, stuck together, and my tongue was making little clicking sounds against the parched roof of my mouth. Here was the gold, but where was the cave mouth I'd seen in the vision Merit had given me so long ago?

And then I remembered.

It had all been covered when Isis lost her power to the stars.

Suddenly, the gold line flickered in front of me, snapping back into my chest with a blow that knocked me backwards, stunning me for a moment.

I would have sobbed, but dehydration had robbed me of tears. I did the only thing I could. I crawled forward in the moonlight and started to dig with my hands where I'd last seen the gold, scrabbling and scraping at the sand and rock in front of me with the last of my energy. A nail tore off, and then another, and another as I went deeper and deeper, driven on by something more than human. I could actually feel the power below, pulsing like a second heart, drawing me on. And then I was falling, sliding, tumbling downward, into heat and a still, ancient darkness. I tried to speak, but I couldn't. My tongue was also swollen, choking my words off.

Something hissed at me. I froze. Was it a snake? I had left the protective amulet Cabar had given me back at the camp. I hadn't thought about taking it with me. Two golden eyes opened in the darkness in front of me and blinked. They were human eyes, fringed with long, dark lashes but much bigger than any mortal would have. Around them, the air started to glow, gradually revealing a woman's face, huge, impassive, with a living serpent uraeus – crown of gods and pharaohs – hissing and swaying over her forehead. Slowly, a naked torso and shoulders appeared, and then the rest of her body. The lower half of her wasn't human at all. I saw a lion's chest with gigantic, claw-tipped paws outstretched in front of it, and a curling tail wrapped around them, twitching backwards and forwards. Power radiated off her like a furnace, and she yawned, showing a set of perfect white teeth and a throat like a cavern.

I would have swallowed if my throat had not had a whole desert in it. I would have run if my legs had not been boneless jelly. Instead, I lay there and stared back at her, my eyes arid as the dust underneath my broken body. Even through my dried-out nostrils I could smell her – the pungent, feral reek of big cat mixed with a sweeter scent that might have been roses.

I'd forgotten that the treasure in the Old One's tomb was guarded by a ferocious protector. No wonder foul Tebu had come out of the cave with those deep gashes on his chest.

This was a living sphinx.

I was in trouble.

'I would be pleased if you answered my riddles, Cleopatra Chosen,' she said. Her voice was a high howl overlaid by streams of dark honey, and the force of it stirred my robes like a great wind.

I'd been expecting this. Sphinxes always asked riddles.

How can I answer a riddle if I can't speak? I thought, and almost as I did, the air shimmered in front of me and a small cup appeared. It seemed that someone was reading my mind. I got painfully to my feet and took it, willing my ruined hand not to tremble as I brought it to my lips. I sucked the cool water into my mouth, feeling my lips crack even more as I moved them on the rim of the cup. There was something sweet and herby in it, which soothed my swollen tissues, making me able to swallow. It was still painful, but with every small sip it improved a little until, as I put my head back and tipped the last drop onto my tongue, I knew I was healed enough to talk.

I looked at her, waiting patiently for me to finish, bent and set the cup down by my feet. It was no use arguing that Isis and her grandmother needed me. This was part of the testing.

'I will answer if I can, great lady,' I said. But I didn't bow my head. She was a servant of my goddesses, just as I was. I had to get past her if I was to reach them. I was good at riddles. I had that kind of mind. But I knew she wouldn't make it easy for me.

'Very well then,' she said, her voice more of a growl this time. It still made me stagger back. 'For the first, tell me this. What may you alone possess, and yet lose if you take it?'

I had so hoped that she would ask me the old Oedipus riddle about four legs and two legs and three. I knew the answer to that one. This was harder. What did I have that was mine alone? My skin? My hair? No. That didn't feel right, somehow. The sphinx's question didn't make sense, but then riddles weren't meant to. Power? Again no. I could take that and lose it, but it wasn't mine alone. I wondered what would happen to me if I failed to answer. Would I die? Would I lose... My mind snapped at the answer like a Nile perch after a minnow, and caught it.

'My life,' I said.

'Very good,' the sphinx purred. Her paws kneaded the ground with pleasure. 'Now for the second one.'

'Wait,' I said. 'There's a second one? I thought the tradition was one.'

The full lips smiled. It was a dangerous smile, full of teeth.

'There is no tradition here. Only what Blessed Isis

163

and Iusaaset Skyborn, Blessed Iusaaset of the Acacia, will.'
I had not heard the name Iusaaset before. I knew I hadn't.
And yet, as soon as the sphinx said it, I knew I was
privileged above all women. I had been gifted with the true
names of the grandmother of the gods. To me, she would
never be the Old One again. She would be Iusaaset Skyborn.

This time I did bow my head.

'Whatever my goddesses will,' I said.

The creature bowed back gravely. 'Then answer me this.
Weakener of souls, I make hearts cold. I prey on the timid
as well as the bold. What am I?'

That was easy. I had it in a flash. I was feeling it, after all.

'Fear!' I said, in a rush of relief. But the sphinx wasn't
finished with me yet.

'Then I shall offer you the third and last, Cleopatra
Chosen,' she said. 'I show you a house where thousands lay
up gold. But no man made it. Spears past counting are at
its door, yet no man guards it. What is it?'

I always thought best when I walked. I'd paced for hours
up and down the corridors of the Great Library when I was
a child, trying to work out a problem my tutors had set me,
and again at Philäe. I couldn't pace now on my ragged,
bloody feet. I couldn't even drum my fingers, torn and
swollen as they were. I closed my eyes and felt grit move
uncomfortably under my lids. A house that no one had
made, guarded by spears that no man bore, with treasure
within it. An egg? No. That was a different riddle – one

I knew. This was not one I'd heard before. What had my old tutor Master Apollonius taught me? I heard his cross old voice in my head.

Logic, Little Pest. You must apply logic to every problem. Only then can you solve it.

So, if I applied logic, it had to be about an animal of some sort – something alive, anyway. What animal lived in thousands? None that I could think of, and no animal carried weapons, did it? I felt in memory the sting of a scorpion in my ankle. Insects carried weapons. Insects lived in thousands. So, which insect guarded gold? My mind whipped back again to my childhood, to the sight of an acacia tree, trunk split open by lightning, heavy with golden combs of honey.

'A beehive,' I said.

As I spoke, the sphinx got to her feet, graceful as a gazelle for one so large.

'Pass, child of Isis,' she roared. 'Your goddesses await you.'

10

Iusaaset Skyborn

It was as if I was taken and wrapped in a small whirlwind. I did not have to move at all. The wind held me and me alone, whisking me underneath the great lion body and through a barrier of blue-white light. Now I could see night-black sky above me, alight with uncountable singing stars, feel the softness of grass beneath me, cradling my body. Gold bled out of my chest, my arms, my legs, my mouth, nose, eyes, skin, spiralling up to meet the eruption of silver that poured down out of the skies, twining together into a rope of power, replacing what had been lost so long ago.

Two shining figures floated in the air. The silver-gold rope wrapped around one of them, squeezing tighter and tighter, becoming smaller and smaller, until it was a ball so bright I had to half close my eyes against it. Like an arrow, it sped towards the second figure, slipping within her belly, which immediately swelled and grew, as if she was great with child.

Beloved daughter, she cried out, and Iusaaset Skyborn's voice in my ears was the sound of a thousand temple bells, the smoke of a hundred praise fires, the hum of a million bees. Come to me now. Attend me.

She cried out again, in joy and pain, squatted, and I saw her belly heave. I rose and went towards her, light as air. I knew instinctively what she wanted.

Catch! she said, laughing, and I held out my arms to receive the baby Isis, limned in silver-gold light, which slid out of her, whole and perfect.

I held my reborn goddess in my arms, gazing down at her tiny, flawless face, her exquisite tiny arms and legs, her fingers that reached for mine. There was none of the mess of human birth, no umbilical cord to cut, no afterbirth. There was just beauty and stillness for one long moment of perfection that went on for no time at all, and forever.

Then the baby Isis smiled.

I fell to my knees and, closing my eyes against her glory, I raised her up to Iusaaset Skyborn on my palms. I knew she wouldn't fall. But in a wonder too great for my comprehension, my hands were taken, and I was pulled to my feet.

Open your eyes, my Chosen, said a voice I knew, one I'd known all my life. I opened them a crack, fearing that I would be blinded, to see a full-grown Isis and her grandmother-mother standing before me, one of my hands clasped in each of theirs. It was too much. I began to weep, not from sorrow, but because my heart was so full of joy.

I had fulfilled my promise. Isis was restored to herself, and now she could begin to heal Egypt. The plagues and the rot would stop, the people would not starve. All would be well. I let myself feel it, basking in the golden light of their benevolence until a tiny thought wormed its way into my brain like a dot of ink in water, spreading tiny tendrils everywhere.

Ma'at *is still broken.*

Yes, beloved daughter, it is, Iusaaset Skyborn said. War is still coming. And you still have a reckoning to pay. The breaking of *ma'at* is not a small thing. Even though your intention was good, your actions led to unbalance. The cost will be great, but it must be met.

I made myself look up at my goddesses. It was so hard. I should be trembling on my belly, not standing with them like an equal.

'What do you want me to do, blessed ones?' I asked.

It was Isis who spoke this time.

You must go back to Sobek's city, my Chosen. I will give you a tongue of honey, so the words from your mouth will hearten the army of the Ibis and your sisters. But do not delay for long there. One army will not be enough. The demon god's power grows stronger with each drop of blood he sheds. You must bring the flute player home across the Great Green. Only when the hound is thrown down and you are on the Double Throne beside your father will *ma'at* be restored. That is the price of forgiveness, demanded of you by the Ennead.

The Ennead. I had to earn forgiveness from all nine gods. It was a task to make the strongest person feel weak. I brought both their hands to my forehead and went to my knees. I would not be weak, though, not if I could help it.

'I-I will do it, blessed ones. Whatever you command.'

The price is high, my Chosen, but if you succeed, we will make your name remembered forever. You will be the greatest Pharaoh who ever lived.

The greatest Pharaoh who ever lived. Greater than Nefertiti? Greater than Hatshepsut? Greater than Ramses or Ahkenaten or great Alexander? It was hard to imagine. It was not something I'd ever wanted, but I would take up the burden of it because I couldn't allow myself to fail. Suddenly, I remembered Charm's vision.

'M-may I ask a question, great goddesses?'

You may, beloved daughter, said Iusaaset Skyborn. We may answer, or we may not.

'My...my...Charm. Apedemak showed her my death. He told her that it was Shai's plan, but that she could prevent it by helping me not to make the wrong decision. And then the oracle of Amun told her to beware the silver voice on the waves. How...how can I avoid Shai's fate? And who is the silver voice?'

There was a brief silence, then Isis spoke. I heard sadness in her voice and at once my heart felt like a stone, falling towards my feet.

Shai weaves his loom as he wills, and all of our threads are upon it, but your choices are your own to make. Whether this doom falls on you or not, if you succeed in doing as we have asked of you, what we have promised will come to pass. I can say no more than that.

I hadn't really expected a straight answer.

Go now, beloved daughter, said the grandmother of the gods. You will find things not quite as they were outside. This will again be a place of sanctuary, a place where a goddess may rest in peace. We will not meet again, not in this life, but you still carry my gift within you. You must learn to use it the hard way.

Iusaaset Skyborn's hand withdrew from mine, and then Isis was gone as well. Once more the whirlwind took me and I found myself in the glowing darkness of the sphinx's lair again.

She bowed to me, inclining her head in a deep gesture of respect.

'Tell no one of me, Cleopatra Chosen,' she said, smiling that dangerous smile again. 'I like it to be a little surprise when people visit.'

I laughed, a small crack of sound, and noticed that it didn't hurt. I looked down at my hands. The nails were restored, I hadn't got a mark on me. The wounds of my journey were healed, and I was clean all over and dressed in a soft white robe. I knew exactly what Charm would say.

That's what you get for having the favour of deities, O Chosen of the Goddesses.

She was right. It was, and I was grateful not to have to contend with my wounds. The task they'd given me was going to be quite enough to deal with.

I bowed back to the sphinx.

'I won't say a word,' I promised her, and then I walked out into the cool, pure light of dawn.

I entered a world of light and colour, very different from the moonlit one I'd left. Everything was green and lush, with palm trees growing all around a pool, where a flock of white ibises called and bobbed through the shallows. Just to my left there grew an enormous acacia tree, laden with clusters of white blossom. The gentle breeze brought me the honey scent of it, and I could hear bees humming in its branches. I remembered the vision I'd had before I answered the third riddle, and laughed again. I knew from her title that the acacia was Iusaaset Skyborn's tree. Had she cheated the sphinx and put the picture of her bee-laden symbol into my head when I was stuck for an answer?

A movement caught my eye, and I saw Lashes, now plump and healthy-looking, move out from behind a thorn bush, chewing busily, a leaf-laden branch sticking out from the side of her mouth. She was saddled, and loaded with water bottles, and as soon as she saw me she trotted over with a welcoming *hoooarrr* and lay down. There were two leather satchels hanging from the saddle, and after I had made a big fuss of her, I opened one, finding fresh flatbread and soft cheese mixed with honey and dates, along with food for the journey. I sat and ate it, and then, after wiping my hands free of stickiness, I took a long drink before climbing up into the saddle. I had no fear of getting lost: I knew that my goddesses would see me safely back to my friends. If they had the power to create this brand-new oasis out of nothing, then that should be a drip of power so small they wouldn't even notice it was gone.

Although I knew I ought to be daunted, somehow having clear instructions on what I had to do made me feel a little more in control of things. And, best of all, they had told me to go back to Crocodilopolis. I would see Khai again. We could finally sort things out between us.

I let Lashes have her head and rode out of Iusaaset Skyborn's resting place. As I crested the next hill, I looked back, but the oasis was nowhere to be seen. All that appeared to be there was the silent shimmer of sand. But I knew better. Sisters would come to guard it again, and this time there would be no betrayals. I would make sure of it.

I'm not going to pretend the journey back to the Oasis of the Oracle was pleasant. Dust and sand still got everywhere. It was still hot as a breadmaker's oven. But my body felt strong and sure, and my muscles didn't cramp and stiffen too much. That first night, we stopped at dusk, and I made camp near some rocks. There was even a bedroll tied behind the saddle, and I unrolled it, and lay looking up at the sky after I'd eaten and seen that Lashes had a drink. As the moon rose, I frowned. Surely it had been full last night? But now it was a few days off full again. How could that be? I blinked and looked at it again. I wasn't mistaken. It was a waxing moon. I had lost nearly a month.

'Oh, no,' I said aloud, as Lashes snorted. Perhaps she didn't believe it either. Charm and Iras and the two warriors would be beside themselves. I'd told them to wait, but by now they would think I was dead, lost in the desert, eaten by jackals and gone to dry bones and dust. As if to echo my thoughts, I heard howling in the distance, first one jackal, then more, joining in a great chorus to the moon above. I closed my eyes and shivered. Well, there was not much I could do now except try to contact Charm with Iusaaset Skyborn's dreaming gift – and pray to the goddesses that they were still at the oasis.

I tried to use the gift that night, and on the one following, but like a muscle that had been too long asleep, it was weak and unmanageable without the force of her will behind it. I only managed to hover over my body the first time, and on the second, I managed a short, wobbly trip over the desert. Then I snapped back into my body, and lay there, panting as if I'd run a race. Well, she'd said I must learn to use it the hard way, so I would keep practising.

* * *

I rode into the oasis at dusk on the third day, looking around me anxiously. Then I heard a short, high scream of joy, followed by running feet. I slid down off Lashes's back, and braced myself, tugging down the scarf that covered my face. Charm crashed into me, laughing and crying at the same time, pounding me with her fists.

'I told them,' she sobbed. 'I told them you'd be back. I kept watch every day. I knew you wouldn't leave me, Cleo. I wanted to come after you, but they wouldn't let me, not after your message said to wait.' She pounded on me some more.

'One word! You could have left me more than one word. And I nearly didn't see that. I nearly stepped on it and rubbed it out.'

I hugged her tightly.

'There was no time. And I keep on telling you I'll never leave you. When will you believe me, O most Faithful of Friends?'

'Well, it is halfway through Mechir now,' she said into my chest, her voice muffled. 'The planting is nearly done here. You've been away since Tybi. It…it's been a long time. I've missed you. It's the longest we've ever been apart.'

I felt a small jolt of shock. Definitely a month then, as the moon had told me. Had I really been with my goddesses that long? It had seemed like only a night.

Charm pulled back, examining my face, running her thumbs over my cheeks.

'You look different,' she said, frowning a little. 'Older. What's happened to you? What have you been doing all this time? Did you...did you find Isis?'

I nodded.

'I did. I've got so much to tell you.' I put my hands over hers, my voice serious. 'I *am* different, Charm. But never to you. There are things I have to do now for Isis and the rest of the gods. It'll be hard. Isis wants me to bring my father home. You were right about the oracle. It'll mean going over the Great Green Sea, over the waves. I'm so sorry, Charm.'

The shadow of the task she'd been given in the labyrinth hung over us for a moment. I could almost hear Shai's loom clicking and shuttling in my head.

Charm's lips firmed and her eyes hardened.

'Don't you even think of leaving me behind, Cleo,' she said. 'I'll be with you, wherever you go. I'm not letting us be parted again, even by a goddess. And I won't let you make the wrong decision when it comes.' She dropped her hands to my shoulders and squeezed hard. 'Believe that, O Holder of my Heartstrings.'

I did believe it, but I still didn't like her carrying the burden of it.

We led Lashes to drink and got her a big pile of fodder, then hobbled her and went back to the camp. As we walked,

I told Charm of everything but the sphinx. That was a secret I would keep, as I'd promised. None of it seemed to surprise her – but then Isis had been a part of her life through me for a long time.

'I'm glad you succeeded,' was all she said. 'But I knew you would, Cleo. And I've always known you were going to be Pharaoh.'

When we finally arrived at the camp, I was surprised not to be scolded by Corporal Geta at least, given his over-protective tendencies, but as soon as he saw me, he saluted and dropped to one knee, as did Warrior Sah.

'We are glad to see you back with us safely, Chosen,' he said, and I could see the held-back curiosity in his eyes. 'May the blessing of Isis be upon you.'

'And on you,' I said, and meant it. I looked around. 'Where's Iras?' I asked.

'She's at the other side of the oasis. She'll be back soon,' Charm said. 'We didn't know which direction you would come from, so we decided to have someone at the north and south one day, and at the east and west the next.' She looked down. 'She's been wonderful. She…she had faith that you would return, just as much as I did. She even went to the oracle for you, not that it did her much good, either.' She snorted in a very Charm-like way that made me smile. 'It basically told her to wait here and mind her own business.'

'Which she took to mean that she should train Warrior

Sah and me till we dropped,' said Corporal Geta.

'Yes,' said Warrior Sah. 'We can both fight as well as girls now.' I stared at him. Had he just made a joke? Iras must have taught him more than just her soldier skills. Sah had always been one of the more serious of my warriors.

Just then Iras herself arrived. Her face split into a wide, white grin.

'Chosen,' she said, tumbling towards me faster than my eye could follow and presenting me with her dagger, hilt first. 'My blade is yours as always. Welcome back.' She came close, and whispered in my ear. 'Pretty Girl and I are getting along *very* well now. She missed you a lot.' Then she winked, and went to put an arm round Charm, who blushed. She was clearly much more comfortable with Iras now, and I was glad. At least Charm had had someone to worry with while I'd been gone.

While we ate I gave the two warriors and Iras a highly edited version of what had happened to me – either Charm or I could fill Iras in properly later on. When I had finished, their eyes were wide and their mouths hung open.

'If I had not seen what I have seen already…' Warrior Sah said.

'What?' asked Charm, quick as a striking cobra. 'You'd think the chosen was lying? Telling children's tales? Can you not see the greatness that hangs about her like a cloak?'

'Leave the lad alone, Charm,' said Corporal Geta. 'We *have* seen what we have seen. And we believe in the power of the chosen and of our goddess, especially now.' He pointed to the recently planted fields. 'The crops are springing forth thicker and faster than I've seen them for the last five Peret seasons. When the Shemu season returns, it will be a fine harvest. Blessed Isis is already healing the land.'

I soon discovered that the blue-veiled tribesmen had left us, taking an extortionate amount of silver for the permanent loss, as they saw it, of Lashes.

'They said either you'd stolen her, or you were dead in the Great Sand Sea,' Charm told me. 'After only four days, they said they didn't believe you were ever coming back. Iras shouted at them a lot, but in the end we had to let them go.'

We hired other guides for the return trip to Crocodilopolis. I was glad to set out, eager to discover what Isis had planned for the army of the Ibis and the sisters. Of course, I wouldn't exactly be unhappy to see Khai either. Every night of the journey, I practised using Iusaaset Skyborn's gift and, each time, I could go a little further. But when I tried thinking of Khai, tried going to him directly, I failed. My dream muscles weren't strong enough yet.

I still hadn't managed to reach him by the time we came in sight of Crocodilopolis for the second time. As we approached the temple, halfway through the month of

Phamenoth, my heart tried to batter itself out of my chest in a way that I'd almost forgotten. Would he be here? Would he be cured? Would he still love me?

I had to put all that aside now, though, as I steered Lashes up the great processional avenue to the House of Sobek. I'd learnt that lesson the hard way, back in Alexandria. What my goddess wanted came first. So, once again, I put on my princess mask and greeted the high priest of Sobek and the solemn child who was Sobek's voice, and then I asked for the new army of the Ibis and for the sisters of the Living Knot to be assembled in the chamber of the labyrinth. I did not ask directly for Khai. I hoped that when he heard I was here he would come anyway.

With Iras and Charm at my side, I went down through the twisting passages, down into the heart of the labyrinth, and waited.

As the ranks of my new army assembled – warriors with ibis-marked shields and spears, sisters with their deadly twin bracelet blades – I saw faces shining with zeal and determination. Merit was there, and Captain Nail with his men. I tried not to look for the face I most wanted to see. I tried and failed miserably, my eyes darting over the gathered ranks. When I didn't spot him anywhere, my heart felt as if it was being squeezed in a vice, but I ignored it. I wouldn't let his absence prevent me from doing my duty to Isis. He would come to me or not, and if he didn't, I would still go on to Rome and try not to care.

I stood before them, with the dirt of my journey still on me, and I felt my goddess's new gift sprout within me. I knew instinctively what words would hold them, would shake them, would make them laugh and weep and pray. My voice was coated with honey, it cut like a newly sharpened blade, it was soft as a mourning dove's cry, loud as a stallion's trumpet.

I spoke for an hour at least, praising, encouraging, applauding all their hard work. I walked among them, touching each on the forehead – and where I touched, a golden ibis appeared for a moment and then sank into their skin. I laid hands on four sisters, and summoned them to go into the desert and be the new guardians of Iusaaset Skyborn's tomb. I was all white flame and glory to them, and by the time I was halfway through, they would have carried me to Alexandria on a wave of fierce determination and put me on the Double Throne themselves. By the time I had finished, they would all have lain down and died for me then and there.

Hail to the chosen of Isis! they cried, over and over.

The power of it filled me like liquid diamonds in my blood, seized me and lifted me on wings of fire, until I felt that I could do anything, even conquer the world. Finding another army, going to Rome to persuade my father to come back – with what I was feeling here and now, it would be easy. And then, as my first army was cheering me to the painted roof, I saw Khai at last, standing silent in the shadows beside Sobek's golden statue, his eyes fixed on me as if he would devour me in one bite. I made myself stay where I was, smiling, as the warriors and sisters filed out. As the presence of Isis drained away from me, and I became just Cleo again, Khai came to me. He was so thin now, much too thin, I thought.

'Chosen,' he said formally, dropping to one knee and raising his palms as if I were the goddess to be worshipped. 'Will you give me the blessing of Isis? Will you forgive me for failing you?' His river-dark eyes were calm and peaceful, not full of pain and anger as I'd last seen them. I laid my hand briefly on his hair, feeling the silk of it slip under my fingers. I allowed myself one caress, and then I bent down to him. The last of the warriors and sisters had now gone, and we were alone. Even Charm and Iras had slipped away to give us some privacy.

'There is nothing to forgive, Khai,' I said, meaning it with all my heart, and I brought my lips to his forehead. It was a chaste kiss, nothing like the sweaty fumblings of previous times, but here at Sobek's feet was not the place for that. As I raised him to his feet, his arms went around me. He just held me close, saying nothing, trembling a little, as I was. It was enough for now that we were together again.

'You are well, then?' I said a little while later, after we'd both stopped shaking. He nodded, his chin knocking against the top of my skull.

'I am well. It took a long time. The fever came back a bit, and I couldn't eat properly for a long time, because anything except the simplest food made me sick. But all through it I held on to the thought of you, the thought of our goddess. I would not let Seth back in, and finally I think he gave up and went away. He found better things to do, perhaps.' He stepped back, still holding me and looked down at me. 'Where you went, Cleo – did…did our goddess say anything about me?'

She hadn't, but as he asked, I felt a cool touch on my mind, and I knew what Isis wanted him to do as if she'd painted pictures on a wall for me. I bit my lip hard, so as not to cry. It wasn't exactly what I would have planned – not one little bit, but our goddess would not be disobeyed. I tugged at his hand.

'Come and sit down,' I said. 'I think you'll need to.' I knew I did.

Minutes later he was staring at me again, his eyes wide with shock.

'I'm not to come with you to Rome, then?' he asked.

I shook my head. 'Isis needs you here,' I said.

'But it's such a big job. I don't know if I…' He scrubbed both hands through his hair, messing it up. I'd missed seeing him do that.

'Yes, you can. Isis wouldn't have asked it of you otherwise,' I said.

'Asked what of him?' said Charm's voice from the shadows.

'Yes, what does the goddess want you to do, Inky Locks?' Khai's breath huffed out on a small laugh.

'I might have known you wouldn't have got rid of them, Cleo,' he said. 'They follow you round like a jackal's tail.'

'Hey,' said Charm, coming forward and punching him on the arm so that he winced. 'Remember who looked after you all the way here? Who hauled your sorry body into bed when it fell out? Who bathed your sweaty brow and held your hand when you were screaming nonsense?' She sniffed. 'Jackal's tail, indeed. Just catch me doing *anything* for you again. Now tell us, Spy Boy. Are we going to have to put up with you all the way to Rome?'

'No,' he said bluntly. 'I have another task to do for our goddess.' He looked at me, as if for permission, and I nodded. There were no secrets between the four of us.

'Blessed Isis has honoured me with the task of calling on Shoshan of the Spear and the marsh people to fulfil their promise to the Chosen,' he said, his voice strong and sure, without a trace of the uncertainty he'd shown me. Khai too could put a mask in place when he needed to.

'They must rendezvous with the army of the Ibis, then guide our warriors into the reeds to hide until it is time for us to attack the city. I must also raise an army of street rats of Alexandria in secret, go amongst the poor and the neglected and whisper to them to be ready, train them to sneak into the barracks of the palace guard and the city soldiers and spoil food, cut harnesses, steal weapons, so that they are weakened. I will earn the title of Spy Boy by the time I've finished, I assure you.'

If he isn't caught and killed by that demon Am-Heh first, I thought.

I didn't say it aloud, though. That would not be helpful.

Isis had just made me give him the most dangerous job in my whole army.

No, I didn't like it one little bit.

11

The Army of the Ibis

Iras was uncharacteristically silent as we made our way out of the labyrinth. She had that faraway look in her eyes again – the one that told me she was listening to Sobek. As we reached the small door she'd taken me out of before, she turned to Khai, putting out a hand to stop him.

'Great Sobek, in his mercy, would not have you fight alone,' she said abruptly. 'My knife-sister and -brother, Shadya and Alim, will accompany you to Alexandria.' She smiled cheerfully. 'I think you will like them, Inky Locks. They are twins, and also good at sneaking and slithering. I will introduce you to them tonight.'

If I hadn't been looking, I wouldn't have caught the flash of relief in his eyes.

There was a feast to celebrate my return. After I had bathed away the dust of the journey and dressed in clean robes,

Merit and Captain Nail reported to me. The army of the Ibis would demonstrate their skills for me early tomorrow morning, on the practice fields. But before that, I would visit Petsuchos again.

Meanwhile, in the great Hall of Sobek, I ate and drank without fear, though Am still offered to taste everything before I did. In the months between Choik and Pharmuti, he had gone from a lanky, indolent boy, to a sun-bronzed and muscled young man, greeting me shyly when I saw him behind my chair. When I asked after little Mamo, Captain Nail told me that he was now vowed to Sobek's service, and was training as a priest after the god himself had spoken to him in the labyrinth. I was glad for him. Perhaps life in this temple would be kinder to him. Maybe the pain of leaving his brother to Berenice's tender mercies would fade with time. I hoped so.

Merit told me that the four sisters I had chosen had already begun their preparations to ride for the Oasis of the Oracle, and then onwards.

'Isis has spoken in their minds,' she said. 'It is a great honour.'

'Do you wish it was you?' I asked her. She smiled stiffly, as if it was still hard for her to do so in front of me.

'Maybe in time,' she said. 'Meanwhile, there is work for me here with the army.' She shook her bracelets. 'I find I am becoming quite proficient with these.'

I looked at her.

'Will you fight with the warriors, then?' I asked.

She shook her head. 'No, at least, not at first. Now that we are trained, we sisters will go straight to all the temples in Egypt and remind those who may have forgotten our goddess that she is back in all her glory.' Her face became fierce. 'I myself intend to go to the temple of the Pharos. I believe that many, many reminders are in order there. I will see to it personally that no one forgets what is due to Isis again.'

I believed her. Maybe the wish Cabar had expressed to me all those months ago – to have Sisters of the Living Knot around her again – would come true now. If all went well, Isis would be restored to her proper place in the island temple – and Merit would be useful backup for Khai, too.

The next morning, seated again on the back of the white desert mare which had brought me from Heryshaf's temple, I watched the warriors of Isis's new army at their drill practice. It was an impressive sight. Many of Sobek's soldiers had also joined the army of the Ibis, and as they wheeled and turned in the dust, spear and sword tips flashing in the sunlight, I turned to Captain Nail.

'You have done well in such a short time,' I said.

He bowed, correct as ever. 'It is an army fit for a goddess – and for our next Pharaoh,' he said. 'If I may be so bold.'

'I'm not on the throne yet,' I said quietly.

'But you will be, Chosen,' he said. There was no doubt in his voice.

'I will,' I said. It was the first time I'd confirmed it out loud, and I felt the words hang in the air, coalesce around me, become real. I would be Pharaoh, because my goddess had decreed it, and there was no other way I could pay the debt I owed.

After Iras had taken me to Petsuchos to pay my respects, and give thanks to Sobek for his help, we met for a council of war in one of the temple rooms. Khai, Charm and Iras were there, along with Captain Nail, Merit, and the two young soldiers Iras had talked of. Shadya was tall and willowy, with the wary, slanted eyes of a cat. Alim was also tall, but stockier, with a coiled and dangerous air to him that made me a little wary. He had the same eyes as his sister.

'By the time we get to the coast, it will be the sailing season again,' I said. 'There are always ships from Leukaspis. We can go from there to Rome.'

'I will detail warriors to go with you,' Captain Nail said. 'An honour guard of twelve should be enough to protect you.'

I shook my head sharply. 'I will take only Charm and Iras, plus Corporal Geta and Warrior Sah if I must. They both work well with Iras. We need to move fast and without fanfare. I will be just another traveller on the road – if

I have a whole troop of warriors with me, I will be noticed.'

'But Chosen…' He started, the familiar frown drawing his black brows downwards. I waved a hand at him, cutting him off.

'No, Captain. My best hope of safety is to remain invisible.'

'She's right,' said Khai. 'Much as I hate to admit it. Nobody will be looking for such a small party.' He turned to me. 'Will you go by river again, my Chosen?'

A small tremor went through my heart to hear him call me that again. I so wanted to say yes, because it would mean more time with him. But he would have to go his way, and I would go mine.

'No,' I said reluctantly. 'We'll take the shorter route over the desert mountains. The river has too many eyes on it, and I don't want to go anywhere near Alexandria, with Am-Heh's shadow prowling the streets and killing people.' The minute I'd said it I wished I hadn't. I could have been more tactful.

'What do you mean, a shadow prowling the streets and killing people?' said Alim. His voice was a rasp, with a slight accent I couldn't place. His sister nudged him. 'I mean, if you would be so kind as to tell us, Chosen,' he added, bowing.

How best to explain? This soldier boy of Sobek didn't know me at all. Was he aware that I could see the gods, as the others here must know by now? I felt an old ghost of fear fall upon me. My mother's early lessons in secrecy ran very deep. I could almost feel her whip across my back.

'You may not actually see him,' I said, hedging a little, 'but Isis has shown him to me in a dream.'

I looked at Khai first, and then at the others, willing them to believe me. 'It's something that all of you who go to the city will have to be wary of. That vile demon is out there, I promise you, maybe with Berenice in tow, taking street children for sacrifice. If any of you see a dark shadow or a cloud that fills you with fear, one that doesn't seem to be in the right place, then run. You must stay alive to do what Isis has commanded. You will not be able to save everyone.'

My eyes were particularly on Khai as I said that last bit. I knew how he'd feel about street children being taken down to Am-Heh's dungeon. I felt horribly sick about it myself. But he couldn't endanger his mission by trying to mount a rescue operation.

'You can warn everyone,' I said. 'But that's all. Remember, Isis has given you a mission.'

He nodded reluctantly.

'Is it only the children on the streets?' he asked. 'Or does he go into buildings too?'

'I've just seen him on the streets and within the palace,' I said. 'But that doesn't mean he can't go into other places.'

'I suggest each of you is paired with a sister,' said Merit. 'That will afford you a certain amount of our goddess's protection, as well as someone to watch your backs. And once I have cleansed the Temple of the Pharos, that will be a safe place for the street children to go.'

Khai nodded.

'Make sure the sisters who go with us are good fighters,' was all he said.

After a lot more talk, we had decided what each of us would be doing. Merit would start sending the sisters who were not going to Alexandria out to the other temples right away, so that the presence of too many priestesses of Isis moving about at once would not cause comment. She, Khai, Shadya and Alim, along with another three sisters, would go to the marshes and then to Alexandria to start raising the streets in secret. Captain Nail and Sobek's soldiers would keep training the army of the Ibis, and also arrange for barges to be ready for them to go downriver when Shoshan's messenger arrived. Timing would be crucial. We could not afford for Berenice to hear of our plans too early.

Merit had news about Berenice.

'I had a dove from Cabar a few days ago,' she said. 'It appears that our false Pharaoh is not just occupied with her foul demon god. A proclamation will reach all of Egypt soon, commanding us to rejoice at her marriage to a priest-prince of Pontus. It is a marriage of state, in name only, Cabar suspects, but the prince will come to the city soon for the formal ceremony.'

I frowned.

'My father won't like that. At least...did she get his permission to marry?' I asked.

Merit shook her head. 'From what you tell me of her, she has an unstoppable taste for power now. She thinks your father, the true Pharaoh, is far away in Rome and so doesn't count. I don't think she has asked permission,' she said. 'Not this time, and not last time either. You have heard about that, haven't you?'

'How would I have heard?' I asked. 'I have been in the desert for three months. News was scarce.'

Merit sighed.

'Soon after you left Alexandria, she married one of your Seleucid cousins. It only lasted a few weeks. Apparently he wouldn't dance to her tune, so she gave him to Am-Heh's priests as an offering. That's not widely known, of course.'

'I'll make sure she realises her mistake when I bring my father home,' I said. It might be the way in. If I could make my father angry enough about Berenice's actions, he would come back to Egypt with me, I was almost sure of it.

Later, I walked alone with Khai in the shade of a secluded grove of palm trees, their leaves whispering secrets into the small, hot breeze.

'I wish...' he said, then stopped. I put a hand on his arm.

'I know,' I said. 'I wish too. But when I come back, when we've given Berenice what she deserves, then we can be together.'

He caught my wrist, pulling me round into his arms, ducking into a small shrine to the snake goddess Renenutet, where we couldn't be seen. The shrine was dark, apart from one lamp before the goddess's cobra-headed statue, and I eyed the floor uneasily, hoping that there were none of her slithery worshippers around.

'Will we, Cleo?' he asked, snapping my attention back to him. 'Will we really be together? When you're Pharaoh and on the Double Throne? Do you think your father will really let a lowly scribe like me near you? A scribe who is well known to the court as your sister's ex-pet? And that's not even mentioning what Seth's priests will do to me if they get hold of me.'

I hadn't seen my father for years. I didn't know what he would do, how he would act. Would he go back to his old ways of flute-playing debauchery, his shady politics, his extravagant ways and his unwise borrowing? I hoped not. I hoped he had learned his lesson. But if I was to be Pharaoh beside him, I would be watched every moment of every day. I would have to play the political games of the court. I would have duties, letters to sign, laws to make, scrolls to read, endless meetings with ambassadors and bureaucrats. A life in private would be impossible, and it would be very hard to have a lover or consort who was not part of that world. I knew it, but I hadn't wanted to face it till now. Not really. I also hadn't faced up to the fact that Khai would be a wanted man. The Brotherhood of Embalmers did not like it when anyone betrayed their secrets to outsiders. They would be after him as soon as they got wind of his presence in the city – unless Seth really had let go of him. But would his priests know that?

'You will have served the throne like no other,' I said, my voice fierce. 'When I am Pharaoh, I will make you my personal vizier. I will give you land and title. I will have you by my side, and I will protect you, with armed guards if necessary. We *will* find a way.'

One hand crept up to my neck. I felt warm fingers caress my nape, making me shiver with pleasure as they stroked the sensitive skin behind my ear.

'I so want to believe you, my beloved,' he whispered. 'But, just in case it doesn't work out, I will take enough kisses from you now to see me through.' The rough sandstone blocks of the wall pressed into my back as I put my arms around him and pulled him closer till his breath mingled with mine.

'That might take quite some time,' I said against his lips, feeling the roughness of his cheek scrape mine. He pulled away for a moment, and started kissing my closed eyelids, my neck, and then back to my lips again. His arm slid around and down, his large hand pressing me tightly against him. I could feel the blade he wore at his hip digging uncomfortably into my waist, but it didn't matter. I was much more interested in the hand which had now moved downwards to explore my curves, making me gasp and hitch myself even closer to him.

'I intend to make sure it does,' he mumbled against my mouth.

All too soon, though, it was time for him to leave me and pack. He would go just before dawn, slipping away unnoticed with Shadya and Alim. Merit and her small band of sisters would leave separately, and meet him at the river. He walked me back to my rooms in silence. We had said everything there was to say for now.

As I put my hand on the latch, he stopped me.

'I will come to you for Isis's blessing before I go,' he said. 'It won't be long now.' With one last, long kiss on my swollen lips, he turned and left me.

'Well,' said Charm, looking up from the cushion she was sitting on, mending a torn robe. Iras was behind her, braiding her hair into small rows. 'Look what Bastet's cat finally dragged in. Is this any way for the chosen of the goddess to behave?' she asked, mock-stern. Then she saw my face, and was up off the cushion in an instant, wrenching her hair from Iras's grasp with no heed for her own pain.

'Oh, Cleo,' she said, taking my hand. 'I'm sorry I teased you. He'll be all right. He will. He's done this before.'

'No, he hasn't,' I said, my voice thick and choked. 'Not

like this. He has to raise an army right under Berenice and Am-Heh's noses. If they catch him…' I didn't have to say any more. Charm knew what awaited him if he got caught.

'Shadya and Alim will watch his back,' said Iras, taking my other hand. 'And don't forget he's got the Cold Streak on his side, and all those other assassin sisters. He'll be fine.'

I appreciated them trying to cheer me up, and I knew Isis would protect him for me as much as she could. But her eyes couldn't be everywhere, and she was going to be busy repairing the damage to the land. One young spy could easily slip from her gaze.

I didn't sleep much for the rest of the night, and when Khai slipped into the room in the lamplit gloom near dawn, Charm nudged Iras and herded her away through an alcove to give us some privacy for our goodbyes. I bit back a cry as I saw him come across the room to me. He looked quite different. All his beautiful hair was gone, shaved down to the scalp, and the shadows made deep pools under his eyes and in his cheeks. He looked harder, more dangerous, a lean-muscled weapon going out in the service of our goddess. I would not weep, I vowed. I would not let his last glimpse of me be full of tears.

I reached a hand up and stroked the strange new smoothness, trying to smile.

'I said once that I'd love you just as well with a shaven head. It's true, I do.'

'I won't let it grow till I see you again, Cleo.' He pressed something into my other hand. It was a tiny, flat papyrus packet, tied with a dried palm frond. 'Open it when I'm gone.' He knelt before me, as he had previously.

'Bless me, before I go, my Chosen. To me, you are Isis on earth, and I want nothing more than to serve you and her with every last drop of blood in my body.'

How could he expect me not to weep after a declaration like that?

I laid both my hands on his head, holding his shaven scalp gently, as I would something infinitely precious and breakable.

'Whatever blessing I may give is yours,' I said, and I felt Isis move within me as I spoke. 'Isis guard and protect you, may her light and Ra's shine upon you. May you smite her enemies, and may all the gods guide your hand and keep you safe from harm.' As I touched him, a golden ibis flared on his forehead, as it had on the other warriors, sinking in and disappearing.

'S-see?' I said, the emotion making my voice break. 'She has marked you twice now. Never think again that you belong to any other but her.'

'Only to her and you, my beloved,' he whispered, as he rose and left me, brushing a kiss on each of my palms.

When he was gone, I did weep, and Charm and Iras comforted me as best they could. Eventually, I opened the tiny packet, and saw a lock of his hair coiled inside it, sealed at each end with red wax. I raised it to my nose and sniffed. It smelt of him, very slightly. Then I put it back in its covering, tied it up again and stowed it in my breastband. Its slightly scratchy presence against my skin would be a constant reminder of him till we met again.

Keep him safe for me, Isis. Please, keep him safe.

I came to the steps of the temple at dawn, with Charm and Iras at my side, and my two warrior guards following. The army of the Ibis was waiting there at attention, with Captain Nail at its head. The previous night, as I tossed and turned, I had decided to do something – my first public act as Pharaoh-to-be. I beckoned him over.

'Kneel,' I hissed. Then, as he did, I raised my hand for silence.

'Be it known,' I called out. 'Be it known that this faithful servant of Isis shall now be known as General Nail. He will lead you into battle. Obey him as you would me.'

His black eyes flew up to mine, startled. He had not expected this. I raised him to his feet, and set his left hand high in the air, in the salute of victory. The troops cheered and whistled, calling his name as he turned to me.

'Chosen,' he said, 'it is—'

'It is what you deserve,' I said. 'And, anyway, Isis can't have a mere captain leading her army, now can she?'

His mouth quirked up in that half-smile of his, and he bowed.

'I suppose not, Chosen,' he said. 'But you still do me too much honour.'

We rode steadily north-westwards across the mountains of the desert, me on Lashes again. There were fewer dunes and more rocks on this journey, and the camels picked their way carefully. We were caught in a *simoom* once, but it was not a bad one, just inconvenient. I didn't sleep well for worrying, and every night, as I fell asleep, I tried and tried to contact Khai using Iusaaset Skyborn's gift. Sometimes I got glimpses of the river and a felucca sailing northwards. Mostly I didn't. Every morning I railed at her in my head.

Please. You gave me this gift. Why can't I use it? What use is it if I can't see what's happening?

But there was only silence. I would have to keep working at it.

Khai's absence pulled at me, and all the more so because with every day that passed Iras and Charm became closer. It was as if this new part of our journey had somehow given them permission to be easier with each other, to begin to have their own private code of glances and smiles. I didn't begrudge either of them their fledgling happiness – but I'd be lying if I said I didn't envy them just a little. I withdrew to my bedroll early every night, saying I wanted as much dreaming time as possible. Really, I wanted to grant them a little privacy – not that there was much hope of that with four guides and two warriors huddled round our small fire.

On the second night before we reached the coast, it finally happened. I found myself hovering over my earthly body, linked to it by that shining silver cord.

Khai, I thought, and immediately the land blurred beneath me and I was flying eastwards. I found him in a small hut made of bunched and tied reeds, at the southern end of Lake Mareotis. He was awake, sitting up with his hands on his knees, surrounded by sleeping bodies. I could see his eyes shining, staring out of the door at the stars reflected on the still water.

As before, my emotions were dampened in this form. I felt somehow empty, as if a part of me had been left behind. But it didn't matter. I was here, with him.

Khai! I said into his head, remembering how to do it at once. His head went up like a sighthound marking prey.

'Cleo?' he murmured.

Yes. I found out how to use my gift again, but I don't know how long it will last. Tell me what's been happening.

He rose quietly and moved out of the hut, walking a little distance away.

'It feels odd, this...' He made a confused gesture to his head.

I know. Maybe it'll work differently if you're asleep.

He shrugged. 'I don't sleep much. Too many things to think about. And...and I miss you, Cleo.'

I miss you too. But, Khai...I don't know how long

I can hold this for... It was true. I could feel the tug of the silver cord. I saw his eyes widen, and he began to talk, rapid and low.

'We got here yesterday. Shoshan has been gathering her marsh tribes since we left her. They're all armed and, even better, they know secret ways into the city. Merit has already left for the Temple of the Pharos, and we've worked out a way of leaving messages for each other. Shoshan's son will take the rest of us in tomorrow night, and then we'll rouse the street rats. A messenger has already gone upriver to Crocodilopolis.' He stopped, running his hands over his shaven scalp in a move I knew very well, then gave a choked-off laugh.

'I never thought I'd miss my hair.'

The tug was much stronger now.

Khai. I have to go. I'll come again when I can. I stretched out a misty hand towards him, but of course he didn't see it.

'Wait, Cleo...I need to tell you...' he said. But it was too late. I was being pulled back to my own body. Whatever he had been going to say, I couldn't hear it. I landed back in my own body, and spent the rest of the night worrying and trying to get back to him. But Iusaaset Skyborn's gift was capricious. However much I tried, that night and the next, I couldn't make it work.

We rode into the port city of Leukaspis at the beginning of

the month of Pharmuti, just as the Shemu harvest heat was beginning to make itself known. It was a place of trade, with many villas belonging to merchants grown fat on the profits from wheat, wine and olives. I said a sad goodbye to Lashes, who we sold to our guides, along with the desert equipment we would no longer need. We had been through a lot together, she and I, but I couldn't take a camel to Rome with me.

The market square was bustling with people as we threaded our way through it. We were travelling fairly light, not knowing what kind of ship we would find passage on, but each of us carried a quantity of gold and silver hidden on our persons. At our last stop outside the town, Charm had helped me out of my desert robes and into the dress of a priestess of Isis. We would give out the word that I was going to join one of my goddess's temples in Rome.

The port itself was even busier than the market. Ships of all shapes and sizes lay at anchor behind the breakwater, and tied up to the loading docks. One, on the far side of the port, was larger and grander than those around it, and had hastily bundled-up sails of royal Tyrian purple. From the hanging ropes and battered planks, I could see that the ship had taken some damage, maybe in a storm. The sails and the foreign shape of the ship stood out as unusual amongst the more everyday merchantmen, with their sails of dirty white. There was a bustle of activity on it, and suspicious-eyed guards stood at attention on the gangway, peering out as if they were waiting for someone. They wore strange conical caps and metal breastplates and carried round, studded shields. I could see the shine of sweat on their faces from where I stood. They must be frying in all that kit.

Most of the other ships had a constant line of laden slaves going up and down, up and down the gangways, carrying heavy jars, sacks and woven, covered reed baskets, loading and unloading. Several treadwheel cranes were in operation, lifting goods too heavy for human hands. Maybe one of those vessels would take us.

I looked around.

'Where do we start?' I asked.

'With the clerk of the harbour, I should think, Chosen,' Corporal Geta said. 'He will have the lists of ships and where they are sailing.'

'And, more importantly, will know whether they will take passengers,' said Iras. She turned to me. 'How long does it take to sail to Rome?' she asked.

I shrugged, trying to remember what I'd learned about our trade routes in my childhood. 'It depends on the wind, I imagine. And whether the ship is heavily laden. These are mostly trading ships, so they may stop off at places like Leptis Magna along the way. Let's go and find out what's on offer.'

Just then, though, I spotted a double line of white-kilted mercenaries shouldering their way through the crowds on the other side of the port. With them was a black-robed priest. I turned my back quickly, muttering a curse. Charm went stiff beside me, so I knew she'd seen them too.

'Charm,' I said. 'Don't stare, but can you see? Are they what I think they are?'

'Yes,' she said. 'Palace guards.'

The three words sent a sickening jolt through me.

Were they here for us?

PART TWO

12

The Great Green Sea

It wasn't far from Alexandria. Had word somehow reached Berenice of our journey? Surely it wasn't possible. Then I heard the harsh blare of trumpets and the slow beat of drums and, as more soldiers and mercenaries marched in, I knew that they were not here for us after all.

They were here to guard the Pharaoh herself. By now, people were on their knees, bowing down, faces pressed flat to the dirt.

'Get down,' I hissed. 'All of you. Right now. She can't notice any of us.'

Berenice was here, for what I had no idea, but there were many festivals and ceremonies that she would have to attend as Pharaoh. Perhaps it was for one of those.

'What day is it?' I whispered.

'The tenth of Pachons, I think,' Iras whispered back. 'Why?'

I was doing frantic calculations in my head. The tenth of Pachons was the feast of Anubis, wasn't it? But there was no major temple to Anubis round here, as far as I knew. It must be something else. I remembered the strange ship. Did that have something to do with Berenice's visit? I couldn't see with my face pressed into the ground, and I wished I knew what was going on. I tilted my head to the side and through a gap in the crowd, I saw her, in an open litter, carried high on the shoulders of her slaves.

Berenice was all in gold, with the white diadem of the Pharaoh around her brow. She was decked in jewels that sparkled and danced in Ra's bright light, though I could see a darkness around her. She looked as if she was dressed for—

Of course. This must be the ship of her intended, the unknown prince of Pontus. She had come to greet him before their marriage. Why he was here, though, and not in the harbour at Alexandria, I couldn't work out. Maybe his ship had been blown off course. Maybe they'd got lost. Navigation from the Pontic kingdom across the Great Green Sea to here was uncertain and chancy, even using the stars. And storms were frequent. The sailing season was not long open and he must have set out long before it was safe to do so.

I froze as my horrible sister's voice rang across the square.

'Bring them,' she said, pointing with one sharp,

gold-nailed fingertip. 'Great Am-Heh himself has summoned them. He is merciful and kind.'

'He is merciful and kind,' shouted the priest and the mercenaries, banging spears against shields.

And then they began to come in our direction.

Charm's arm came down on the back of my neck as I made a panicky lurch to my knees.

'Stay down,' she said, fierce and low. 'Stay down, Cleo. It's not us. They're taking those poor people over there.'

I slumped flat, once again turning my head to the side in an effort to see. Charm was right. A small group near the front of the crowd was being herded away by the black-clad priest.

Berenice's voice rang out again.

'Rejoice,' she said. 'Why are you not all rejoicing? Your Pharaoh commands you to be happy on this auspicious occasion.'

The mercenaries were moving through the crowd again, spears and sandals dealing out blows and kicks, and everywhere they went, a dull, muted cheer went up, growing louder and louder.

I felt a spear haft thump down by my head, and closed my eyes. It was happening all over again. I almost let the rage in my blood take me. I wanted to jump up, to challenge Berenice for the throne right now, save those poor people from their fate as crocodile food. Surely if I did, Isis would come to my side, would protect me? But a sullen ache in my belly told me that she wouldn't – that I must obey my goddess's command and go to Rome. If I was taken now, *ma'at* would still be broken and I would have lost any chance of mending it. So I stayed flat, forcing a cracked cheer out of my unwilling throat in order to stay alive. I vowed it would be the last time I would bow to Berenice, the last time I would stay on the sidelines while she took people away to sacrifice them to her foul demon god. The people knew, I could tell. All around me amongst the sour cheers were soft murmurs of fear and small sobs. Nobody wanted to be next for Am-Heh's mercy. Maybe Khai wouldn't find it hard to raise the streets after all. I remembered the way my father had been tipped off his throne – but then he had only borrowed money from the Romans. Fear and uncertainty were much more powerful ways of keeping people in line, but there was only so much they would take from their rulers.

Berenice kept us grovelling there for a long, hot hour while she greeted her new prince with all the pomp and fanfare of a ruling Pharaoh. It was a display of pure arrogance and complacent power, and I hated her for it. I wondered if the priest-prince of Pontus knew what he was marrying. If he didn't, he was in for a nasty surprise. Finally, though, it was over. The litter was lifted again and carried out of the port, with the prince riding at its side on a black horse. He carried a short, curved horn bow slung across his back, banded with gold, and behind him came his guard, then slaves carrying boxes and bundles – presumably his gifts to his wife-to-be.

Gradually, stiffly, as the last mercenary marched out of sight, the crowd got to its knees and stood up. A low hum of chatter began, rising to a roar.

'We need to find a ship and go,' I said quietly. 'We'll take the first one out that's going in the right direction – I don't care how much it costs. Use gold if you have to.'

Corporal Geta bowed.

'Right away, Chosen.'

I stood at the rail of the ship, looking back, letting out my breath properly for the first time since Berenice had left. Leukaspis was nearly out of sight, the white houses of the port fading into the distance under a bright blue sky. Soon all I could see was the endless white sand of the coast, with the occasional village scattered here and there. The ship was a smallish merchantman, carrying a cargo of wine and lentils, and was crowded with passengers taking advantage of one of the first sailings of the season. The square sails flapped and bellied in the brisk breeze from the east, which was blowing us along at a good rate. The five of us had been lucky to obtain a tiny cabin as far as Leptis Magna. From there we would hope to find a ship bound for Rome.

Charm and Iras stood to either side of me, with Corporal Geta and Warrior Sah at my back, hemming me in. Charm's hand crept into mine, as the ship dived into the waves, making it hard to keep our feet. A fine spray made everything slightly damp and sea-scented – and this was when it wasn't even particularly rough.

'Isis preserve us,' Charm said. 'Is it always like this?'

Iras said nothing but her face had a greenish tinge to it, and suddenly, mumbling an apology, she ducked under the arm of the person next to her and pushed her way to the back of the ship. By standing on tiptoes, I could just see her leaning over the stern rail and retching. This was not the adventure she'd been anticipating back in the desert.

'Should I go to her?' said Charm, her face anxious. 'Has she eaten something bad?'

Corporal Geta gave an amused grunt as he moved into the place Iras had left beside me.

'No, lass,' he said to her. 'Leave her be.' He jerked a thumb at the stern. 'She won't be the only one, not by a long way. It's just a bit of seasickness. She'll get over it. But it's maybe best if she doesn't spend a lot of time in that cabin.'

I wasn't sure I wanted to spend a lot of time in it, either. It was dark and although above the waterline, its one slit window was covered in hide and didn't let in anything but the smallest bit of light. The stench of sour wine and damp, overlaid with traces of human waste and vomit was not appealing. There were two rough wooden bunks, just planks held up by iron chains, really, and a chest seat nailed to the floor, which was covered with our bags and bundles, so only some of us could sleep at any one time.

I could see that Charm was torn. She wanted to stay with me, but she also wanted to go to Iras. The two of them were nearly inseparable now.

'Don't worry,' I said. 'Geta is right. It's just seasickness. It will pass.'

But it didn't. Iras could keep nothing down but sips of water for the seven days of what soon seemed like an interminable journey.

The sky darkened an hour or so after we set sail, and the wind began to blow off the land in vicious gusts, rolling the ship from side to side. I could feel Seth's malice behind it, as sea spray mixed with sand stung our faces and covered the deck in a fine grit. Waves slapped the ship from all directions, and the crew ran about with white, set faces, turning the sails this way and that before the wind. Passengers wailed and huddled at the rails, clinging on, being sick, their faces screwed up with fear.

'Ask Isis for help,' Charm shouted over the scream of the gale. 'Please, Cleo.' Her skin was ashy-grey with fear and cold, and she held Iras's head in her lap to shield her from the worst of the weather.

I called on my goddess with everything I had, hoping that her power extended this far out to sea. Almost at once, lightning flashed a blinding green-white against the water, and thunder growled and roared like a gigantic lion of the sea. The mast crackled and snapped as blue fire limned it, making the hair on my head prickle and rise, as if I had suddenly grown Medusa's snake locks. Now the wails around us had turned to moans of terror. A man had been swept overboard, disappearing into the maelstrom of the waves.

'Isis!' I called aloud, raising my arms. 'Blessed goddess! Save us and see us safe to shore!' Blue fire trembled on my fingertips for a moment, and then went out, leaving a fizzing feeling within me. The air smelt hot, sharp, like burnt seaweed and salt.

Ride the storm, my Chosen! Learn from its power. Fair winds lie ahead.

I didn't know whether her voice was in my head, or whether the wind itself had spoken. Suddenly it was blowing from behind us, filling the sails, sending us scudding over the sea westwards. The feeling of Seth's malice snapped off as if it had never been. Now it was just weather – just a spring storm. I raised my palms in gratitude, knowing that Isis would not let us die – not yet, at least.

'Thank you, great goddess,' I whispered, trying to work out what lesson she wanted me to learn. Was it to take power when it offered itself? Was it to show implacable ruthlessness? I worried at it in my head all the way to our landing place.

Unfortunately, although the storm itself eventually stopped, the wind was still strong, and Iras's seasickness did not go away. Her round face grew gaunt, and in the end we put her in the bottom bunk of the cabin, rather than tending to her in the fresh air on deck, because she became too weak to stand and was shivering harder than an acacia in a *simoom*. We swaddled her in all the spare robes, but we'd sold our bedrolls along with Lashes, not thinking that we'd need them.

Several times Iras asked us to let her die, moaning pitifully as she retched up yet another bitter mouthful of yellow bile. It was only then that I saw Charm's calm facade begin to crack.

She dipped a cloth into the small clay jar she held and pressed it to Iras's lips, wetting them again.

'Don't you dare die,' she snapped. 'I'm not losing you now. You went to all that trouble to make me love you, so fight like Sobek taught you to. Don't even think about going to Anubis's realm. Because if you do, I'll make your afterlife so miserable when I finally get there that you'll wish you hadn't.'

Iras groaned and retched again.

'Can't hear him,' she whispered. 'Can't hear him any more.'

'That doesn't mean he's not watching,' said Charm, her face implacable as she dripped in more water.

We took it in turns tending Iras, and shared the top bunk out between the four of us. It was hard and uncomfortable with no bedding and nobody got much sleep. Although I tried to use Iusaaset Skyborn's gift whenever I did doze off, I was so exhausted that if I did go anywhere in my dreams, I didn't remember it. I missed Khai as if I was lacking a limb, and I worried constantly that he was in danger. All I could hope for was that Berenice would be so occupied with her new shiny Pontic prince that she wouldn't be scouring the streets for new victims.

On the seventh day we sailed into Leptis, past the lighthouse, which was not nearly as impressive as the Pharos. The ship would be docked there for a day, unloading passengers and cargo, before going on to Carthage. We were all glad to get off her, especially with Iras in such a state. Corporal Geta and Warrior Sah carried her down the gangplank and laid her down on the quay, before going back for our bags. She groaned.

'I can still feel the rocking,' she whimpered. 'Sobek help me, will it ever stop?'

When we were all disembarked, I sent Warrior Sah to find us lodgings for the night and to seek out a physician before bringing back a litter for Iras. People swore at us. We were taking up a lot of space and it was a busy place

'Move, Ra curse you,' said a drunken man with a brass earring, who was wheeling a barrow full of sacks.

I glared at him. 'We will move when we're ready,' I said, forgetting my accent. 'Can't you see we've got a sick girl here?'

He spat again.

'Foreign scum. Isis-blasted Greeks.'

That was too much. 'I am a priestess of Isis,' I snarled at him. 'If she accepts me, I see no reason for you not to. And don't use my goddess's name like that, either. It's not respectful.'

'What do you know about it?' he sneered, weaving off towards a stall selling jugs of barley beer. 'Greek cow.'

'Quite a lot, as it happens,' I said. But I said it quietly.

Charm just looked at me.

'Keep ourselves invisible,' she remarked, looking somewhere over my left shoulder. 'I'll be an ordinary traveller. Don't attract notice. I believe that was what you said, O Sovereign of Sneakers.'

There was a weak chuckle at our feet. 'She's got you there, Cleo Blue-Eyes.'

'I'm sorry,' I said, my voice stiff with embarrassment. 'He just annoyed me, that's all.'

It was amazing what a difference being on land for an hour had made to Iras. She got off the litter and walked to our chamber by herself, with a little help from Corporal Geta and Warrior Sah. When the physician arrived, he inspected her and prescribed barley gruel till her inside-out stomach settled itself, and his own concoction of bitter herbs to be taken at hourly intervals.

'Will you be going on a ship again?' he enquired. Iras looked at me pitifully, and I grimaced with sympathy.

'I think we'll have to,' I said. 'Is there anything more you can give her?'

He nodded, rummaging in his leather satchel. He got out a small pot that rattled slightly, and a tiny sealed bottle, which had a small reed brush attached to it. Opening the box, he beckoned me over and showed me what was inside. Several gold beads, each as big as two grains of sand, rolled about inside it. He licked a finger and delicately fished one of the beads out, then with his other hand he seized Iras's left ear. Applying the bead just where the lobe narrowed, he pressed firmly.

'Just here,' he said, 'there is a point which controls the humours of the stomach. Use one of these before you go on board and it should take care of the problem.' He grabbed the bottle and, taking the small stopper out with his teeth, he set it down one-handed and gently dipped the reed brush into it.

'This is acacia gum,' he said. 'A small drop painted onto the ear will hold the ball in place.' He demonstrated. 'If you lose the beads, then you can use a stylus or something sharp to press on the same point.'

'It…it's like magic,' Iras said as I paid him. 'The sickness is nearly all gone. I almost feel hungry.'

The physician sniffed, offended. 'I am not a charlatan. I do not deal in magic, only in the principles of Hippocrates,' he said haughtily. 'It is simply an ancient technique I learned from one who had travelled in the east. It is medicine, lady, not mumbo-jumbo.' He stalked out clutching the silver coin I'd given him.

Iras giggled. It was good to hear her do that again. 'What an old nose-in-the-air,' she said. 'You'd think I'd insulted his sacred mother's chastity or something.'

It was taking a while for Iras to get back on her feet so, two mornings later, I walked down the street, lightly veiled in case of spying eyes, with the Knot of Isis firmly at my shoulder. Charm was at my side with a large basket borrowed from our lodgings, followed by Corporal Geta. I would not go to my father improperly dressed, so I was in search of a new kohl pot and other necessary items, such as hairpins. Before we made our purchases, though, we would go to the harbour and search for a suitable ship to take us on to Rome.

As we hurried towards the clerk of the harbour's office, I felt eyes on me. Glancing about through the thin linen, I had a hazy view of a stocky young man with the short, cropped hair of a Roman soldier, standing by the prow of a galley, a fast trireme of the sort the Republic used for conveying messages up and down the Great Green Sea. I had seen them often in the years when my father had dealings with Rome. He was directing a bustle of activity around the ship, which had a sharp prow decorated with eyes that seemed fierce and warlike. She was high-sided, long, narrow and had a curving stern in the shape of a swan. Wine and water jars, along with flat round loaves of barley bread in string bags and bunches of dates were being manhandled aboard by a line of crew in red tunics, and received by men with muscled shoulders and backs, who I assumed were the rowers.

The young man's clean-shaven, square chin had a stubborn jut to it, and his deep-set brown eyes looked over at me with sharp intent. Somehow I had caught his interest. He was older than me by quite a few years, but he was definitely handsome, in that patrician way that said without words Rome owned the world and didn't care who knew it. I disliked him on sight. He gave me a funny feeling at the pit of my belly. I hurried over to the harbour offices, trying to ignore him.

The clerk of the harbour was a small, bent man with the face of a surprised ibis. He had a long, curved nose, a sloped-back forehead and a frill of white hair at the back of his bald, brown head.

He shook his head and tapped his teeth with a stylus, unrolling his scrolls with painfully slow fingers.

'No, lady priestess,' he said in a nasal whine. 'Nothing for Rome just now. It's too early in the season.' He cocked a feathery brow at me. 'Unless you want to ask the decurion?'

I looked where he was pointing. 'What decurion?' I asked, though I knew very well to whom he was referring.

'Him out there giving orders as fast as a chattering

crow,' the clerk said. 'Carrying important letters for Rome, he says, for the consul himself, if you believe him. He's only here taking on stores and water for his rowers. Then he'll be off again.' He tapped his long beak knowingly and waggled an eyebrow. 'A nice lady priestess like you, well, if your journey is so urgent, I'm sure he'd be open to a little compensation, if you get my drift. I could ask him if you like.'

One bony hand hovered in the air in front of me, waiting hopefully. I sighed and put a coin in it – a small one.

'Monetary compensation only,' I said firmly. 'I want that made very clear. There'll be five of us, plus baggage, and I want transport from Ostia to Rome included in the deal. If you persuade him, there'll be a bonus in it for you.' I bent close to his ear, smelling ink and the sour reek of someone who hadn't been to the baths in too long. 'Silver,' I said.

He scurried out without another word and I saw him approach the decurion, grovelling a little.

'Was that wise, Chosen?' asked Corporal Geta. 'A ship full of Roman soldiers is not…well…' He stopped.

'They'll be too busy rowing to bother with us,' I said. 'We'll keep ourselves to ourselves and with luck they'll hardly notice we're there. We'll buy everything we need and have it with us. If we need the, er, necessities, we will go with either you or Sah to protect us. I have not heard that the Romans rape women other than after battle. If the decurion proves troublesome, I shall tell him who my father is. He wouldn't dare harm a princess of Egypt.'

'What if he hears that and holds you for ransom?' Charm asked.

'Either way, my father will hear of my presence in Rome,' I said calmly. 'And I have the protection of Isis. She stopped Seth from drowning us. She will not let me fail.'

'Are you sure this is a wise decision?' she asked. 'I mean…'

I knew what she meant.

'I don't think we have a choice, Charm,' I said. 'We need to get to Rome, and if this is the only way, we have to take it.'

She nodded reluctantly.

By this time, the clerk was back.

'The decurion would like to talk to you, lady priestess. He is interested in your proposal. Very interested. But he would like to discuss the sum with you personally.' He winked. 'Young officer like him, he'll have debts, mark my words.'

I stepped past him. 'If you speak true,' I said, 'you shall have your silver.' I sniffed, then wished I hadn't. 'Use some of it on hot water, perhaps.'

I walked towards the decurion. Suddenly the air was very still, almost as if the world was holding its breath. He took a step towards me, away from his men, and bowed his head in the Roman manner.

'Do you speak Greek, priestess? I have little Egyptian.' His voice was deep and mellifluous, like dark honey over silk, but he spoke my mother tongue as if he was attacking it with an axe. I heard Charm give a little gasp behind me.

'I speak perfect Greek,' I said. Well, I did – a lot better than him, if I'd cared to say so. 'Now, I believe you are amenable to taking passengers to Rome. Name your price, decurion.'

He smiled at me, openly flirtatious. His eyes had sun-crinkles in the corners, and his teeth were square and white. Handsome older men of his sort were a mystery to me. He made me feel uneasy in a way I couldn't identify.

'Will you not take off your veil and give me your name before we bargain?' he asked.

'My name is…' I hesitated. I hadn't thought of this. 'My name is Priestess Charmion,' I said hurriedly, picking the first name that came to mind – Charm to the rescue yet again. 'And my face is hidden to all but servants of my goddess – whose name is Isis, may her blessing be upon you.'

'Very well…Priestess Charmion.' I could tell from the curl at the corner of his mouth that he didn't believe it was my real name. 'My name is Marcus Antonius, decurion of Aulus Gabinius's legions. And my price is a gold talent for each of you, with two more for getting you to Rome safely.' His smile grew wider, full of the lazy assurance of one who knows he holds all the senet pieces, and he leaned forward and took a step towards me. I could smell him now – metal and oiled leather, and the rank sweat of a long voyage, mixed with cedarwood and lemons. It was not unpleasant. The strange, uneasy feeling settled in my belly and intensified. 'If you'd only take that veil off and let me see what's underneath, I'd ask for a kiss on top, but as you won't…' He let the sentence hang, as Corporal Geta stepped in front of me, blocking my view.

'The priestess won't be kissing anyone…sir,' he said in his rough but serviceable Greek. 'You'll get three of your five talents when we're on board, and the rest when we're in the city. No arguments. We'll treat you fair if you'll do the same to us. The lady is in a hurry.'

Marcus Antonius raised his hands in mock surrender.

'I can see you have a fierce defender, Priestess Charmion,' he said, and then his face turned serious and he was all business. 'Be on board by sunrise tomorrow. We leave just after first light. If any of the rowers fall sick your men will take their place for the duration of the voyage.'

'My men are not slaves—' I began.

'Neither are mine,' he said. 'Freemen all, or soldiers. And that was not a request, priestess. Take it or leave it.'

I nodded.

'I'll take it,' I said.

Iras looked nervous when we boarded the Roman galley. It was early morning of the third day and she was recovered and able to eat properly again. Charm had applied the physician's bead to her ear before we left our lodging, carefully pressing it into place and glueing it down.

The night before, Charm had tried to persuade me to renege on my bargain with the decurion.

'He's too smooth,' she said. 'I don't trust him.'

'I don't trust him either,' I replied. 'But he's all we've got.'

'I know,' she said. 'But he gives me a bad feeling. You just keep away from him.'

'I will,' I said, and meant it. I had no intention of spending any more time than I could help with Marcus Antonius of the Gabinian legions. I didn't tell Charm about my own uneasy feelings around him, though. I didn't want to worry her.

Of course, he was waiting on the gangplank to escort us on board. He introduced us to the commander of the ship, a swarthy fellow from Thrinacia with slightly shifty eyes and a rolling walk.

'I have vacated my own sleeping place for you,' the decurion said. 'It's best if you and your people keep to that part of the deck for the most part – there's not much room for spare bodies.' Then he looked at me sideways. 'Unless you wish to take the air on deck with me, Priestess Charmion,' he added with that wide-toothed smile again. 'I promise not to molest you and to talk of only the colour of the waves and the sky.' He was very charming, and I just couldn't put my finger on why he made me feel this uncomfortable.

'Perhaps my maidens and I will join you later in the voyage,' I said, keeping my voice cool. 'I thank you for your kindness to us.' It didn't hurt to be polite, though of course I had no intention of following through. I held out a hand. 'The money, Corporal Geta, if you please.' The corporal handed me a small purse. 'Three talents, sir, as agreed.'

He took it from me and, as our fingers touched, I felt a small jolt, as if someone had burned me with a tiny lick of flame. I snatched my hand back hurriedly.

'How long will the journey take?' I asked. A small frown had appeared on his face and he was looking down at his hand. Had he felt it too?

'Six days or so, maybe less if the rowers put their backs into it and the wind is with us,' he said, turning abruptly and leaving the captain to take us to our places. I didn't tell him that my goddess would almost certainly make sure that the weather cooperated. She had promised me fair winds, after all.

The decurion's 'sleeping place' was a cloth shelter tied to rings on the ship's sides and deck, open to the breeze and with nothing in it except a folding military stool and a tied-up bedroll. After these had been removed, there was hardly room for all of us to squeeze in. We sat on our bundles with our backs pressed against the heavy linen, as squashed as a shoal of sardines in a net.

The best that could be said was that it was not much

worse than the felucca we'd come downriver on from Philäe. At least it didn't smell anything like the cabin on the merchant ship and the deck was very clean. Perhaps there was something to be said for military neatness. Luckily, we'd bought more bedrolls in Leptis, learning from our previous experience, and also some food, hopefully enough to last us. When we reached Ostia, I knew that Rome was at most half a day's journey by road from the port, but once inside the gates of the city, we would be on our own. It was time I made a plan to get to my father.

As soon as the captain had left us, I folded back my veil. I didn't think the decurion or any of the crew could see me in here. I was sweating and a fly buzzed above me, battering itself hopelessly against the heavy material. It was stuffy with so many bodies inside the shelter, but that would soon change when we got going. Iras leaned against Charm, with Warrior Sah beside her. I was on the other side of the shelter, with Corporal Geta beside me. I looked around. The commander was behind us but he was busy, pointing up at the sails and talking to the steersman. My Latin was rusty – I'd never spoken it other than in lessons – but I could just about make out that he was giving orders to make a course westwards for Carthage.

I leaned forward, beckoning everyone to do likewise. There would be little privacy here to discuss things, so we would have to be discreet.

'I don't know if my father will recognise me,' I said in a

low voice. 'It's been nearly five years since he left and I've changed a lot since then. It shouldn't be difficult to discover where he is living, though. We can easily bribe someone to find out. But actually getting in to see him will be hard, once we do find him. The guards may think I'm lying about who I am, and I can't rely on Isis to manifest a sign like she did when I arrived in Alexandria. She may not have as much power in Rome. I'll probably be on my own.'

'What about sending him a letter asking for an audience?' Charm asked.

I shook my head. 'No. I want to take him by surprise. I don't want him to have too much time to think about why it's not a good idea to see me. I know the Pharaoh. He doesn't like to feel guilty – and he will. He'll know that my mother is dead. And he will also have heard that I am too. If news of my return didn't get through before the last ships sailed, he will almost certainly think I'm an impostor.'

Just then, the deck beneath us creaked and rocked, and a drum began to beat. There was a scraping noise as the oars pushed us off the dock, and the sound of shouted orders behind us. I could just see the decurion at the bow, gesturing furiously at someone in the harbour below to get out of our path.

We were on our way.

I was going to Rome to find the true Pharaoh at last.

13

Rome

Iras tensed as the ship lurched, putting a hand to her ear.

'Is it working?' said Charm, giving her an anxious look.

'I think so,' Iras said. 'I don't feel all green like I did before.' She bounced up and down a couple of times on the bundle. 'We'll soon see, Pretty Girl.'

An hour later, in the open sea, she was still fine, and we all breathed more easily. The thought of spending even a few days with the smell of vomit around us had not been something any of us had looked forward to – Iras least of all. But the physician's eastern remedy seemed to be worth the silver I had paid him. As the ship got properly under way, and the slap and splash of the waves hit the planks of the hull, we settled ourselves in for an uncomfortable ride.

Most of that first morning was passed in telling stories of the gods, or making plans for every contingency we could think of when we arrived in Rome. Iras amused us by teaching Sah more hand movements for fighting with a knife in close quarters, teasing him as he overbalanced and nearly stabbed his own leg when a wave hit us amidships. By midday it was stifling in the small space, and we could all smell each other's sweat.

'I have to get some air,' Charm groaned. 'And, well… other things.' She wriggled uncomfortably. I was fairly uncomfortable too, as it happened.

'We'll take it in turns,' I said. 'You go first, with Warrior Sah, and then I'll go with Iras and Corporal Geta.'

She nodded. 'All right,' she said, giving me an odd look as I put my veil down again. 'But don't you talk to that decurion while I'm gone – Marcus whatever his name is.'

'I won't,' I said.

I could see him, still at the bow, perhaps keeping watch for unexpected rocks or obstacles ahead. As Charm ducked out, followed by Warrior Sah, he seemed to sense the movement and turned round. He wove his way towards us, round ropes and sailors, agile as a drunken monkey, and I hurriedly fixed my veil back in place.

'Did you need something, soldier?' he asked. He'd clearly noticed the covered shields and spears that we'd brought on board.

'The necessary for the lady,' said Sah bluntly. 'If you wouldn't mind, sir.' I could see the back of Charm's neck flush darker with embarrassment.

'Ah, yes,' he said. 'The comfort of the ladies. Of course.

That way. Down the ladder.' He pointed Charm and Sah towards a narrow hole in the deck.

Charm looked back at me, frowning a warning, but I gestured to her to go on, and soon the top of her head had disappeared down into the lower part of the ship.

'Perhaps a small turn on the deck, Priestess Charmion,' the decurion said to me, offering his hand. 'You could tell me of your goddess.'

I *was* desperate for some air.

'Very well,' I said, deliberately ignoring his offer of support. 'I'm sure my guards would appreciate the exercise.'

I saw the twitch at the corner of his mouth. He wasn't fooled.

I started immediately to talk of Isis, her beauty, her mercy, her power – especially her power. I emphasised that a lot.

'You have such a beautiful voice,' he said, when I drew breath. 'Intoxicating. Enchanting. I wish I could see your face.'

'I told you,' I said. 'My face is my own business, and that of my goddess.'

For the first time, I wished that Isis had not given me her voice of gold and storm.

'Aren't you hot?' he asked, honest curiosity on his face.

'Yes,' I admitted. 'But it doesn't matter. I've been hotter.'

'What is your purpose in going to Rome?' His voice whipped out, fast as the slash of a sword.

My heart began to beat faster. Should I tell him? Maybe he knew my father. Maybe he could help…but no. I couldn't risk it. Not yet, anyway.

'I must go to the shrine of Isis and Serapis,' I said. 'My goddess has summoned me to serve there.'

'That would be the one near the Capitol, I suppose. Are you sure it still exists?' he asked.

I stopped, making Iras nearly run into my heels. It was not at all what I'd expected him to say.

'What do you mean?'

'There has been some talk in Rome,' he said. 'There is an Egyptian there, one of your rulers. He has been causing trouble for years, stirring things up, interfering in our politics, bribing people – even murdering a whole embassy from his own land, or so I heard. Soon after he arrived, the gods struck great Jupiter's statue with a thunderbolt, and then the oracle of the sibyl was consulted about him.'

My heart felt as if it had been struck with a thunderbolt. He was talking about my father!

'Tell me more,' I said, keeping my voice smooth with a considerable effort. 'What did the oracle say?'

'I don't remember exactly – I was in Athens at the time, studying – but something along the lines of, "Welcome the Egyptian king with open arms, but do not give him an army or it will be the worse for Rome." Since then, the people have turned against all things Egyptian. There has been rioting. It is possible that your shrine has been destroyed or damaged.' He looked down at me, a warning in his eyes. 'You may not find that your Isis is all that popular in Rome. Nor your king, come to that.'

'Do you know what this Pharaoh's name is?' I asked. 'Maybe I should visit him first. Find out what the situation is, perhaps, and pay my respects.' I held my breath.

'I do know,' he said. 'His name is King Ptolemy. I carry letters to the consul concerning him from my commander, General Gabinius. If you wish to see him, I can take you there.'

If it hadn't been quite improper, I might have hugged him. Instead I bowed.

'That is kind, Marcus Antonius,' I said, as if it was a thing of no importance. 'I will give it my consideration, but of course I must pray to my goddess on this matter first.'

What I really needed was time to think. My father had been bribing people? Playing politics? Murdering ambassadors? How had I heard nothing of this? And what was in those letters the decurion carried to the consul?

He bowed in his turn. We were nearly back at the tent.

'Of course,' he said. 'Pray as you will. You will not be disturbed. I will see you when we stop for the night,' he said, turning to go back to his post at the bow.

Charm came up the ladder as he passed. Her eyes went between me and the decurion's departing back. She tutted disapprovingly.

'I thought I told you not to talk to that man.'

'I needed air,' I said. 'And I found out something very interesting, so it was worth it.' Quickly, I told her and Sah about my father.

'Well, I suppose that's useful,' she said. 'But don't talk to him again. There's something about him—'

I broke into her scolding.

'What's it like down there?' I asked.

'Ugh,' she said, with a little shiver. 'You have to sit on two planks with a hole in between, and your…' – she gestured behind her meaningfully – 'is right out over the sea. I got splashed.'

She was right. I took the opportunity to relieve my own needs, and it was not a pleasant experience. Walking through the breathless catcalls of the upper tier rowers on their greased cushions, straining at the oars, was not pleasant either, even with Iras and Corporal Geta close by me. I vowed to hold on until I was bursting in future.

My mind was buzzing, of course. I would have to talk to the decurion more, get all the information out of him I could. Charm must see that, however much she disapproved of our spending even a single moment together, I told myself.

But when I broached the subject, she disagreed vehemently. Iras and Corporal Geta backed her up.

'I know his type, Chosen,' said the corporal. 'Sees a mystery and can't rest till he's solved it, even if he breaks it in the process.'

'Stay away from him, please, Cleo,' Charm begged me. 'He's the one. He's the silver voice on the waves, I just know it. If you don't talk to him, he can't make you do something you shouldn't.'

'He sounds more like a seagull than a silver voice to me, but he does make me want to punch him, Cleo Blue-Eyes,' said Iras. 'Something about that smug, good-looking face of his. He's just too cocksure and arrogant.'

I knew they were right. But I couldn't help following the decurion with my eyes every time he came near us, wondering what else he knew about my father, wondering who General Gabinius was and what the letters to the consul were about, wondering if I should tell him that I was Ptolemy's daughter. Most of all I wondered guiltily about the tiny spark of fascination he had lit within me.

After that, Marcus Antonius tried every day to get me to walk with him again along the deck to the prow, but I heeded Charm and the others and resisted firmly, getting Charm to tell him that my goddess required long hours of prayer and seclusion. I would smother that spark so that it died for lack of air, I decided.

The voyage took on its own rhythm. Each night before dusk, we would head for a beach or a small port and anchor for the night, taking on water and buying supplies where possible. The rowers slept, ate, rowed, slept, ate, rowed, and we learned to take sleep where we could in our small allotted space, and hoard our supplies until we were really hungry. I did pray to Isis a lot, reminding her that she'd guaranteed me fair winds, asking for her protection for my friends, telling her my fears. She didn't reply, but I felt her presence nearby every time the wind filled the sails.

Before I slept, whether day or night, I would always close my eyes and try to reach Khai. I only managed it once, for a brief moment.

I rose up from the beach my friends and I were huddled together on, the silver cord of light anchoring my spirit to my sleeping body. Then I was rushing over the waves, back the way we had come. Everything blurred, until finally I dipped down over the Pharos, and dived through walls and roofs and deep underground. Khai was huddled by a cistern. If I could have tensed in this form, I would have. He was in the slave tunnels under the palace. He looked tired and wary, and there was a dirty bandage round his upper left arm.

Khai, I said into his mind. He jumped as he had before.

'Cleo,' he whispered, the sound only a thread. 'Where are you?'

On a beach, near Carthage, I think. What's happening? Are you all right?

'Fine,' he muttered. 'Not a good time to be distracted.'

What's going on?

'Something strange in the palace – stranger, I mean. Archelaus is…' He shook his head. 'Too hard to explain.'

Who's Archelaus?

'Berenice's consort. He's…they say he speaks with the voice of the demon god. I'm trying to get close enough to find out. I'm sorry, Cleo, but you have to go. I can't risk being heard by anyone. I left Shadya and Alim on guard back there, but it's still dangerous.'

Be careful.

He nodded, then darted forward, into an alcove I thought I recognised. There were steps leading upwards. I followed him. I hadn't been here since I was six years old. I slid my formless body through the tiny spyhole opening, and into the throne room, rising up to hover over the people gathered there.

Torches were blazing, but the shadows they threw were unnaturally large, giving the scene the flickering feel of a nightmare. The bejewelled and richly clad courtiers were abased before the throne. Berenice sat on the left, and beside her was her consort. Darkness hung around him like smoke, and his skin had an unnatural green pallor to it, as if he was newly dead and didn't know it yet.

'Who wishes to have the blessings of eternal power and riches? Who is courageous enough to offer themselves to walk the paths of the dead with Blessed Am-Heh?' he asked, a harsh, heavy rasp overlaying his Pontic accent. I had heard that rasp before, coming out of Berenice's mouth. It tore my frail ethereal body to shreds, sending it fleeing down the silver cord, past Khai, his face shocked, mouth open.

Run! I shrieked into Khai's head. *Run! It's him. It's Am-Heh!* As I landed back in my mortal body, I prayed desperately to Isis that he'd heard me.

I sat bolt upright, shaking in every part of me, Khai's shocked face imprinted on my brain, the voice of my sister's foul demon-husband in my head. I needed to move, to run. Before I knew what I was doing, I was up and fleeing into the dunes. I tripped and would have fallen, except that a pair of strong hands caught me. I clung on to them, half sobbing, and found myself clasped against a chest that smelt of oiled leather and metal mixed with salt. Underneath was that faint tang of cedarwood and lemon.

'Priestess!' he said, sounding surprised. My veil was tangled in my hair, put back for sleeping. Marcus Antonius gazed down at my face in the half-light of a waning moon. 'Beautiful as Diana herself,' he said. And then he bent forward, swooping on my lips like a bird of prey, capturing, ready to conquer, and kissed me.

For one brief moment I kissed him back, Khai's image still floating before my closed eyes. I was with him…he was here…but no! These lips felt hard, assured, knowing, totally different from the chapped roughness of my beloved's. The spark inside me roared to flame, and I came back to myself in an instant, smothering it instantly with shock and guilt.

'No!' I choked out, battering at him. It was a small, weak thread of sound on the night air. 'No! Let me go. I don't want you…I…' My voice tailed off, breathless, as he stepped back from me as swiftly as if the flame between us was real – as if I'd burned him.

I thought I heard a god's laugh, and the click of a shuttle.

'I said I would have one kiss from you,' he said. 'That debt is now paid a thousandfold.' He swallowed unsteadily, all his lazy assurance gone. 'I...I think you have bewitched me, priestess. I am not myself. I would kneel at your goddess's feet and worship her for just one more taste of you. I would sink a hundred ships, send ten thousand men to their deaths...'

The words burst out of him as if he couldn't help himself, then he stopped, shaking his head as if to deny them, and offered me his hand again, unsmiling. This time I took it. It trembled in mine for a moment, then closed around my fingers in a firm grasp.

I was still unsteady on my feet and also in my mind. My breath was coming in small, shocked gasps. I couldn't seem to pull myself together.

Khai! Khai! I'm sorry. I didn't mean to...I didn't want to...it just...

Marcus Antonius escorted me back to my bedroll without saying another word, turning away with a heavy sigh to go back to his own. I lay down, shaking and panting as if I'd run a race with a cheetah.

'Oh, Cleo!' Charm's voice caught on a sob beside me. I had woken her. 'Oh, Cleo! What have you done? What have you *done*?'

As she asked the question, I remembered that immortal laugh, that click. Had it really been the sound of Shai's loom as he shuttled my fate in a new and grimmer direction? Charm's broken sobs seemed to indicate that she thought it was. Iras and I held her in our arms till dawn, trying to persuade her that it didn't matter, that what was done was done.

'Such a little thing can't possibly make a difference, Pretty Girl,' Iras said in her usual forthright manner. 'I don't believe a word of it. You're wrong.'

But Charm just turned away from her and sobbed harder. I wasn't totally convinced myself. Surely one unwanted kiss wasn't enough to send us to the death Charm had seen?

We boarded the ship again as Ra's chariot rode over the horizon, red-eyed, tight lipped and unspeaking.

That was the day the wind dropped, and all my prayers to Isis to revive it were in vain. The rowers cursed as the sail lay heavy and limp in the unnaturally still air. The drum that set the stroke sounded like doom.

'It's not your fault, Charm,' I said, over and over, till we were all weary of the words. 'You couldn't have stopped him. You couldn't.' But she still wouldn't hear me. She sat in a huddle on her bundled bedroll, sniffing quietly, fending off both Iras's embrace and her futile attempts to make Charm laugh again.

At least it was a distraction from my burden of guilt

about Khai. Had he escaped? And what had happened in the palace? Had that foul demon really taken over Archelaus's body? And what had he meant by 'walking the paths of death with Blessed Am-Heh'? I went over and over what I'd seen in my mind's eye and wished I could have some privacy to discuss it with Charm and Iras – well, that and whether what had happened with Marcus Antonius last night had really sealed my fate. But there was no privacy to be had, so I had to sit and watch the land slide by in slow, painful fragments of time, till the wind picked up again two days later.

The decurion kept his distance for the rest of the journey and I was glad of it, though I caught his eyes on me now and then, the blaze of them like a torch against my skin, continually fanning that spark I was feeling inside. I couldn't help thinking of his words, though I tried not to. How could he have said such things? He didn't know me. Had he just been flirting? Did he say the same to every woman he kissed? I vowed never to find out.

We slid into Ostia on the cool breeze of very early morning, past the salt beds with their conical mounds of grey sludge, and into the bustling harbour. The noise was indescribable: a babble of Latin, Greek and other languages, the cries of fish sellers bidding for catches, the shouts of merchants urging their porters and slaves to load or unload faster, faster.

Marcus Antonius was calling out orders even before we docked, in the part of the harbour reserved for ships of the Roman navy. We stood ready to disembark, bags and bundles at our feet. The ship rocked to a halt, bumping the thick rope fenders with a jolt. The gangway was slid down and then the decurion was beckoning us forward.

'I have messages to deliver, as you know, priestess,' he said, now formal and remote. 'But I will guide you and your people to the house of Ptolemy if you still want to go there. He lives in the villa next to the consul Gnaeus Pompeius Magnus, near to the Temple of Tellus in the valley of the Subura. It is not far from there to your own shrine – if it still stands.' He raised an enquiring eyebrow at me, while managing to look straight over my head.

I nodded. 'We do wish to go there,' I said. I didn't look at him either.

A few hours later, dusty, hot and thirsty, we trundled into Rome, following the long, straight road up to a gate in the high wall of grey-brown stone. I sat with Charm in the back of an oxcart with the baggage, while the men and Iras marched beside us. There was a constant stream of people going in the direction of the city, laden with fruits and vegetables from the countryside, flapping chickens, squawking geese and herds of cattle, sheep and goats. Everything looked so different from Egypt. Everywhere there were trees with floating tops like deep green clouds, taller than any I'd ever seen. The earth was dark reddish-brown and rich-looking, with drifts of bright spring flowers everywhere, and the Tiber flowed green and placid down to the sea. When we finally came to the gate, before midday, we were stopped by leather-armoured legionaries with plumed helmets, spears and short swords by their sides. One stepped forward.

'Name and business,' he barked.

Marcus Antonius brought his forearm to his chest in a salute. 'Hail to the heroes of the Fourth Legion,' he said. 'I am Marcus Antonius, decurion, bringing messages from my general, Aulus Gabinius, to the consul Gnaeus Pompeius Magnus.' He gestured behind him. 'These people are with me.'

The legionary saluted in turn.

'Pass, friend,' he said, gesturing us through. 'Wouldn't want to delay a message to old Magnus, eh? I served with him in Africa. Impatient old beggar.' He winked as we passed under the high arch, and then we were in Rome.

My heart started to beat faster than the rowers' drum. Charm and I had done our best on the ship to make me look presentable, but I was not at my cleanest after the dusty journey. The houses, tall and crammed together like crumbled clay blocks, seemed to press in on me, constricting my breathing. I fumbled for Charm's hand.

'What if he won't see me?' I whispered, as we wound our way past a large horse-racing track, and then up and up the hilly streets. But before she could answer, we were stopping in front of a house that overlooked a bustling cluster of temples and other buildings, with wide streets paved with dark reddish stone. It had an arched gate, palms in large terracotta pots and a pleasant pillared atrium beyond. Patrolling inside the entrance were two men in a uniform I recognised – the short, white kilts of my father's palace guards.

Marcus Antonius came to stand in front of where I sat, enthroned on bundles.

'This is the place,' he said. 'Your King Ptolemy lives here.'

I looked for Corporal Geta and nodded my head at him. He and Sah had got their sea-tarnished shields and spears out of the baggage, polishing off the worst of the black with pee and vinegar. They were now fully armed, and looking as much as possible like warriors again.

'Pay the decurion what we owe,' I said, reducing him to the level of a flunkey. It was unfair, but all I wanted now was to break the strange, unsettling connection between us; to be done with him and never see him again. 'Two gold talents and not an obol more. He has fulfilled his side of the bargain.'

But Marcus Antonius shook his head. 'No,' he said, placing his hands on the cart, as if he would grasp my ankles and hold me there. 'I will take no more from you, priestess. Only...' His sun-dark skin flushed, and he looked at me directly, so that I too blushed under my veil. 'It is not coin that I want from you, Priestess

Charmion,' he said in a lowered voice. 'You know that.'

I blushed even harder than him, hot anger rising. How dare he say that in front of everyone? How dare he? But it was too late to do anything about it, even though I wanted to, because now the guards had seen our party, and were coming out, spears pointed towards us.

'Halt,' said one. 'You can't come in here. No supplicants allowed in without an appointment. There's nobody on the list for today.'

Fury took me then, hot anger turning to a cold, focused rage that straightened my limbs and firmed my shoulders. I was no supplicant.

My princess mask fell into place without my even thinking about it. I put out an imperious hand for Corporal Geta to hand me down from the cart, as if I was descending from a royal litter dressed in the finest silk and jewels, instead of a white robe stained with sea-salt and the dust of the road.

I should have waited for Charm to attend me. Instead I stalked past Geta, past the decurion, and over to stand before my father's hard-eyed guard, knocking aside his spear.

I put back my veil with a decisive flip.

'I am Cleopatra, priestess of Isis and princess of the royal house of Egypt,' I said. 'I am here to see Ptolemy XII Theos Philopater Philadelphus Neos Dionysos. My father. You will let me in or I will have Blessed Isis see to it that you pay for it with your skin.'

I would not be denied.

Not when I'd been through so much, come so far to find the man who had left me behind all those years ago.

14

Ptolemy Auletes

My voice carried the full-forged iron weight of a royal command, backed up by my goddess's gift, and the man gaped at me, hard eyes suddenly wide and awed.

I heard laughter behind me, and the sound of slow clapping.

That Isis-cursed decurion was *laughing* at me.

'Bravo, priestess. Or is it "princess" I should call you now? I knew you weren't a Charmion the minute the name left your lying lips.'

I spun round to see Marcus Antonius walk past the side of the cart and come to stand in front of me. He tipped up my chin with his forefinger, and stared down at me hungrily, as if he would devour me in small, delicious bites. I shook him off and slapped him, hard, just before Corporal Geta moved to stand between us, silver-tipped spear and silver-decorated shield angled threateningly

'Don't touch me again, decurion,' I said, biting off each word as if it were thread. 'Or I will have my men take your fingers off, one by one. Slowly.'

'Is that who you really are?' he asked, quite unafraid, a smile tugging at his lips as he fingered the red handprint that had appeared on his left cheek. 'The daughter of King Ptolemy?'

'Yes,' I said, and I filled that one word with ice and scorn as I turned my back, ignoring him, and faced the still-gaping guard again.

'What are you waiting for, idiot?' I snapped. 'Take me to my father immediately, and have my bags brought.'

If I was to be Pharaoh, it was time these people started to obey me.

The man gave one fearful glance at his silent colleague, who was also staring at me, then bowed.

'At once, great princess. At once.' But then he hesitated again, looking at my warriors. 'Excuse me, Your Highness… but none may bear arms in the presence of the Pharaoh except his own loyal guard…your men…' He stopped, casting down his eyes.

I glared at him. 'I am the marked and chosen of Isis,' I snapped. 'These are warriors of the goddess. Are you suggesting that they are not loyal to the throne?' I tried to summon up the power of Isis in my fingertips, to burn the two of them as I had Shoshan and her people, but it would not come. Very well, then. I would manage on my own.

The guard had recovered himself somewhat, and remembered his duty.

'Rules are rules, Your Highness,' he said. 'You may come in, but the warriors must stay behind unless they leave their arms at the gate.'

Both my warriors carried hidden daggers now, so I shrugged. There were some battles it was not worth fighting.

'Very well, then. But those weapons belong to Isis. Touch them at your peril.'

With no more than a small frown, Sah and Geta propped their spears and shields against the sunny wall and fell in behind me. Charm and Iras were hovering under the arch of the gateway.

'I assume you have no objection to my maidens attending me,' I said to the guard, beckoning them in.

He lowered his eyes respectfully. 'None at all, Your Highness,' he said, as they came to join me.

I could feel the decurion's eyes on my back as I walked into my father's house. They burned into me like those of Ra himself, but he stayed silent. It was a small mercy and I was thankful for it. For all my outward confidence, inside I was a small child, desperately craving a father's love and fearing it would be withheld.

Our little procession entered a wide corridor, painted with frescoes of the Roman gods seated between arches. I sent up a quick prayer to the queen of heaven, Hera –

who was called Juno here, I remembered. Just as I was about to cross the courtyard garden, a girl came running out of the door in front of me, followed by two young boys. She skidded to a halt, her mouth open.

'Who's this, Aka?' she asked the guard rudely. Then her eyes widened as she got a good look at me, and her dark brows snapped down in a ferocious frown. 'You!' She spat at my feet.

'Yes, Arsinöe,' I said, keeping my voice calm. 'Me.' My little sister had grown, but she still looked like a sly, skinny weasel. The boys clustered around us, their eyes big.

'Who is it, Sinny?' asked the bigger of them – my brother Lem, I thought.

'Who do you think?' she snapped. 'It's our so-called sister, Cleopatra. The Pharaoh's little bastard.' Her mouth curled into a grimace of disdain. 'I should have known you weren't dead. I suppose you're here to see Father. Well, you can't. He's busy. Go away.'

I sighed inwardly. Her manners hadn't improved by much since I'd last seen her.

'You will show respect to the chosen of Isis, sister,' I said softly. 'Or you will regret it, believe me. Now take me to the Pharaoh.'

'Chosen of Isis?' She spat again. 'You always did give yourself airs and graces.'

I reached out a hand and gripped the front of her robe, dragging her nearer. The guard twitched once towards his weapon, but then he saw the look on my face and took his fingers away from his sword hurriedly.

'Do *not* dare to question my goddess,' I roared at her. Isis's gift made my voice a thing of crashing thunder.

Arsinöe flinched back, throwing up an arm to protect herself. Her mouth was hanging open in fear, but her eyes were pure poison.

I let go of her, wiping my fingers on my robe. She was a snake – a young one, but she would grow. I would have to watch my back with her around.

A small hand tugged at my robe. It was Tol, the younger of my two brothers.

'I'll take you to Father. He missed you. He was sad when you died. He cried.' Tol's face looked puzzled. 'How are you alive again? Did you see the underworld? Did you meet Anubis?'

'It's a long story,' I said, taking his hand and squeezing it. He'd been so young when he left, just a baby. I was surprised he knew anything about me. My mind was suddenly all tangled up in his words. My father had cried when he thought I was dead? A tiny seed of hope began to grow inside me. Maybe he would listen to me, after all. Maybe he did love me.

'Lead on,' I said. 'I'll tell you the whole story later.'

The two of us brushed past Arsinöe and my other brother, Lem. Both of them were glaring at Tol as if he was a beggar who had just stolen a tasty crust from their feast.

He stuck a small pink tongue out at them.

'I hate them,' he confided. 'They're mean to me.'

Welcome to the joyous world of the Ptolemy siblings, I thought.

The villa was in no way as luxurious as the palace my father had been used to ruling from. It was more of a large house. Servants bustled about, giving us curious looks as we passed.

'He's in here,' Tol announced, pushing open a carved door through which the familiar strains of a flute seeped out into the hallway.

I turned to face Charm and the others. Charm's face was tense. She knew how much this meant to me. Iras's eyes were darting about like swallows, looking for danger. The warriors were impassive as always – but I saw that they were blocking the kilted guard with their bodies.

'Wait here, please,' I said, willing my voice not to break. 'I need to see the Pharaoh alone first. Don't let anyone in.'

My heart fluttered in my chest like a caged linnet. My breath came in small, nervous gasps. What if he wasn't the man I remembered? What if he threw us all out into the street? Or into some Roman dungeon? What if I failed to bring him home, failed the Ennead?

No, I told myself fiercely, touching the small packet of Khai's hair for reassurance and luck. *No. You* will *do this. You must. He is the Pharaoh, but he is also your father. He will listen to you. You must make him.*

I straightened my spine, and then, holding my head high like the princess I was meant to be, I followed my brother into a room full of light and shade.

My father looked smaller than I remembered as he stood at the open window, bathed in sunlight, playing a tune that conjured up my childhood. The instrument fell from his lips as we entered.

'Ptolemaios!' he said, laying the flute aside on a table as the boy ran to him. 'And who have you brought to see me today?' It was so lovingly informal that I almost gasped. Gone was the entourage of courtiers, the lickspittles and lackeys that surrounded a Pharaoh. Although he was finely dressed, my father almost looked like an ordinary man – almost, but not quite.

'It's Cleopatra,' Tol said. 'She's not dead, Father. Now you don't need to cry any more.'

My father's face changed in an instant, becoming hard and suspicious, then it was as if a shutter rolled down over his face. He stared at me in silence, his impassive court mask in place. I recognised it. It was the one I wore myself.

'Come here, girl,' he said, in quite a different tone. 'If you are lying, I will throw you down from the Tarpeian Rock with my own hands.' It was his Pharaoh's voice. I had no idea what the Tarpeian Rock was, but I obeyed, falling to my knees at his feet and bowing my head.

My chin was tipped up by a finger for the second time that day. I stared into my father's eyes, Ptolemy eyes, blue-green and full of power. They searched my face minutely.

I forgot to breathe. At that moment, I was not the chosen of Isis. I was just a girl who'd been left behind, abandoned by the parent I loved. I blinked frantically, trying to hold back the tears, but it was no good. One spilled over and ran down my cheek.

'Well, well,' said my father, at the end of a long, unblinking moment. He took his finger from under my chin and tapped the proud Ptolemy nose which mirrored his own. 'If it isn't my little pusscat princess after all. You have your dear mother's mouth.' And then I was raised up, held tight in his arms, and we were both sobbing. My father always had been an emotional man.

When we had recovered ourselves a little, the guard was summoned, and then sent to find servants to take Charm and the rest to our new quarters, and to bring refreshments. Tol was given a swift pat on the head and dismissed with the promise of a treat before bedtime. My father sat down on a padded bench in the cool shade of an alcove.

'Come, daughter,' he said, offering me a dish of fat olives, glistening with oil and herbs. 'Tell me your news. I know you will not have made this journey without need. How are my people? How is my beloved Alexandria faring under its thieving new rulers?'

Abruptly my stomach sank like a stone in deep water, and the sourness of the olive curdled in my mouth. He didn't know about Tryphena. I closed my eyes and drew a deep breath.

'The news is not good, Father,' I started.

By the time I had finished, he was up again and pacing the room like a caged lion, his hands clenched into fists.

'So,' he said. '*Ma'at* is broken, and your sister sits alone on her stolen throne with this Am-Heh-possessed Pontic princeling?' I nodded.

'And you really have been marked and chosen by Blessed Isis?' I nodded again, pulling the shoulder of my robe open to show him the throne glyph on my shoulder. It was glowing softly, and he reached out with one finger and touched it cautiously. A spark of blue drifted gently up his arm, and I saw him repress a small, superstitious shiver.

'You are highly favoured, daughter. The goddess has done our family great honour by choosing you.' He sighed. 'And you say she wants me back in Alexandria?'

'Yes, Father. She sent me to fetch you home. *Ma'at* will only be restored when you are on the Double Throne again.'

He looked at me, head tipped on one side in a gesture I remembered well. 'With you beside me, I suppose?'

Whatever else he was, my father was not stupid.

'Yes,' I said simply.

'And what of your sister?'

For one moment I thought he was talking about Arsinöe – and then I realised he meant Berenice.

'She deserves to die,' I said, a breath of winter chill frosting my voice. 'Let her be given to the mercy of foul Am-Heh, as she has given so many others to it.'

He chuckled.

'So fierce, my little pusscat,' he said. 'A true Ptolemy.'

I met his eyes.

'In this case, yes,' I said.

I had let one sister die by mistake. But there would be no mistake about the second one's death.

As soon as I told my father about the letters Marcus Antonius carried, he summoned his advisers. I disliked them on sight – and it was clearly mutual. Achillas looked down his soldier's nose at me and Theodotus ignored anything I said by talking over me. To them, I was simply a pawn on the chessboard of their ambitions. However, since I wanted to be included in whatever plans they were making, I simply smiled sweetly, bided my time and listened. If I was going to be Pharaoh, I would have to learn to play the game of politics, and this was a new land and a new set of rules that I was not yet familiar with. I found it strange to see my father not as Pharaoh but as supplicant to the powers in Rome.

It appeared that my father had been in communication with Aulus Gabinius for some time, and that the consul – Gnaeus Pompeius Magnus – was already backing his bid to retake the throne. My coming simply accelerated matters. The problem was the Roman people. They would not agree to give my father an army of legionaries because of that Ra-blasted sibyl's oracle. That – and of course the fact that armies cost a lot.

The two armies I had at my disposal did not seem to count with anybody.

'How do you know that this so-called army of the Ibis will even appear?' Achillas said with a superior sneer that let me know his opinion of women interfering in military matters. 'And an army of street rats? They'll be cut to pieces in the time it takes to slaughter a cow.' He let out a crack of incredulous laughter.

I looked at my father. Was he really going to allow this disrespect to our goddess?

'I think you underestimate my daughter, Achillas,' he said, frowning. 'She is a Ptolemy, and a priestess of Isis. The goddess is on our side in this matter. You need to remember that.' It was not the absolute rebuke I could have wished for, but the iron in his tone made it clear that Achillas had overstepped the mark.

He bowed to me grudgingly. 'I apologise, Your Highness. I am a simple man and not used to the gods interfering in mortal matters.'

I looked at him consideringly, as if he was a scorpion about to sting and I was deciding whether to crush him or not.

'I hope you are a quick learner, Achillas. If you don't

believe in the army of the Ibis, perhaps you should ask Corporal Geta and Warrior Sah what happened at Crocodilopolis. They are soldiers, after all.'

He nodded. 'I will indeed, Your Highness. A warrior of Isis would not lie about military matters.'

Which suggested, of course, that I might.

The arguments went back and forth till I wanted to scream with frustration.

Then it got worse. A messenger arrived from Gnaeus Pompeius, as unwelcome to me as a rat in a granary.

As Marcus Antonius walked into the room I saw that he had clearly been to the baths in the short time we had been apart. The dust of our journey was gone and he wore a clean tunic. I, in contrast, was still dressed in the less than pristine clothes in which he had seen me last.

He nodded briefly and I noticed the slight twitch at the corner of his mouth as he acknowledged me.

'Princess,' he said formally, before turning to my father with a rather more fulsome salutation.

'I bring greetings from the consul, Your Majesty,' he said. 'He begs the indulgence of an urgent private meeting, and then he invites you to a feast.' He looked at me. 'The Princess Cleopatra is of course welcome to join you. Shall we say at sunset?'

I wondered if that particular part of the invitation had been his idea. There was still a slight redness on his face where I had slapped him. I shivered slightly. He was a dangerous man and I wanted nothing more to do with him. Unless my father insisted, I thought I would plead extreme tiredness after our journey and give the consul's feast a miss.

Unfortunately for me, my father did insist.

'If you are going to sit beside me on the Double Throne, you must be seen,' he said, after everyone had left the room. 'I need this man, this Pompeius. As consul, he is a powerful voice in the Roman Senate and he pulls the strings of the man who will pay for my troops. Gaius Rabirius Postumus is his name, and he will be there tonight. You will charm him, my little pusscat. You will make him see the importance of restoring me to my throne. Now hurry. You must be bathed and changed within the hour.' It was an order.

I nodded.

'Yes, Father,' I said, as meekly as I could manage. I would do whatever I must to obey Isis's command.

A slave took me to my new quarters. Warrior Sah and Corporal Geta stood outside, their weapons restored to them.

'Have you eaten?' I asked.

'Yes, Chosen. We have eaten well.'

I dismissed the slave and lowered my voice.

'A man called Achillas may come to see you. Do not trust him – but tell him of Crocodilopolis and the army of the Ibis if he asks. He must believe it will come to the Pharaoh's aid.'

Corporal Geta bowed.

'As you wish, Chosen.' He opened the door and ushered me in, then shut it behind me. It was a good-sized room with, behind it, a sleeping chamber separated by an olivewood door with marble pillars either side. The furnishings were rich but much simpler than those I had had in Alexandria. The windows looked out onto an internal courtyard, which had a small rectangular pool in it, and some lemon trees, still heavy with fruit, providing shade.

Charm got up from a polished wooden couch and ran to me, arms outstretched.

'Oh, Cleo. You look worn out. What happened with the Pharaoh?'

'Here, sit down, Cleo Blue-Eyes,' Iras said, patting the seat beside her. 'Have a honeycake – they're good.' She smacked her lips and patted her stomach at the same time, making me smile.

'I'll tell you everything,' I said. 'But first I need a dress to charm a moneylender with, and a quick bath.'

I had no idea what to wear for a Roman feast. Charm had already unpacked and sent my sea-stained clothes away to be laundered, so I summoned a slave and asked for the housekeeper in my rusty Latin. She turned out to be a plump, comfortable-looking woman who spoke reasonable Greek.

'Oh, dear,' she said, hands fluttering. 'A dress for the consul's feast? Within the hour? Well, Your Highness,

I'll do my best.' She bustled out, shouting orders.

Before the door could be shut behind her, Arsinöe slipped into the room. News clearly travelled fast in this place. I had only left my father a short while ago.

'Why is Father taking *you* to the consul's feast?' she asked in her sullen whine. 'He should be taking me. I'm the princess. You're only a bastard.' Before I could reply, Iras stepped forward.

'I expect it's because of your lack of manners, youngling,' she said calmly. 'You should apologise to your sister. Not only does the Pharaoh see her as a princess, but she is also a priestess and the chosen of Isis. You should have more respect for your elders.'

Without warning, Arsinöe launched herself forward, her screams a high, piercing whistle, arms and legs flailing, nails outstretched to tear.

'How dare you speak to me like that!' she shrieked. 'Daughter of a dunghill rat! I shall have you whipped till you bleed!'

Iras stepped neatly aside, catching Arsinöe's arm and flipping her so that she landed on her back on the painted tiles. All the breath went out of her with a whoosh, and she lay there, glaring and wheezing for breath, winded and finally speechless.

I stood over her, princess mask firmly in place, and looked down at her, offering a hand to help her up.

'There will be no whipping, and Iras is right. You should

have more respect. Now get up. When you have learnt to curb your tongue, maybe Father will take you with him. Until then, go back to your nursemaid.'

'Ganymedes is not a nursemaid – he's a proper tutor,' she choked out, scrambling to her feet and ignoring my hand completely. 'And I'll get you back for this, you'll see.'

'Isis bless you and send you wisdom,' I said as she flung herself out of the door, crashing into Corporal Geta.

'That is a very angry child,' said Charm. 'You should take care around her, Cleo. I wouldn't put it past her to put poison in your food.'

'She's my sister,' I said. 'What did you expect? All of them except Tol hate me for being the Pharaoh's bastard. And he's too young to understand.'

'If that viper attacks me again, I will sting her bottom for her,' Iras said. 'Pharaoh's daughter or not. If only I could give her to Petsuchos for an hour or so.'

Charm looked at her seriously.

'You should be careful too, Iras. She may be young, but she knows this place and we don't. Don't underestimate her. She's had the Pharaoh's exclusive attention for four years, and Cleo's taken it away from her in a few hours. It's no wonder she's acting like a hornet poked by a stick.'

'I have swatted angry hornets before, Pretty Girl,' Iras said. 'I can take care of myself. Now, where's that bathhouse? I smell worse than a fart in a lead box.'

We had the bathhouse to ourselves – posting a warrior

at each door to prevent intrusions. We quickly stripped off our grubby robes with moans of relief.

'So,' Charm said. 'Why do you have to charm a moneylender?'

I sighed, and began to fill them in.

'Do you think this Achillas person would enjoy a lesson in how long it might take to skin a man with a blunt knife?' Iras asked when I had finished. 'Because I'm sure I could oblige.'

'And I could hold him down for you,' said Charm.

I looked at her disbelievingly. 'When did you get so bloodthirsty?' I asked. 'You'll be joining the warriors next.'

Charm giggled, her eyes roving over Iras's curves.

'It's being around this one,' she said. 'She's a bad influence.'

Clean robes were waiting for us in the drying room. I had never seen Iras in a dress before. She made a face as she tucked the simple tunic around her. It did not suit her as well as her soldier's attire.

'Not many places to hide a knife under here,' she said.

'I find tucking one down the back of the breastband works for me,' I replied.

Her eyes went round. 'Charm isn't the only one full of surprises today,' she muttered.

While Charm helped me dry and dress my hair, working at speed, Iras moved restlessly round the room, picking up things and then putting them down again.

'Will you stop it?' Charm said crossly. 'You're worse than a hopping sandfly.'

Iras sighed.

'I'm sorry,' she said. 'I need to stretch my legs. I'll go and take a look around. See the lie of the land.'

'Don't get into trouble,' I said.

Her grin burst out, whiter and wider than a new moon. 'When do I ever get into trouble, Cleo Blue-Eyes?' she asked, somersaulting out of the door.

'That girl,' Charm said. 'I don't know why I put up with her.'

'Because you love her?' I suggested.

'Oh, well – there's that, of course,' she said.

A surprisingly short while later I was dressed in a Roman-style stola of yellow silk, with a matching palla to go round my shoulders. I pinned my golden Knot of Isis at my breast, and Charm threaded a blue ribbon through my hair. Since leaving my mother's necklet and armband at great Alexander's tomb before I left Alexandria, I had no jewellery – it would have to do.

Attended by Corporal Geta, my stomach in knots again, I walked to find my father. What if I was sitting next to Marcus Antonius? Would it be horribly rude to ignore him? How important was he to my father's plans? And what was I to say to the money man, Rabirius? On the way, I passed a tall, thin man I thought I recognised. He turned his shoulder to me with a curl of his lip and stalked away.

'Oh, really!' I muttered. 'Does everyone in this house hate me?'

The guard at my father's door let me into his antechamber. It was a pleasant room, painted in ochre, with pictures of musicians cavorting over the walls. I sat down to wait and soon my father came striding in, dressed in a Roman tunic with a golden key pattern at its edge. He held a box in his hands.

'Ah,' he said. 'My little pusscat.' He looked me up and down. 'So like your dear mother. But it needs a little something extra.' He held out the box and I took it. 'Open it, open it,' he urged me. So I did.

Inside lay a broad necklet and bracelets of gold and lapis, with matching pins for my hair. The necklet was in the shape of a flying black kite, sacred bird of my goddess, and the bracelets were shaped like royal snakes with lapis eyes. They were beautiful.

'Thank you, Father,' I said, blinking back tears so as not to smear my kohl. 'Will you help me put them on?'

His fingers were gentle as they fastened the catch at the back of my neck. The weight of it was comforting, and I remembered the kite which had accompanied me into Isis's realm at my first testing. The Pharaoh offered me his hand.

'Time to charm the Romans out of an army,' he said. 'Are you ready?'

'I am,' I said, hoping it was true.

15

Feast and Fear

Although Ra's chariot had not yet driven into the west, great torches flamed outside the next-door villa, occasionally sputtering and spitting out gouts of oily black smoke. It was a strange building, with what looked like the rams from ships built into its walls, sticking out like enormous bulls' horns. My father told me that they belonged to the Cilician pirates Pompeius had defeated some years before – spoils of war for all to see and marvel at. Achillas and Theodotus had joined us, along with four kilted guards and a couple of lesser advisors I didn't know. It was a small retinue for a Pharaoh. Things were clearly arranged differently in Rome. I looked for the tall, thin man who had sneered at me, but could not see him.

Naturally, Marcus Antonius was there to greet us once we were past the legionaries at the gate. At least I was properly dressed now. It was armour – of a sort – against his hungry, knowing eyes.

'This way, Your Majesty. The consul is waiting for you,' he said to my father with the normal Roman salute. I had noticed by now that bowing was not really the Roman way. My father did not seem to mind. Perhaps he had got used to it by now. We followed him into a pillared chamber, painted with martial scenes, where the consul waited. Gnaeus Pompeius Magnus was a man of some years, built like a sturdy bull, with a pouchy, weathered face, grizzled locks and a nose that looked as if it had been broken one too many times.

'Good,' he said, his Greek accent thick as melted tallow. 'You're here. Greetings, Your Majesty.' Then he turned to me.

'And who is this charming young lady?' he asked, in what was clearly meant to be an avuncular way.

If I'd been a dog, my hackles would have bristled at his patronising tone.

'May I present my daughter, the Princess Cleopatra, priestess of Isis, Consul,' said my father, his tone now only slightly warmer than a chilled sherbet. 'She has brought me important news from Alexandria.'

'Ah, yes. I believe Marcus Antonius mentioned her.' He gestured, looking slightly uncomfortable. 'Perhaps she might be more comfortable in the women's quarters while we discuss business. Gaius Rabirius Postumus will be here shortly. Women don't really understand these things, do they? Finance and all that? Not to mention the soldier stuff.' He laughed, as if it was some joke that only men would understand.

I stiffened. Was I to be shuffled off and hidden away until wanted, like some chattel? I knew the Romans allowed their women no public power, but surely my father wouldn't permit this. We were of Egypt. Women were treated as equals with men there. If I was to be ruler beside him, I would be so with equal power, female or not.

My father drew himself up and made a short, sharp gesture of dismissal, Pharaoh again to his fingertips.

'The princess stays,' he said, in his most regal voice. 'She has a brain, and she has already raised one army for me, perhaps two – which is more than I can say for you, Pompeius, despite your promises.'

The consul frowned, giving me a considering look. Talk of raising armies was clearly something he understood – even though he thought I didn't. I wished fiercely for General Nail to be at my side. If nothing else, his respect for me would convince this stupid Roman that I was not some feeble girl who fell into a faint at the thought of war and blood.

'The will of the Roman people is hard to thwart, I would remind you, Your Majesty. I am doing my best. Armies are not so easy to come by, especially' – he gave my father an almost sly look – 'if you have a temporary shortage of denarii and nothing to pay them with.'

My father laughed. It was not a laugh of amusement.

'"A temporary shortage of denarii." Is that what you're calling it, Consul? I hear the enormous sweeteners I've paid you have all gone into that ridiculous building of yours. What do they call it? The Theatre of Pompeius? Not to mention the gardens and that big new house overlooking the Forum. You might almost be a king yourself, your ambitions are so large. No wonder I can't pay an army, with you and your pet senators being so greedy for my gold.'

'There are no kings in Rome, saving Your Majesty's presence. *Senatus populusque Romanum* is what we live by. The will of the Senate and the Roman people. I and my friends merely have many expenses which must be covered, as you very well know. The payment for any army must depend on our friend Rabirius's goodwill.' The consul had a smile on his face, but I could see the iron behind it.

As if Pompeius's words had conjured him up, another man entered the room, his tall frame stooped and hunch-shouldered. A waft of some spice preceded him – sandalwood I thought – as if his tunic had been kept in some rich chest. He was very pale, with sunken brown eyes and a balding head.

My heart plummeted into my sandals. This must be the moneylender himself. He didn't look like a man who would be easily charmed.

'You summoned me, Consul,' he said in Latin, and my

heart dropped again, to somewhere below the tiled floor. The Roman tongue was not a language I spoke particularly well. If this whole meeting was to be conducted in it, I might have difficulty in understanding, and even more in speaking. That would not improve my status in the consul's eyes, one little bit. It didn't matter, though. I would do what I had to. So I smiled beguilingly at Rabirius, and inclined my head to him graciously, following my father's orders. He nodded back, but then took absolutely no further notice, ignoring me completely. Clearly, he too felt that a woman had no place in the negotiations.

With little further ceremony, we sat down at the table, me at my father's right hand, which I could see did not please Achillas and Theodotus, who were left standing behind us.

The consul cleared his throat. 'I have today had letters from Aulus Gabinius in Tyre. Since the Roman people have spoken, and the legions are not officially available, he has gathered an army of mercenaries and is ready to move on Egypt to restore the Pharaoh as soon as the funds are in place.' He looked at Rabirius meaningfully.

'And what guarantee do I have that the...' The moneylender paused delicately. 'That the promises made to me by the Pharaoh will be kept? If His Majesty should be, let us say, hurt in any way...if there should be an unfortunate incident...' His voice tailed off suggestively.

'By Ra's holy seed,' my father swore, slapping his palm

on the table so that it shook. 'I am Pharaoh of Egypt, not some begging street scum. I keep my promises. You will be repaid as agreed, in grain and in gold, as soon as the keys to the treasury are in my hands again. And if you are asking what happens if I should meet Anubis in the afterlife... well, I have children.' He gestured towards me. 'This one will be on the throne beside me. If I die, she will make good on my debt, won't you, Cleopatra?'

I thought of the rotting fields and mould-covered wheat I'd told him about earlier and wondered if my father truly realised what he was saying. He'd never seen Egypt as it was now. If Isis did not keep her promises, if the harvest failed because the gods were displeased, there would be no grain to send, and no gold – not until *ma'at* was restored. I nodded in agreement though.

'My word on it as a Ptolemy,' I said in my slow Latin, looking directly into Rabirius's shrewd eyes. 'Blessed Isis forfend, but if my father should go to the afterlife, I will keep his promise and the debt to Rome will be paid in full.'

Egypt was a rich land. Once my father and I were ruling together (and I refused to consider any other possibility), the gods would forgive us and it would recover. The Roman would get his money in the end, I supposed, though I wondered what our people would have to say about it. It had been borrowing too much money from the Romans and not repaying it that had got my father exiled in the first place.

Rabirius let out a small snort, almost as if he couldn't help himself, and let the corner of his mouth twitch up. He was most certainly noticing me now.

'Very well, then. I must be mad, but you have an honest face and a voice to make a man lose any sense he might have had.' He looked over at my father. 'You must hurry to Alexandria, though, Your Majesty. The Roman people are becoming impatient with your presence. I think our good consul will not be able to guarantee your safety here for very much longer.'

Pompeius nodded slowly.

'It is true. There is increasingly bad feeling in the city, whipped up by the anti-Egyptian faction, and that idiot Marcus Tullius Cicero, with his orations against you. They claim we have given you shelter for long enough. The sooner we get you on a ship, the better, or there will be more riots.'

As the talk and bargaining over troop numbers, tactics and ships went back and forth, with little or no reference to me – apart from my father asking me to repeat my news about the army of the Ibis – I studied the men around me. What made them so sure of themselves? I had the power of a goddess behind me, and yet most of them considered me less than they were. Even my father considered me his subordinate – but perhaps that was the nature of a relationship between a parent and child. He had not yet had time to get used to the person I was now. I was young still, yes, but how many of them could say that they had crossed wits with a sphinx and won, let alone survived twice in a goddess's realm? I wondered if they would really believe it if I told them what had truly happened to me – or if they would dismiss it as a young woman's fantasy, a dream brought on by a fevered imagination.

Oh, Isis, I thought. *I wish you could hear me. I wish you were with me now.* Suddenly the kite necklace grew faintly warm at my throat, and a tiny breeze tickled my nose. It smelt of the desert, of home. Perhaps my goddess wasn't as far away as I thought she was. It was a small comfort in the midst of this strange new world of bickering old men.

At last, thank all the gods, the final deal was made. Rabirius would not only provide the gold to pay General Gabinius's mercenaries, but would also pay for the transport they would need to get to Egypt. Pompeius also agreed (very reluctantly) that the legions would be on standby, just in case. My father would take ship as soon as it could be managed, sail down the Great Green via Crete, and be in Tyre by the time the Shemu season started. After that, the Pharaoh and his new army would reembark immediately for Alexandria.

I kept silent about my own plans, which differed somewhat from my father's. He obviously assumed I would be going all the way to Tyre with him, but I had different ideas. I did not think he would be pleased if I told him in front of the Romans that I had every intention of finding a ship in Crete and going back to Egypt to join Khai, General Nail and the army of the Ibis. That was something he didn't need to know – not yet, anyway.

There was, of course, a fly in the wine cup. Marcus Antonius would be escorting us, carrying Pompeius's letters to his commander. I had managed to avoid looking at him till then, but as Pompeius announced that piece of news I couldn't help my eyes flying to him for a moment. He was, of course, staring straight at me. I flushed and looked away immediately, but it was too late. He had seen.

The feast seemed strangely intimate to me, after the overpopulated events I had attended in Alexandria. The room had a mosaic floor with dolphins and fish frolicking in the waves. The walls were painted with pictures of Neptune, Nereus and various heroic scenes, and in the alcoves stood statues and busts – mostly of Pompeius, it seemed. In the Roman manner, we lay about on couches to eat, set around a long table laden with oysters and other shellfish, stuffed songbirds, a peacock served whole with its tailfeathers, and a hare decorated with wings to resemble Pegasus. More and more food was brought, until the table was literally groaning under the weight. The plates were made of silver, decorated with rock crystal, and the wine cups were decorated with scenes of a nature that made me blush and avert my eyes. My couch was made of ivory and bronze, and most uncomfortable, digging into me in several places.

Gnaeus Pompeius's young wife, Julia, fluttered and flitted about, ordering the slaves to do this and that, although she didn't need to. She had a perfectly good overseer – a young man who quietly directed operations so that they ran smoothly in spite of his mistress. I felt sorry for her. She didn't know what to make of me at all – a highbred girl who had come in with the men. I could see from her pursed lips and sideways looks that she found me shocking – unmarried Roman girls did not act in such a bold manner. She would have placed me in an out of the way corner, but my father insisted I be put between Gaius Rabirius and himself. Since he was the guest of honour, she didn't dare disobey. At least I wasn't beside Marcus Antonius. He was on the other side of the room, next to a woman who seemed to be very familiar with him, from the way she touched his shoulder to get his attention. I felt his eyes on me again several times during that long evening, but I didn't look at him once, ruthlessly stifling the tiny spark of fascination he continued to light within me. The sooner he learned that I wasn't interested in him – would never be interested in him – the better. If I kept on telling myself that, I might actually believe it.

I made conversation in my halting Latin with Rabirius, setting out to charm him further, as my father had instructed. We got on better once he asked me politely if I would not prefer to converse in Greek. I found he was a cultured and amusing man, with a fund of scurrilous stories about members of the Senate and other figures in Roman society. I didn't know half the names of course, but the stories were fun, and he also recited some scandalous poetry – apparently about a well-known senator's wife – by a man he called Catullus. I enjoyed it so much that I asked him to send me a scroll of it, if he had one. He promised to do so, and also to send his own guards and his oldest daughter, Calpurnia, to guide me round the famous Forum, which I had expressed a polite desire to see.

'If my father will allow it,' I said.

'If I will allow what, my little pusscat?' said my father, turning to me with his most benevolent smile.

Rabirius hurried to explain.

'I can't see any harm in it,' my father said. 'But you and your women will have to dress as sober Roman matrons, Cleopatra. Pompeius was right – there have been riots against my presence here. It is best not to take any risks by dressing as an Egyptian princess.'

I did not tell him that it would have been hard to do so – the clothes I had brought with me weren't exactly princess class. I would have to do something about that.

It was late when we returned. I could see that Warrior Sah and Corporal Geta's eyelids were drooping, though they tried not to let it show. I turned to the guard escorting me.

'My men need to rest,' I said. 'Send two of your best to relieve them. The Pharaoh has ordered it.'

Well, I had ordered it really, but it wasn't a lie. I would be Pharaoh soon.

The man nodded.

'At once, princess,' he said.

Corporal Geta tried to protest as soon as he had gone, but I overruled him.

'You can't serve me if you fall asleep on duty,' I pointed out. 'If it makes you feel better, you can sleep inside, across the doorway.'

He nodded stiffly.

'We won't leave you alone here, Chosen. The Princess Arsinöe's tutor tried to sneak past us earlier, saying he had a message for you. But I didn't like his looks, so I denied him entry.'

'Was he a tall, thin man with a sneer?' I asked.

'Yes, that's him. Ganymedes, he said his name was. I'd trust him as far as I could throw a camel.'

I smiled over my shoulder as I went into the bedchamber. 'Maybe not even as far as that.'

Iras and Charm were curled up together on the bed like two entwined snails, and I hadn't the heart to wake them. So I stripped off my clothes and clambered in beside them as quietly as I could. It was a tight squeeze, and I lay on my back with my arms pinned to my sides, rejoicing that I was back with my father again and that he was pleased with me.

As I drifted off, though, my thoughts turned to Khai. I had not managed to dream of him in all the time since

I had left him in the palace. Iusaaset's gift was hard to manage at the best of times – and every night since then it had eluded me. I tried not to think that maybe it wasn't working because I felt so guilty. I brought up a hand and scrubbed drowsily at my lips. Would Khai be able to tell that another man had kissed me? Would he care that it hadn't been my fault, that Marcus Antonius had given me no choice? Even as I had the thought, I was above my body and flying down the silver cord that bound me to it. But I didn't cross the sea. I hovered for a moment over the dark mass of Rome, then with a sharp tug downwards, I found myself in a strange bedchamber. Where was I? The shutters were open and dying candles flickered before a tiny altar set into an alcove, where a large painted statue of Mars, god of war, kept watch over the room. In front of it knelt a man, quite naked, with the wide white slash of a healed sword wound across his lower back. It was Marcus Antonius.

'Witch,' he groaned aloud. 'Sorceress. Oh, great Mars, protect me from her beauty. I want her so badly.'

I knew at once who he meant. Me. Had he summoned me somehow? Or was it my own thoughts that had brought me here? But this wretched decurion had no right to desire me in such a way, despite that small spark I couldn't deny between us.

No, I snarled into his mind. *I'm not yours. I'll never be yours, however much you want me. And you won't be the death of me, whatever Sobek and that oracle said to Charm.*

His head turned, and then he leaped to his feet, eyes searching the room.

'Cleopatra?' he said hoarsely, passionately. 'Princess?'

Khai! I thought desperately, averting my eyes. *Khai, where are you?* And as quickly as that I was gone from the Roman, and out over the sea.

Now I was in the dark. Total dark. My invisible eyes couldn't see a thing beyond the silver cord that led back to my sleeping body.

Khai! Khai! Are you here?

There was no reply, but all at once I could see a faint blue glow, which quickly brightened to show me my goddess, standing in the corner of a windowless room filled with bodies – some big, some small, all young, sleeping restlessly in the heat of an Alexandria night. Khai lay at her feet, dressed only in a loincloth, with Shadya and Alim at his left and right hands. He had shaved his head again. To my great relief, I could see his chest rise and fall. I wasn't able to fall to my knees in my invisible state, or I would have done so. Then Isis smiled at me. If I had had an actual heart here, it would have stopped at the beauty of it.

My Chosen, she said. Your Khai is safe here in my brother Serapis's temple as you see, and he does good work for me. Many of these young souls are safe and not sacrificed to the demon because of him.

She stretched out one fingertip, letting fall a curling

thread of blue light, which settled just over Khai's heart, sinking into his skin.

What further protection I can give, he has. Now, come.

At once I was drawn to her side. Even in my disembodied form, I could feel her angry power like the buzzing rage of uncountable bees. The windowless room blinked out, and I was somewhere else – somewhere I knew immediately I didn't want to be at all.

I was in a large room painted with pictures of my goddess, except that where her face should have been was now the head of my sister's foul demon-god. Through the small window high up in the wall, I could see the familiar flicker of the Pharos light, and I realised with a small, numb shock that we must be in her temple on Pharos Island. To my horror, five embalmers in stained red robes were working frantically on a row of about a hundred naked corpses, both men and women, laid out on benches. The face of each corpse was stretched in a uniform grimace of terror, dark clotted blood oozing from their nostrils, ears and eyes. I thought I recognised some of them as courtiers and, with a growing sickness, I realised that one was the slovenly priestess who had shown me to Cabar's room on my previous visit.

Over the five embalmers stood the Pontic princeling, Archelaus, and my sister Berenice – except, of course, it wasn't Archelaus any more. It was vile Am-Heh given human flesh. Surrounding them in a dark line around the edges of the room was the same number of black-robed priests, chanting. The sound of their toneless voices oozed over the room in a thick, oily veil of power – like lamp oil mixed with rotting blood.

There was something odd about the embalmers. Then it came to me. They were not wearing the amulets of Seth. They had gone over to the evil demon instead. Am-Heh's mark was burned into their throats like a fiery brand, though none of them looked as if they were enjoying the task their new master had set them. Each pair of hands was a shaking, bloodied blur as they swiftly cut out dead hearts with curved iron knives and stowed each in strangely shaped canopic jars, which they then set beside each body. Then they went back and stitched the corpses up with large bone needles and coarse linen thread.

As soon as each chest was sewn shut, Archelaus laid his hands on it and muttered something I couldn't hear. Am-Heh's burnt mark appeared on every body, but over the place where their hearts used to be. What in the name of blessed Anubis was he doing? This was more than sacrilege against Isis. This was vile. This was so depraved and wrong that I couldn't find the words.

Berenice stood beside the demon as he worked. The triumphant smile on her lips seemed entirely enchanted by what he was doing. It was also entirely insane.

Although my emotions were partially numbed, as they always were when I was out of my body, I wanted to scream at my goddess, demand to know why she couldn't stop this obscenity in her own place. Why did she want me to see this? As if she had plucked the thought out of my head whole, I heard her answer.

This temple has not been mine for years, and now it has fallen to the demon through the neglect and betrayal of my priests and priestesses. All here have rejected me and embraced the demon – except for two. This is the price of that betrayal.

Her voice was no longer in the realm of raging bees. It was now the searing heat of pure white lightning. It was a merciless flame which would destroy everything in its path. It was utterly terrifying, and I wished for fingers to block my mind against it, as I might block my ears. But my goddess continued, inexorable. I could no more stop hearing her than I could halt a desert storm.

Others have come here through their own greed for eternal life and riches. The Ennead has decreed that this abomination must happen, as part of the cycle of their lives. To watch and not be able to save those here is part of your own punishment for breaking *ma'at*. This is the beginning of the demon's army. These are the Burnt-souled Dead, the blood-kilts. Watch and you will see.

I did see, much as I wanted not to. The first of the bodies sat up. Each horror in turn came to life, got off the bench and shambled towards the priests. Each one, man or woman, was given a rusty sword and a blood-red kilt, which it fumbled carelessly around its naked and bloody hips. Then they lined up by the wall with the real priests, their faces now gone blank and slack, and Archelaus turned to face them. His voice hissed and crackled like wet fire.

'I have taken you and given you the power of a new life. I have given you the riches of a body that will not fail you. So the merciful promise of Am-Heh is fulfilled. You will be my unstoppable army. None in Egypt will be able to stand against me or my queen. Now go forth into the streets. Bring me more souls, more hearts to fill my jars. The willing shall feel my mercy, the unwilling shall feed my sacrificial fire.' His eyes flicked up to the window.

Berenice cackled madly.

'Obey your Pharaohs' command,' she said, and I could see the fires of Am-Heh's lake already burning in her eyes. 'More souls. More hearts. Hurry!'

The creatures – for I could not call them people any more – nodded expressionlessly and marched out of the door. I winced to see the women's breasts exposed. Even with my emotions numbed, it bothered me to see them so uncaring of their nakedness. Had all of them been priestesses of Isis? It was unthinkable – and yet I had to think it, and consider whether the price for betraying my goddess was a fair one.

Thus your sister and her consort think to rule, by fear of their undead army. All of these lost souls thought to gain eternal power and riches by pledging allegiance to the demon and his Pharaoh bride. Their greed undid them, as it will undo others. Am-Heh's sister, Ammit, would have weighed their souls against the justice feather and found them wanting. They would not have passed the test and gone on into the afterlife. They were always destined for the fiery lake.

But what about the unwilling ones they're going to take off the streets now and sacrifice?

I couldn't cry, but I knew that would change the minute I got back to my body.

This is a monstrosity. I want to stop it. I want to help them.

But Isis's voice was implacable.

You cannot stop it, my Chosen. Their fate was sealed the moment they let Am-Heh into their hearts. Willing or not, these creatures are what your armies will face, along with the mercenaries and city guards your sister employs, and their numbers will now grow daily. Hundreds have already been sacrificed to provide the blood to fuel the demon's power, and more still will die unless you can stop him. The streets of the city are not safe at night now, and soon they will not be safe by day either. Our people stay locked and cowering in their houses, with the shutters drawn against the dark. You must warn both your own troops and those the Romans bring. These abominations cannot be killed. If struck down, they simply rise again. Only fire will stop them, or the destruction of the demon himself. For he has made an error by taking a human body of his own, and in his assumed human frailty lies your chance to end him. He too can be burned and brought to judgement.

I will find him, I promised her. *I will find him and burn him to ash with my own hands. I will destroy them all.*

Isis nodded.

Good, she said. It is a hard lesson we gods ask you to learn, my Chosen, but it is necessary. We see in you the potential to be the greatest Pharaoh Egypt has ever had, but *ma'at* must never be broken again. The Double Throne must be in balance, or the Egypt you know and love will be gone forever, and strangers will rule in your place. Bring your father home soon, and kill the demon, or all will be lost. We gods will not step into this fight. You have passed my second test – now you must pass theirs. Be brave, my Chosen. The path ahead is full of death and danger.

Her voice had changed. It had the timbre of prophecy about it. It filled my head, my heart, my soul. But before I could say another word, the silver cord tugged at me, Isis was gone and I was flashing over water and back into my bed beside Iras and Charm.

I just made it to the earthenware basin before I began to vomit up everything I had eaten that night, and more. I threw up until I thought my stomach would come up through my throat.

'No! No! No!' I gasped between heaves, trails of snot

and tears pouring from my nose and eyes until I could barely breathe.

'No! No! No!'

I retched until I was empty and aching and sore and there was nothing left in me, but still the horrible images flashed before my eyes, over and over and over.

Am-Heh and Berenice were making an army of the Burnt-souled Dead out of *my* people.

And I had to convince my father and the Roman generals that they were real.

More than that, I had the impossible task of killing the demon god.

I never, ever wanted to dream again. But I was going to have to try. I must get a warning to Khai and the others.

16

The Tarpeian Rock

All at once I felt the comfort of Charm's cool hands holding back my hair, and Iras gripping my shoulders, supporting me.

'What is it, Cleo?' my best friend whispered, her voice shaking. 'Did they poison you at the feast?'

I wiped my mouth with the back of my hand and spat the last of the bitter bile into the overflowing basin.

'Water,' I croaked. 'Please.'

Iras's hand appeared in front of my face, holding an earthenware beaker. I took it and rinsed my mouth out several times, spitting again and again, then held it out for more.

There was a hammering at the door and the two warriors burst in.

'I heard noises,' said Corporal Geta. 'Are you all right, Chosen?' His eyes fell on the basin and widened. 'Have you been harmed? Should I call a physician?'

I waved a hand weakly.

'No. I am well. Just a temporary sickness. But come in, both of you. I have something to tell you all.'

Once I had finished, I could tell from their eyes that it sounded unbelievable. It *was* unbelievable. But if I couldn't convince those who were closest to me that an undead army stalked the streets of Alexandria, then I had no chance of convincing my father – let alone the Romans.

'So,' Iras said. 'We will need to carry fire with us. You say these things can be burned?'

'And we need to find the Pharaoh's consort and destroy him, Chosen?' Corporal Geta asked.

I nodded to both of them, grateful beyond anything that they were treating what anyone else would have called a bad dream as something practical to be overcome.

'Yes,' I said. 'And that's why we need to find Khai and General Nail and make a plan of attack as soon as we're back in Alexandria. Khai is the best positioned to know where to trap Archelaus. If his army of street rats is as good as I think they will be, they will be able to find out.' I closed my eyes for a moment.

'Thank you,' I said then. 'I know this is not an easy thing to hear.'

Warrior Sah went to one knee, looking up at me as I sat on the bed.

'We believe in you and our goddess, Chosen,' he said

simply. 'If she has given you the power to travel in dreams, then why should you lie about what you see there? It is like the oracle – except that you speak the truth in plainer language.'

My throat went thick and choked. What had I ever done to deserve trust like this?

'I will do my best to live up to your faith in me,' I managed to get out, swallowing and blinking against the tears which threatened to spill over my lower lids.

'The chosen needs her sleep if she's going to tell the Pharaoh about this in the morning,' Charm said, squeezing my hand tightly. 'And so do you two. We'll take care of her. Go back to your posts.' She handed Sah the earthenware bowl, now discreetly covered with a cloth, and told him to get rid of it, then closed the door firmly behind the two men.

'Poor Sah,' I said, as I crawled into bed again.

'Poor Sah nothing,' Charm said. 'All he does is stand outside the door all day, leaning on that spear of his.' But her voice was fond and I knew she didn't really mean it.

'You've got a hard task ahead of you, Cleo Blue-Eyes,' said Iras.

'I know,' I said. 'But I'm going to have to make them believe me. And I'm going to have to get a message to Khai and General Nail and Merit as soon as possible. They all need to know what the street rats and the army of the Ibis are facing.'

'Can't you…' – Charm wiggled her fingers and made a mysterious face as she straightened the covers – '…you know, dream it to them?'

I tried not to retch again at the thought.

'I'll try, but I still can't control it properly,' I said. 'I mean, last night I ended up in Marcus Antonius's bedchamber.' I clapped my hand over my mouth. I hadn't meant to say that. It had just slipped out. But now that it had…

Charm stopped what she was doing abruptly, slapping a hand onto the sheet with an angry crack.

'I thought I told you to keep away from him,' she said, almost growling the words.

'Look,' I said. 'I know you think that kiss with him was the thing the oracle was talking about – the thing that will lead to all our deaths. But I don't believe our threads on Shai's loom cannot be diverted into a different pattern.' Then I told them both what Isis had said to me. 'If I restore *ma'at*, if I sit on the Double Throne beside my father, Isis and all the gods will support us. Kissing one Roman soldier isn't going to lead to anything – let alone decide the fate of all Egypt.'

Charm looked even unhappier when Iras agreed with me.

'I don't care. I hate him,' she said. 'And I believe that oracle. He'll have you if he can, sooner or later. I've seen the way he eats you with his eyes. He's bad news any way you look at it.'

I remembered the decurion's passionate words and shuddered. I knew it was true. I would just have to keep even further away from him, that was all. I dared not let myself be tempted to fan the spark that lay between us, to see what would happen if I did.

'Don't worry, Pretty Girl,' said Iras, slinging an arm around Charm's neck and planting a smacking kiss on her mouth. 'If he comes near her I shall stab him with my sharp little knives where it will hurt him most. He won't try again, you'll see.'

'You'd better,' said Charm, as we all snuggled down in the bed and prepared for the few hours' sleep we would get before dawn.

I smiled to myself as I closed my eyes. The way they were with each other made me happy. Even if I couldn't be with Khai right now, at least two of my friends could be together and in love. It did make me miss him terribly, though. I remembered him lying in that crowded room tonight, asleep, and wished for nothing more than to go back there now and press my body against his, skin to skin, soul to soul, and to wake him gently with a kiss – well, more than a kiss if I was honest with myself. I thought of the poem Gaius Rabirius had recited to me earlier.

Da mi basia mille…

I wondered if I would ever have the freedom to give Khai even one kiss again, let alone a thousand. My fingers went to my lips, remembering our time together in Renenutet's shrine. I fell asleep counting every single place he had touched me with his lips and hands, hoping and also fearing that my dreams would take me to him again.

But they didn't. And until they did, he would have no warning of the new threat he and his street rats faced.

I managed a little breakfast next morning, although my stomach was still tender and my throat sore. Then I went in search of my father. I didn't want to put off what I had to do any longer than necessary.

He was at his own breakfast, surrounded by piles of scrolls. He was waving one at one of the men who were hovering nervously about him when I walked in.

'Redraft this, and take it to the consul at once. He promised that I could call on the legions if I needed extra men. This makes no mention of it.'

'But Most High…' the man said, wringing his hands.

My father just looked at him. 'Do you dare to disobey your Pharaoh?' he asked, deadly as a cobra. The man shook his head.

'No! No, Most High! Of course not. It shall be done as you wish.' He backed away, holding the scroll.

My father waved his hands in a shooing motion at the rest of them.

'Be off with you. I want to talk to my daughter.'

Well, that's one problem solved, I thought, as the room emptied. I hadn't relished the thought of telling my father about the Burnt-souled Dead in front of a room full of onlookers.

As soon as we were alone, he gestured to a seat.

'Come. Sit, daughter,' he said. I did so, staring at him openly as he fidgeted and avoided my eyes. What was the matter with him? There was an uncomfortable silence.

'I dreamed last night,' he said finally, the words spilling out of him like wine from a too full jar.

'What did you dream, Father?' I tried not to let hope fill my voice. Maybe he already knew.

'Blessed Isis came to me,' he said. He leaned forward and took my hands. His palms were damp and sweaty – with fear not heat, I thought. 'It was a true dream, Cleopatra, I know it. There have been Pharaohs before me who dreamed true. She was so beautiful I could hardly look upon her.'

I knew how he felt.

'Did she say anything?' I asked hopefully.

'No. But she showed me a man in a red kilt, with a terrible mark over his heart.' He frowned. 'I'd never seen him before in my life. What does it mean? Have you something you wish to tell me, Cleopatra?'

My shoulders slumped. I was going to have to explain after all.

'Yes, Father,' I said. 'And however strange it seems, you must believe me.'

He didn't – not at first, not until I'd stood over him and shouted what I'd seen into his face.

He was so surprised that his mouth fell open like a fly-hungry toad's. I don't think anyone had ever raised their voice to him like that – not for a long time, anyway. He blinked at me.

'But how can they be dead and yet live?' he asked, like a plaintive child seeking comfort.

'I don't know, Father,' I said, my voice soft now. 'But I will stake my life that it is true. Even now our people and our city suffer under these creatures of Berenice and her vile consort. The gods want *ma'at* restored. They want us on the Double Throne together. So the sooner we set sail for Tyre and that army we've promised to pay for, the better.'

He looked at me, the old charming smile I remembered so well on his lips.

'You would have made a fine son, Cleopatra.'

'I make just as fine a daughter,' I retorted. 'And anyway, a Ptolemy son like me would probably have poisoned you by now.'

'True,' he said, unable to stop a swift, nervous glance towards the remains of his breakfast.

I laughed.

'Don't worry, Father. I wouldn't dare poison you. Isis would strike me down if I did. She wants you back in Egypt very badly.'

If anything, that made him look even more nervous.

Unable to keep my mind away from the terrible things I'd seen, I spent the rest of the morning fretting, biting my tongue so as not to snap at the housekeeper, Lydia, who wanted me to try on my new garments cut in the Roman style. She had clearly kept the dressmakers up all night sewing. Charm and Iras had new outfits too, though Iras scowled at the length of hers and hitched it up at once. I remembered my manners enough to thank the woman, who flushed with surprised pleasure. Her surprise told me without words that my sister and brothers had never thanked her in their lives. Probably my father hadn't either.

'The Pharaoh commanded it, Your Highness,' she said. I had a sudden thought, and turned to Charm.

'Where are my priestess things?' I asked.

'The laundry still has them,' she said, raising a questioning eyebrow. 'Shall I go and get them?'

I shook my head and turned to Lydia again. 'Get the dressmakers to copy the robes I came here in,' I ordered. 'In the finest white linen. See that they make four sets. I want to take them with me, so they should be ready by tomorrow.'

She bowed and scurried away to do my bidding.

Almost immediately there was a tap at the door. It was my brother, Tol.

'You look nice,' he said. 'You smell better than when you arrived too. I came to bring you a message.' He cleared his throat importantly and stood up very straight. 'The Princess Arsinöe commands you to attend her apartments to meet the Lady Calpurnia Rabiria.' He frowned. 'I think I got that right. Calpurnia Rabiria is a difficult name to say.

I don't like Latin. It hurts my tongue.'

'You did it perfectly, Tol,' I said, trying not to grind my teeth at Arsinoë's cunning. How had she got hold of Rabirius's daughter? She had been supposed to be coming to see me, not my sister. 'Will you run back and tell Arsinoë that we will be with them shortly?'

'Do you want me to say just that?' he asked, his face falling a little.

'Tell her that the Princess Cleopatra, marked and chosen priestess of Isis, will attend on the Lady Calpurnia Rabiria just after the midmorning hour, then,' I said, putting out a hand and ruffling his hair. 'Will that do?'

He nodded eagerly and skipped off. I don't think he even noticed that I had carefully omitted Arsinoë's title, or even any mention of her. How dare she use Tol as her personal errand boy?

'That will make the little madam cross,' Charm said, her eyes dancing. 'But you still need to be careful of her, Cleo. She'll bite, just you see if she doesn't.'

'She needs to be taught manners, that one,' Iras said. 'And I would be only too delighted to oblige again.' She flexed her palm meaningfully.

'Behave,' I said. 'I shouldn't have done that. It wasn't very Pharaoh-like.'

I had a surprise when I stepped outside the door. Both of my warriors were armed in the Roman way, with leather corselets and kilted tunics. Short swords were belted at their waists, and the spears they carried were not silver, but iron-tipped.

'We were told that Egyptian dress was not wise if we were to accompany you out, Chosen,' Corporal Geta said, before I could speak. 'The Pharaoh himself ordered it.'

A tall young woman with a thin face and her father's slightly mischievous brown eyes was standing awkwardly in front of Arsinöe, who was lounging on a couch, the tall, thin man standing behind her. His face was, yet again, set in a disapproving sneer. Ignoring him and my sister, who hadn't even had the manners to ask the young woman to sit, I went to her, my hands outstretched. Did Arsinöe not realise how important it was to be polite to the family of the man who was paying to put our father back on the throne?

'You must be the daughter of Gaius Rabirius Postumus, whom I had the pleasure of meeting last night. Calpurnia, is it?'

The young woman nodded.

'I'm sorry, Your Highness,' she said, in very good Greek. 'I hadn't realised there was more than one princess in your house. The servants brought me here, but when I explained, your sister kindly sent a message. I would have come to you myself, but…' She gestured helplessly.

After last night, the last thing I wanted to do was to go sightseeing, but it was vital that Rabirius's daughter took back a good report of me. So I put on my princess mask and smiled.

'I understand completely,' I said. 'You have come to show me your marvellous Forum, have you not?'

Immediately, Arsinöe bounced up.

'The Forum?' she squealed. 'I love the Forum. I haven't been there for ages. I want to come too. I can, can't I, Ganymedes?'

'Certainly, Your Highness,' he said, his voice as dry as a dead riverbed. 'Would you like me to accompany you?'

'No,' she said rudely. 'You'll only want me to learn things. Cleopatra can look after me. She's got nothing better to do.'

I didn't like the way she had reduced me to servant status so easily, but I couldn't very well stop her without making a scene, so I nodded. Luckily, she too was wearing Roman dress today.

'Very well,' I said. 'Shall we go?' I would do whatever I must to ensure my father got Rabirius's money – and maybe the sights around the Forum would take my mind off the terrible memory of those undead bodies for a while.

In addition to my warriors, we had four other Roman guards, all tough-looking men who would stand for no trouble. And there was Iras as well, of course, though nobody except me, Charm and the warriors knew about her knife skills.

The Forum was only a short downhill walk away, down

the narrow street Calpurnia called the Argiletum. She was a good guide, pointing out the ancient temple of Tellus with its frieze of giants, and the next-door house of Quintus Tullius Cicero, the brother of the great lawyer and orator, who she said was her father's friend.

'It's so sad you won't hear Marcus Tullius speak,' she said. 'He is a marvellous rhetorician, but I believe he is on his country estates just now. Some dispute over politics, I think.'

I didn't feel it was polite to tell her that Pompeius had called her father's friend an idiot the night before.

The forum itself was a boiling mass of people, pushing and shoving their way past each other, shouting out greetings, carrying baskets of food or just gawping as we were. The smells were rich and ripe, with a whiff of something very unpleasant occasionally breaking through. Our guards formed a rough ring around us and shoved their way through, as a flock of seagulls added to the noise, screaming and fighting for scraps overhead.

'Oh, dear,' Calpurnia said. 'It's nearly noon.' She stopped and stood on tiptoes. 'Yes, look,' she said, pointing to a raised platform where a group of men in white robes stood waiting outside a large stone building. 'There are the senators ready to go into the Curia.'

'What's the Curia?' I asked.

'The building where the senators make the laws, stupid,' Arsinöe answered, her voice a contemptuous sneer. 'Don't you know anything?'

'I know a great deal,' I said. 'Since, unlike Your Highness, I have had the privilege of being educated in the Great Library, and at Philäe. However, I am always happy to learn new things.'

A Pharaoh would *not* rise to her baiting.

'Look,' said Calpurnia, hurriedly, clearly not wanting to get into a fight between two sisters. 'There is the famous fig tree under which Romulus and Remus were suckled by the wolf.'

By the time we had walked all round the place, my feet were tired from slipping and sliding over the large red-cobbled roads.

'Let's go up to the Capitol,' Calpurnia said, oblivious to my discomfort. 'You can see Gnaeus Pompeius's new theatre being built from there.'

As we climbed the steep marble steps upwards, I sighed. I didn't care about seeing the consul's stupid theatre. The need to warn Khai about what was facing him was becoming more and more urgent within me. How soon could I get back to the house and try to use Iusaaset Skyborn's gift again, I wondered.

But after we reached the top, just past what Calpurnia was busy telling us was the mighty temple of Jupiter, I saw a familiar figure away to the left.

'Oh!' I said loudly. 'Look! There's Blessed Isis!' There was a large statue of my goddess standing outside a pillared shrine, her hand outstretched to me. I started to move towards her. Too late I noticed the crowd of rough-looking men loitering nearby.

'Oi, bitch!' said one aggressively, spitting on the ground. 'Are you one of those filthy Egyptian Isis-worshippers or something? We know what to do with your sort.' And as quickly as that, they were surging forward, picking up stones.

'Quick,' said Corporal Geta. 'We must get the chosen away from here.'

I felt Arsinöe stiffen at the idea that I was more important than her, but before she could protest, our guards were hustling us away, down the hill and towards two other temples below. The path was rough and narrow, and I was in constant fear of stumbling and falling. I could hear the nearby *plock* of thrown stones and the baying of the mob behind us.

'This is all your fault, Cleopatra,' Arsinöe panted, as she ran beside me. 'You and stupid Isis!'

If I'd had the breath to chastise her for her stupidity, I would have done. How dare she be rude about my goddess? I shuddered. What if Isis had heard her? I'd seen at first hand what my vengeful goddess was capable of doing to those who rejected her.

'Jupiter curse it,' said the Roman guard in the lead. 'We can't get down. They've blocked the steps. Form up, boys, they're nearly on us.' We had come to a sheer drop which overhung the Forum, the people down there oblivious to the drama happening above them. More of the terrible smell I'd noticed below wafted into my nostrils, and I nearly gagged, but there was no time to see what was causing it. The five of us were hemmed in behind the men's bodies, their shields upraised against a small rain of stones, rocks and other less pleasant things. I felt the splat of something rotten spatter my foot, and a sharp-edged rock whistled by my head, soaring out over a large building below and clattering onto its roof.

'Let's be having them, lads,' called the man who had spoken before. 'You're good Roman citizens. You don't want to be protecting Egypt-loving scum, now do you?'

Suddenly Calpurnia was shouldering her way past me, her face set and determined.

'Let me through,' she said loudly. 'I am Calpurnia Rabiria, daughter of Gaius Rabirius Postumus, friend of the consul Gnaeus Pompeius Magnus. I am a true daughter of the Republic and a Roman citizen. How dare you treat me and my friends like this?'

It was so brave that my mouth dropped open.

The man laughed, but I could see his eyes shifting uneasily.

'Prove it, little girl!' he said, trying to brazen it out. There were jeers of encouragement behind him. 'Women aren't proper citizens, anyway.'

'Very well,' she said, ignoring his last comment. 'My father is with the consul at this very moment, down at the new theatre. Let us go and find them. You may ask him yourself.' She stuck her chin in the air and stared him down.

'That's all very well,' the man said, blustering a bit now. 'But what was all that about Isis?'

'My friends are Greek,' said Calpurnia, carefully not answering the question. 'Daughters of one of the rulers of Athens, who is here to make a trade treaty with the Senate. Do you truly want to jeopardise the future prosperity of the Roman Republic by offending them? I'm sure the consul will be delighted when I tell him.' It was a clever lie – clever enough to be believable, I hoped.

By now, the men at the edges of the mob were slipping away, back up the hill. Their leader stood there for a moment, unsure of what to do.

'Oh, if it's a question of the prosperity of the Republic,' he said, his eyes sliding away shiftily. 'Very sorry, I'm sure, lady. Mistaken identity. Let's not bother the consul, now.'

Calpurnia just stood there, ramrod straight, in silence, until he too turned and backed away. As soon as he had gone her shoulders slumped. I was about to go to her when I felt a small hand push me sharply backwards towards the drop. With a cry of surprise, I lost my balance and felt myself falling, my ankle turning with a pain like the stab of a needle. All in a flash, with a rip of material, Iras had grabbed the shoulder of my tunic and was pulling me back, whirling me away from the edge. I fell to my knees, panting with the shock, my heart racing so fast I thought it would burst. Iras advanced on Arsinoë menacingly, a knife in each hand.

'You will die for that, youngling,' she said quietly, absolute menace in her voice.

My sister screamed, the high, thin wail of a child.

'Get her away from me!'

'Iras!' I said. 'Stop!'

Reluctantly, Iras stepped back to stand beside Charm, whose face wore a leopard snarl of anger. I was back on my feet now, ignoring my throbbing ankle and smarting knees, rage replacing the fear. I took my sister's shoulders and I shook her like a rat, back and forth till her eyes rolled.

'What were you thinking?' I said through my teeth. 'Did you imagine you would be rid of me that easily, you nasty little snake?'

'Father said,' she mumbled.

This time my heart nearly stopped. My father had ordered this? No! I could not believe it. I wouldn't.

'Father said what?' I snapped, digging my fingers into her.

'Tol heard him. Tol said he told you he would throw you down off the Tarpeian Rock with his own hands. I thought I'd do it for him. Rid him of his bastard spawn, like he wanted, just like they execute the worst criminals here.' Her face was a mask of slit-eyed, pinch-mouthed hatred, and her spittle hit my face in a fury of tiny droplets.

Relief filled me, even as I understood what the overpowering stench must be. Tol had merely reported what our father had said, not understanding the consequence his words would have. My father didn't want me dead at all. A murderous sibling I could deal with – I was used to that, after all. I let her go with a contemptuous flick of my fingers.

'Control yourself,' I said, as I turned my back. 'This is not how a Ptolemy princess behaves.'

Calpurnia put a trembling hand on my shoulder. Her face was white, and she was sweating.

'W-we should probably go back now, princess,' she said.

'We should,' I said, taking her hand and squeezing it. Her eyes were no longer mischievous, but scared and shocked. 'What you did just now took a lot of courage. I am sure my father will want to reward you in some way.' Somehow I needed to repair the damage I'd done. Would Rabirius be so angry that he would withdraw his offer?

She shook her head, smiling with an effort.

'It was nothing,' she said. 'Please don't say anything to your father. I'm not going to tell mine, either. I don't want a fuss. I just want to go home.'

But I knew I would have to tell him. My father needed to know that the anti-Egyptian sentiment in the city was indeed growing.

The sooner we were away from Rome, the better.

* * *

17

Fair Winds to Crete

The journey back to my father's house was long and trying. As we edged down the narrow steps that led from the rock to the Forum, I tried not to shudder as I noticed a criminal who dangled from a wooden cross which leaned against the wall of the prison. His body was smashed and broken, with arms and legs sagging in all the wrong places. The sickly smell of his rotting flesh made my nostrils wrinkle with disgust and even after all I'd seen last night in that dreadful chamber of the dead, my stomach heaved and roiled, and I had to work hard not to lose what little breakfast I'd eaten. I tried not to imagine the terror as he was thrown down from above, and then nailed up through wrists and ankles. Had he still been alive? It was easier to concentrate on the throbbing pain in my ankle instead, stepping carefully so as not to turn it a second time. I was limping badly and leaning on Corporal Geta before we were home again.

Back in our rooms, Charm cleaned out the grit and blood from my knees, muttering grim threats against my sister, before she set my ankle to soak in hot water with herbs steeped in it. Then she replaced the hot with cool, and inspected it.

'It will go purple, but not too badly if you keep it raised,' she said, wrapping it in a linen bandage which smelt pungently of yellow bruise-flower.

'Oh, Ra curse this wretched foot! I have to see my father before my serpent of a sister does,' I said. 'Will you take a message, Iras? And remember to be polite – he is the Pharaoh.

She looked at me, solemn for once.

'Do you think it's wise to send me, Cleo Blue-Eyes? If the snakeling does get to him before you do, he'll probably throw me in chains for trying to stab her. I would have done it, you know. I take my promise to be your protector seriously.'

'I know you do, Iras,' I said. 'If you hadn't been there…'

'Well, you're safe now,' said Charm, sitting back on her heels, as I repressed a shiver. 'But she's right. It's better if one of the warriors goes.'

I scribbled a hurried note to my father and gave it to Warrior Sah. I could only hope that its contents made my father hurry to me. Arsinöe had scampered off, not even bothering to say goodbye to Calpurnia at the gate, making wild threats against me over her shoulder. According to her, she would throw me into the amphitheatre and set the lions on me. I knew it was bluff and bluster, but still…if my father didn't discount what she said as childish jealousy, I could be in trouble.

Still unable to sleep or dream, I waited in ever-increasing pain and discomfort for the whole of that long afternoon before he came, shouldering past his guards and through the door with a word for my warriors and a careless nod at Charm and Iras.

'Well, daughter,' he said. 'I come back from more dusty meetings with the consul to find you have been in the wars.'

I had thought carefully about how much to tell him. I didn't want to be seen as a telltale. That would make me look like a child, not a chosen. I knew he was intelligent enough to read between the hieroglyphs, though. When I had finished, he looked at me.

'Your sister's tutor tells a different tale,' he said. 'If I am to believe him, you put Arsinöe and Rabirius's daughter in danger, and should be chastised with a thick stick and locked up with nothing but a stale loaf and water for a week. I just hope it doesn't get back to Rabirius, that's all.'

I opened my mouth to protest, to say that Calpurnia wasn't going to say anything, but he held up a hand.

'If I have learned anything, it is that a Pharaoh never defends himself against vile slander, Cleopatra,' he said, his face stern. 'A dignified silence is best.'

I closed my lips firmly, and he nodded.

'Quite right,' he said. 'But I think no more expeditions till we leave. That decurion of the consul's – Marcus Antonius, is it? He tells me that the ship will be ready to depart the harbour on the afternoon tide tomorrow.' He glanced down at my swollen ankle. 'I will order a litter to take you to the barge – it's just as well we are going down to Ostia by river.'

'Thank you, Father,' I said, then paused. 'And will the children be coming with us?' It had just occurred to me that there were a lot of opportunities on a ship for murder.

He shook his head.

'They will be living in the consul's house,' he said. A sour look crossed his face. 'Gnaeus Pompeius thinks he can use them as bargaining chips to ensure my debt to him and Gaius Rabirius is paid, but I will send for them as soon as I am restored to the Pharaoh's throne. I had to promise them to him to keep you at my side.' He gave me a sideways glance. 'I hope our goddess will be pleased.'

I didn't know about Isis, but Arsinöe would be about as delighted as a cat trapped in a pit full of cobras.

'Did you tell him about...you know – the army of the Burnt-souled Dead?' I asked.

'No. There'll be time enough when we reach Tyre. Don't want to frighten the camels, now do we, pusscat?'

'I suppose not,' I said. I still didn't know how to tell him that I wouldn't be coming to Tyre.

Packing up the household of a Pharaoh in less than a day meant a whirlwind of slaves and servants running about and shouting, with bags and boxes in the corridors. In the end, I had my warriors bar the door against them. And I knew precisely the moment Arsinöe received the news she would be staying behind with my brothers – the screams of her tantrum filled the whole house for hours. If she hadn't hated me before, she certainly did now.

'One less danger to guard against, Cleo Blue-Eyes,' was all Iras said.

'Unless she gets in tonight and stabs me,' I said.

Iras grinned. 'My fierce Pretty Girl would never let her anywhere near you,' she said. 'Would you, my pomegranate?'

Charm looked up from the bundle she was tying with long strands of twisted hemp.

'If you are not careful, O Annoying Queen of Warriors, I shall take this rope and smack you with it,' she said. 'Hard.'

I felt a sudden pang. That was the kind of thing Charm used to call me, the kind of conversation we used to have together. She hadn't done that for a while. I knew I hadn't lost my best friend – would never lose her – but maybe our relationship would be different now she had Iras. Perhaps that was one of the prices I had to pay for power. I knew that my father too would change when he got to Alexandria. The prescribed pomp and ceremony around the Pharaoh would mean that the relaxed and informal man he was here would disappear, as if he had never been. I realised that the me I was now would disappear too when the royal diadem was bound about my brow. Khai's words came back to me.

Do you think your father will really let a lowly scribe like me near you?

I had promised him I would find a way for us, but would I be allowed to keep Charm and Iras as near me as they were now, or would Alexandrian politics dictate that I must be surrounded by the well-bred Greek ladies of the court instead? I brought my fist down on the arm of my chair with a crash, making Charm jump.

'No, I will *not*!' I growled.

'What in the name of Osiris's beard…?' she said, eyes wide with alarm.

'You won't leave me, Charm, will you?' I asked, reaching for her.

'No, O Sultana of Silliness,' she said, taking my hand and holding it to her cheek. 'Of course, I won't. Not ever. What made you think I would?'

I smiled.

'Nothing, O Princess of Packing,' I said.

The less said about the journey back to Ostia, the better. The consul himself accompanied us, with half a century of legionaries, so there was no trouble, but the litter journey was hot and oppressive, the barge was cramped, and my father was in a foul mood, having had to peel Arsinöe off him at least twice before he left. In the end Ganymedes had had to physically hold her by the arm and clamp a hand over her mouth to stifle her screams of rage. Lem and Tol had not made a sound, but Tol's big eyes had overflowed with silent tears. They too knew that the years of being able to see the Pharaoh whenever they wanted were at an end. I felt sorry for them. I knew what it was to be left behind by our father.

Marcus Antonius was already at the harbour, overseeing the loading of our goods. I eyed the decurion warily, telling myself that he was a lecher and a philanderer with no respect for royalty, and that on this voyage I would have nothing more to do with him. We were on a fast merchant ship this time, with more room, so it would be easier to avoid him. Charm, Iras and I were squashed into a tiny cabin near the narrow bow, while my warriors were huddled in below with the legionaries accompanying us. And my father could not be expected to hunker down on deck as we had on the journey from Leptis, though as I passed them on my way to my own cabin, I noted Achillas and Theodotas did not look too happy with their accommodation in the bowels of the ship.

I prayed to Isis as I limped on board, supported by Charm on one side and Iras on the other.

Please, dear goddess. Give us fair, fast winds, and help me get to Alexandria quickly.

It appeared she had heard me. As soon as we were out

of the harbour, a brisk breeze blew up from the north, sending us scudding down towards Thrinacia. We stopped only to take on water and food at Syrákousai, before turning eastwards and heading for Crete. Iras had fixed the physician's seasickness remedy to her ear, and once more it proved effective.

'The best silver I ever spent,' I said to her.

'You only did it because you were tired of holding my head over a bucket, Cleo Blue-Eyes,' she said, juggling a knife from hand to hand.

'We were all fed up with holding your head over a bucket, Iras,' Charm retorted.

I stood at the ship's bow watching a pod of dolphins race the lace of spray thrown up by the prow. We were approaching the busy harbour of Phoenix in Crete after a miraculously fast journey. Well, the sailors all said it was miraculously fast. I knew that Isis had been tampering with the winds again. I could almost smell her desert herbs on the breeze.

I raised my hands to the heavens, feeling the warmth of Ra's rays heat my palms.

Thank you, beloved goddess.

Even as I gave praise to her, I scanned the ranks of tied-up boats anxiously. Would there be one we could take passage on to Egypt? I would send Corporal Geta to enquire as soon as we landed, I decided.

I felt the pull towards Khai like an eternal tug at my

midriff. I had finally managed a very brief glimpse of him in my dreams, staring up at a dawn sky, with a trail of pinch-faced children behind him. He was outside a building I almost recognised, and Merit was beside him. I had just time to notice a new scar pattern on her cheek – scabbed and startling against her brown skin.

Khai... I said into his head. *Beware Am-Heh's new army. They wear blood-red kilts. Tell General Nail...* But I didn't have time for any more, and I didn't know if he'd heard, because suddenly I was elsewhere, whisked away to a large painted room full of soldiers. General Nail was bent over a tray full of sand and pebbles, with Shoshan of the Spear at his side, when another scrawny child appeared. My general looked up, frowning. He didn't seem surprised.

'How many have been taken this week?' he asked.

'Fifty-four children, seventeen women and thirty-eight men,' she recited, rattling off the numbers like shrivelled beans pouring from a jar. 'Khai is getting as many as he can away to Sister Merit and the others at the temple of Serapis, but it's dangerous with the...the Pharaoh's new army on the streets.' I saw her swallow, making a trembling gesture against evil with her fingers.

I had no time for finesse. I spoke into both their minds.

This is the chosen. Do not approach the blood-kilted ones except with fire in your hands. They cannot be killed unless you burn them. Tell Khai. Spread the word. I will be with you as soon as I can. Set watch for my coming. And then

I was gone, back to my own body. I just hoped the message had got through to one of them – though it was obvious from her words that the street-rat girl knew that there was a new army in town. I snapped back into my body, grinding my teeth with frustration. *Why* could I not control Iusaaset's gift better? I couldn't even reach Merit – and she was a fellow priestess.

Please, Blessed Iusaaset, I prayed, as I had done ten thousand times before. *Help me.* But I knew she couldn't hear me. She was sleeping in her desert tomb, deep in her own dreams.

'It's very simple. Just inform the Pharaoh you're not going with him to Tyre, Cleo Blue-Eyes,' Iras said the next morning, her jaw tight with an impatience I was unaccustomed to. 'You are the chosen. He can't tell you what to do.' She whisked a whetstone over her dagger to emphasise the point. The high, grating sound made my teeth hurt.

We had been arguing back and forth for some time about the best way to break the news to my father. It was hard to get time alone with him on the ship, because Achillas and Theodotus were stuck to his heels like sandflies on a week-old camel corpse.

'You don't understand, Iras. He's the Pharaoh. I'm not – yet. I can't just dictate to him like that.' Also, though I didn't say it out loud, he was the father I'd just found. I knew the political implications of me landing in Egypt and taking charge of my own armies would not escape him. I didn't want to cause a rift between us. I had to do this right.

'Oh, for Bastet's sake,' said Charm. 'You're both giving me a headache. Say you've been summoned by Isis in a dream. He'll have to believe that – and he won't dare oppose Isis's will. He's scared of your goddess, you know.'

I did know, and while I was glad of it in some way, I didn't like how it made my father behave when he was reminded of my link to Isis. I didn't like how his fear of our goddess sometimes transferred into an awed incomprehension of what his daughter had become. I was still his pusscat princess inside, wasn't I? It shouldn't have made any difference – but it did.

'All right,' I said. 'I think that's the best plan, O Queen of Schemes.'

'It's lucky you have me to be the voice of reason then, isn't it, O Chosen of the Goddess?' Charm smiled, clearly pleased that she'd solved my dilemma.

'You're both too devious for a plain soldier of Sobek,' said Iras grumpily, and she stomped off to practise dagger work with Warrior Sah.

'She doesn't mean it, you know,' Charm said, gazing after her with worried eyes. 'She just feels a bit like a lioness in a snare here.'

I sighed. 'I expect she just wants to get to grips with the enemy. I know I do.'

Charm nodded slowly, biting her lip. 'Just don't get yourselves killed, all right?' she said. 'I-I love you both.'

The night before Crete appeared on the horizon I managed to get my father alone, and put Charm's plan into action while his toadies were otherwise engaged.

After I'd explained that I would be leaving the ship, I took his hand and looked up at him through my eyelashes, the way I'd often seen my mother do it. I wasn't above a little manipulation and flattery.

'Don't you see, Father?' I said. 'I'd just be preparing the ground for your return. And it would be wrong to waste the gifts Isis has given me.'

The corner of his mouth twitched, and he grunted.

'Don't try those tricks on me, girl. I'm not convinced. You'll be better off coming with me to Tyre.'

I fought to keep my temper.

'Look, if Isis helps me to get the demon and Berenice out of your way, all you and the Romans will have to do is mop up any of their fighters who remain and ride in at the head of your troops. The people will see you as their saviour after all they've suffered, and the Romans will see a triumphant and much-loved Pharaoh welcomed home by his adoring subjects. It makes good political sense.'

It wasn't exactly a lie. After a bit more arguing he capitulated, though reluctantly.

'I should send somebody with you, pusscat,' he said.

'Perhaps Achillas. He has a good military mind…'

I shook my head. The last thing I wanted was disdainful Achillas interfering – or curtailing any time I might have with Khai. This was my time to prove to myself whether I could be a leader of my people – or not.

'But you will need him, Father. Who else will deal with the Romans and make them do what you want? I couldn't possibly take him from you.'

What I didn't tell him was that I had only my dreams to go on when I got to Egypt. I knew Khai and Merit were still in Alexandria, and that General Nail and the army of the Ibis had reached Shoshan's marshes, but I couldn't be certain of anything else. It made me very nervous, but there was nothing I could do unless I learned to gain proper control of Iusaaset's dream gift.

My father stared at me broodingly. I knew what he was still thinking. If I was in Egypt before him, I would have two armies to his one. Despite all I'd said, might I try to take the throne from him? It was the sort of question a Ptolemy ruler was always asking about his relations – we didn't exactly have a good reputation where treachery was concerned. I needed to convince him that betrayal was the last thing on my mind.

I laid a hand on his. The skin was warm and soft – the skin of a man who had never done a day's hard labour in his life. Not like my Khai.

'I will be waiting every day for news of your safe passage

home,' I said, and I looked into his eyes, hoping that he could see the truth in mine. 'We must mend what has been broken, as Isis has commanded. I cannot defeat Berenice and Archelaus's armies all on my own, Father. We will take back our city together and then rule side by side, with our goddess's blessing, and in her name.' I found that I wanted him to believe me terribly.

He nodded, lips and eyes narrowed, brows frowning.

'Together, then, in the name of Blessed Isis, pusscat. And may she protect us both from harm.' Then he sighed, rubbing his forehead with his fingertips till it wrinkled. 'I suppose you'll want me to warn Aulus Gabinius about the Burnt-souled Dead, then?'

It was something that had been preying on my mind. I had thought and thought, and come to a decision I didn't like at all.

'No, Father,' I said. 'I will tell the decurion myself. If I can make him believe me, then between you, you have a better chance of convincing General Gabinius.'

I didn't want to spend any time at all with Marcus Antonius. However, I would do it for Egypt's sake – or, at least, that was what I told myself. As soon as we were safely tied up at the dock, I had him summoned to my father's cabin, and greeted him standing at the Pharaoh's side. Unfortunately, Achillas and Theodotus were crammed into a corner, giving me disapproving stares. I was not looking forward to this at all.

I caught a whiff of metal and oiled leather, cedarwood and lemons as he entered. I did not find it tempting. I did *not*.

I made my face devoid of all expression, locked down my princess mask so that he would not be able to read me. As his arm was falling away from that formal Roman salute, I spoke, using Isis's gift to the full, making my voice honey and ivory and the harsh caress of desert sand.

'Hear me, decurion of the Roman legions. I am the marked and chosen of the goddess Isis. May she strike me down if I do not speak true. You will face a greater danger in Alexandria than all the armies of Scythia and Parthia combined.'

He couldn't help his jaw dropping a little as I spoke on, his eyes turning first incredulous and then wild and wary, as if I was some untamed and unpredictable beast from the gladiators' circus which might rip his throat out without warning. Achillas and Theodotus had the same look on their faces but, out of the corner of my eye, I saw my father gesture them to silence with one sharp movement of his hand.

'You cannot expect me to believe this,' the decurion spluttered after a small, heavily charged silence. 'It is ridiculous. It is a tale for children.' He turned to my father, whose face was as impassive as my own. 'Your Majesty, don't tell me you and your advisers believe this pile of donkey dung too?' Clearly Isis's gift wasn't working as well as I had hoped. I hadn't convinced him.

'But I do, decurion,' my father said, his voice calm and cool. 'And my advisers believe what I believe. Would you doubt the word of the goddess's own chosen?'

Marcus Antonius spluttered some more, incoherent with disbelief. My father's advisers looked as though they had eaten a particularly tart lemon and then vomited it back up.

Isis! I called in my mind. *Beloved goddess. Help me out here. Please.*

But there was no response, not even a whisper. But as if she had put it into my mind, a plan came to me. I would have to risk everything on this one last throw of the senet pieces.

'I have never been to your house in Rome, have I, decurion?'

He shook his head, puzzled by this sudden change of tack.

'No, princess, but what has that to do—?'

I forged onward, interrupting him.

'So I would have no way of knowing that you keep a statue of Mars in the altar alcove at the right-hand corner of your bedchamber? And no way of knowing that on the second night before we left Rome, as you were praying to your god, you had a strange experience, as if someone had spoken in your head?'

His mouth was fully agape now, his jaw hanging down like loose washing. I saw the slow tide of red rising up his bronzed neck, as he remembered his lack of attire.

I nodded with satisfaction.

'Only the power of my goddess could have shown me these things. Would you like me to repeat to you the words you heard – and the words you said?' I asked.

He shut his mouth and let out one short bark of embarrassed laughter, shaking his head.

'Yet again, you have ambushed me on my weak side, princess,' he said. 'Witch I called you that night. My opinion hasn't changed. I have no notion what sort of sorcery this can be, but if I believe one tale, then I must believe the other, I suppose.' His hot, hungry eyes roamed my body one last time before he looked at my father, shutting me out as if I no longer existed.

He squared his shoulders and sighed as if going to an execution.

'Very well then, Your Majesty. I will order a torch carrier with every ten men,' he said. 'And if General Gabinius questions it, I will say that you have had word of some new and deadly weapon which can only be tackled with fire. That is the best I can do.' Then he turned and left without so much as a backward glance at me.

I stamped on the small flare of disappointment so hard that it never had the chance to grow. I would be on my way to Khai soon. He was the one I loved. He was the one who mattered to me – not some leather-smelling Roman who insulted me and couldn't keep his eyes where they belonged.

I squared my own shoulders and turned to my father's advisers, who by now were both red in the face and seething with the need to speak.

'Not a word,' I said sharply. 'Once again, I call on Blessed Isis to strike me down if I have said a word that is untrue. Do you really believe that she does not have the power to turn me to dust where I stand if I lie in her name?'

I pointed a finger at them, drawing in a breath to say more, when two small blue sparks erupted from my fingertips, fizzing across the cabin to land precisely in the spot between their eyes.

Theodotus gave a strangled shriek and rushed out of the cabin as if a pack of jackals was on his tail. Achillas clapped a hand to his forehead and turned the colour of muddy milk. Hurriedly, he bowed low.

'My apologies for doubting you, Chosen,' he said, forcing out the words through stiff lips. It was the first time he'd deigned to use my title. Then he too left. I saw him reach the rail and vomit over it into the sea below.

'That was not easy to watch, Cleopatra,' my father said. 'They will not love you for it.'

'I don't care,' I said. 'Perhaps they will have more faith in their Pharaohs and our goddess next time.'

* * *

Saying farewell to my father just after dawn on the next day was hard – much harder than I'd expected. Kneeling before him, I squeezed his hands tightly, bringing them to my forehead in the time-honoured sign of obeisance and fealty to a Pharaoh, before kissing them.

'Come as quickly as you can,' I said. 'I will have the army of the Ibis waiting.' And Khai's army of street rats, though I didn't mention them again. Not even my father believed that they could or would fight against normal soldiers – let alone an army of the undead.

'Whatever blessing I can give goes with you, daughter. May Isis guard and protect you. Do not take any unnecessary risks.'

I looked up at him, my eyebrows shooting upwards before I could stop them. I would take any risk to stop Am-Heh's army of horrors and kill Archelaus – even if it meant my own death.

'I'll try,' was all I said, however, as I touched the little packet of Khai's hair for luck. As always, it was tucked inside my breastband. Then I walked down the gangplank to where Charm, Iras and the warriors were standing.

We had another ship to catch, and I had a goddess to pray to for more than just favourable winds.

18

Egypt Again

Five long days later, at sunset, I stepped off the aggravatingly slow ship we had found, onto the soil of Egypt and into the end-of-the-day, fish-and-fermenting-grain smell of Canopus harbour. I peered over Corporal Geta's shoulder.

'It all seems so normal,' I said, putting back my veil and fanning a hand in front of my face to disperse the damp heat which had hit us as soon as we landed. Somehow, I had been expecting hordes of blood-kilted, sword-wielding undead to greet us off the ship. But everything here seemed unchanged. All I could see around me was the piled-up plenty of the fields, bathed in the red light of Ra's chariot sinking into the west. It was late in the month of Payni, and the harvest was coming in – a very good one. At least that was an encouraging sign. Maybe Isis had used some of her regained power to make sure the people were fed.

Suddenly I heard Iras exclaim softly behind me, as a tall, willowy girl with the slanted eyes of a cat scurried sideways out of the small crowd of merchants and shoppers. As she looked worriedly over her shoulder and then directly at us, I recognised her. It was Shadya, who I'd last seen in a dream, asleep at Khai's side. Without stopping, she crooked one finger in a beckoning gesture, and then put the same finger to her throat and drew it lightly across.

'We need to follow her, Chosen,' said Iras urgently. 'Right now. There is danger coming.'

All in a scramble, we set off after Shadya's rapidly disappearing figure. Luckily we had travelled light and had only a small bundle each. Soon we were in a narrow alleyway, with rickety mud and wood houses leaning towards each other on either side, shutting out Ra's eye so that the light was dim. The air was close and fetid, not helped by high piles of rotting rubbish which we had to pick our way around and over. I tried not to think about the unknown substances squelching under my feet, oozing over my sandals and between my toes. With a sideways jerk of her head, Shadya disappeared into a blue-painted door with a red hieroglyph of a reed scrawled on its pitted surface. It was the sign for shelter.

'I'll go first, Chosen,' said Corporal Geta. It was his no-nonsense warrior voice. As he ducked through the opening, a knife sprang into his hand. Iras had taught him well. A few seconds later, his head poked out.

'Come,' he hissed. 'Quickly.' As the words left his mouth, I felt a shiver of cold sickness run through my whole body. I knew the danger came from behind us. I didn't have to be asked twice. I threw myself through the door, reaching out and dragging Charm with me, our bundles catching on the rough wood. Iras and Warrior Sah followed immediately after and, as soon as they had appeared, Shadya leaped at the door, closing and barring it. Her teeth were bared in a rictus of disgust and fear, and her eyes looked old and tired.

'I have to get you out of here, Chosen,' she muttered. 'Khai will kill me if I let you be taken.'

Almost immediately there was a thump on the door.

'Open in the name of great Am-Heh,' said a soft, unnaturally sibilant voice with absolutely no emotion in it. Then there was another thump. The door shivered visibly. Shadya put her finger to her lips and grabbed my hand, tugging me forward.

'This way,' she mouthed.

We followed her on tiptoe, into a house full of overturned furniture and other signs of hurried departure. A lone lamp was burning in an alcove, a small statue of Osiris beside it. I was close by her side as she stopped beside an open trapdoor, gesturing us through and downward.

'Is it the blood-kilts?' I asked softly.

She nodded, not questioning how I knew about them.

'How many?'

'Just two,' she breathed. 'They followed me from Alexandria, but I thought I'd lost them. I'm so sorry, Chosen. I've led them straight to us.'

There was no time for apologies. There were crashing noises behind us. The door wouldn't hold much longer. I made a decision to test what Isis had told me.

'Get the lamp NOW,' I whispered. 'We can defeat them with fire.'

Immediately Iras was running into the next room. She grabbed the tiny lamp and a bundle of the papyrus reeds that were lying scattered all over the floor. Working quickly, she tore a piece off her tunic and wrapped it around them. Tipping some of the oil out of the lamp onto the makeshift torch, she touched the now flickering flame to it. It blazed up, burning fast. As soon as I saw what she was doing, I took off my veil and started tearing it into strips, bundling it around reeds. Charm did the same. Shadya, Corporal Geta and Warrior Sah were scrabbling for their own reeds and material.

Just as the last of the torches flared into life, there was a final thunderous crash.

Shadya gave me a push.

'No time,' she said. 'Down you go, Chosen. We'll hold them off for as long as we can. Alim is waiting with a boat at the end of the tunnel. Go! You at least must be safe. You're too important to lose.'

I had a brief flash of memory. Brave Sergeant Basa

standing at the door to my former palace apartment, guarding my back with just broken sticks and courage as I ran down the slave passages to safety. I would not run this time.

'No,' I said fiercely. 'No. We stand together and fight.'

It was too late anyway. The feeling of cold sickness within me intensified to a peak and then two of the undead horrors were in the room with us. One had a sliver of wood as long as my arm through his shoulder, a crippling wound on any mortal body. But he stalked forward, the brand of the foul demon above his heart scar, the other beside him. It was a woman, and the sight of her breasts hanging untrammelled and free, smeared with dirt and flakes of blue, was almost more shocking than anything else.

Iras darted forward, smashing her torch against the man's kilt, just as Shadya did the same to the woman's. The crisp linen flared and crackled, and then went out.

'Again!' I cried, surging forward with my torch held high. But Charm held me back.

'No, Cleo!'

I shook her off, stepping forward again, but my warriors were before me, whipping their torches at the kilts and then at the woman's hair.

'In the name of Isis, BURN!' I screamed, my torch-free hand pointing forward, fingers stiff, willing blue sparks to erupt. But none came.

Now Shadya had slipped round behind them, creeping

forward, trying to come on them unnoticed. With a crackle, and without any warning, both horrors erupted into columns of flame. The blood-kilted woman whirled, tripped and fell onto Shadya, clutching at her with hands limned with orange light.

'Come with me to Blessed Am-Heh's fire,' she croaked.

Shadya screamed and tried to roll away, but she was pinned and helpless. Within a blink, her clothing too was a ball of flame, then her hair went up in a roar of acrid, crackling sparks. The two undead bodies tore apart with a flash of darkness and disappeared with a smell of rot and flame, leaving Shadya shrieking in a high, thin wail as the horrible roast pork smell of burning human flesh filled the air.

Charm tore apart her bundle, and threw a robe towards Iras.

'Smother the fire, hurry,' she shouted. But as if time had slowed, I saw the sharp blade in Iras's hand, saw it plunge downwards through the flame and dart back, leaving a raw, red-spurting mouth where there had been none before.

The wailing cut off abruptly.

'No,' Charm gasped. 'Iras, why…?'

Iras got up and faced us, cradling her singed hand.

'She would not have survived the burns,' she said fiercely, wiping her blade clean. 'Better a quick death from a friend than a long-drawn-out agony. She would have done the same for me.' Moisture glistened on her cheek, but she didn't wipe it away. Instead she walked towards us. 'Come on,' she said, as she lowered herself through the trapdoor. Her voice was unnaturally steady. 'Down into the tunnel, all of you. Alim is waiting for us. We will tell him that his sister died bravely. She may have neither tomb nor grave goods, but Sobek will take her home. I know he will.'

The room was now full of choking smoke and flame. It was either do as Iras said or perish ourselves.

'She will have the blessing of Isis as well, when she stands before the scales,' I said, before I hurried down the ladder into the darkness. 'I will make sure of it.'

I had made that promise too many times before. Dennu, the lotus pot girl, the girl with blue flowers in her hair, Sergeant Basa, Mamo's brother, even Tryphena...too many deaths because of me. I felt the wetness on my own cheeks, but I dashed it away. I would not allow myself to weep with Iras. I would grieve when this was over. Because this would not be the only death in this war – of that I was horribly certain.

Alim's eyes went black and flat when Iras told him how and why his sister had died at her hand, and the air of danger around him magnified. He asked for an exact description of how to kill the blood-kilts, but after that he said not one word to any of us in the four slow days we took to reach the place where the army of the Ibis was encamped. None of us talked much, in truth. It was a cramped and uncomfortable journey, making our slow, tortuous way down narrow canals, and then sneaking and doubling back across what seemed like endless bits of country on foot to avoid notice, before we finally reached the marshes at the southern end of Lake Mareotis. I wasn't surprised to see a crowd of black-veiled marsh people materialise as if out of the damp, heavy air. Alim gestured to us.

'Take them to Nail,' he said, in a voice gone husky and difficult with disuse. 'I'm done here.'

Then he turned his back and began to walk away.

'Alim…' I said. I didn't know what to say, but I had to say something. He was too good a fighter to lose.

He rounded on me like a sand viper striking.

'Don't,' he said. 'Don't say anything about sacrifice or souls or Isis. She was my twin, and I loved her more than anything. More than Blessed Sobek, even. Now I'm going to avenge her by burning as many of those things as I can find before I die myself.'

'Stop!' I said, putting a Pharaoh's command behind that one word. Slowly, he turned, setting down his foot with a kind of hopeless deliberation.

'What?' he asked. 'What more have you to say to me, Chosen of Isis? Haven't you done enough already?'

'This,' I said, stepping forward and taking the strong, calloused hands which had fallen limp at his sides, as if that last word had taken all the energy out of him. 'Yes, you can go after them on your own and die if you want to. I know the anger you carry inside, Alim. I feel it too. My own sister has allowed these horrors to exist. Will you not fight them with me, with Iras, with Khai? However good a warrior you are, if you fight the blood-kilts alone they will take you – make you into one of them. Would Shadya really want that for you? Would Sobek?' I let my voice fall into gentleness. 'I know I don't.'

He wrenched his hands out of mine.

'I don't care,' he said flatly. 'I don't care about any of it.' Then he turned and walked away.

A black-veiled woman was in front of him before I had taken a single breath.

'Give me your tongue,' she snapped. He reared back in surprise.

'What?'

'Give me your tongue, Sobek's child. If you are captured, you will tell all. I will not risk my people or the Chosen's for one coward who deserts his commander. Give your tongue to me and I will cut it out.'

Suddenly I realised I knew that voice. It was Shoshan herself.

There were blades in both Alim's hands now, and he began to laugh like a hyena.

'Come and take it, then, eater of frogs!' he said, slicing the air as if he would cut a hole in the fabric of the world itself. And then they were fighting. I had never seen one of the marsh people in action before. Shoshan flowed like

333

water across a dry desert, here one minute and gone the next. But then, so did Alim. He was a crashing waterfall to her sinuous stream.

'Iras!' I said. 'Stop them.'

'No, Chosen,' she said. 'See – she is not trying to hurt him. She is giving him an outlet to express his grief.' The sorrow in her voice told me that she too wished she had such an outlet to express her own.

It was beautiful to watch, in a terrifying kind of way. But the conclusion was inevitable. Alim ended on his face in the mud, both arms twisted up behind his back, with Shoshan crouched on top of him like a malevolent black eagle. He turned his head to one side and spat.

'Nobody calls me a coward,' he growled.

'Then don't act like one, Sobek's child,' she said, climbing off him and offering a hand to help him up. 'Men fight and obey their orders. They don't run off at the first sign of trouble.'

Alim surged up.

'My sister *died*, curse you,' he yelled.

It was enough. I stepped forward.

'Do you think others have not lost sisters, brothers, mothers, fathers already?' I asked hotly. 'Do you think there won't be more deaths before the end? This is a *war*, Alim. And we win it together or not at all.'

I looked at him down my curved Ptolemy nose and waited.

He stared back for a moment, then dropped his eyes.

'I suppose I do get what Khai sees in you,' he muttered. 'Very well, Chosen. I will stay. But you'd better have a *lot* of torches ready for me. Those things are going to die in flames.'

Shoshan and her people led us deep into the marsh, and then out into the lake itself in a flotilla of little reed boats which wobbled at the slightest movement. I learned from her that the army of the Ibis was now encamped on the large island within the lake itself.

'We encouraged the current inhabitants to join us,' she said, with a flash of teeth. 'They started to believe in Isis's cause and open their storehouses almost as soon as we pointed out to them that death was always another option available to them. My people have been making boats since you left us, Chosen. We have enough to land everyone at the gates of Alexandria itself.'

'Thank you,' I said. 'You have fulfilled the command of our goddess. She will be pleased.'

Shoshan unfolded her palm and looked down at the mark I had put there with the fire of Isis.

'It will be fulfilled when the false Pharaoh is thrown down, and her consort with her,' she said. 'And it won't be easy. Khai says there are more blood-kilts on the streets every night, and they're spreading to other places now. The city is emptying fast. Soon there will be none to unload the harvest – and none left to eat it but the mercenaries and Khai's street rats.'

'I will be interested to hear his report,' I said, trying to keep my voice even and calm. 'I assume he will be coming to give it to me in person.'

Shoshan chuckled, looking at me sideways.

'He's been here since dawn yesterday, fretting that you hadn't arrived yet. Who do you think set up a network of watchers at every port, Chosen? Once he'd confirmed we'd heard your warning too, he was busier than a fish laying eggs.'

A rush of pride warmed my bones. He was indeed my king of spies. Then the warmth turned to heat. He was here. I would see him. But I knew I wouldn't be able to greet him as I really wanted to. Shoshan had used the word 'commander'. I would have to act like one and put my personal feelings aside until we could be alone. I would have to be a Pharaoh now.

We landed at a wharf just below a low hill at the western end of the island around mid-afternoon, with the Eye of Ra riding high in a clear blue sky. There were troops everywhere, all wearing Isis's sign on shield and tunic. Even though I was muddied and crumpled from travelling, I tried to walk among them as a future Pharaoh would, straight and as tall as I could manage. Each face I saw was filled with purpose, and they bowed down before me. Soon I could hear the whispers all around me like desert wind.

Cleopatra Chosen is with us.

Praise be to Isis.

Praise be to Sobek.

As I approached the large white villa which Shoshan told me served as a command post, the whispers rose to a roar, and I saw the uphill path was lined with yet more troops, banging the hilts of their spears against their shields. It was awe-inspiring. They were all here for me, for Isis, for Sobek. For the first time, I really felt that we might be able to topple Berenice and her foul consort. For the first time I actually felt like a Pharaoh. These people were my responsibility. I would not let them down.

At the top of the steps, I saw General Nail together with a crowd of people I didn't recognise. But I only had eyes for one face – a face with deep brown eyes dark as Delta mud, and skin the colour of burnt honey; a face with a curved nose and slightly chapped lips that I wanted to run my finger over immediately. All that was missing was the hair. Khai's head was still shaved as smooth as a kite's egg.

I couldn't do as I wanted and run to him, so I tried to let my eyes do the talking for me. One corner of his lip quirked with the familiar dimple and he inclined his head a bare fraction.

I turned to face my army knowing he had understood, and raised my palms to them in a Pharaoh's blessing. They cheered me so hard that I feared Berenice would hear it all the way up the lake. I held up a hand and spoke to them.

'Save your energy for the battle ahead, my warriors of the Ibis. It will come soon enough.' Then I went inside and called a council of war.

It didn't go quite as I had hoped.

'Pharaohs don't lead their troops from the front,' General Nail said stubbornly, right after I'd told him of my intention to kill Archelaus. 'You're not trained as a fighter. You must stay here where it is safe, Chosen. Where you can be protected. Surely one of us can kill the demon?'

If it hadn't been unPharaoh-like to stamp my foot, I would have done it. Instead, I just gripped the edge of the sand table we were leaning over a little tighter. There was a rough but recognisable map of Alexandria's main streets and the palace on it, with the lake, the coastline and the Great Green outlined in black around it. Differently coloured glazed pottery counters represented the army of the Ibis; Khai, Shoshan and Merit's people, and our foes in the palace. Pharos Island was a sea of enemy red. Khai had found out that the false Pharaohs were almost permanently based in the temple they had stolen from my goddess – and that the Pharos itself ran with the blood of sacrifice. The only good thing about that was that now I knew where to find them.

'My father and the Romans will land near the east of the city in a few days,' I said, reaching for a green counter and placing it out in the sea. At least, they would if all went to plan. 'If we do nothing before then, we risk Berenice and

Archelaus taking more sacrifices, and making a bigger undead army than we can handle. From what Khai has told us, those blood-kilts may be untrained, but they are strong, and they'll keep on going even with a spear in the guts. We have to begin to move against the false Pharaohs by tomorrow night at the latest. I don't want them to sacrifice any more of our people than I can help.'

'But, surely, now that we know the blood-kilts can die by burning, we can—'

I interrupted General Nail ruthlessly.

'Yes. But we risk setting the city on fire if we draw them out from the Pharos and start throwing blazing torches around. My father won't thank me for returning him to a throne of ashes. We need to hit them at their source. I am the only one of us protected by a goddess. I must go with you to Pharos Island to find the demon, and destroy his mortal body. Isis herself has commanded it.'

General Nail's jaw tightened in a familiar way.

'Pardon me for saying so, Chosen, but you are the most stubborn woman I have ever met.'

I aimed my most charming smile at him.

'Why, General,' I said, 'I take that as a great compliment, coming from you. I'm quite sure you yourself were born of a long line of stubborn women.'

Khai leaned forwards.

'She'll go whether you like it or not, Nail,' he said. 'I've protected her before, and I'll do it again. Merit and her priestesses are in the city too. They're lethal with those wrist knives now, and my street rats are ready to rise as soon as I give the word.'

'I'll be with her as well,' said Iras. 'Sobek himself appointed me as the Chosen's protector.'

'And me,' said Alim, looking grim and more dangerous than ever.

Corporal Geta stepped forward.

'Me and Warrior Sah have come this far with our Chosen, sir,' he said. 'We'd appreciate it if we could finish the job.'

'That's settled, then,' I said, blinking hard as my eyes threatened to overflow again. 'I will have more protectors surrounding me than Isis herself. All you have to do is get me to Archelaus, and burn the blood-kilts where it will do least harm. After that you'll only have the city guard and the mercenaries to deal with – and hopefully my father and the Romans will have arrived by then.'

Khai looked at me, his face sombre and full of pain.

'Those Ra-cursed blood-kilts tried to storm the temple of Serapis two nights ago – where we're hiding the youngest of the street-rat children. Merit and I couldn't stop them snatching a few of our younglings right out from under our noses.'

I laid two fingers gently on his wrist. It was as much as I could allow myself. 'We'll save as many as we can, Khai,' I said, as his shoulders slumped. I knew he felt the weight of each of those young deaths as a personal failure. Because there was no doubt that they would be dead now, sacrificed on the bloodstained altars of Am-Heh's ambition.

He straightened again, cleared his throat and continued, walking over to General Nail and pointing on the map to a gate marker at the west of the city.

'The most urgent thing is to take the Moon Gate here and the fort near the Heptastadion, and get our troops in,' he said. 'If we hold that side of the city, we can burn any new blood-kilts that come across the causeway, and any that try to return there – and it gives us a good base to storm the temple and Pharos from. We'll have to leave the Gate of Helios side of the city to the Romans when they come.'

General Nail sighed and started drawing arrows in the sand with his finger. Like every good soldier, he knew when he was beaten.

'Very well, then. Your street rats will overpower the sentries and let us in, Khai. We'll use the pincer movement we planned earlier and attack the fort from both land and sea.' He turned to Shoshan. 'You and I will lead. Start readying the boats, and make sure every squad of soldiers carries oil-soaked torches and a firepot. We'll come up the lake in darkness and attack before dawn the day after tomorrow. If we attack from two sides, it will confuse them.' He fixed me with a stern look that had a hint of pleading in it.

'Chosen, if you insist on coming, we will work out the

best way to keep you safe until the last minute. I will not risk you further than I absolutely have to. I would rather burn in Am-Heh's fire myself than see you hurt.'

He allowed no time for me to argue, but started rapping out orders, pointing to the map and moving counters here and there, stabbing a thumb into the sand for emphasis. I had definitely promoted the right man to head up my army. My former captain was taking to the generalling business like a river horse to water.

We discussed plans late into the night until all of us were dropping with tiredness. I covered a large yawn with my hand, but my general noticed. He noticed everything, I had found. Beckoning one of the soldiers, he ordered the man to take me to my quarters. Then he looked at me.

'Get some rest, Chosen. I thought you might like to address the troops tomorrow. Like you did at Crocodilopolis.'

It was a good idea. It was what a Pharaoh should do.

'Gather them on the hill just before sunset, then,' I said, before following the soldier out.

It would not be quite the same as at Crocodilopolis, of course. This time I would be taking Isis's army with me to fight and, if necessary, die – against opponents who were already dead.

I swallowed past the sudden icy lump of fear in my throat.

19

The Broken Jar

In the small, hastily prepared chamber I'd been taken to, Charm wrestled my pack open, pulling out the linen robes I'd had made in Rome. Iras had gone to talk to the soldiers of Sobek, and I'd dismissed my two warriors earlier to go and rest. If I wasn't safe here, I wouldn't be safe anywhere.

'These all smell of smoke and river,' she said, shaking one out and wrinkling her nose. 'How am I ever to get them washed and dried in time for tomorrow?'

'Don't worry about it, O Queen of Cleaning,' I said absently, staring out of the window. It faced north-west and I could see the roaring flare of the Pharos burning brightly in the far distance, with the city silhouetted against it. Now that I looked closely, I could see it burned an unnatural brownish-red instead of its usual clear yellow-white, and a column of black smoke obscured the familiar flash of the golden statue of Zeus at its summit. I shuddered, knowing that even now, there might be the blood of sacrifice running down its three hundred steps.

Soon, Isis, I promised silently. *I will stop it soon.*

In contrast, the stars were very bright in the sky, and Thoth swung lazily inside the curve of the crescent moon. Would we really be able to take the throne back? Could we really defeat Am-Heh's unnatural army? I needed to talk to Khai in detail about how exactly we were going to sneak up on Archelaus and kill him, but he had stayed in the war room to go over the fine details. I tried not to mind. Of course he needed to know what all Shoshan and Nail's plans were, and to coordinate his own with them. That was what a good leader did.

Was I a good leader? I remembered what Isis had said. This was both my punishment and my testing ground. The gods would not step in. I would have to find out on my own whether I was fit to rule my people.

'Do you think I can do it?' I asked Charm abruptly.

'Do what?' she asked.

'Take the throne. Be Pharaoh. Lead an army. Defeat my sister. Kill the demon.' My fingertips pressed hard into the cool white marble until they matched it for colour and temperature. I felt two arms go round my waist and squeeze hard.

'Of course you can,' she said. 'You are Cleopatra the Brave, Cleopatra the Chosen of Isis. Didn't you hear them cheering you today? You should believe in yourself more.'

'But what if I can't, Charm? What if I let the gods down?'

She moved her hands to my shoulders and gave me a little shake.

'Stop it,' she said. 'You faced Am-Heh down once – and Seth too. You can do it again. Remember, you're not alone. You have Khai, and all Merit's Sisters of the Living Knot, and your warriors and Alim and Iras – and two whole Ra-blessed armies as well until your father gets here, and then it'll be three.'

'And you,' I reminded her.

'And me,' she said, but her voice was suddenly trembling. I turned to look at her.

'What?' I said, seeing the tears on her cheeks. She wiped them away with the backs of her hands, fanning them in front of her face.

'Nothing. I'm being stupid.'

'What?' I asked again. She wasn't fooling me. There was something big behind those tears.

'Oh, Hathor curse it, I promised Iras I wouldn't do the crying thing,' she said, half-laughing. 'You know me too well, Cleo. It's just…I don't know how to tell you this any other way than straight. I'm not coming with you to Alexandria.' I opened my mouth to protest, but she held up a damp hand. 'No, Cleo, let me finish. I'm not a fighter. I'd just be in the way and both you and Iras would be worrying about me. I *won't* be a distraction. I can't. What if Berenice takes me like Tryphena did? I'm your weak side, Cleo, and

I know it.' She looked at me, biting her lip to stop it trembling.

I wished I didn't understand. But I did. I folded my best friend in my arms.

'You are my strongest side, dear one. You always have been. But you're right. I won't risk you again. It will make both me and Iras stronger, knowing you are safe.'

She nodded, sniffing.

'I will be on my knees to Isis and Sobek and every other god there is, begging them to keep both of you safe, every minute you are away,' she said.

'You will be a veritable Princess of Praying,' I said. 'Let's just hope Isis at least is listening.'

There was a soft knock at the door.

'Who is it?' I called, before remembering that a Pharaoh should probably let someone else do that.

Charm went to the door and opened it a crack, then she turned to me.

'I think you'll want to let this one in,' she said. 'I'll just go and check on Iras. I may be some time. Possibly all night. Remember to be careful like I told you!' With a stern shake of her finger and that irrepressible giggle of hers, she swung through the door, pushing the person outside through into the room before closing it with a distinct click of the latch.

It was Khai.

We stared at each other awkwardly for a moment.

'Cleo…'

'Khai…' We both spoke in unison. Then he laughed.

'Look at us both. Shy as if we'd never met before.' He took a step towards me, and then I was in his arms. He no longer smelled of ink and papyrus, but that unique Khai-scent was still there. I buried my nose in his neck.

'I missed you,' I mumbled. 'Every minute of every day.'

His arms tightened around me.

'I missed you too, my Chosen. And the times you came to me and I couldn't touch you made me miss you more.' He hesitated. 'I wish…'

My heart began to thump even harder than it was already, banging against my ribs like a bird against a cage. What did he wish?

'I wish your dream gift didn't always come when I'm in danger. I wish it could be like the old days – when you were in Philäe. At least then, even if we were apart, we could be together all night without interruptions. I know Isis didn't let me remember much of it then, but…'

He was babbling and I knew I should probably stop him. I knew I should make a final plan with him on how to kill Archelaus. I knew I should be responsible, sensible, Pharaoh-like. I glanced over at the bed and made my decision, putting one finger to his lips, hushing the flood of words. I was absolutely calm and absolutely certain.

'Now is what's important, Khai. You and me, together, here. We should make the most of it…in case we don't get another chance.' I stared into those beautiful dark eyes, and saw myself reflected in them. I swallowed hard, and said what I really meant. 'In case one of us dies in battle.'

For one agonisingly blissful moment he just held me and we stared at each other, relearning each other's features with our eyes. I'd imagined us being together for so long, imagined his body loving mine, mine loving his, wanted his kisses to wipe out the touch of the man I'd successfully blocked from my mind for days. But at the thought of the decurion it was as if my lips took on a life of their own.

'A man kissed me,' I blurted out. 'A Roman. I didn't mean him to. I didn't want him to. I'm so sorry, Khai. It just happened.'

I felt the long muscles either side of his spine tense under my hand, and I heard that strange clicking, shuttling sound in my head again. Oh, no! What had I done? Why had I told him? Had I just moved another thread of fate on Shai's immortal loom?

The calmness of a moment before left me, and I began to cry, all the fear and tension of the time we'd been parted bubbling up inside me. It was my turn for broken, incoherent words to spill from my lips, making not one iota of sense.

I wept and snuffled until I was drained and empty, and the shoulder of Khai's tunic was soaked dark with my tears. Through it all, his arms held me close, curved around me like a haven of safety.

When I had come to a choking, snivelling halt, he stroked my hair, then put a hand on either side of my face, making me look at him. His eyes were calm and steady, and I thought I saw a new and unwanted regret in them.

'I shouldn't have said all that, earlier. It was wrong of me. Selfish. I've thought a lot since you've been away, Cleo,' he said, all trace of babbling gone now. 'Whether you give me rank or not, you're going to be Pharaoh with your father. You and I...' He paused, running a hand over his scalp in that familiar gesture I loved, fingers blindly searching for the hair that was no longer there. 'You and I will never be ordinary lovers. We'll never have the happy ever after that normal people do.'

I made a convulsive gesture of denial, but he lowered his hand. It was his turn to put a finger against my lips.

'Hush. You know it's true, Cleo. The throne and Egypt must come first for you, not me.' I saw the muscles in his throat move as he swallowed. 'This Roman,' he said tightly. 'Is he an important man?'

I wriggled free. Important? What had that to do with anything?

'Why?' I burst out. 'Why would you ask me that? No. He's not important. He's just a decurion.' Again, that shuttling noise in my head.

'But there will be other important men,' Khai said. He was the calm, certain one now. 'You will need to make alliances. You will need to ensure the stability of your reign by making a marriage of state. You cannot do that with a scribe at your side, however high his rank becomes.' His voice was matter of fact.

Each sensible word stabbed me, deflating me like a burst water skin.

'Don't you love me any more, then?' I said in a small voice. 'Is that what all this is about?'

There was a moment of tense silence, like the quiet before a storm. Then he stepped forward, grabbing my upper arms. A dark tide of red rose in his face.

'Of course I love you, stupid girl,' he roared, giving me a tiny shake to punctuate every word. 'But I'm trying to be…'

'Trying to be what?' I snapped, anger and hurt welling in me like a tide as I stepped back, shoving him hard in the chest so that he let go of me. 'By all the stars, Khai, you're being so noble you make my teeth ache. I know I'll have to make alliances. I'm not stupid. But it's you I want. You I love. I told you before. We'll work this out. We'll be together even if it kills me.'

'How?' he spat at me. 'I told *you* before too. I won't be the Pharaoh's lapdog again.'

I let out a scream of frustration.

'Do you really think I'd do that to you? Do you really think I'd have you sitting at my feet like Tryphena did, for all the court to jeer at? Do you think so little of my love for you that you compare me to my *sister*?' I spun on my heel, picked up a pottery wine jar and flung it at his head. It missed, shattering on the wall in a shower of shards and purple spray, so I picked up the cups beside it and flung them too.

'I'm naming you my vizier right now, Khai,' I shouted. 'Do you understand me? I may not be Pharaoh yet, but I'm making that the first edict of my reign. See, I'm even signing it.' I marched over to the wall, and, dipping my finger in the dripping wine, began to write.

There was a small silence as he looked at the words on the damp plaster.

So be it.

The traditional phrase a Pharaoh used to sign an official document of state, and then the cartouche of my name, with one small addition. The number seven. Because I would be the seventh Cleopatra to reign.

I didn't even see him move. His lips were on mine before I could draw a breath, and then heat flared between us, hotter and sweeter than ever before. His hands shaped me as mine shaped him; the hard, muscled slope of back and thigh; the soft curve of breast and hip; backwards, always backwards towards the bed.

'Isis help me, I tried,' he mumbled, nibbling at my upper lip in a way that stole the breath right out of my mouth. 'As she is my witness, I tried to do the right thing, Cleo…but I've wanted you for so long. I can't…' His voice was low and husky with longing.

I clasped my hands at the back of his neck and pulled

him down on top of me, feeling the faintest prickle of stubble under my palms, feeling the weight and heat of him settle along my whole body as if it was designed by our goddess herself to fit there.

'This is the right thing,' I murmured, pressing my nose into his neck again so that all I could smell was him. I would not let the threat of any future alliance steal this moment from me. Lying with Khai was my choice and I would take my newly appointed vizier as my first lover, knowing everything I risked, with both hands. Even if I died tomorrow, even if I never became Pharaoh and had to answer for my sins before the scales of Osiris, this one night would be worth every punishment the gods could throw at me in the afterlife.

I stood on top of the low hill at sunset and felt as if Ra's pink glow was reflected in my own body. I was dressed all in white, with the golden knot of my goddess at my breast. I shone like a star both within and without. Isis herself had never burned so bright.

General Nail had gathered my army below. They stood in steady, disciplined ranks, and the silver of their shields and spear tips was washed in Ra's red flame. Every eye was on me, and the air was still, holding its breath.

'Warriors of the Ibis,' I began. 'There is evil abroad in this beloved land of ours.' I swept a hand to my left, where the Pharos once more flared sullen brown-red in the sky above Alexandria. 'The blood-kilts of the Burnt-souled Dead stalk the streets of our royal city. There are false Pharaohs on the Double Throne of Egypt. The balance of all things is broken and disturbed. It is up to other Pharaohs to put things right. My father, the mighty Ptolemy, will bring the legions of Rome across the Great Green Sea to join us. Soon the army Vizier Khai has gathered will rise from the city streets to help us too. Together we will crush this threat to dust and ash.'

I lowered my voice so that they all strained forward to hear, and I shaded my eyes, looking at them, turning my head back and forth as I surveyed their ranks.

'Only the bravest men and women will do,' I said softly. 'Only those who are prepared to lay down their lives in defence of the gods will pass the test. And make no mistake – this test will be the hardest any of us have ever faced.' I raised my voice again, and let the full power of my goddess's gift ring out over their heads, spilling out of my mouth like cream and honey over a steel blade.

'Do I see the bravest and the best before me now? Shall we defeat the false Pharaoh and her vile demon god and throw them down? Is my army ready?'

As one, their fists pumped into the air, then came down on their shields with a sound like crashing boulders in a flood.

'AYE!' went up the shout.

'Then we leave for Alexandria before tomorrow dawns!'

I cried. As I said it, I felt myself lifted high into the air and settled onto strong male shoulders.

'CHOSEN!' shouted the shoulder on my left. It was Corporal Geta.

'CHOSEN!' shouted the shoulder on my right. It was Warrior Sah.

'CHOSEN!' shouted General Nail and Iras and Charm and Alim. Then it was a wave of sound, travelling through the ranks, spreading like wind through grass, like thunder through a clear blue sky.

'CHOSEN!' shouted the army of the Ibis.

I felt the power of it shake my bones.

Surely even the gods would hear.

'Vizier?' Charm asked, as she helped me into a tightly belted tunic the colour of dusk. 'You made Spy Boy a vizier?' She looked at me sideways. 'When did that happen? I thought you'd have had other things on your mind than titles.'

I blushed, still feeling that hot glow in my body, remembering long, slow caresses on my bare skin. My new vizier had left me at dawn, kissing both my closed eyelids with a slow passion that nearly made me pull him back into the bed. But he murmured that Charm and Iras wouldn't be gone forever, and so I'd snuggled into the warm hollow his body had left in the narrow bed and gone back to sleep, before waking late to face another session of military planning, and of working out what I was going to say to the troops.

I knew Charm would be cross with me for ignoring her warning. We had not been very careful at all, though Khai had tried his best to protect me. And once she found the bloodied sheet I'd hurriedly stuffed under the bed she would know for certain what he and I had done. It would be too late for her to scold me once I'd left, though.

'His head will swell to the size of a gourd,' Iras said, grinning, as she handed me a pair of sheathed razor-sharp daggers to thread onto my belt, and knelt to lace my sandals more tightly to my feet. 'No one will be able to live with his pride.'

'I made him vizier last night,' I said, ignoring both the blush, and the words that were still clearly written on the wall. 'Even if I cannot have him beside me on the throne, I *will* have him behind it. Now my whole army knows. It cannot be undone.'

'And what will your father the Pharaoh say, O Great Granter of Titles?' Charm asked, braiding my hair and pinning it to my head so closely that no stray curl could escape.

'My father the Pharaoh is a tiny bit intimidated by my close relationship with Isis,' I said lightly. 'If he complains, I'll just drop another blue spark on him.' I inspected my fingertips doubtfully. 'If I still can, that is.'

Those fair winds bringing us to Egypt had been the last

thing Isis or any of the gods would give me until Berenice was overthrown. I knew that as if it was written on the faint breeze that scuffed the surface of the lake.

The boats began to leave the island soon after midnight, each poled by one of Shoshan's people. After he had left me, Khai had gone straight back to Alexandria to rouse the street rats and alert Merit to our plan of attack. The bulk of the army of the Ibis would creep into the west of the city at dawn. Led by Nail and Shoshan, they would break through the Moon Gate and take the fort by the Heptastadion, then converge on Pharos Island. The street-rat army would raise barricades, set booby traps and generally hinder and cause mayhem among the mercenaries and city guards who would be pouring out of every barracks when the fighting started. They were to avoid the blood-kilts, though, as their job was to draw attention away from me and my small party. We would first make for the temple of Serapis to meet Khai and Merit, before sneaking up the canal to join Nail and Shoshan at the fort when we received a message to say it was safe to do so. Then, with our backs guarded, we would march up the Heptastadion and storm the temple and the Pharos. That was the basic plan at least.

'So many senet pieces,' I muttered, as the small boat slid silently through the water. I felt a hand grip my shoulder.

'Just enough to defeat the enemy,' Iras whispered.

In the starlight and faint glow of the crescent moon,

I saw boats breaking away in front. Our own two boats curved left, following them for a while, then hung back, waiting to let them get ahead of us and a good way onto land before we entered the lake canal.

Oh, Isis, I prayed as the moon sank lower and lower in the sky. *I know you can't help me openly, but please. Keep as many of them as you can safe.*

I felt the weight of responsibility for so many lives as I never had before. For all my fine words to the army, I didn't feel at all like their commander-in-chief. Had great Alexander felt like this before his first battle as leader? Had his belly roiled, his skin prickled, his limbs felt like they had lead weights attached, his heart beaten faster than a stick on a hide drum? I sent a prayer up to him as well. If anyone could help me with courage, it would be my martial ancestor.

Then it was time. The reed boats crept on and on over the silent water, silken ripples arrowing out from their prows. Now I could just see a small forest of masts in the port of the lake, silhouetted against the star-spattered sky like bare-branched trees. We were close.

My heart tried to force its way up into my throat as I fought to keep my breath slow and even. A true Pharaoh would not show fear. I must not either. A sudden horrible, fetid smell of rot and night soil slid into my nostrils, making me want to clap a hand to my mouth and nose. Alexandria had never smelled perfect, but this was worse than a pack of week-old dead dogs in a midden. I tried not to choke on it as the blank-faced houses on either side of the lake canal began to hem us in, narrowing the stars to a strip of sky above us and shutting out the sinking crescent moon entirely. The minute we had crossed the boundary from lake to city, I began to feel cold all over in patches, and I knew as if Isis herself had shouted it in my ear that this was a warning. I had felt the same when the blood-kilts came at us in Canopus, but now the feeling ebbed and flowed strangely. Chill, chill, chill, ice. Chill, ice, chill, moving both within my body and outside it. Then, as we passed under a bridge, I heard the far-off clash of weapons, screams, ululations, and then saw a roar of sparks up ahead, which blinded my precious night vision. Nail and Shoshan's troops must be attacking the Moon Gate. Or maybe they were through already and at the fort. I couldn't tell in the confusion of darkness.

As we rounded the third bend, a small light flashed. Once, twice, pause. Once, twice, pause. Once, twice, pause.

'That's the signal,' I breathed softly, but Alim was before me, opening his small thieves' lantern in reply. The boat bumped the side of the canal, and then he was swarming out and up onto dry land, almost invisible.

A young voice came out of the darkness, softer than a dove's coo.

'Hail to the Chosen.' And then, as Alim gave the response, I was out too, pushed up by Iras as the boat rocked dangerously. Almost as soon as I found my feet, the boat was replaced by another, and my two warriors were beside me as well.

'Come,' Alim whispered. 'The youngling will guide us. Khai and Merit are waiting.'

We slipped through the dark streets and alleys in single file. I could feel a growing knot of cold to my left, moving away from me to where I thought Shoshan was. Other, further-away knots, were moving south and east, away from the centre. I tried not to think about what my army was facing. I had to focus on finding Archelaus and destroying him.

Abruptly, the body in front of me stopped, and I nearly crashed into it as Iras's hand pulled me into the shelter of an alley. The tramp of at least ten sets of marching feet was suddenly close, and I flattened my back against a mud wall, feeling crumbling bits of loose clay work free and patter on my heels and down my neck. I loosened the dagger at my waist and tried not to breathe as Iras and Alim pressed up close beside me, guarding me with their bodies.

'I can't see a Seth-cursed thing,' said a voice in the street outside. 'Why can't we have torches, sarge?'

'No torches,' a harsh Nubian voice replied. 'Pharaoh's orders. The blessed blood-kilts don't like them, apparently. Don't worry, soldier – it'll be dawn soon.'

There was a hawking sound, and a wet splat.

'Pharaoh's orders?' said the first voice. 'Consort's orders, more like. Nothing's gone right since he appeared. All the bread in the kitchens rotted yesterday. I had green mould for my breakfast.'

There was another wet sound, a gurgle and a thud, as of a body falling, then scrabbling sounds, like heels kicking on the earth.

'Any of the rest of you want a taste of that?' said the harsh voice. 'Or would you prefer to be given to the black priests? They're running short of sacrifices up at the lighthouse, I hear.'

Murmured responses reached my ears.

'Then march, you misbegotten sons of jackal dung. There's trouble up by the fort. The gold is good. We don't question the bosses. We don't interfere with the priests or the blessed blood-kilts. You know the rules.'

The tramp of feet resumed for a little while, before a chorus of surprised male shouts, pained groans and then a series of splashes came to my ears from a short distance away. Khai's street rats were in action.

I had never considered feeling even a little bit sorry for my sister's mercenaries before. Now I wondered how many of them were as committed to her as they seemed – and whether we could use that against them. Perhaps I was beginning to think like a general after all, though what practical use this thought could be put to right now, I didn't know.

We met nobody else. Our progress was painfully slow

and cautious, but apart from the muffled sounds of fighting far off, the city was as quiet and dead as a mausoleum. Every shutter and door was barred, and I could almost feel the fear seeping out from within each house.

Just before dawn broke, we crept into the temple of Serapis, our guide having given the agreed signal. Once in, I saw that the back of the temple was cram-full with small sleeping bodies. Four armed sisters paced before the barricaded main gate, along with a squad of warriors and priests of Serapis. There was a stack of torches and a large amphora of oil ready next to a glowing brazier. A lone lamp flickered in front of the large golden statue of Serapis which gazed out, bearded face impassive under its laurel wreath. There was a smell of rot and flame in the air, which I had last smelled in Canopus. I glanced round, made uneasy by the unmistakeable scent of dead blood-kilt. Where was Merit? Where was Khai? And then the door of the sanctuary opened.

'Hurry, Chosen,' came Merit's familiar high, cold voice. 'There is one here who would speak with you before death takes her.'

20

The Burnt-souled Dead

I almost didn't recognise Cabar at first. One of her eyes was now a pit of unhealed tissue, and four of the fingers on her left hand were missing the top joint. She had fresh scars on her cheeks, similar to those on Merit's. What little I could see of her body was mottled with old bruises, and her left arm had shards of bloody white bone poking through, one at the forearm, one at the wrist. Her belly was a bloody mess. I knew she couldn't live long.

I went to her, dropping to my knees by the rough pallet where she lay.

'Chosen,' she whispered, through teeth that were either knocked out or broken off. 'Poison...in my pack...green bottle...it will...' She broke off, gasping with pain. I put a hand on her shoulder and stroked it.

'What about the poison, Cabar?' I asked, keeping my voice very soft.

'Got it…for you. Your weapons. Coat only the tip. It will kill with one nick. No antidote.' Her right hand squeezed mine hard. 'Use it on his embalmers. His priests. Him. It will kill his human body. Our goddess…g-gifted me with vision.' She moaned, high and full of pain, then began to thrash back and forth. 'Isis. Isis, take me. Don't let them hurt me any more.'

I drew myself away gently and stood over her. I was full of an icy determination. My goddess could not, must not deny me now. I raised my palms to the sky.

'Blessed Isis,' I said aloud, not allowing my voice to tremble. 'Lady of gentleness and mercy, mother of us all. Take the soul of your servant Cabar into your hands. Stand by her at the scales of judgement.'

As the silver form of Cabar's *ka* rose from her lips, I saw the door to the afterlife open, saw jackal-headed Anubis stretch out a hand, welcoming her. And then my goddess reached around his shoulder and drew Cabar into her arms. As the door snapped shut, one small, bright blue spark drifted downwards and landed where Cabar's mortal heart had just stopped beating.

I met Merit's eyes and saw a silver tear fall on her spiderweb scars. I reached out with my thumb to brush it away, but she moved back impatiently, shaking her head.

'No time to cry, Chosen,' she said. 'We cannot waste the gift she gave her life to bring us.' She bent to Cabar's body and drew the thin sheet up over her face. 'It is not Cabar who concerns us now, but the demon and how to kill him.' She drew out a small pack from beside Cabar's body. 'The demon's priests tortured her when she refused to renounce Isis, but she escaped, and brought us valuable information. Then she had the vision and insisted that she sneaked back into that devil's pit to get this.' She handed me a small green glass bottle and nodded towards the gate. 'The blood-kilts caught up with her just outside. We burned them, but it was too late. Her body had taken too much damage in the fight. Just before you came, she told us that Berenice stays permanently in the Pharos to oversee the sacrifices, but that the demon is below the temple, in the room which used to be our sanctuary.' She gave me the cold look I remembered, but I recognised the passionate hatred for Am-Heh simmering underneath. 'Cabar wanted to atone. To make up for what happened in our goddess's temple.' There was a pause. 'As do I.'

I remembered what Isis had said.

All here have rejected me and embraced the demon – except for two.

I knew now who she had meant.

Khai was at my side now, and he nodded, his face grim.

'She was the bravest of the brave,' he said. 'We will avenge her.'

I looked at Merit, who was twisting her wrist knives in a purposeful fashion, her lips drawn back in an unconscious snarl.

'You will not sacrifice yourself deliberately,' I said, knowing exactly what she was thinking without having to be told. 'I don't care how much shame you feel. Isis still needs you. I still need you. And so does the sisterhood. You have a job to do, Merit. Neither Isis nor Iusaaset will allow you to shirk it.'

She met my gaze, and just for an instant there was more pain in her eyes than I'd ever seen before in anyone.

'Why didn't I act sooner?' she asked, her voice a bitter lashing. 'I knew they had lost their way. I just didn't know how far they'd gone in betraying our goddess. Cabar tried to warn me, but I didn't listen. I was too busy. Too important. Too arrogant. Sobek made me look at myself in his mirror. I have failed Isis. I have failed everyone.' She stroked the new scars on her cheeks. 'See these? Cabar and I marked each other so that all would know our shame.'

I went to stand in front of her.

'Enough, Merit,' I said sharply. I was the one in charge here, not her, and I wouldn't allow her to chastise herself any longer. 'None of that matters now. What is done is done. The traitors chose their path, and they have been punished. Their souls are lost and there is nothing any of us can do about it except to kill the demon who led them astray.'

The coldness was back in her face now, and the pain was shuttered away as if it had never been.

'As you wish, Chosen. I am at your command.'

Khai was bending to listen to a skinny boy who had just entered the room. Standing upright again, he dismissed the lad with a pat on the shoulder and a word of thanks.

'We have to go now, my Chosen. Riaz here has just brought word. The fort is ours. But we must hurry. Some of the barricades are down, and the mercenaries are scuttling like weevils out of every barracks across the city. It will be hard to contain them.' He looked at me, lips suddenly thin with strain.

'Are you sure you should come, my Chosen? It will be—

I interrupted him before he had a chance to say any more.

'I don't care how dangerous it is, I will fight beside my army and die with them if I have to.'

I took his hand, not caring who else was in the room, who else saw, and lowered my voice to a whisper. 'I will fight and die beside you, my Khai, my vizier, my love. Whatever danger we face, we face it together or not at all.' He brought my hand to his lips, pressing them against it and giving me a look I knew I would treasure for the rest of my days. Then suddenly he was all decisiveness. He turned to face Merit and the rest of our little band.

'I have runners on nearly every street corner and hidden in every alley and on every rooftop all the way up to the Kibotos harbour. If we take the canal again, we will be warned of any danger long before it is near, and can take evasive action. The citizens have all been told to keep inside and bar all doors and windows until the city is won or lost.'

'What about the children here?' I asked.

'This is the safest place for them. It is guarded by fifteen of our most able sisters, and twenty warriors,' Merit replied. 'We are prepared. Not one more child will die as a sacrifice if I can help it.'

'Then we should go.' I said. 'If Riaz is right, Shoshan and Nail have the fort and maybe even the causeway by now. If anyone gets lost or separated, they should head there.' Then I looked round at everyone, fixing each familiar face in my memory. Merit, Iras, Sa, Geta, Alim…and Khai.

'Whatever happens, whatever we face next, the most important thing is to kill Archelaus and destroy his body. If one of us falls, the rest carry on.' I cleared a sudden lump in my throat. 'But I don't want any of us to fall. Each one of you is precious to me, so be careful and guard each other's backs.'

I squared my shoulders and took a step, then realised I didn't know where we were going, so I gestured towards Khai, making it look deliberate.

'Lead on, my vizier,' I said, but Iras raised her hand and pointed to the green bottle I still held clutched in my hand.

'You should use that on your weapons, Cleo Blue-Eyes. We all should.'

I wanted to kick myself. How could I have forgotten Cabar's poison, so dearly bought?

We each dipped the tip of our weapons gingerly in the

viscous white liquid in the green bottle, being careful not to get even the tiniest drop on ourselves. Then Merit jammed the stopper in the glass neck and stowed it in the tiny pouch at her waist. The wrist knives glinted, sharp and dangerous as her hands moved, checking that the now-poisoned daggers in her belt were sheathed securely.

'Just in case I get a chance to pour it down that foul demon's throat,' she said, fingering the fresh scars on her cheeks again.

I could feel the knot of ice in my body growing, shifting. The blood-kilts had gathered up ahead on the Heptastadion. We were crouched down in the boats, keeping our heads low as we poled into the small Kibotos harbour behind the fort. Thick, oily smoke poured down the sides of the Pharos, and the reek of it coated the inside of my mouth and nostrils with a greasy grey taste that made me want to spit and spit. Our troops filled the land around the fort, and I could hear shouts and screams along with the clash of metal on metal and the twang and hiss of bows.

'Land here,' said Merit sharply, making the boat rock dangerously with her gesture. The soldiers nearby had their backs to us, waiting to be called forward into the fray, but as Khai gave a low one-two whistle, they turned. Immediately they snapped into ready position, spears pointing forward, shields up, but then one man recognised us. I recognised him too. It was Warrior Rubi, one of Nail's men, his feet shod in oversized sandals as usual.

'Halt!' he called. 'It's our Chosen.' Within a blink, helpful hands were pulling us onto dry land and hustling us forward towards the fort. There was a red burst of flame ahead, then another. I was bumped and jostled by hard male bodies, the edges of shields. Iras was on one side of me, shouldering her way through, Khai on the other. Alim was out in front, eager to join the fight, but the rest surrounded me in a tight ring of protection. The iron reek of blood was in the air, and now I heard groans amid the screams. It was a scene of total madness. I could see no order in it at all. A swell of men came backwards at us, as if pushed from in front, then surged forwards again, screaming war cries.

'CHOSEN!' I heard, and 'ISIS!' and 'SOBEK!'

I felt like a piece of flotsam bobbing in a huge sea over which I had no control, then Khai seized my arm.

'Make way!' he shouted. 'Make way for the chosen!' His face was an iron mask of determination, and, pushing and shoving against the flow, we crept towards the gate of the fort. Inside was not much calmer. Dead bodies lay strewn about – both the white kilts of mercenaries and the grey tunics of our own troops. There were wounded everywhere too, some silent with pain, others moaning in agony. Khai's street rats darted about, carrying bandages and water, directed by a band of priests and sisters of the Living Knot. Silver *ka* forms hovered everywhere, snapping in and out of view as Anubis took them to the afterlife, although, as always, I was the only one who could see them.

'Up!' I said. 'We must go up!' I needed to see what was happening so that I could judge what to do next. There was a narrow stair across the courtyard and, picking my way through the bodies, I made my way to it. A hand grasped at my ankle and I nearly fell, coming face to face with another man I recognised. His belly was sliced open, a spill of viscera oozing through the yellow fat that marked the gaping mouth of the ragged wound.

'Please, Chosen,' he groaned. 'The blessing of Isis before I die.'

'You have it, Warrior Haka,' I said, leaning down to trace the Knot of Isis onto his forehead. With a sigh, his *ka* slipped from his mouth, tall and proud. I felt it as a whisper of cold as it passed through my body and disappeared.

After that, I knew the only way I would get through this day was to shut all feelings away, to become my numb dreaming self while still awake. So, as I ran up the steps, avoiding bodies and slippery patches of blood, I imagined a large iron-banded chest, stuffed all my grief and sorrow into it, and locked it tight.

The fire of Ra's eye hit me as I came out onto the narrow rampart high above the fighting. Bodies lay here too, already beginning to swell and attract blowflies in the heat. The smell of blood and excrement was indescribable. Down below, the army of the Ibis were fighting for their lives. The white kilts of a line of mercenaries pressed them from behind. In front, thronging the causeway, was a roiling mass of blood-kilts, faced by a line of flaming torches. I craned my neck, searching for a sail on the north-eastern horizon, a mast, anything that would tell me my father's army was here. But the city and the rising smoke blocked my view.

'Sobek curse it,' said Iras, pointing. 'Look! There's Alim.'

'But he promised he wouldn't…' I said, then stopped. Sobek's young soldier had a torch in each hand, and he threw himself into the front line, smashing his fire down at the undead enemy, over and over, in a manic frenzy. Even over the racket below, I could hear him screaming.

'For my sister! For Shadya! Die, you unholy monsters!'

Rank after rank of blood-kilts caught fire and burned, as Alim, torches now gone, grabbed the ones already on fire with his bare hands and threw them into each other. Still they came on, uncaring, swords swinging and spears stabbing wildly, men and women together, bare-chested, blank-faced, bloodied, burning. And then I saw him go down, caught by a spear thrust to the chest.

I heard Iras shriek with rage beside me, and I caught her arm as she began to move.

'No!' I said, cold and fierce as Merit. 'No, Iras. He is gone.' Khai was at her other side, holding her back. Even as I spoke, I saw that the tide had turned. Alim had done that for us with his passion and fury. The flame was now spreading from blood-kilt to blood-kilt, back down the causeway, towards Pharos Island. My army poured forward like a torrent, unstoppable, hacking, stabbing, pushing the burning bodies off the edges of the road and down onto the green-edged rocks below, where the Burnt-souled Dead were torn apart as the fire took them, and disappeared in a haze of smoke and flesh. I could see General Nail urging on his troops, leading them from the front, and an arrow of fear for him stabbed out of my locked box. I shoved it back ruthlessly, as Shoshan's black-veiled figures erupted, seemingly out of nowhere, on the faraway shoreline of the island with a flare of new-lit torches, pinning the remaining blood-kilts between two remorseless walls of flame. Shoshan had joined the fight again.

The bigger knot of ice in my body was finally loosening, melting, dying. There was still an aching patch of chill up ahead in the temple, but the nearer threat was almost gone. I turned to Khai and the others.

'It's time,' I said, turning back to the stairs, and loosening the poisoned weapons at my belt. If Cabar spoke true, Berenice's demon consort would be waiting for me in the temple. I didn't intend to let him leave the island. Isis would reign again in Alexandria before the day was done.

There was still fierce fighting behind us, as some of Berenice's mercenaries tried to break through the spears and bowmen to Pharos Island. General Nail had gone back with his victorious soldiers to lead the rest of the army of the Ibis in a charge against them, but Shoshan was waiting up ahead, holding the line in case there was a sudden rush from the temple.

I stopped just once on the causeway, to kneel by Alim's broken body. He had been wounded so many times that his tunic was sodden black with blood. His bare brown arms were scorched and burned, almost to ash in places. The spear that had killed him at last drooped over his chest, as if its very victory over his mortal body was a defeat. His face, so dark and dangerous in life, was smooth and at peace in death.

'Sobek will guide him back to Shadya through the halls of the afterlife,' Iras said quietly. 'I know he disobeyed you, Chosen, but...'

I didn't answer her, but instead turned to two of the large troop of soldiers behind me, who had fallen in around us on General Nail's command to guard my passage across and defend the causeway.

'Take his body and put it in a place of safety till it can be embalmed,' I said. 'He shall have a tomb of honour and grave goods enough for two.' I knew Iras would understand. Shadya too would have her portion in the afterlife.

I walked straight and tall, my princess mask (or should I call it my Pharaoh mask now?) firmly in place. Inside me, that locked box of emotions bulged and tried to burst its bonds, but I wouldn't let it.

As I stepped onto the bare rock of Pharos Island, I felt the cold jolt back into place with a renewed fierceness.

I stopped, and Shoshan and her marsh warriors swirled into place around me like black mist.

'What is it, Chosen?' Shoshan asked.

'There are blood-kilts up ahead,' I said, in my new, not-to-be-disobeyed Pharaoh voice. 'Have the torches ready.'

They didn't ask how I knew; they just obeyed without question.

We moved cautiously towards the sea-bleached white of the temple, Shoshan's people fanning out to either side to scout, torches blazing in one hand, weapons in the other. I tried not to shudder as the shadow of the Pharos blocked out Ra's rays for a moment. Black smoke was still pouring from it. My sister was up there somewhere, but I would deal with her later. If I survived.

I felt, rather than saw, Iras's movement as we approached the open gates. She barrelled into me, knocking me to the ground and covering me with her body, as I felt a hiss of air by my ear, and then another and another. There was a jolt, and Iras cried out, just as a wall of shields surrounded us, and Shoshan's warriors let out warlike shrieks, storming past us and through into the temple.

I just had time to think that Charm would kill me if I'd let Iras get hurt, when she rolled off me with a groan and a curse, plucking out a black-feathered arrow from the meat of her upper arm.

'Let me see,' I said, but she brushed my hand away.

'It's nothing,' she said. 'Just a graze.' Her mouth was set and grim in her round face – a contrast to her normal happy expression. 'There are more important things for you to attend to, Cleo Blue-Eyes.'

'Bind it at least,' I ordered her, but Corporal Geta was there before me, wrapping the arm in a strip of linen torn from his tunic as more shrieks issued from inside the temple.

'Come on,' I said, pushing at the wall of shields in front of me.

'No,' said Khai, pulling me back, as more arrows hissed overhead. 'You go in protected or not at all.'

I heard the fear for me in his voice, but I shook him off. Fear had no place here. It was courage we needed.

'Forward, Ibises,' I screamed. My blood was up and I would not be denied. If he wouldn't run with me, then I would leave him behind.

But he did run, charging beside me with a battle cry of 'CHOSEN!'

Then they were all shouting it.

My wall of shields broke over the threshold like the crest of a wave, to be met in turn by the countershock of a line of white-kilted mercenaries crashing into them. Up on the walls, a band of black-veiled bodies were swarming the last archer, who fell with a gurgle and a knife in his throat. Other black-veils were fighting the blood-kilts who had appeared out of a door to the left, setting them on fire with howls of triumph. Merit was slashing left and right, cutting throats with her wrist knives. Iras, despite her wound, was using her poisoned daggers to deadly effect. Khai was in front of me, guarding my front, as Sah and Geta stabbed with spears and then knives behind me. Men fell like cut papyrus fronds before us, some gurgling and frothing at the mouth as Cabar's deadly poison took them. One of my own daggers took a man in the throat. His eyes bulged and he went down like a rock, limbs thrashing. Then, as I pulled the blade out with a foaming red gush of lung blood, quite suddenly, the fight was over.

The courtyard was still apart from the crack and pop of flame, and the groans of the wounded. The smell of rot and burnt blood filled the air. Most of my troops were leaning on their spears, looking around bewildered, as if they couldn't quite believe there was no enemy left to fight. I ordered them back down the causeway to aid General Nail. What I had to do now would not take many.

That door to the left beckoned like an open mouth, and a sense of urgency seized hold of me, pulling at me like eager fingers. There was a god waiting for me.

I whirled round, looking for Merit. There she was, flicking the blood off her knives with a disdainful snap of her wrists.

'The sanctuary,' I called. 'Where is it?'

She was with me in an instant.

'Down there,' she said, pointing.

Time seemed to pass in strange, disconnected jolts as I fumbled my bloody dagger back into its sheath, careful not to touch the point.

They were all gathered around me now: Merit, Khai, Iras, Sah and Geta – out of breath, yes, but with determined faces. Sah had a cut across his cheek, Geta was limping from a slash on his calf. Shoshan and some of her black-veils were busy cutting the throats of wounded mercenaries, but I called her over.

'Bring fire and come with me,' I said.

There was another disconnected jolt of time as I turned and led them into darkness.

I could feel him ahead, like a sickness in my veins, like ice soaked with rotten blood.

One step, two, three, four, down and down. I wouldn't allow myself to think about what lay ahead.

There was a sort of high-pitched buzzing in my ears, which turned into screaming. It came from a room which should have been holy.

But the two statues of my goddess on either side of its door had no heads, and they were covered in a glistening, roiling mass of flies, feasting on the blood which covered their carved robes in stinking black clots.

I drew my unused dagger and held up a hand.

'Kill or burn anything you find in there, but leave the

consort to me,' I said, and then I stood back as Shoshan and her black-veils kicked in the door.

I knew what I would find.

Rows of ravaged bodies.

Renegade embalmers.

Jars of hearts.

Priests.

But I let the others deal with them.

I had eyes for only one man.

My sister's consort.

Archelaus.

He stood there, arms upraised, howling like the rabid dog he was, the light of a mad demon god in his eyes.

The blessed battle rage came out of nowhere, filling me with a glorious surge of energy.

I ran forward, dagger upraised, aiming to stab up under his ribs for a heart blow, as Iras had taught me. But his flailing hand caught me a vicious thump on the head, and I stumbled and missed, knocking my wrist on the jewelled belt he wore. The dagger fell to the floor with a clatter, and then he was on me, clasping me around the waist as if he was my dearest lover, squeezing me to him so that my breasts squashed flat against his chest. His breath was death and graves and the darkest imaginings of men.

'Oh, little sister,' he whispered in my ear. 'I have been waiting for you so long. I have so much planned for you.'

His voice was worms and filth and things long decayed.

I struggled frantically against him, and we spun and whirled in a macabre dance, knocking into those horrible jars of hearts, smashing them onto the floor so that it became wet and slippery and filled with the scent of putrefaction, bumping and twirling into knots of fighting warriors and priests and then away again.

I heard the buzz of flies, felt their wings, their pricking tongues, their filthy feet. They covered my head, my hair, crawled into my ears, my nostrils, my eyes, my mouth.

My ribs were cracking.

I couldn't breathe.

I began to see black stars behind my closed lids.

But still I wouldn't give in. Still I fought him with teeth and body and everything I had. If his death meant my own, still I would make the sacrifice willingly. Because die he must.

'I will take you to the fire. I will see your soul scream forever in my lake. I will make you bow before me and clean my middens with your tongue. And that will only be the start.' He began to whisper words in a language I didn't understand. But I could feel the power rising, could feel him begin to trace a symbol on my back.

'No,' I gasped, spitting out fly bodies, trying to wrestle a hand free. 'Isis help me!'

'She is not here,' he hissed triumphantly, breaking off his chant, his finger stilled. 'Your puny, puling goddess has not been here for a long time. This place is mine now. Mine.'

That vile insult to Isis gave me the last bit of strength I needed. I brought one knee up between his legs, then down to stamp on his foot, hard, grinding it under my sandal. He collapsed onto me with a strangled scream, and in that second, I wrenched my right hand out of his grip and pulled at my second dagger, feeling it stick and then come free. With a single hard thrust, I slammed it up under his ribs at the back and into his kidney, praying that there was still enough poison on it.

He wailed and let go of me, falling backwards, and I dropped to my knees in a buzzing fury of flies, scrabbling for the dropped dagger. My hand closed on it seconds before his flailing foot came down where it had been.

My goddess's words came back to me.

For he has made an error by taking a human body of his own, and in his assumed human frailty lies your chance to end him. He too can be burned and brought to judgement.

Very well, then. It was time.

I rose to my feet, a strange, high ululation coming from my mouth, and, two-handed, I raised the dagger above my head, bent forward and shoved it into his eye, feeling a pop as it slid deep into the demon god's frail human brain. The flies rose from me in a buzzing cloud, then they dropped to the floor, blanketing Archelaus in an iridescent purple-green cloak.

As I stumbled back, retching, spitting, Merit was on him, growling our goddess's name deep in her throat as she hacked at him, butchering him until Berenice's former consort was an unrecognisable bag of blood and bone smeared with crushed insect bodies.

But still the demon god wouldn't let go of Archelaus. His limbs continued to flail and grasp, his lips to mumble.

'Merit,' I yelled, thumping her in the shoulder. 'Merit! Stop! We have to burn him!'

Somehow she heard me through the fog of rage, and drew back. Quick-thinking Khai grabbed a torch from Shoshan and handed it to me, before ripping cloth off the dead and piling it around the wreck that had been Archelaus. Iras took all the oil lamps in the room and poured the contents over the twitching, grasping body.

I took Merit's hand. It was trembling.

'Together,' I said, and we threw the torch onto the pyre.

The flames rose high and hot at once, and with a last wail, the demon god exited his host body and fled as a *ka* of dark mist. I saw the door in the air snap open, but this time Anubis was not on the other side. Ammit, goddess of divine retribution reached out a flaming hand and snatched her brother through. Then she bowed to me, and the door shut with an ethereal slam I felt right down to my soul.

The demon god was gone, to be judged and punished as a human would have been. I hoped Ammit and the Ennead would make him rot and burn forever.

* * *

I stumbled out of that room of death and flame and up into the cleaner air above. All I wanted was to get away, to put that desecrated place behind me. I knew the others felt the same. Once again, that high keening sound erupted from my throat as I led my people out through the gates, far from the temple, out to where the clean light of Ra burned in a blue-white sky and vultures were circling and circling above, their wings outspread, waiting for dead flesh. Pharaoh's chickens, the people called them, the very symbol of the throne itself. Somewhere in my clouded mind, that seemed appropriate.

Falling to my knees in the dust, I raised my bloodstained palms to the heavens.

'Isis!' I called out, my voice cracked and dry with screaming. 'Beloved goddess! You are avenged.'

And, out of nowhere, the wind came, and with it the lightning.

It swept over us and through into the gates behind, and it fanned the flames of Am-Heh's passing into a white-hot inferno which engulfed the temple in a column of fire. I smelt the singed scent of burning hair.

I felt someone's arms lifting me, felt him running, calling, saw the blur of other bodies running beside us, smelt desert herbs and hot, dry sand and roses. There was a bright, hot shimmer of intense heat that passed over my body, and then I was dropped, grunting with the impact as the earth shook and shook underneath us. The arms holding me fell away and collapsed under me, and everything went dark.

I woke what must have been moments later. Ra's eye had not moved in the sky, but the circling vultures had been joined by more, black dots lazily riding the air, wings outstretched. I sat up to find a ring of prostrate bodies around me, foreheads in the dust, in the position of obeisance. I looked down at my body, my hands. The blood and filth and flies had disappeared, and I was dressed all in priestess white, with a blazing golden Knot of Isis at my breast. My right shoulder was bare, and on it the throne glyph glowed.

'Isis,' I whispered, as Ra himself seemed to wink approvingly at me. Then the blue of the sky coalesced into one bright spark and fell to earth.

'Isis-chosen,' whispered those around me. Iras, Merit, Sah, Geta – even Khai, who loved me for myself, not for who I would be. After I was crowned Pharaoh, I knew I would be worshipped as a goddess come down to earth. But I wasn't Pharaoh yet. I wouldn't be till I sat on the Double Throne beside my father. There was still work to be done. *Ma'at* was still broken.

'Rise,' I said softly, going among them, pulling them to their feet. None of Shoshan's black-veils would meet my eyes, and some of them flinched away when I laid hands on them. I had been touched by the goddess right in front of them. I was holy now. I was apart. I knew that the story of my transformation would spread faster than the fire that Isis had brought down from the sky, and that it would change things forever.

I made myself look at Khai. Would he too flinch away and stare at the ground? I didn't think I could bear it if he did. But his mud-brown eyes stared steadily into mine. He was bloodied and smoke-streaked, and he had never looked more beautiful to me. Merit too met my eyes, so did Iras and Sah and Geta. Shoshan flicked a quick look at me, then lowered her veil. I knew it was a sign of respect.

Khai cleared his throat.

'My Chosen,' he said. 'What would you have us do now?'

I looked up at the Pharos. The black smoke had gone, and it was wreathed in a shimmering haze of dust.

'Now,' I said. 'Now we go to take down a false Pharaoh.'

21

The Double Throne

The Pharos was a good way away, across a narrow spit of land to the east of the island. As we walked cautiously up the ramp and under the sixteen vaulted arches to the entrance of the tower, we saw a huddle of tethered donkeys, surrounded by panniers still loaded with bundles of papyrus root for the fire. Their handlers were nowhere to be seen – either fled, or taken by Berenice and her priests for a last desperate round of sacrifice.

Round and round we went, ever up and up, past rows and rows of naptha oil in jars. Berenice had not been in danger of running out of fuel to burn her prey, I thought. There was a little resistance from the black-robed priests on the second floor of the tower, who were guarding the few sacrifices still left alive. Shoshan and her warriors put them down without mercy, despite their screams, and escorted the poor, uncomprehending victims downwards towards the donkeys.

My small band and I carried on climbing, up, up, up, circling round the spiral of iron stairs to the topmost level. The air was dead and still, and the iron was streaked with dried runnels of blood.

We found Berenice slack-jawed and drooling, on her knees by the huge brazier she had turned into a sacrificial pyre to her evil god. It was still glowing, and the stench of burnt flesh was so strong that despite all I had seen that day I nearly retched again. The huge burnished bronze mirror above the fire was tarnished and streaked with black soot. My sister was dressed in filthy embroidered robes, her Pharaoh's white diadem slipped over one ear, long hair straggling and unkempt. Her eyes were blank and filled with unending horror. She was a broken thing, unrecognisable as the murderous, scheming Berenice I had known just a few months ago. I didn't feel one shred of sympathy for her.

She threw herself at my feet, fingers scrabbling at my ankles.

'Mercy,' she mumbled. 'Mercy.' But there would be no mercy from me for her, the false Pharaoh. She had done too much evil. However, I would not kill her now. The people of Alexandria would need an example made. They would need someone to pay publicly for what they had endured.

I bent down and ripped the Pharaoh's diadem off her

head, folding it between my fingers before stepping back from her clutching hands and throwing it onto the embers of the fire. No future Pharaoh would ever wear it, I decided. It was too tainted. I would have a new one made.

'Bind her and take her down to the bottom,' I ordered. I couldn't bear to look at her for one more instant, so I turned my back on her and walked round to the open arch which framed my city. 'She will face the Pharaoh's justice when my father returns.'

As if the very saying of his name had conjured him, I saw the Roman galleys which had already slid up to the pier on the other side of the Great Harbour, saw the ranks of marching soldiers rushing forward, heard the harsh sound of orders on the breeze and the flap of banners. From where I stood, so high, the whole city was laid out before me. There were still many knots and clusters of hard fighting in the streets, especially on the Gate of Helios side of the city. The army of the Ibis was hard-pressed, and the street rats had all but disappeared, leaving nothing but dismantled barricades behind them. I was not experienced at reading the ebb and flow of a battle, but even I could see we were losing badly until the Roman troops joined the fight.

Their disciplined squares moved forwards as one, shields and spears a deadly glitter, and they cut through the ranks of the remaining mercenaries and city guards until they scattered and ran, laying down their weapons and crying for quarter. My father had paid a high price for Aulus Gabinius's help – but if it had saved only one soldier in my army, it was worth it to me. No doubt the Romans would now try to interfere in the running of Egypt, power-hungry as they always were. But I would not let them, I decided – not if I could possibly help it.

I looked down at the Heptastadion. The fighting there had moved eastwards, towards the marketplace. Tiny, doll-like bodies lay strewn in its wake, and I could see that the circling vultures had landed, their clumsy bodies hopping and flapping as they fought for the best bits of dead flesh. Pharaoh's chickens would have their due, and so many bodies had to be disposed of somehow.

I knew I should make myself go down, should find my father and greet him, but the locked box was opening inside me. For all that Isis had clothed me and taken away the outward stains of war, inside I was still human, still Cleo. I wanted nothing so much as to find Charm and curl up beside her and weep till my heart was clean again. But she was not here. I felt the hot tears spill over onto my cheeks, put out my hands and clutched at the gypsum-covered brick in front of me, feeling the gritty dust of it rasp under my fingers. I must not cry, I told myself. I was the Pharaoh-to-be, the commander-in-chief. I must be strong.

Even as I thought it, I felt a hand on my shoulder, the warm press of fingers a comfort. I didn't have to look to know it was Khai.

'My Chosen,' he said in my ear. 'Berenice is gone. Merit and the others have taken her downstairs. It is just us now.'

I turned to face him. It was true. He and I were alone, here, above everything – on the fiery tower, as the oracle had said.

Would I find truth here?

'I'd wipe away your tears,' he said, 'but my hands are filthy.' He glanced down at them and grimaced. 'More than filthy.'

'It doesn't matter,' I said. 'I don't care. You're alive.'

'We both are,' he said simply. 'And whatever happens now, I will rejoice in that for all my days.' He reached out with one grimy finger to stroke a lock of my hair back into place. 'You are so beautiful, my Cleo. You are my bright, shining star. You are the true heart of me. You always will be.'

I knew what he was trying to do. I heard the regret and the farewell in his voice. Why did he have to keep trying to make noble sacrifices after all we'd said and done, after all we'd been through together? Why couldn't he see that he was the one who made it all matter?

'No,' I said.

I wouldn't make it a Pharaoh's command. I didn't have the right to do that to him. But I would fight for him the only way I knew how. With the truth.

I reached out and took his chin in my fingers, squeezing

hard. 'If you leave me, I will set Iras and Charm on you. And Merit. And possibly some cobras as well. I know how much you like those. How many times do I have to say it? I need you. I want you. I love you. And I can't be Pharaoh without you. You keep me real. You keep me Cleo.'

For one awful moment I thought he was going to deny me, then his eyes crinkled at the corners, and that dimple of his appeared as his lips twitched upwards.

'Please. Not the cobras.' Then he gently put my hand aside and dropped to one knee, his face turning serious again as he brought it to his forehead in love and homage.

'Very well, O Beloved Pharaoh, heart of my heart,' he said. 'If you're really sure you want me that much. I'm not sure I'd survive without you, anyway.'

'Isis be my witness,' I said, bending to kiss his bowed head. 'I'm sure.' And I was. If I was the true heart of him, then he was of me. That was what the oracle had been trying to tell me. I raised him to his feet, and kissed him again, very gently. Then I let him go to begin the long climb down the iron stairs, secure in the knowledge that wherever I went now, he would follow.

I do not know where they found the chariot, nor the flowers which decorated it. Ra's eye was sinking westwards, and I was being pulled along the Canopic Way by a band of my warriors and some of the children from the temple of Serapis. Merit, Shoshan and the Sisters of the Living Knot walked at my left hand; Khai, Iras, General Nail, Geta and Sah at my right. Berenice was chained to the chariot's tail, stumbling along and mumbling to herself in a high, mad voice. The remainder of my triumphant army followed us, along with Khai's street rats and what seemed like the whole populace of Alexandria, all throwing flowers and cheering as the statues of my ancestors looked down on me. The ancestors had not approved of me in beggar's robes. This time, I thought their expressions were more approving – even benign – as cries of 'CHOSEN' and 'CLEOPATRA' filled the air.

As we approached great Alexander's tomb in the Sema, burial ground of the Ptolemys, the cheering grew louder, deeper, amid a sea of lit torches which glittered on Roman arms and armour.

'AVE! AVE PTOLEMY! AVE GABINIUS!' The Third Army in front of me called.

From my vantage point in the chariot, I could see a man, dressed in Tyrian purple hemmed with gold. He was being carried on the shoulders of Roman soldiers. It was my father, triumphant in his return.

They set him down on the steps of the tomb, just as I climbed down from my chariot. I walked the few paces towards him, and faced the crowd, holding up a hand for silence. I knew that I would need to use Isis's vocal gift to its fullest extent to make myself heard.

'Let us welcome back the true Pharaoh,' I cried out, and

my voice was sharp-edged steel cloaked in molten gold.

'Hail Ptolemy Theos Philopater Philadelphus Neos Dionysos!'

The crowd took up my words with a shout of approbation that I could feel from my soles to the crown of my head. I crooked my finger at four of Shoshan's black-veiled fighters who now held Berenice, bound in chains of iron. They came forward, throwing her down at my father's feet, and her mad voice rose and fell, praying, cursing, begging, until Shoshan herself stepped forward and stuffed a rag in her mouth, silencing her.

'I bring you the false Pharaoh,' I said to the crowd. 'The demon worshipper. The killer of innocent souls, the mother of the Burnt-souled Dead. I do not call her sister, for she has forfeited all claim to kin and kindness.' I turned to look up at my father, lowering my voice. 'Shall she face immortal justice, great Pharaoh? Shall she die and be judged?'

He looked at me, holding my eyes, and then he nodded and turned to the crowd.

'The chosen of Isis has spoken. Let it be so,' he shouted. 'Let her be given over to the justice of the gods.'

As the crowd screamed its approval, Merit and the sisters walked forward. Over one shoulder, the High Sister carried a double-headed silver axe. The sisters stretched Berenice's body out, holding her still. One of them grasped the traitor's long, dirty hair, wrapping it round a fist. She pulled hard, up and over, so that it revealed the bare, pale nape of the false Pharaoh's neck, forcing her forehead down onto the tall bottom step beneath us.

Then Merit's axe rose and fell, and rose again, rimmed red with blood. For just a second I saw Berenice's *ka* rise and hover above her headless body. It was not silver, but a kind of dirty brown. Then, with a flash of flame, it was gone. I knew that Anubis had not come for her, but Ammit. The false Pharaoh had gone straight to the fiery lake, where she would suffer for all eternity. The gods had already made their judgement.

'Let her body be given to her own crocodiles,' I said, my voice colder than frost. 'Then release the beasts to the care of Sobek's priests.'

It was a fittingly bloody ending for one who had been a traitor to the name of Ptolemy, I thought, ignoring the spatters of red on the hem of my white robe as the body was dragged away like the carrion it was.

I bent and reached my hand through the delicate bars which surrounded great Alexander's tomb, fumbling for a moment as I searched for what I had left there so long before, praying that nobody had stolen them. But no. There they were! My mother's jewels felt warm in my hand as I pulled them out from the hiding place where I had stowed them, back in those desperate hours when I was trying to save Khai from Berenice's dungeons. I shook the rose petals off them, and put them on with a prayer of thanks to my ancestor for protecting them. Just for a moment, I thought I felt a soft hand stroke my hair.

Then I turned to the true Pharaoh and took his hands in my own, dropping to my knees before him.

'Welcome home,' I said. 'Welcome home, Father.'

He inclined his head to me gravely, raising me to my feet.

'Daughter,' he said. 'Come, take your rightful place beside me. You shall henceforth be known as Cleopatra Thea Philopator. For it is your love and courage which have brought me and Isis home to our people.' Then he smiled, and whispered for my ears only, 'My little pusscat Pharaoh.'

A month later, my father and I sailed upriver on a golden barge, floating on the music of a thousand mizmars and sistrums, and dressed in robes sewn with enough jewels to ransom all of Egypt. We were officially crowned Pharaohs together at Memphis, amid great celebration and pomp – he for the second time, I for the first.

It was the day on which my birth star Sihor rose in the sky. Exactly a year before, I had faced the testing of Isis at Philäe. The blessing of the flood had come early this year, and the temple of Ptah was filled to bursting, as the High Priest Paserenptah led the holy chants.

'*O Amun the Great, O Shu, O Tefnut, O Geb, O Nut Skyborn;*

O Osiris, O Isis, O Seth, O Nephthys, O Bastet, O Sobek the Warrior;

O Nekhbet, O Tauret, O Thoth, O Nefertem of the Lotus;

O Serapis, O Seshat, O Anubis of the Door, O Horus of the Wings;

O Hathor in the Great House, O Ptah, O Ra, O Grandmother Iusaaset;

O Great and Little Companies of the Gods of North, of South, of East and West;

O ye of Heaven and Earth, grant ye these diadems of purity to the reborn Pharaohs.

To Ptolemy Theos, to Cleopatra Thea, God-presences on Earth,

Grant strength, destroy evil.

Pure are the praises in the house of gold.

Praise be to the Pharaohs, to the gods...'

On and on and on it went, till my eyes stung from the incense, and I ached from sitting still on the uncomfortable carved stone of the Double Throne and keeping my Pharaoh mask in place. It was hard not to let my mind drift...

Most of the Roman army had left some days before, marching overland to Tyre and onwards to other wars, leaving a small force behind 'to back up the Pharaohs'. I knew exactly what that meant. They would report straight back to Pompeius Magnus in Rome.

I had, of course, been introduced to General Gabinius

immediately after our victory, and he had patronised me in the way that only a Roman could until I stopped him in his tracks with a few well-chosen words. Marcus Antonius had stood at his shoulder, whispering into his ear during the whole of the triumph feast that my father and I had provided, and I didn't think much of what he said was complimentary from the looks both of them gave me. The decurion had been promoted, I heard, and was off to some wild island in the north to join Julius Caesar in more conquering. He had spoken to me only once, a few jeering words about how the torches had not seemed to be needed after all.

'Luckily for you, my armies dealt with the problem before you arrived,' I said, my voice as full of disdain as a midden is with muck.

His eyebrow had lifted, and he smirked in that annoying way of his that I did not find in the least bit attractive.

'If you say so, princess.' I didn't bother to correct him about my title. He was nothing. He was as unimportant as a grain of dust under my foot. That's what I tried to tell myself, anyway, as the weaver god's loom clicked and shuttled inside my head.

I had been stubborn about Khai's appointment as my vizier and, as predicted, my father had given in once I pointed out the mark of Isis's favour on his chest. Khai had gone a deep red and nearly choked when I demanded he show it to the Pharaoh, but he had done so. Now my beloved had title, lands and a grant of monies from the treasury. He also had rooms near to the royal quarters, and all I will say about that is that the slave passages proved very useful to both of us.

The first sisters had sent messages that they were safe in Iusaaset's oasis. The Skyborn was guarded again. Merit was undertaking a journey there and then round all the temples of our goddess in Egypt, and the remaining warriors of Isis had gone to guard her, recruiting on the way to replace their depleted ranks. They had suffered heavily in the fighting. Before she left, I had promised her that the Pharos temple would be cleansed and rebuilt, bigger and better than before, and that Cabar would have her own memorial there. The old, cold High Sister was gone forever. I knew Isis had visited her in a dream, forgiving her, and now her twice-scarred face shone with a new inner light and purpose as she left, kissing me on both cheeks.

'I will return, Chosen,' she said, and I smiled.

'I will look forward to it,' I answered – and meant it. Even as all-powerful Pharaoh, I would need all the friends I could get around the court.

Sah and Geta wished to stay with me as my bodyguards. I promoted them both, Geta to captain, Sah to sergeant. I thought they would both burst with pride as I announced it before their fellow warriors, and handed each of them a heavy purse of gold. Iras, of course, remained, pledged to me as she was by Sobek. She did accompany Sobek's priests downriver with the demon's crocodiles, though.

'I need to tell Petsuchos what happened, Cleo Blue-Eyes,' she said, irreverent as ever. 'He likes a good story.' Then her eyes went serious. 'And I need to say goodbye. I won't be going back to Crocodilopolis again. My place is here with you and my Pretty Girl.'

Shoshan and her people went back to the marshes, but nearly every man and woman in the army of the Ibis pledged to remain with my father and myself. With Berenice's mercenaries dead or fled, and the city guard mostly under arrest or executed for treason, we needed a force we could trust around us. General Nail would become head of the palace guard, though unfortunately my father had insisted that Achillas be given the post of head of the army. I didn't like it, but my father overrode my objections.

'He and Theodotus have been good servants to me. They must have their reward.' Theodotus too became a vizier. He and Khai hated each other on sight, and Theodotus made endless gibes about rats dirtying the court with their inky fingers until I wiggled my fingers at him meaningfully. He turned pale and silent then. He hadn't forgotten Isis's blue spark between his eyes.

Charm became my foremost lady-in-waiting. I signed the decree for her freedom almost as soon as I returned to the palace, sealing it before witnesses, and sending a copy to the archive in the Great Library. I would have done it years before if I'd had the power to do so, but only a crowned Pharaoh could free a slave.

When I handed the scroll to her, she cried, first on my shoulder, then on Iras's.

'I never felt like your slave,' she sobbed. 'I didn't mind.'

'I minded for you, O Sister of my Heart,' I said. Naturally, that made her sob even more. But she soon got used to her new position, bossing around the ladies of the court as if she'd been born to it – which of course, she had. She delighted in finding ever more elaborate names for me when we were alone. The latest was 'Peerless Pharaoh of the Passages' after an abortive trip to see Khai, when I'd nearly got caught sneaking out to his rooms one night, but the less said about that, the better.

The sound of chanting intensified suddenly, assaulting my ears with noise, and I came back to myself with a jerk, quickly stifled. The priests were dancing now. It was nearly time. The High Priest was approaching, his hands held high, holding a jewel-embroidered cushion on which lay the two white symbols of power.

'Lord and lady of the uraeus crown, come forth!
The Lady Isis hath made a way for thee.
Thou shalt be as great as the sovereign chiefs before thee.
Thou shalt vanquish thy enemies,
And they shall be as chaff under thy sandals.
Thou shalt be as mighty divine stars in the land,
And thy diadems shall shine forth as the rays of Ra.'

As the new, gold embroidered white diadem of the Pharaoh was bound about my brows by Paserenptah, I heard a noise like the beating of a thousand wings. Then, quite suddenly, all the gods were there, crowding among the people, unseen by all but me. Isis led them, so glorious in her beauty that I was almost blinded.

Time slowed and stopped.

I slid out of my throne and onto my knees, prostrating myself at Isis's feet.

Her hands raised me, burning like the heat of a Shemu day, cool as the green waters of the Nile.

My Chosen, she said in that immortal voice which flowed through my body, filling me with the song of a hundred bulbuls, with the roar of a thousand lions, with the silence of a white crescent moon on a night full of stars. Ma'at is restored, and the Double Throne is no longer empty. You have fulfilled your promise to us. Now we will keep ours to you. Whether your reign be short or long, all the nations of the world as yet unborn shall sing songs of you and praise you forever. Neither light nor darkness shall extinguish your name, not wind nor rain, nor anything visible or invisible. You, my Chosen, will never be forgotten till the Great Green is dry, and the stars fall.

The throne glyph on my shoulder flared a bright white, blinding me. I could not speak. I had no words. I found myself back on the throne with the world moving around me again, as the people sang praises and cheered my father and me till the walls trembled.

Isis and the other gods had disappeared and I understood, without knowing how, that I might never see any of them again.

My gifts would remain, but that part of my life was over.

I had passed the test.

Isis would always be my goddess, and I would always be her chosen.

But I was the Pharaoh Cleopatra now, and it was time to reign.

Who is Who, Where is Where and What is What in CHOSEN

The Main Players:

Berenice Ptolemy: the evil false Pharaoh, and worshipper of Am-Heh, demon Devourer of Souls

Charmion (Charm): best friend, body servant and the person Cleo thinks of as her real sister

Cleopatra Ptolemy (Cleo): Princess of Egypt, marked and chosen of Isis, later known as Pharaoh Cleopatra VII Thea Philopator (meaning 'father-loving goddess' in Greek)

Iras: former Crocodile Child, worshipper of Sobek and bodyguard to Cleo

Khai: scribe, librarian, spy, all-round hot guy and lover of Cleo

Marcus Antonius: decurion and Roman officer serving under Aulus Gabinius. Handsome pain in Cleo's neck

Ptolemy XII Theos Philopator Philadelphus Neos Dionysos, also known as Auletes (the flute player): Cleo's Pharaoh father who was exiled to Rome, leaving his family, his people and the Double Throne

Tryphena Ptolemy: wicked Pharaoh half-sister of Cleo, now dead, poisoned by Berenice

The Minor Players:

Achillas: military adviser to Ptolemy XII

Ahkenaten: famous Pharaoh of the 18th Dynasty

Aka: a royal guard to Ptolemy XII

Alexander the Great: royal founder of Alexandria and first Greek Pharaoh

Alim: warrior of Sobek and twin brother to Shadya

Am: Cleo's food taster

Archelaus: prince and priest from Pontus, married to Berenice (a fate worse than death – almost literally)

Arsinöe: Cleo's youngest half-sister, and a nasty little snakeling

Aulus Gabinius: Roman general and wielder of armies

Brotherhood of Embalmers: red-robed, Seth-loving cutters-up of dead bodies

Cabar: Sister of the Living Knot, priestess at the Temple of the Pharos and ace poisoner

Calpurnia Rabiria: daughter of Gaius Rabirius Postumus

Captain Nail: Warrior of Isis, and head of Cleo's guards

Corporal Geta: Warrior of Isis, and one of Cleo's two main guards

Crocodile Child: the child who is chosen as the Voice of Sobek on earth

Dennu: one of Cleo's eunuchs, killed earlier by Berenice and Tryphena

Dhouti: another of Cleo's eunuchs

Gaius Rabirius Postumus: important Roman moneylender

Ganymedes: tutor to the three younger Ptolemy children

Gnaeus Pompeius Magnus: consul and triumvir of Rome

Hatshepsut: famous female Pharaoh of the 18th Dynasty

Julia: fluttery young wife to Gnaeus Pompeius Magnus

Lashes: one of Cleo's camels

Lem (Ptolemy): Cleo's younger half-brother

Lydia: Roman housekeeper

Mamo: slave boy and fanbearer from Ethiopia, gift to Cleo from Berenice

Marcus Tullius Cicero: a Roman orator and troublemaker

Master Apollonius: Cleo's old tutor in Alexandria

Merit: High Sister of the Sisters of the Living Knot

Nanu: healer in Sobek's temple at Crocodilopolis

Nefertiti: famous Egyptian queen and wife of Ahkenaten

Paserenptah: High Priest of Ptah at the Temple of Memphis, and cousin to Cleo

Quintus Tullius Cicero: younger brother of Marcus Tullius Cicero

Ramses: famous Pharaoh of the 19th Dynasty

Riaz: messenger street rat

Seleucid cousins: an ancient Greek royal dynasty who ruled Syria and intermarried with the Ptolemies

Sergeant Basa: Warrior of Isis, killed by Berenice's mercenaries while covering Cleo's earlier escape from Alexandria

Shadya: warrior girl and twin sister to Alim

Shoshan of the Spear: head of the marsh bandits who live in Lake Mareotis

Smelly Camel: the name says it all

Temehu: a nomadic tribe from the Sahara desert

Theodotus: adviser to Ptolemy XII

Tol (Ptolemaios): Cleo's youngest half-brother

Warrior Haka: Warrior of Isis

Warrior Sah: Warrior of Isis and one of Cleo's two main guards

Warrior Rubi: Warrior of Isis

The Gods and Goddesses:

Am-Heh: also known as 'The Devourer of Souls' – hound-headed, crocodile-clawed, river-horse-reared demon of all things evil. Lives mostly in a lake of fire

Ammit: judgemental underworld goddess and sister to the demon Am-Heh

Amun: king of the gods and the wind

Apedemek: lion-headed warrior god, worshipped in Nubia

Aphrodite: Greek goddess of love

Apollo: Greek sun god

Anubis: jackal-headed Lord of the Underworld, who ushers souls into death

Bastet: cat-headed goddess of protection, music and dance

The Ennead: group of nine powerful Egyptian gods and goddesses

Geb: god of the earth, brother of Nut

Hathor: cow-headed goddess

Hera/Juno: Greek and Roman queen of the gods

Heryshaf: ram-headed god

Horus: falcon-headed god of the sky, son of Isis and Osiris

Isis: goddess of motherhood and thrones, protector of all Egypt

Iusaaset Skyborn/The Old One: mysterious grandmother to the Egyptian gods, whose symbol is an acacia tree

Khonsu: moon god

Mars: Roman god of war

Nekhbet: hook-nosed vulture goddess

Nefertem: god of the blue lotus flower

Nephthys: goddess of death and rivers

Nut: goddess of the sky

Osiris: god of the afterlife, husband of Isis

Petsuchos: living crocodile incarnation of Sobek

Ptah: god of creation and fertility

Ra: god of the sun

Renenutet: snake goddess, wife of Sobek

Serapis: bull-headed god

Seshat: goddess of wisdom and writing

Seth: god of storms, chaos and the desert, murderer of Osiris, enemy of Isis

Shai: god of fate, and weaver of threads

Shu: god of the air

Sobek: crocodile-headed god of war

Tauret: river-horse-headed goddess of childbirth

Tefnut: goddess of rain

Thoth: god of the moon

Other Ancient Egyptian and Roman terms:

Amharic: language spoken in Ethiopia

Atrium: a Roman courtyard

Bruise-flower: another name for arnica, a healing herb

Cartouche: official hieroglyphic

Cilican pirates: sea marauderers defeated by Gnaeus Pompeius Magnus

Denarius/denarii: Roman silver coins

Decurion: a Roman army officer

Diadem: ornamental silk headband worn by Egyptian royalty

Egyptian seasons and months: there were three seasons, *Akhet* (flood), *Peret* (spring) and *Shemu* (harvest). The months, in order of season, are *Thoth*, *Phaopi*, *Athyr*, *Choiak*; *Tybi*, *Mechir*, *Phamenoth*, *Pharmuti*; *Pachons*, *Payni*, *Epiph* and *Mesore*

Felucca: a sailing boat, usually with a high stern

The Great Green Sea: what the ancient Egyptians called the Mediterranean

Haboob: wind which brings sandstorms in the desert

Hieroglyphs: ancient Egyptian symbols

Ka: the spirit form of a person, the soul's life-spark

Ma'at: balance of the universe, life and the Double Throne – must not be broken

Mizmar: a wind instrument

Obol: a small bronze coin

Palla: a Roman shawl

Papyrus: paper made out of a reed-like plant

Quanun: a stringed musical instrument

River-horse: what the ancient Egyptians called a hippopotamus

Senet: an ancient Egyptian board game

Sihor: the star of Isis, which rose in late June or early July to herald the Nile flood

Sistrum: a percussion instrument

Simoom: a hot desert wind, also known as 'poison wind'

Stola: a long Roman robe

Talent: golden coin

Uraeus: serpent crown worn by gods and Pharaohs

Places:

Alexandria: capital city of the Ptolemy pharaohs in Egypt

Argiletum Street: main route from the Roman Subura district to the Forum

The Canopic Way: main thoroughfare of Alexandria, lined with statues

Canopus: port city to the east of Alexandria

Carthage: conquered Roman city in North Africa

Crocodilopolis: temple city of Sobek, with a hidden labyrinth underneath it

The Forum: main marketplace in Rome, and location of the Senate and other important buildings

Gate of Helios: eastern gate into Alexandria

Great Sand Sea: large desert region in western Egypt

Harbour of the River: southern harbour of Alexandria, bordering Lake Mareotis

Heptastadion: long causeway connecting Alexandria to the island of the Pharos

Herakleiopolis the Great: city on the Nile, sacred to Heryshaf

Hill of the Cow: hill sacred to Hathor at the Shore of the Sea Oasis

Kibotos Harbour: small, enclosed harbour by the Moon Gate fort in Alexandria

Lake Mareotis: large lake to the south of Alexandria, home of Shoshan of the Spear and her bandits

Leptis Magna: port city on the coast of North Africa, near Khoms, Libya

Leukaspis: port city west of Alexandria. Also known as Antiphrae

Memphis of the White Walls: city on the Nile, sacred to Ptah, god of craftsmen, creation and fertility

Moon Gate: western gate into Alexandria

Naucratis: trading city on the Nile, famous for pottery

Oasis of the Oracle: oasis in the Sahara desert, now known as Siwa. Home to the famous oracle of the god Amun

Ostia: Mediterranean port city at mouth of Tiber, serving Rome

Parthia: ancient region in north-east Iran

Pharos of Alexandria: one of the Seven Wonders of the World – a huge lighthouse in Alexandria, standing on its own island

Philäe: island in the southern Nile, with a temple to Isis on it. Previously home to Cleo and Charm for four years

Phoenix: harbour town in southern Crete

Pontus: area on south coast of the Black Sea, now part of modern Turkey

Rome: capital city of the Roman republic

Scythia: ancient region

The Sema: Alexandrian burial ground of the Ptolemy pharaohs and their families, also probable site of Alexander the Great's tomb

Shore of the Sea Oasis: ancient name for Bahariya Oasis in the western desert region of Egypt

Subura: valley area of Rome between the Esquiline and Viminal hills, where Gnaeus Pompeius Magnus and Pompey XII live

Syrákousai: the ancient name for Syracuse in Sicily

Tarpeian Rock: execution place above the Roman Forum, from which criminals were thrown

Temple of the Pharos: temple to Isis on the island of the Pharos

Temple of Tellus: temple in Rome, dedicated to the earth goddess

Theatre of Pompeius: the first permanent theatre in Rome, built 55 BCE

Thebes the Great: city on the Nile, dedicated to Amun, god of the invisible and winds; king of gods

Thrinacia: ancient name for Sicily

Tiber: river running through Rome

Tyre: city in ancient Phoenicia, now Lebanon

Author's note:

Nobody knows much about Cleopatra's path to the Pharaoh's throne, beyond the bare minimum of speculative dates, and even those are disputed. Who her mother was, when exactly she was born, what she really looked like are all mysteries. Her early life is a big fat hole in history, which I have jumped into with both feet and tried to fill. Where possible, I have done my best to make the known facts about life and culture in ancient Egypt and Rome at that time historically accurate, but this is a work of fiction, so any small twistings and turnings to suit my story will, I hope, be forgiven.

Acknowledgements:

This feels like the end of a very long journey, and to those of you Lovely Readers who have travelled with me this far, I'd like to say a heartfelt thank you. Many of you have been incredibly generous in your praise of the first part of Cleo's story, so I hope this second and final offering will help you forgive me for that cruel cliffhanger ending in Book 1!

As always, I have been helped and encouraged to make this the best book it can be by the efforts of a whole raft of amazing people, and huge thanks are due to the following:

- My fabulous Orchard editor, Emily Sharratt, who asked all the right questions and whose continuing enthusiasm and support for *Chosen* has been such a bright constant throughout this project.

- Maurice Lyon, heroic copy-editor, who spotted all my terrible inconsistencies, and saved me the embarrassment of Being Found Out When It Was Too Late.

- Megan Larkin, fantastic publishing director of Orchard, who nearly made me cry when she said I'd finally made her 'get the Egyptians'.

- The whole enthusiastic Orchard and Books With Bite team.

- As always, the Most Kickass Agent in the Universe, Sophie Hicks, of the Sophie Hicks Agency, who is my rock and my confidence-booster (and also my secret ninja weapon, obvs).

- The magnificent Michelle Lovric, finder of fabulously arcane facts, and the Best Nile Party Planner and Provider Ever.

- The wonderful and generous communities of UKYA bloggers, librarians (both school and public), reviewers and booksellers who do so much to promote books and reading. Your support has been humbling.

- Mary Hoffman, Nicola Morgan, Liz Kessler, Candy Gourlay, Teri Terry, Anne Rooney, Tanya Landman, Amanda Craig, Nicky Schmidt and all my other dear Nonnywrimo, Scattered Authors' Society and SCBWI friends for encouragement, tea, cake and emergency St Bernards in times of writing crisis.

- Deborah and Bob of the highly recommended Retreats for You in Sheepwash, who provided space and time to concentrate on the race to The End (and also judicious glasses of red wine).

- Nikki R-S (without whom I would not function) for keeping the home fires burning.

- The patient, long-suffering and lovely men in my family, Richard and Archie, and my dear old mum, Prue, who put up with snarling, grumping and late/missing meals due to 'yet another writing crisis'.

- And last but never, ever least, my brilliant daughter Tabbi, my first, most enthusiastic and also most critical reader, who always tells me the truth about my writing. This book would never have happened without her constant help and insight.

Lucy Coats,
Northamptonshire, March 2016

About the author

Lucy Coats writes stories for all ages, and has also worked as an editor, journalist and bookseller. She loves all things mythological, and is fascinated by the magical place where history meets legend. Lucy lives with her husband, three out-of-control dogs and far too many books.

You can find out more at www.lucycoats.com and also on Twitter at @lucycoats

Cleo is also on Twitter @CleoTheChosen